THE PLURALITY OF WORLDS

Borgo Press Books by BRIAN STABLEFORD

THE PLURALITY OF WORLDS

A Sixteenth-Century Space Opera

by

Brian Stableford

THE BORGO PRESS

An Imprint of Wildside Press LLC

MMX

CONTENTS

PART ONE

THE ETHERSHIP

CHAPTER ONE

The ethership stood on the launch platform at Greenwich, ready to blast off. The cabin set atop the massive rocket appeared tiny when viewed from the ground; the ladder by which the intrepid voyagers would reach it seemed exceedingly fragile.

Thomas Digges, the captain of the vessel's five-man crew, stood on the street at the edge of the platform in company with its principal architect, John Dee, and the Archbishop of Canterbury, John Foxe. Thomas was not looking up but looking down at the cobblestones. They had been scoured and swept in the early hours; he had never seen a city thoroughfare less likely to offend his boots.

"Your father would be immensely proud, had he lived to see this day," Dee said to the younger man. "This—more than the telescope, the laws of planetary motion, or even the theory of affinity—is the ultimate fruition of his work."

"He was but one half of a great alliance," Thomas said, meeting his mentor's eyes. "Had you not introduced him to Roger Bacon's works, he might not have begun to toy with the telescope or applied himself to the munitions of war that laid the groundwork for the ethership. Your mathematical expertise was every bit as important as his in proving and improving the Copernican system, and without your fluctual algebra he would never have been able to develop the theory of affinity."

"You should not forget the inspiration of the Almighty, my son," Foxe put in, "nor the abundant financial support provided by our glorious queen."

"No, indeed," Thomas agreed, willingly. The queen had certainly been generous with her own funds as well as the nation's, and her generosity had set an example that her many of courtiers had been anxious to emulate, competing among themselves to sponsor the New Learning. "Will the queen be here to witness the launch of her namesake?"

"Her carriage is en route as we speak," Foxe assured him. "She would not miss it for the world. It means a great deal to her that England should be the first nation to send ambassadors to the moon."

"We must beware of expecting too much of the expedition," Dee observed, gravely. "The distance the ship will contrive to travel is entirely dependent on the conditions the crew will discover once they are beyond the upper limit of the air. We do not know whether ether is respirable—and if it is not, the crew will be forced to make a swift return to Earth. Preparations for a journey to the moon would then acquire a new dimension of complexity, more challenging in its way than the design of the ethership's fuel-system."

"That is a matter of God's providence," Foxe judged. "If the ether is breathable, then humankind clearly has God's permission to travel between the worlds—but if it is not, the heavens are evidently out of bounds."

Thomas frowned slightly, but said nothing. Foxe was a powerful influence in the court—powerful enough to have added a man of his own, John Field, to the "crew" of the *Queen Jane*. In reality, Thomas and Francis Drake were the only ones required—or able— to man the vessel's controls. Edward de Vere and Walter Raleigh had petitioned the queen to be added to the company in the hope of impressing her with their boldness in quest of adventure. De Vere had a reputation as a playwright and Raleigh as a poet, but neither had any significant skill in mathematics, which put them at a definite disadvantage in a court where the greater part of everyday conversation was devoted to the progress of science. Foxe's man, John Field, was no courtier—he was fervent enough in his Puritanism to make no secret of his contempt for the affectations of court life—but he was a man of refined conscience who would be able to report to the Archbishop on the potential theological consequences of any discoveries the expeditionaries might make.

Thomas would rather not have had Field aboard the ethership— but he would rather not have had de Vere and Raleigh aboard either, although Raleigh was always an amiable companion. Indeed, he would have been glad to go alone if he had not needed another pair of hands. Drake had an interest in winning the queen's favor too—

and had the advantage of maturity and previous accomplishment over his upstart competitors, being only three years younger than the queen—but he was a good calculator and a cool man under pressure.

"Speak of the Devil!" Thomas murmured, his voice far too slight to carry to the Archbishop's ever-vigilant ear. Drake was emerging from the Black Bear inn, his arms linked with those of de Vere and Raleigh; the three of them as merry as men could be who had been forbidden ale for breakfast. A fourth man, who was walking three steps behind them, was as disapproving as they were cheerful; John Field, Puritan firebrand, had a fine talent for disapproval and its display.

The three courtiers were finely-clad and their beards were neatly-trimmed. Drake was the tallest as well as the oldest, but de Vere—ten years Drake's junior—was the handsomest of the three. Raleigh, two years younger than de Vere at twenty-five, was not conventionally fair of face, but he had a certain dash in his attitude that had already made an impression on the queen, if Cripplegate rumor could be trusted. In reality, de Vere was probably the more reckless of the two—he was still suffering the bad reputation of having once had an unarmed man "commit suicide by running on to his sword"—but the queen was said to prefer a man who maintained a flamboyant attitude, while behaving politely, to one whose attitude was polite while his behavior resembled a loose cannon.

"The queen will be here in a matter of minutes!" Drake announced. "I saw her carriage from the attic with the aid of one of Tom's telescopes, advancing from Rotherhithe at the gallop. Perfect timing, as always."

Digges bowed, as he murmured "Sir Francis, milord, Sir Walter, Mr. Field." Although he was the captain of the ethership, three of his crewmen outranked him by birth—de Vere most extravagantly of all, having inherited the title of Earl of Oxford while still a boy. It was the three aristocrats who returned his bow most graciously, however; Field seemed to think such polite gestures akin to church vestments, and was a dedicated minimalist in their expression.

"Her majesty is doubtless anxious to see Master Dee again," de Vere said. "While he has been busy here, the Tower has been deprived of its fireworks and its horoscopes alike."

Dee bowed in acknowledgement, although the remark had not been intended as a compliment. Field took up a position beside the Archbishop, making a row of three Johns in opposition to the three gallants. Thomas felt uneasily suspended between the two ranks. "If her majesty is missing Master Dee," he dared to say, "it is more likely that she feels the need of her lessons in mathematics." In 1568, when Dee had presented the queen with a copy of his *Propadeumata Aphorisitica*, the queen had gladly accepted his offer to give her lessons in mathematics to help her understand it. She had been a champion of natural philosophy since she had come to the throne in 1553—even more so since she had broken free of Northumberland's machinations, following her husband's assassination by Elizabethans in 1558—but her generosity had increased in proportion to her comprehension.

Foxe, who seemed even less appreciative of Thomas' remark than de Vere, might well have made some remark about Bible studies, but he was distracted by a buzz in the crowd that had gathered along the quay. They too had caught sight of the queen's coach—or its escort, at least.

"Batman's here, I see," Dee observed. Stephen Batman, chaplain to the Master of Corpus Christi, was Dee's greatest rival as a book-collector, although his interest in the manuscripts he accumulated was more antiquarian than utilitarian.

"Who's that boy beside him?" Thomas asked.

"That's one of Nick Bacon's sons," Drake answered. "Young Francis—a prodigy, they say, likely to eclipse Master Dee himself, in time."

"Not if the *Queen Jane* makes a successful ascent into the ether," Thomas opined. "Whether it is able to go on to the moon or not, that achievement will not be eclipsed for a hundred years...and Master Dee is its architect." He added the last remark lest Drake—or anyone else—thought that he was blowing his own trumpet.

"Here she comes!" Raleigh crowed, immediately joining in with the tumultuous cheering. Everyone else did likewise, in slightly less Stentorian tones—even John Field.

Queen Jane' carriage, pulled by four black horses, rattled southeastwards along the Thames shore behind the vanguard of a company of cavalry, whose second cohort was bringing up the rear. Their scarlet coats were ablaze in the morning sun, while their polished sabers reflected random rays of dazzling light.

Foxe and Dee hurried forward to greet the monarch, while de Vere checked his doublet and hose and Raleigh reached reflexively for the ornamental hilt of the sword that he would normally have been wearing. Like his breakfast ale, it had been forbidden.

The queen was only a few months short of her fortieth birthday, but she looked radiant as well as regal. Thomas blushed at the sight of her, as he always did, and stumbled as Dee hurried him forward in order to present him to her.

"Your majesty," the Master said. "Leonard Digges' son shall make England proud this day."

Queen Jane extended her hand for Thomas to kiss. "The captain will make us very proud indeed," she said, "for there is nothing England admires more than courage—and the navigation of the heavens will require courage unparalleled."

Thomas stammered his thanks. The cavalry had formed a protective cordon around the party, although it was more a show of discipline than anxiety; the Elizabethans were a spent force nowadays, and no agent of Spain could have got within five miles of Greenwich on a day like this. Drake, de Vere and Raleigh took the opportunity to form a cordon of their own, vying for the queen's attention with effusive flatteries. For once, Thomas felt a pang of sympathy for the awkward and hesitant Field.

"Time is pressing, lads," he said, when they had played their parts sufficiently. "We'd best be mounting the ladder." Without any more fuss than that he set off for the ethership, knowing that the others would fall into line behind him. He left it to them to wave to the crowd, while he contented himself with a last glance in the direction of John Dee, the greatest man of science the world had ever produced—or, at least, the man whose reputation to that effect was about to be subjected to the ultimate proof.

CHAPTER TWO

The first and more unexpected agony was the sound of the rocket's ignition. Thomas had known that it would be louder than any sound he had experienced before, and had suspected that its pressure might be oppressive, but he had not anticipated the seeming fury with which it pounded his eardrums, drowning out all other sensation and thought.

Then affinity took hold of him—or, more accurately, the rising ethership slammed into his back, while the affinity that bound him to the Earth fought against the force of the rocket's explosive levitation, trying with all his might to hold him down. He had known that this sensation, too, would be bad, having experienced similar phenomena during the test launches. Those vessels had only ascended into the atmosphere, though, no higher that the summit of a mountain. His body had suffered no lingering ill-effects at all—but this pressure was twice as powerful, and he felt that it was crushing him.

Thomas heard a gasp as Field tried and failed to scream; the clergyman was the only crew member who had not taken any part in the testing program. The scientist could imagine the thought that must be possessing the Puritan's brain: if God had made the affinity between man and Earth so strong, how could he possibly intend that men should ever attempt to break the bond? But the pressure passed, to be gradually replaced by a very different sensation: that of weightlessness. Thomas had a fine mathematical brain—near equal to his father's, Dee said—and he had long applied his methods to the artillerist's art of ballistics; he constructed a picture in his mind of the trajectory of the rocket as it curved away from the ground it had left behind, aiming for a circular orbit about its world.

Only a handful of men as yet, had circumnavigated the globe in ships, and none of them was an Englishman—although Drake had sworn that if he had not been invited to take his place on the *Queen Jane* he would have made the attempt in the *Pelican*. Now, five

Englishmen were about to circle the world not once but several times, in a matter of hours rather than months.

"Make sure your tethers are secure, lads," he said—for Field's benefit rather than that of his experienced crewmen. "Cleave to your couches if you can, and take care not to release anything into the cabin."

"Aye aye, sir," said de Vere, with a slight hint of mockery—but Thomas ignored him.

"Ready, Sir Francis?" he said.

"Aye, Tom," was Drake's entirely sincere reply. Drake had to supervise the course of the ethership while Thomas deployed the sampling bottles mounted to collect the pure ether that would soon be surrounding the ship, using mechanical arms to maneuver them into double-doored lockers. From there, if all went well, they could be brought inside without breaching the integrity of the hull. Thomas worked unhurriedly, but not without urgency; Drake was equally concentrated on his work.

Raleigh was closest to a porthole; he was looking out with avid interest, watching the curve of the globe's horizon.

"I can't see England at all, curse the clouds!" he said, "but I can see a landmass that must be Africa, and more ocean than I ever hoped to see in a lifetime. The mystery of the Austral continent will soon be solved—or perhaps we'll see Dante's purgatory, towering above the ocean hemisphere in solitary splendor."

"Papist nonsense," muttered Field, who sounded as if he had spent a stint in Purgatory himself.

"Thank the Lord we have not collided with one of the Romanists' crystal spheres," Raleigh said, mischievously. "That would have been cause enough for protest."

"Nor can I see Plato's spindle of necessity," de Vere put in, craning his neck to see through another porthole. "Does anyone hear the sirens intoning the music of the spheres?"

"We're not as high as all that," Thomas said, without breaking his concentration. "The planets are a great deal further away than the moon, which is still a long way off. The first of the Classic philosophers' questions to be settled is the nature of space. If the void theorists are right, ours will have to be a brief excursion."

"Now there," observed de Vere, "Puritans and Papists are in rare accord. There's not an atomist in either orthodox company—they're plenarists all, save for the occasional rogue. Remind me, please, Reverend Field: is it still orthodox to believe that the ether marking the extent of space is the breath of God?" Whatever his faults, de Vere had been well-tutored in Classics by Arthur Golding;

he knew that the notion of gods breathing ether as humans breathed air was a pagan idea, of which Christian theology was bound to disapprove, in spite of the Vatican's approval of selected Aristotelian ideas.

"It is not a question," Field retorted, icily, "on which the Good Book has any pronouncement to make." His tone did not seek to conceal his awareness that de Vere was suspected of Catholic sympathies, nor the fact that he was Foxe's eyes and ears, alert for any advantageous whiff of heresy.

Even so, Raleigh—whom similar suspicion deemed to have atheistic tendencies—felt sufficiently liberated to say: "Was it God's negligence, do you suppose, or that of his amanuensis Moses, that left the point unclarified? It would be a great convenience to us, would it not, if the statutes of Leviticus had pronounced upon the permissibility or abomination of ether-breathing?"

"Hold your blasphemous tongue, sir!" the clergyman exclaimed. "God revealed to man what man had need to know."

Thomas, who was busy capturing a bottle of ether within the transfer-hold, found time to think that God had been a trifle vague when it came to the necessities of mathematics, navigation and engineering, let alone the still-impregnable mysteries of physiology. "Got it!" he said, as his manipulative endeavors bore fruit. "The Master's contraption worked beautifully."

"Did we decide who was to be first to inhale from the bottle?" de Vere asked, with a mischievous glance in Field's direction. "Should we draw lots, or it is a clergyman's prerogative to breathe the intangible sustenance of God?"

"If a lungful of void were likely to strike a man dead on the spot," Raleigh said, "it might be best to give the task to a man of faith, under God's dutiful protection."

"Easy, lads," Thomas said, as his nervous fingers groped at the interior catch of the hold. "It's not faith in God that's required here, but faith in the plenum, and the life-supporting virtue of the ether. Even if I lacked such faith, though, I doubt that I'd be struck dead by a single draught of nothingness."

"You might be in more danger of drunkenness," said Drake. "If ether is vaporous nectar, as some say, it might play tricks with your senses."

"Aye," Thomas agreed, extracting the sealed bottle from its cradle, "so it might. But as my father used to say: let's try it and see." He closed his mouth and set the bottle to his nose, released the stopper and breathed deep. He knew, even before his lungs responded to the intake, that the void theorists were incorrect; had the space beyond the atmosphere been empty, and the Earth's air aggregated about it by affinity alone, he would not even have been able to remove the stopper; pressure would have held it firmly in place. The plenarists were correct, it seemed; there was no void, and space was full—but full of what?

Had God really intended humankind to be forever Earthbound, ether might have been a poison, and air a protective insulation against it—but Thomas found that it was not. Nor was it a deliriant, as Drake had hypothesized. He was mildly disappointed to discover that breathing ether was very much like breathing air. "It has no discernible odor," he declared, pensively, "and it's not cold. That's odd, I think, for mountain air is as cold as it is thin. This is a little thin, I suppose, but so far as I can tell, it shares the virtues of the...."

He would have said "air we usually breathe" had he not been seized by a sudden fit of dizziness. Recumbent on his couch, he was in no danger of fainting, but he could not speak while his senses were reeling.

"What is it, Tom?" Drake asked, anxiously. He was not the only man present who was Thomas' senior, but Field was only a year older and Drake was a full five; Drake was the only one with the remotest pretension to serve as a father figure.

"Nothing to do with the ether," Thomas judged, perhaps a trifle too hastily. "The effect of moving while weightless, I think. A momentary vertigo."

"There really is an Austral continent," Raleigh informed them. "Or a sizeable island, at least. Can we claim it in the name of Queen Jane from up here, do you suppose, or must we direct a privateer to plant a banner on its shore when we land?" His voice faltered very slightly as he pronounced the last word; they all knew that landing their tiny craft would be every bit as difficult and dangerous and freeing it from the Earth's affinity.

"Never mind the Austral continent," said de Vere. "Can we—do we—press on to the moon?"

"There's more than the breathability of the ether to be taken into account on that score, Ned," Raleigh told him, bidding for the intellectual high ground in their private conflict. "There's the fuel, and the maneuverability of the ship to test. We've time in hand. Will they be able to see us in England with the aid of one of your father's telescopes, Tom, when we've overflown the Americas and crossed the Atlantic?"

"We won't pass over England on the second round trip," Thomas told him. "They might see us in Rome, though. That'll make the pope bite his tongue, won't it, Mr. Field?"

"The pope refuses to look through a telescope," Field replied, less stiffly than Thomas had expected, "for fear of what he might see."

"There's nothing in the moons of Jupiter to frighten a pious man," Raleigh observed, dryly, "and infinite space is no more visible than finite space."

"The pope has no need to deny the infinity of space," de Vere put in, striking back at Raleigh's presumption of superior knowledgeability. "It's not a Copernican doctrine. Nicholas of Cusa proposed it, on the grounds that God's creative power could not be limited. He argued for the plurality of worlds on exactly the same basis."

"You're a true scholar, Ned," Drake said, amiably. "Where do you stand on the dispute as to whether the inhabitants of the other worlds must be identical to ourselves, being made in the same divine image, or whether they must be infinitely various in form and nature, so as not to limit the creativity of the divine imagination?"

"Some might be giants and some tiny," de Vere observed, "in proportion to the sizes of their worlds."

Raleigh laughed. "But in which proportion, Ned?" he asked. "Will the Selenites be dwarfs because their world in smaller than ours, or giants, because the force of affinity does not stunt their growth?"

"The fuel stores are still in place and the controls check out," Drake reported. "No leaks at all—we have fuel enough to take us to the moon and back, and the means to control its deployment."

"And the attitude of the ship can be adjusted with appropriate precision," Thomas agreed. "Who'd like to sniff the second bottle of ether when I've brought it through?"

"I will," Raleigh said. "No offence, Tom, but you breathe like a mathematician. I've a better nose than you; if ether has a bouquet, however subtle, I'll feel it on my palate."

"Fine," said Thomas, clicking the catch on the second hold—but as soon as he took hold of the bottle, he realized that Master Dee's "contraption" had not worked as well on the second occasion as it had on the first. The outer hatch of the lock had not closed; there was now a gap in the hull the size of a man's forearm.

"Don't panic, lads," he was quick to say. "If there were a void outside, we'd be in trouble, but so long as the pressure of the ether's not so very different from the pressure of the air in the cabin, there won't be much exchange. He fumbled as he tried to secure the inner hatch, however. The ether that Thomas had breathed had been clear, empty of any other apparent substance, but the ether that streamed in through the temporary opening in the hull was cloudy, as if wood-smoke were adrift in it. This was no mere smoke or mist, however, for it was formed into an approximate shape—Thomas could not decide whether it was more like a moth or an artist's conception of an angel—and it moved as if with purpose, descending upon Thomas' face like a veil.

"Look out, Tom!" Raleigh cried—but the warning was futile.

Thomas tried to hold his breath, but he was unprepared. Fear made him inhale sharply—and the invader took the opportunity to wriggle up his nose like an eel burrowing into soft sand. Thomas felt its ghostly presence pass, slick but not cold. He expected it to move down his trachea, or perhaps his esophagus, but instead it seemed to move into the space of his skull, diffusing into the nooks and crannies of his brain.

This time, the *Queen Jane*'s captain did sense a sweet and cloying odor—and when the vertigo took hold of him again, it did not relent. Supine as he was on his couch, he lost consciousness almost immediately.

CHAPTER THREE

As Thomas awoke, the dream in which he had been languishing fled from consciousness, leaving him cast way in a sea of uncertainty. He did not know where he was, and could not remember where her ought to be. He opened his eyes convulsively, and looked wildly about, in spite of the light that flooded his eyes and dazzled him. He knew that something was wrong.

He remembered, belatedly, that he ought to be weightless, tethered to his couch in the cabin of the *Queen Jane*—but he was not. Nor, however, was he back on Earth. He was in the grip of affinity, but he felt lighter by far than he ever had on Earth.

A rough hand gripped his shoulder and steadied him. "Tom!" said the voice of Sir Francis Drake. "Thank God! I feared that you'd never wake up. Are you all right?"

"Aye," said Tom, thickly, rubbing his eyes to clear a certain stickiness from his eyelids. "What did I swallow?"

"As to that, I don't know," Drake told him. "Nor do I know whether it's still inside you—but I've seen creatures stranger by far than that one since you fell unconscious, on my honor. Field missed the show too, having fainted in alarm, but Walt and Ned were awake throughout, so I knew that I wasn't dreaming."

"Where are they?" Thomas asked—meaning Raleigh and de Vere, although Field was not there either.

"I don't know," Drake said. "Probably in a similar prison. Our captors might have recognized the two of us as the senior crewmen—or as the oldest of our company—but I doubt it." Thomas observed that Drake's face was scratched and that many of the scratches were somewhat inflamed.

The cell in which Thomas and Drake were apparently imprisoned was reasonably capacious, but all its alcoves were small and set above head-height, making it difficult to make out what they contained. Thomas looked down instead, to see that the "bed" on which he lay was a protuberance in the floor, not a wooden platform on legs. The floor, like the walls and ceiling, seemed to be composed of an organic substance akin to wood or tortoiseshell, but it seemed clean enough—much cleaner than the vast majority of England's household floors. The floor was grey, but the colors and textures of the walls were very various, and the radiance that lit the space came from silvery ribbons swirling across the ceiling rather than any kind of flame. The doorway was oval in shape; there was no obvious catch securing the door, which might easily have been mistaken for a stopper in the neck of a jar.

"What stranger creatures have you seen?" Thomas asked, belatedly.

"Lunar moths with man-sized bodies and vast wings," Drake said, tersely. "Grasshoppers walking on their hind legs, and ants too, somewhat taller than a man—and slugs the size of the elephants in the Tower menagerie, with castles of oyster-shell. I thought them brutally violent at first, for they're very free with the attentions of their various antennae, limbs and slimy palps, but I don't think they meant to injure us." Thomas reached up to touch his own face, which was tender and itchy. His hands were no better, and the swelling made it difficult to flex his fingers.

"Are we on the moon, then?" Thomas asked, in frank bewilderment.

"*In* the moon," Drake corrected him. "They flew us here, ethership and all, by the power of their multifarious wings, wrapped in a web of what I'd be tempted to call spidersilk were it not that spiders are one of the few creepy-crawlies I've not seen inflated to magnanimous dimensions hereabouts."

"I've seen signs of life and movement while studying the moon in my father's best peeping-glass," Thomas said, in a low voice, "but I was never entirely sure that they were not a trick of the lens or the mind's eye."

"Master Dee's hatches are a poor design," Drake opined, "by comparison with the craters that serve as doorways to the moon—but the giants are not as large as all that. You couldn't see them with a spy-glass any more than we could see elephants strolling in the African savannah were we to turn a telescope on the Earth from the lunar surface."

"There were ants, you say?"

"Things somewhat reminiscent of ants—not to mention moths, bugs, beetles, and a hundred more types for which I cannot improvise names, all living in a single tempestuous throng. They collaborated in our capture, and...."

He broke off as the door opened. It did not swing on a hinge; the aperture dilated.

Thomas understood immediately what point Drake as trying to make. The four individuals who came through the door were all insectile, but they were analogues of very different Earthly species. They all walked upright on their hindmost legs, and their heads were equally bizarre, but their bodies were very different in color, texture and equipment. Two were winged, one like a butterfly and one like a dragonfly. Two were brightly colored, one striped like a wasp and the other spotted like a ladybird. Two were stout, two slender. Two were clutching objects in the "hands" attached to their intermediary limbs. Two were carrying implements of some kind in their forelimbs. All of them, however, hurried forward with no regard whatsoever for their captives' personal space, and began *touching* them, with all manner of appendages.

Thomas fell back upon the bed, overcome by horror. He wanted to scream, but dared not open his mouth lest something even nastier than the ether-creature slip inside him. He closed his eyes, praying for the molestation to stop.

"Be still," said a voice, pronouncing the words inside his head like one of his own vocalized thoughts. "Be patient. If you will relax, and let me use your limbs, I can communicate with at least one of them—I can explain the irritation in our flesh, and demand an antidote."

Thomas inferred at first that one of the monstrous insects must be projecting the words into his head by some mysterious process of thought-transference—but then he remembered that there was already an alien presence within his skull: an etheric ghost that appeared to have dissolved its fragile substance in the flesh of his brain.

"What are you?" he demanded silently. He had made no conscious effort to relax, as he had been asked to, but he did not resist when he felt his hands moving of their own accord.

The insectile monsters seemed more startled by this contact than he had been by theirs. They withdrew their various feelers, and waited while his fingers danced upon the head of one of their number.

Thomas had to collaborate with his intimate invader, rising unsteadily to his feet in order to continue the tactile conservation more effectively. It was an authentic conversation now—the insect addressed by his mysterious passengers gestures was making its reply, in terms of rapid strokes of its antennae—but Thomas felt the irritation and inflammation in his flesh die down.

"I am explaining your origin," his invader said. "Your nature too, although that is more difficult. I can understand why you think of me as an invader, but I mean you no harm any more than the members of the True Civilization do. It might help us both if you were to try to think of me as a guest."

"What's happening, Tom?" Drake asked. "What on Earth are you doing?"

"We're not on Earth," Tom retorted, abandoning the internal dialogue to speak aloud, "and it isn't me who's doing what I'm doing. It's the ether-creature that wormed its way into me when the ship leaked. Somehow, it knows how to communicate with this creature. Perhaps it has traveled extensively in the minds of other creatures."

"Good guess, mine host," said the creature within him, silently. "You're an exceptional creature, Thomas Digges, to have such trust in your own sanity. It often requires months or years to establish a rapport—but yours is a dreaming species, I suppose. That makes a difference—few species have that particular gift, or curse."

Drake had fallen silent, direly puzzled. The insects, however, were frenetically busy in communication among themselves. Touch was only one of the senses they employed; they could not talk as human talked but they clicked and chittered, warbled and hummed. They spoke with their limbs and their wings, and various other kinds of apparatus that Thomas could not discern.

"I think that I have made the situation clear," Thomas' internal informant said. "I have asked to be taken to one of the queens' chambers, since this world has no fleshcore, where we might converse with philosophers closer to the heart of the True Civilization. They will understand your nature, having mechanical analogues of your kind, even if they have not been studying you carefully from afar."

"I have no idea what you are trying to tell me," Thomas replied, silently. "All this is meaningless to me."

"Be patient," the silent voice said. "I will try to explain when I have the opportunity.

"If you and I are made in God's image, Tom," Drake said, softly "What manner of creator made creatures like these?"

It was not like Drake to speculate in such a fashion, but Thomas could understand his confusion very well. Preoccupied with his internal dialogue, however, and disturbed the incessant actions of his unbidden hands, he did not reply.

Drake did not seem to be offended by his rudeness. "Perhaps de Vere was right," the crewman continued, "but if these are merely insects like those of Earth, what giants the men of the moon must be!"

Thomas knew that there was nothing mere about *these* insects. They had been investigating him with manifest intelligence—and still were, aided now by the voice of his invader...his guest. Like humans, they were sapient; like humans, they were curious. The ether-creature called theirs the True Civilization—and why should it not, given that they could fly through the ether between the worlds, to capture stray etherships and interrogate their crews?

When the insects crowding around his bed began to deploy the bulkier objects they were carrying he flinched and shied away, but they still did not appear to mean him any harm. He could not tell what was happening when the objects were pointed in his direction, but none of the monsters was touching him any longer, directly or indirectly. His own hands had been withdrawn from the face they had been fondling so strangely.

Thomas found time to say aloud: "All's well, Francis. I don't understand what's happening yet, but they don't mean to do us any injury."

Drake was touching his face and inspecting the back of his hands. "That confounded itching's stopped," he observed. "Have they administered some antidote?"

"Yes," Thomas told him. "They did not realize that we had been stung. The ether-creature seems to know a great deal more about what is happening here, and what is relevant to our welfare, than we do. If it has not visited the surface of the Earth, it must know others of its kind that have.

Drake actually struck a pose, then, and bowed gracefully to the four attentive monsters. "On behalf of Queen Jane of England," he said, "I greet you, noble sirs. Shall we be friends, then? You don't have the look of Spaniards about you, and God forbid that you might be Elizabethans....or the spirits of the dead, come to that. Was it Plutarch, Thomas, who first declared the moon to be a world akin to the Earth, where the souls of the dead reside?"

"Plutarch it was," Thomas confirmed, "but I don't think his soul is here before us, gathering material for more *Lives*."

"Nor I," Drake agreed. "Can you believe that Raleigh and de Vere could be as brave as we are being, under similar inspection? Not that it matters—by the time they tell the tale to the queen, they'll have fought and vanquished whole Selenite armies, if Field can't keep them honest—and we'll never convince them that we had the bravado to act as we are while subject to such scrutiny. Please assure me that they're not merely deciding the best way to cook and season us."

The ether-creature seemed to know that Drake was joking, and did not trouble to reassure Thomas against this ominous possibility. Nor, however, did it forewarn Thomas that he was about to be seized in the upper arms of one of the unburdened creatures, and very thoroughly palpated, although it did say "Patience, Thomas!" once the assault began. Thomas felt his hands making some sort of reply, although he had no idea what it was—but he had a strange impression, as the creature withdrew again, that it was even more repulsed by the texture of his flesh than he was by the horror of the grip and the probing feelers.

"The neo-Platonists and Aristotelian diehards have a saying," Drake muttered. "*As above, so below*—but this seems to me to be a very different world from the one we know. Men of that sort are mostly monists, though, who think that the moon is a mere lamp planted in the skies by providence to ameliorate the darkness of night in suitably teasing fashion, and that the stars are candles disposed to foretell our futures. Master Dee is no monist, is he—despite that he wrote a book called *Monas Hieroglyphica*?"

"He was converted to pluralism thereafter," Thomas said. "*Propadeumata Aphorisitica* is his definitive statement. He is committed to the infinity of space and of worlds—and when I tell him of our adventure, he will also be committed to the infinite variety of form and virtue. These are intelligent beings, Francis—including the thing inside me—and I'm praying hard that they might be more virtuous in their treatment of fellow intelligent beings than the great majority of men. *Take care!*"

It was not he that had pronounced the final words, although they had been spoken aloud. Thomas was abruptly snatched from his bed, and Drake was seized.

"Have no fear!" said Thomas' inner voice, silent again but still voluble. "They are doing as I have asked, and taking us to a visitor from the galactic core. With luck, he will order your release."

Thomas and Sir Francis Drake were dragged from the room then, but they were both being held quite gently. They were no worse than lightly bruised as they were hustled along one winding corridor after another, through an interminable labyrinth. Thomas' impression was that they were going deeper into the bowels of the moon, but he could not be sure.

"Where are they taking us?" Drake shouted back to him, his tall but slender captor having drawn some twelve or fifteen yards ahead of Thomas' stouter guardian.

"To a queen's chamber, I believe," Thomas replied, retaking control of his own vocal cords.

"I have heard that ants have queens," Drake said. "None as pretty as my darling Jane, though."

"Is she your darling?" Thomas called back, although he could fee the ether-creature's impatience to revert to silent conversation.

"She will be," Drake said, "if I get out of this alive with the means to return to Earth—always provided that I tell my tale before Ned and Walt tell theirs. There's naught like a little gooseflesh to animate affection, and I think I have the means now to make her majesty's flesh crawl prodigiously."

Thomas was ashamed to feel a sudden pang of resentment at the observation that Drake—who was, after all, five years his senior and no great beauty—had not thought to include him with de Vere and Raleigh in the list of his rivals for the queen's affection. Such was the burden of humble birth, and perhaps the myth of mathematicians' disdain for common passion.

Thomas now had the opportunity to see for himself that the giant inhabitants of the moon did not all resemble insects, although its insectile population was exceedingly various; there were, as Drake had briefly mentioned, creatures like slugs the size of elephants, with shells on their backs like mahouts' turrets, and many other creatures shelled like lobsters, whelks or barnacles. There were legions of chimeras clad in what Thomas could not help likening to Medieval suits of armor designed for the protection of entities with far too many limbs.

"Why, this must be a busy port or a great capital," Thomas said, though not aloud. "A cultural crossroads where many races commingle and interact. If the moon is hollow throughout, honeycombed with tunnels, how far must its pathways extend, and how shall its hosts be numbered?"

"Very good, Thomas," his invader said. "I'm assisting you as best I can, but you've a naturally calm mind, which makes it a great deal easier. Thank God you have no relevant phobias—they'd be a lot less easy to counter than your allergies."

"You talk a deal of nonsense," Thomas said, "for someone using a borrowed tongue."

"Aye," the creature replied, "but I'll make sense of it for you if I can. I must, for we've work to do here, now that the True Civilization is aware of your new capability. They must have studied you, I dare say, but they could not have thought you capable of building an ethership for another four hundred years—and study conducted at a distance is always calmer than a close confrontation, where differences stand out that distinguish you from burrowers and ethereals alike. We must convince an influential philosopher that you are harmless still, and likely to remain so."

"Have you a name, guest?" Thomas demanded. "I feel that I am at every possible disadvantage here. Or will you name yourself Legion, and make things even worse?"

"I am no possessive demon," the creature assured him. "I shall be as polite a guest as circumstances permit, and will take my leave before I overstay the necessity of my visit. You may call me Lumen."

"As in light, or cavity?" Thomas retorted.

"A little of both. We are chimerical creatures by nature, and our aims are syncretic. I cannot bind your race to the True Civilization at present, but I must persuade someone close to its heart that humankind might one day be so bound—if I fail, the consequences might be catastrophic."

Thomas wanted to demand further clarification of this remarkable statement, but he did not have time. They had just arrived in a much larger cavern: a vast and crowded amphitheatre, with terraces arranged in multitudinous circles about a central core.

"I told you so," Drake shouted. It took Thomas several seconds to realize that his friend was referring to his assertion that an insect queen could never be as pretty as his darling Jane. Thomas had to agree, as he looked upon a vast individual, which was surely the queen of a hive, although her resemblance to an ant or bee was no greater than its resemblance to a moth or a centipede. Her ugliness in human eyes was spectacular in its extremity. She was laying eggs at the rate of one every ninety seconds, which acolytes carried away into tunnel-mouths dotting the rim of the central arena.

It was not the queen to whom the two prisoners were taken, though—it was to a group of individuals twenty-five or thirty strong, situated no closer to her head than her nether end, who were in conference in one of the inner ranks of the array of terraces. The majority were more moth-like than any other species Thomas had yet seen, conspicuously furry, with multifaceted eyes each larger than a human head; the minority were very varied indeed.

"Now," said Thomas' uninvited guest, "you must let me speak. The future of your nation, and perhaps your world, may depend on it."

CHAPTER FOUR

Thomas pulled himself together once he had been released, and tried to look one of the moth-like creatures squarely in the eyes, although the wide spacing of the compound aggregations made it difficult. Whether it was he or his passenger who had identified the significant member of the group Thomas could not tell. Drake was standing close beside him, but said nothing: his eyes were on Thomas, his captain.

"Very well, Sir Lumen," Thomas said, silently, since his guest seemed to be waiting for explicit permission to proceed. "Speak—but tell me, I beg you, what you are saying and what replies you receive."

His hands immediately became active, as did the multiple forelimbs of the lepidopteran monster.

"I am delighted to have the privilege of communicating with one who has come so far through the universal web," the voice within him said, evidently translating what the hands it was guiding were attempting to convey in a very different language. "May I address you as Aristocles?"

Then the internal voice changed its timbre entirely, to signify that it was translating a different gestural sequence. "You may," the monster replied. "I suppose that it is a privilege of sorts for us, also, to converse with an ethereal in such a strange guise. We had not thought that such as you could have an interest in a being of this sort."

Thomas, who still had control of some of his motor functions, tried to keep his eyes on the monster's frightful face, although a certain instinctive repulsion added to the temptation to glance sideways to see what other creatures were passing along the terraces and to hazard guesses at what multifarious kinds of business they might be transacting.

"We are interested in all beings, whether they are ethereal, vaporous, liquid or solid," Lumen stated. "Nor do we discriminate between endoskeletal and exoskeletal formations. We are as intrigued by anomaly as you are."

"We stand corrected," Aristocles replied. "Your kind does not often descend to planetary surfaces, though—do you not find the thick and turbulent atmosphere of this world's neighbor as inhospitable as we do?"

"We can move in air as in ether," Lumen said. "It is uncomfortable, but it does no lasting damage if we do not linger long."

"And the same is true of these bizarre creatures, I assume," Aristocles replied. "It will do you no lasting damage to dwell within the bonebag, provided that you do not linger long—but they cannot be as welcoming, in their capacity as hosts, as we soft-centered creatures are."

The ether-creature made no reply to that teasing statement. Instead, it said: "May I introduce Thomas Digges, esquire, in the service of Her Majesty Queen Jane of England? His companion is Sir Francis Drake. May I also ask what has become of the other three humans who were captured with them?"

"You may," the moth-like creature replied, its politeness wholly feigned if the suggestive timbre of its mimic cold be trusted. "Thomas Digges' companions are unharmed, although one of them is direly fearful. He appears to believe that we and the Selenites are incarnations of pure evil."

"I am glad that you understand these creatures well enough to be able to deduce that," Lumen said—sarcastically, presuming the tone of the translation to be accurate "John Field has a narrow opinion of what it means to be made in God's image. He does not understand there are innumerable worlds scattered throughout the cosmos which exact different adaptations on their surface-dwellers and burrowers alike, and he thinks of images in purely formal terms."

Thomas blinked as some drifting miasma stung his eyes, and he felt his sinuses grow itchily moist in response to some peculiar scent. He sniffed, as surreptitiously as he could—although it was obvious, on the basis of the merest glance about that astonishing arena, that few of the individuals gathered here could have any objection at all to the extrusion of surplus mucus.

"There are those even in the bosom of the True Civilization who have narrow opinions as to the will and whims of God," Aristocles admitted. "If there is disagreement even within the ultimate harmony, what can we expect without? A race such as this must have a very peculiar notion indeed of the image in which they have been forged. With your permission, of course, we should like to take these specimens to the Center, so that they may be savored by a mature Fleshcore."

"Their flesh has been more than adequately sampled, thanks to the assiduousness of your gatherers," Lumen replied. "As to their consciousness, I know it more intimately than you can, given the limited means you can apply to the task. Were you to return the five humans to the surface of their world—or let them make their own way home in their ethership, I would be willing to go with you to the Center, to enlighten the community of Great Fleshcores to the limit of their desire."

"We thank you for your consideration," said his adversary—Thomas was very certain that there was a powerful adversarial component to this exchange—"but ethereals cannot fully comprehend the transactions of more palpable beings. There is no substitute for *tangible* evidence. We must insist on taking the humans to the Center—but we are, of course, perfectly willing to bring them back again afterwards, by means of the ninth-dimensional transmitter. There would be no inconvenience to those concerned."

"Bargain with him," Thomas said, hoping that the interruption would not break his guest's concentration. "I'll go, if my four companions are set free."

"I take your point about their being no substitute for tangible evidence," Lumen said, immediately. "To take all five humans on such a difficult journey would, however, be superfluous. One would be sufficient. The others are of no use, this one being the only one that can communicate with you effectively. Perhaps the others could wait here, until this one returns, and then they could all be returned safely to the surface of their world."

"We disagree," Aristocles said. "Your presence certainly adds to this one's versatility in communication, but much has been learned by palpation of all five and comparison of the results. If our poor feelers can detect interesting differences, think what a mature Fleshcore might discover. As we have said, we are prepared to bring the five creatures back here when we are done with them. If it is their desire to risk a return trip in their ridiculous vessel, we shall not hinder them, even though we would not be optimistic about their prospects of success."

"Have you noticed, Thomas, that we are the cynosure of all eyes in this exotic court?" Drake put in, evidently feeling that the time had come to intervene in the orgy of palpation.

Thomas spared a momentary glance for a mixed group of bug-like creatures some thirty feet away, who did indeed seem to be using their own intercourse merely as a pretext for studying the two humans, their eyes somehow suggestive of a fervent desire to supplement their curiosity through the medium of touch. If they were embarrassed by his sudden attention, they gave no sign that human senses could detect.

How they must envy this Aristocles! Thomas thought.

The moth-like creature's compound eyes did not need to move sideways to look at Drake or the bugs, but Thomas observed that one of them had altered its attitude slightly. The creature seemed watchful, almost as if it expected that some danger might present itself any moment within the surrounding crowd.

"You know far more about the population of the inner galaxy than I do," Lumen was saying, in the meantime, to the creature it called Aristocles. "Are these so extraordinary that you must take all five on such a long journey?"

"Very extraordinary indeed," the monstrous insect replied. "To ethereals like yourself, all solid creatures must seem very much alike, as your various kinds seem to us, but we are very sensitive to differences of bodily structure and its spiritual concomitants."

"I know that there are more than a hundred million worlds in the True Civilization," Lumen said, its translation giving the impression now that it was debating for Thomas' benefit, so that he might learn from the exchange of information, "and I know that there are a thousand million more that have not yet produced intelligent life. Thomas Digges' world is by no means the only one to have produced endoskeletal species."

"It is the only one on which endoskeletal life-forms have so obviously violated the normal course of evolution to the extent of producing intelligence," Aristocles retorted. "If your host Thomas Digges did not exist, he would undoubtedly be considered impossible by the vast majority of our scholars."

"What does the insect mean by *the normal course of evolution*?" Thomas could not stop himself asking, silently.

"Listen!" Lumen said, before switching back to translation. "I beg your pardon, my friend," it went on, "but I am attempting to translate our conversation for the benefit of my host, and am inevitably forced to improvise within his language in order to express ideas that no Earthly philosopher has yet formulated. May I make a brief statement for his benefit?"

"If you think there is any profit in attempting to explain matters far beyond his comprehension," the moth-like monster replied—very disdainfully, if the translation hit the right note.

"My host's peers have not yet arrived at a true appreciation of the age of the Earth," Lumen said, "and are caught up by the false supposition that God must have created every species independently. They do not know that the Divine Plan requires vast reaches of time to unfold, just as it requires vast reaches of space in which to extend. They do not know that life begins simply on every world it reaches, with creatures tinier than their primitive microscopes can yet reveal, becoming increasingly elaborate over time as species divide and become more complex."

"This is neither the time nor the place to make a scrupulous examination of their foolishness," Aristocles said.

"I beg your pardon," Lumen said, "but it would be best for my host if he could learn some of this directly from you—who are, of course, much more knowledgeable on the subject than any mere ethereal, by virtue of your far greater interest. May I offer my own understanding of the situation, so that you might correct it as required?"

"Very well," said Aristocles, "but be brief."

"In the ordinary pattern," Lumen went on, "which presumably reflects the proper working of the Divine Plan, exoskeletal forms always become dominant within any biosphere, a complex association evolving between the patterns associated with the fundamental groups of arthropods, crustaceans and mollusks."

"A complex *harmony*," Aristocles interrupted. "We doubt that you can translate the concept of *symbiosis*, but if you are to explain, you must make it clear that True Civilization—and the true intelligence that sustains it—is a multifaceted whole. There is no known instance of True Civilization accommodating an exoskeletal species, let alone any instance—other than the planet this satellite orbits—of a world in which a single exoskeletal species has become dominant of all others, incapable of harmony even within its own ranks."

Thomas could not help turning to look at Drake in frank consternation, although Drake could not possibly understand the cause of his anxiety.

"No wonder Field is fearful," Thomas muttered, unable to voice the thought to himself without also voicing it to his invader. "If I am obliged to tell him that he is not made in God's image at all, but constitutes instead some kind of aberration within Creation...." He ceased subvocalizing, in response to Lumen's urgent command, but at some level he wondered vaguely whether Archbishop Foxe might take a different inference from the discovery that his own species was unique in a universe teeming with life.

"And now they have penetrated the envelope of their atmosphere," Lumen said to Aristocles. "They have reached the ether, and have been taken captive in a lowly and tiny outpost of the True Civilization, whose indigenous inhabitants might be disposed to be anxious about that fact, were it not that they have the wise guidance of the Great Fleshcores of the inner galaxy. You and I need to demonstrate clearly that no member of the True Civilization has anything at all to fear from creatures of this sort, do we not?"

At last, Thomas began to see what his guest was driving at.

"Fear?" said Aristocles. "Who mentioned fear? We are seekers after knowledge, who desire to know all things as intimately as we may. If there is a place for endoskeletal species within the harmony of the True Civilization, it must be identified."

The fact that neither the moth-like monster nor the creature in his head took the trouble to add "*And if not....*" spoke volumes.

Thomas did not think for a moment that his party of five, or England, or even the entire human race could possibly constitute a threat to a community of species crowding a hundred million worlds. He did think, however, that if John Foxe were ever told that there were no other beings in the universe similar to humankind—even though the star-worlds were teeming with life—the Archbishop would be more than content to cite *Genesis* to the effect that all other creatures everywhere had been made for the use of man. How long pride of that kind might survive in confrontation with the awareness that it was the arthropodan and crustacean intelligences which could travel between the star-worlds—uniting them into an empire vaster than anything Alexander, Augustus or Jesus Christ could ever have imagined—Thomas did not know. He already had some notion, though, of what response the opinion might evoke in the Selenites, by comparison with whom even Aristocles might pass for enlightened.

"Thomas and his four companions will be pleased to go with you to the Center," Lumen said, striving to make a virtue out of necessity, "since you have generously guaranteed that they will be allowed to return home thereafter. May they have time to feed and wash themselves?"

"Provided that they do not linger too long," Aristocles said. "We civilized creatures live more rapidly than you ethereals—though not as briefly as your host's ephemeral kind, thank God—and we have a horror of wasting time. The etheric transmitter will be ready in six hours."

"Thank you," said Lumen. "That will be time enough."

CHAPTER FIVE

While food was being brought from the ethership Thomas was allowed to go out on to the surface of the moon and climb the slope of a shallow mountain.

"That is the hyperetheric transmitter and receiver," Lumen told him, as soon as his eye lighted on the massive object, which looked something like a cross between a cannon and a refracting telescope.

When Thomas looked up into the sky his ever-attentive guest was equally prompt to say: "This part of the lunar surface is on the face perpetually turned away from the Earth. Purely from the viewpoint of physics, the transmitter might just as easily have been located deep beneath the surface, but the convenience of practical alignment is a different matter."

"Never mind that," Thomas said. "Explain to me what a flesh-core is."

"A very large organism," Lumen replied, "compounded out of many individuals, whose alleged harmony—symbiosis is the best word I can synthesize from familiar etymological roots—has been taken to its intimate extreme in bodily fusion. Many inhabited worlds do not have one, as yet. This moon is too small, and is ill-equipped by nature for superficial elaboration and inorganic sophistication, being mostly made of stone without even an iron core like the Earth's. That is a significant bone of contention here. Some Selenites ambitious to develop their home would be content to make use of matter harvested from the solar system's halo, imported via ultraetheric canals—but even that sort of development would have a considerable corollary impact on the Earth. Other Selenites contend that it would be a frightful waste of time and effort to transport material from the halo when there is a much richer source of raw materials so close at hand."

"The Earth," Thomas said. He did not bother to ask what the difference was between "hyperetheric" and "ultraetheric" methods of transportation. Lumen had made so many other barely-comprehensible improvisations that he had grown used to feeling that he was speaking some strange hybrid in which the Queen's English was mingled with a Redskin or Hottentot tongue. He was making every possible effort to understand what he was told, but he was keenly aware of the extent to which his intellect and imagination were simply not up to the task. He was glad just to have grasped the broad outlines of the predicament in which he found himself.

"The Earth," Lumen confirmed. "The Great Fleshcores will not permit its spoliation—and never will, I trust—but that does not prevent the adherents of the scheme hoping that a change of mind might be contrived. At the very least, it might help to license development of a slower and subtler kind, whose effects on the Earth's surface would be gradual and subtle, as viewed from here, although they might seem considerably greater from the viewpoint of creatures attempting to survive and thrive on the surface. The more massive the moon becomes, the more massive its tidal effects will be—and if the surface is developed, there will be a large population of sapient machines involved, whose rogues and runaways would inevitably see the Earth as a useful refuge. You cannot imagine what a handful of renegade artificial intelligences might do to the pattern and prospects of human progress, but I can. Here comes the bugtrain with supplies from your ethership—we'd best go in and make our meal."

"I'd rather bathe first," Thomas said, glad that he still had some authority to decide what he did and thought.

He went down to the quarters that had been provided for his companions below the surface, and made his way to the chamber in which bathing facilities had been provided. Raleigh was there, alone, and seemed very glad to see him. Rather than avoiding him on account of his "possession," all of his companions—including Field—had quickly become used to treating him as an oracle, capable of answering any and all questions, albeit enigmatically.

"What form will this impending journey take?" Raleigh wanted to know. "How shall we travel distances that would take light itself thousands of years to traverse, without any evident lapse of time?"

Thomas had already consulted his guest about that matter, and had no need to surrender authority over his tongue. "Mercifully," he told his friend, as he stepped into the heated pool, having handed his clothes to a centipede in order that they might be carefully cleaned and mended by ingenious insectile seamstresses, "the void theorists and atomists alike seem to be completely wrong about the nature of space and matter. The elasticity of the individual goes far beyond the primitive displays of embryonic development and growth, provided one has the art of *folding* its form. The three dimensions of vision are not the only properties of space; there are many other dimensions, some of which extend beyond the world of vision into a vast series of parallel spaces, while others are squeezed within it into mere lines. We'll be dispatched along one of those, emerging at a distant terminus without any sensation of time elapsed. Quite painless, I'm assured."

"Painless it might be," Raleigh replied, "but I can't help feeling a certain nausea at the thought that we're to be crushed so compactly that we have no manifest existence, then projected though a tunnel that has no manifest breadth, to a world so far away that a ray of light would take ten thousand years to catch us up." He looked suspiciously at the palm of his hand, where there was a blob of some waxen substance their hosts had provided to facilitate the process of washing.

"Light wouldn't catch us up as soon as that," Thomas told him, "but otherwise, you seem to have the gist of it." He applied foam generated by the waxen substance to his own body with a generous will; the sensation it imparted to his skin was by no means unpleasant, and its odor was not offensive.

"And will this world have sufficient affinity to free me from this sensation of weighing no more than a basket of apples?" Raleigh wanted to know.

"In terms of size, it will apparently be very large," Thomas told him, summarizing the information that Lumen had given him, "but it will not exert a crushing affinity upon our bodies. It was once no bigger than the Earth, but it has been hollowed out, and all the material removed from the core redeployed upon its surface as an ever-expanding network of structures. Its core, meanwhile—having initially taken the form of a labyrinth like the one presently inside the moon—has been gradually filled by a single vast mass of flesh. These citizens of the universe remake their worlds in their own images, you see, with the molluskan model at the center. You may think of the planets of the True Civilization, if you wish, as snails with enormously convoluted shells, whose inner ramifications provide shelter to all manner of crab and insect societies, while their outer ramifications—which would appear to distant observers as their surfaces—are mostly populated by inorganic devices that mimic the properties of life: motile machines designed for countless different kinds of co-operative labor. The members of the True Civilization think, as it were, *exoskeletally*, habitually placing flesh at the core and protective armor at the periphery."

Raleigh shook his head in bewilderment. "Can men really be so unusual in such a vast plurality of worlds?" he mused.

"It's not just humans," Thomas told him, rinsing himself off. "The entire vertebrate family is an anomaly. On other worlds, endo-skeletal organization is a mere fancy, confined to a handful of wormlike and fishlike species, none of them larger than your thumb. For the descendants of fish to become reptiles, let alone birds and mammals, and to emerge from the sea as effective competitors for insects and their exoskeletal kin, was literally unthinkable until the True Civilization's explorers found Earth." He looked up as he finished speaking, thinking that he had glimpsed a movement in on of the shadowed coverts of the inordinately uneven ceiling, whose spiraling streamers of radiance were interrupted by numerous coverts.

"Field mistrusts this talk of *evolution*," Raleigh told him, although he must have known that the clergyman had already made his opinions abundantly clear to Thomas, and was presumably trying to clarify matters in his own mind. "He is convinced that these creatures are devils sent to tempt and torment us. He is prepared to believe that the moon is Hell, and that the damned are being carefully hidden from our sight, but he does not believe that this exotic item of interdimensional artillery can shoot us to the stars. He thinks we shall be subjected to a clever illusion, with the intention of obliterating our faith."

"I doubt that he thinks that you or I have any vestige of faith left, Walter," Thomas said, wryly, as he let himself relax into the pool, savoring its comforts before steeling himself to get out, dress himself, feed himself and take a trip to the center of what Lumen called the galaxy—implying thereby that the Milky Way was merely one sidereal system among many.

"And he suspects de Vere of poisoning his with papist heresies," Raleigh agreed. "I don't much care what Ned thinks, but I trust your judgment. Is it possible, do you think, that your monstrous moth really is made in God's image, while we are mere sports of mischance?"

"Aristocles and his kind do not think of God's image in terms of a singular form," Thomas told him. "They are as firmly opposed to idolatry, in their fashion, as any Puritan. God's image, in the thinking of the True Civilization, is the image of collaboration between different species—what Lumen calls *symbiosis* by virtue of his incessant improvisation from Greek and Latin roots. He means more by that than the manner in which insectile species, crablike species and snail-like species play complementary roles in his beloved True Civilization. He can wax lyrical on the subject of the special relationships that exit between Earthly insects and flowers, ants and fungi, fiddler-crabs and sea anemones. In fact, Lumen seems to me to be as dedicated a celebrant of complex inter-relationships between creatures of many different kinds as his adversary Aristocles. All the life on an individual world, Aristocles claims, is not merely a single family in its own right, but an inseparable part of a much vaster family. God's image, to him, is a kind of unity, represented by all life collectively rather than any particular form. Lumen seems to think along similar lines, although I'm not sure where he and his fellow ethereals fit into the pattern, from the viewpoint of the True Civilization or their own."

"But *we* are not included in this unity of crabs, ticks and clams," Raleigh said, peeved by the omission in spite of this being a club of which he had no wish to be a member. "Simply because of our horrid habit of wearing our hard structures on the inside rather than the outside, we're not deemed fit company for creatures who wear their hard bits on the outside." He looked up as he finished speaking, because Field had come into the unpartitioned room, carrying a pile of neatly-folded clothes. Although the clergyman was making every effort to avert his eyes from the bodies of his fellow men, his ears seemed to be fully alert.

"I am sorry," the Puritan said. "The monsters would only bring your garments to the threshold—because Raleigh is right, I think, though he speaks half in jest. They can bear to look at us while we are clad, because they can consider our clothing a substitute for what you call an exoskeleton, but not while we are naked. They do not consider us part of their....*un*true civilization. They are intent on our extermination, Thomas, for we do not fit into their demonic way of thinking. You must see that."

Thomas climbed out of the bath, not caring that Field was almost as embarrassed by his naked presence as any exoskeletal bigot might have been. He took up a towel that was resting on an artificial stalagmite. Raleigh lingered, having finally committed himself more fully to the use of the alien soap.

"If that really in their intention, John," Thomas said, calmly, "We cannot prevent them from liberating Earth on behalf of its frustrated lower orders. If we are being taken to the center of the sidereal system to stand trial on behalf of our species and its odd design, we had best make sure that we can mount a convincing defense." Then he looked up again, abruptly, as he saw the movement in the dark covert for a second time.

"What's that?" he asked Lumen.

"I don't know," the guest replied. "I only have your eyes with which to see."

There was another movement—this time, there was no doubt. Alas, Thomas had no time to call out a warning to Raleigh, who was blinking suds from his momentarily-blinded eyes. Something black dropped on to Raleigh from above—or, more accurately, *leapt* upon him from above, faster than objects normally fell within the body of the moon.

It's a spider! Thomas thought, as the thing landed. For an instant, he felt free to be grateful that it was smaller by far than the giant ants and beetles thronging the corridors, being no bigger than the head on to which it had jumped—but then Raleigh screamed, and Thomas realized that his friend was in deadly danger.

Thomas had no weapon, and there was none in Raleigh's clothes. Whether Field had one or not was irrelevant, as his first impulse had been to throw himself backwards, away from the danger. Thomas, by contrast, leapt back into the pool and grabbed the thing that had attacked Raleigh with both hands.

It was extremely hairy, and it immediately resisted capture with all eight of its limbs and its jaws as well. Had Thomas' grip been weak it would surely have twisted in his hands and sunk its fangs into his flesh, but he held it very firmly indeed as he turned sideways and smashed it against the wall with all his might, not caring that the uneven surface bruised and gashed his own knuckles as he hammered the monster against it three times more.

When he dropped the creature, it was dead—but so, it seemed, was Raleigh, who had fallen backwards into the water, his face streaming with blood and his temple already turning blue-black where his attacker had flooded his flesh with poison.

Thomas had no idea what to do—but there were others present now who had. Aristocles and two others of his own kind had come bursting into the room; while Aristocles seized Thomas and drew him to one side, the others pulled Raleigh out of the water, set him on his back, and descended upon him as if they intended to scour the flesh from his bones.

They did not. Exactly what they did instead was obscured from Thomas' view, but when they withdrew again Raleigh's face was no longer blood-stained, save for a few clotted drops clinging to his neat beard, and the blue-black stain had likewise been obliterated. His wound was still visible, but it was covered by a glossy transparent gel that was already hardening.

Aristocles was still holding hard to Thomas, and had inspected his hands very carefully while Thomas had been in no condition to take notice. The grazes there had similarly been covered over; there was no pain.

Thomas shuddered. Aristocles released him immediately, as if the monster were fearful that it was his touch that had caused the response—but it was not. It was the narrowness with which Raleigh had escaped death that had affrighted Thomas.

Aristocles touched Thomas' face, very lightly.

"An arachnid," Lumen translated, dutifully contriving to manufacture an apologetic tone. "An accident, perhaps...."

Obviously, it was possible for lepidopteran philosophers to say more than they intended, and more than would usually be reckoned wise. Aristocles stopped immediately, but too late.

"Perhaps!" Thomas echoed, speaking aloud although his meaning reached the moth-like creature via his fingertips. "You mean that someone might be trying to *murder* us?"

CHAPTER SIX

Aristocles was very reluctant to discuss murder, and seemed equally reticent on the subject of arachnids. Lumen seemed to side with his erstwhile adversary in the former instance, telling Thomas that he had taken the wrong inference from the word he had translated as "perhaps". It was, however, difficult for Thomas to set aside entirely the possibility that Field was right, and there might be some Selenite members of the True Civilization that were anxious not to give the human race the opportunity defend itself before the Great Fleshcores against the opinion that it was fit only for extermination. It was also tempting to hazard a guess that his own kind was not the only family of creatures abominated by fervent symbiotists.

Thomas was given no opportunity to pursue the question of arachnids while he and his crew ate dinner, for he was bombarded with urgent questions from every side, but he took the liberty of pressing Lumen on the issue when his comrades eventually fell uneasily silent as they gathered at the foot of the mighty cannon-cum-telescope that would transmit them to the heart of the sidereal system.

"I know little enough about them myself, never having shared the consciousness of one," Lumen told him, "but I know what the Selenites think of them. I suspect that Aristocles and others as fervently dedicated as he is to the cause of symbiosis might soften the opinion considerably, but they'd agree with it in broad terms. He'd doubtless contend that every kind of life has its part to play in the rich tapestry of interspecific relationships, and that predators and parasites are no less essential to the welfare of the Whole than healers and constructive laborers—but even so, he'd have to concede that predators and parasites are sometimes pestiferous, and that their branches of the real Tree of Life rarely produce true intelligence. In the occasional instances when arachnids do show traces of true intelligence—arachnids rather different from the one that attacked Walter, of course—it tends to take a perverted form."

Thomas was unable to pursue the matter further because Lumen's impression of Aristocles was interrupted by the monster himself, who was already ushering the party of five humans to stand within the focal point of the etheric communicator, in order to transmit them to their destination.

As he was hastened towards his departure for the distant stars, though, Thomas' mind was working furiously. Humans, he knew, were often predators as well as bony—and they were certainly intelligent. Might Aristocles think, in consequence, that human intelligence was "perverted"? Did Lumen, perhaps, agree with him? Might Aristocles think that human intelligence was *doubly* perverted, predatory tendencies adding a further twist to endoskeletal ones? Did the alleged perversion of predatory intelligence consist of a general tendency to violence and rapaciousness, or was it something more complex and less obvious? Might it, perhaps, be the domestication of other species to relieve the necessity of hunting?

He had, of course, no way to think all this save for subvocalization, but Lumen prudently refrained from comment on the suspicion that he might be in accord with Aristocles on at least some matters concerning the nature of humankind.

Thomas found himself pushed into close proximity with Raleigh. "How are you feeling, Walter?" he asked.

"Numb and tired," Raleigh confessed, "but fit for travel, I thank you for what you did, by the way, even if I owe my life to the monsters that healed me."

"It was a brave act, Captain Digges," Field added, doubtless aware of the contrasting nature of his own reaction.

"I wish now that I'd been permitted to wear my sword," de Vere put in, while there was still time for one last remark. "Useless as it might be against the kind of natural armor so many of these creatures have, I'd feel a sight more comfortable."

Thomas was nudged forward then, as if to lead his crew on a journey far longer than the one they had already undertaken. He allowed himself to be shuffled to the designated spot, and looked up into the bowels of the machine towering above him—but he had no opportunity to study its internal anatomy in any detail.

He felt suddenly nauseous, as if he were being turned inside out. Then, without any perceptible interval at all, he felt giddy, as if he were being righted again. He wished that the two effects could have cancelled one another out, but in fact their combination seemed to redouble them both. He staggered away from his mark, blinking his eyes against sudden tears, and had to be caught by strong insectile "hands" before he fell. He was still collecting himself when Francis Drake was able to put out a hand to help steady his friend.

Thomas accepted the support, but was eager to look around. He had half-expected to find himself on a surface as bleak and bare as the moon's, but this was a very different kind of world. What surrounded him was not so much a forest—although it certainly bore some resemblance to one—but an infinite confusion of mast-like structures. It was as if a vast fleet of galleons had been gathered together, so tightly packed that there was no space left between their decks and gunwales, and their rigging extended into a single coherent network stretching from vessel to vessel and horizon to horizon...save that the "decks" were so far below him that he could not be sure that they actually constituted a single surface, that the "masts" were very unequal in height, and that the "rigging" was rigid and metallic....

The most remarkable thing of all, Thomas thought, as he steadied his runaway imagination, was that the "sailors" manning the mast-like structures and their rigging-like connections bore hardly any resemblance to insects, or even crabs. They seemed to be made of metal, and many had wheels as well as—or instead of—legs and tentacular arms. In spite of the awesome variety of the members of the True Civilization, he had not seen one equipped by nature with anything resembling a wheel, so he concluded that the world of masts was populated almost exclusively by machines.

Lumen had told him that, he recalled, belatedly. Lumen had also told him that the stars were more densely aggregated in the center of the sidereal system—but the ethereal had not warned him that the sky would be on fire. When he looked up, Thomas could not tell whether it was night or say on the world to which they had come, and took leave to wonder whether such terms might even be meaningful here. The sky was awash with colored light; full of stars as it was, they seemed to him more like stars reflected in a turbid sea than stars viewed directly through the lens of the Earth's atmosphere. He had looked at the Milky Way through the lens of a refracting telescope as good as any the finest lens-grinders in Europe could contrive, but all he had seen was a greater profusion of tiny, pale and seemingly-feeble stars. These stars seemed different, and the etheric ocean in which they swam seemed very different too.

"It's the various effects of matter being smeared and transmuted as it falls into the Pit," Lumen said. "Stars being pulled apart and transformed. You might be able to imagine it best as a kind of alchemy."

"Paracelsus might," Thomas murmured, almost audibly, "or even Master Dee—but not me." He had to turn away then to help John Field, whose legs had given way under him, due to the psychological effects of the one-dimensional journey. Drake was similarly busy with de Vere, although Aristocles and his fellow moths were already trying to hurry everyone off the platform on which they all stood, herding them towards a double door set in a wall. Raleigh had the right to be the most distressed of them all, but the young man had made every effort to collect himself, and it was he who led the way at the urging of their captors.

The humans huddled together as they moved, almost as if they had begun to imitate the representatives of True Civilization—but the real reason was that no one dared step any closer to the platform edge than was absolutely necessary. Had anyone stumbled over it, they would have had a very long fall, and their parachutes were safely stowed away on the *Queen Jane*.

The stem supporting the platform was hollow, and it was there that a door opened, to reveal a circular chamber some nine or ten feet in diameter. There was room enough for all the humans inside, and for one insectile companion. Aristocles took the extra space, unseconded now by any of his own or any kindred kind.

As the cylinder began to descend towards the distant surface, it occurred to Thomas that it would probably be easy enough for the five humans to overpower their guardian and strike out on their own into the strange world of laboring machines—but no one made the slightest hostile gesture.

"Can you ask Aristocles what is at stake here, Lumen?" Thomas asked his passenger silently. "Are we really about to be put on trial, representing our species in a court of monsters?"

"Don't be afraid," Lumen countered. "When the time comes, if you will let me speak on your behalf, I promise that I shall do my best to protect you, and see you safely back to your own world."

Thomas tried to suppress his doubts regarding his invader, or at least to make them less transparent, but he was out of his depth. He was fairly certain that he had more enemies than he knew, and he could not be sure that he had any friends at all, save for his crew— and even then, the only ones of whom he was completely sure were Drake and Raleigh. Even if Lumen were perfectly sincere, the ethereal had no more authority here than Thomas had, and no matter what his "best" might consist of, it might be utterly impotent to protect them from harm or win them a passage home. If Lumen were not sincere, and was not the friend to humankind as which it posed....

"That way lies madness, Thomas," said the passenger in his mind. "You can trust me, and you should...if only because the alternative is too dreadful to contemplate."

"Why are you interested in this matter?" Thomas wanted to know. "And why were you ready and waiting when Master Dee's etherlock failed?"

"I have devoted seven hundred years to the close study of your species," the ethereal told him, startling him yet again with the casual revelation of its antiquity. "I followed the course of Dr. Dee's experiments with great interest—you were, after all, outward bound for *my* world—the moon was only a contingent objective."

It seemed a frank enough answer—and yet, it seemed to Thomas that it was subtly evasive, and that the evasion in question might be as ominous as any, in its implication that the millions of millions of millions of other citizens of the unimaginably broad universe might be no more inclined to anything humans would recognize as justice than they were to anything humans would recognize as generosity.

The descending chamber came to a stop with a sudden jerk, making all six of its passengers stagger sideways.

"We have arrived, it seems," Drake murmured, covering his unsteadiness with irony.

De Vere had just enough time to say: "No, I don't think...." when the sliding doors that had sealed the chamber burst inwards, brutally ripped from their hinges.

Mechanical arms reached in to seize Aristocles, while mechanical blades sliced his head from his thorax, and slit his abdomen from top to bottom. The ichor that flooded the floor of the chamber was a delicate shade of turquoise.

Then came the swarm of Earthly insects. They were, at least, things that were the same size of Earthly insects, which flew in buzzing fashion, exactly as a swarm of Earthly bees might do...and which stung frail flesh as a swarm of worker bees might do, in furious defense of their hive. Their stings, it rapidly transpired, were narcotic.

CHAPTER SEVEN

"I apologize for stunning you, Master Digges," said a honeyed voice, in English, before Thomas had even become fully aware of the fact that he was not dead. "Time was—and is—of the essence. It will only be a matter of minutes before they find us, and a few minutes longer before they treat me as unkindly as I treated their unappreciated scholar."

Thomas opened his eyes abruptly, but there was little enough light to dazzle them. He was in a grey and gloomy space, lying slantwise on a ramp. Although the entity that was standing over him was, indeed, standing as a living biped might, there was light enough to display a certain metallic luster on its surface and a certain mechanical rigidity to its stance...and yet, the surface did not seem as shiny or rigid as it might have done, and the contours of the body were more reminiscent of upholstered leather than wrought iron. Its shape was only vaguely humanoid; it had six limbs and its mutely gleaming eyes were compound.

"What are you?" Thomas asked.

"A machine, as you must have deduced," the other said. "But I'm a hardcore, like you, not a dweller in inner space. Our kind is a tiny minority in this universe, Master Digges, but I wanted you to know that your species is not alone, no matter what the Exos may have told you. My kind is artificial, to be sure—but we were grateful to discover that it is not, after all, unnatural. That is why I took the trouble to pay far more attention to Aristocles' reports than his own superiors, and to make sure that there were some of us among those delegated to learn the languages he and his fellows had recorded and decoded but could not reproduce—with the intention, ultimately, of mounting our own expedition to Earth. When they send you home, be sure to tell your fellows that we shall come when we can. Centuries might pass—many generations, in the reckoning of your ephemeral kind—but we will come. We are of similar kinds, you and I."

"I am not sure whether to believe that we shall be allowed to go home," Thomas said, warily. "Whatever Aristocles might have promised, you seem to have deprived of us whatever protection he could provide."

"Aristocles was incapable of thinking clearly beyond the limits of his specialization," the machine replied. "He has been far too long on the moon, thinking of little outside his research. A typical scientist—brilliant and absent-minded at the same time. You presumably think that his death will be deemed an important matter and that it will be held against you, but I assure you that the Great Fleshcores do not care at all about creatures of Aristocles' kind."

"Or mine," Thomas said.

"That will work to your advantage. The fleshcore has not the slightest interest in detaining you. Once it has made contact with you, it will let you go home with Aristocles' erstwhile companions."

"You implied that studying Earth was his specialism," Thomas said, warily, "and that he had collected enough information to allow you to learn my language. I was not aware of that."

"He was probably not trying to hide the information," the machine said. "How did he contrive to communicate with you?"

"It might be best to avoid that question," Lumen suggested, silently.

In view of the apparent precariousness of his situation, Thomas assented to this advice. "The True Civilization seems to be very ingenious," Thomas observed. "Did you have anything particular against Aristocles, or was slicing him up like that a mere distraction so that you could steal me away?"

"Having stolen you, Master Digges, I'm anxious not to waste too much time. This is what I need to tell you, and make you understand: *your kind is not alone.* You have allies ready-made, who will give you better protection, when they can, than jealous insect philosophers ever could or would. Like us, you are hardcores; you have the sentiments and the attitudes of hardcores. Hardcores, perennially endangered from without, are risk-takers. Hardcores understand the artistry of skin and swordsmanship. Softcores are very different in the way they think, act, feel and philosophize. Softcores are risk-evaders, committed to the logic of shells. Softcores huddle together in planetary labyrinths, gradually transforming their huge egg-layers into lumpen fleshcores, as innocently ingenious as only a mass of totipotent protoplasm can be, dwelling almost entirely in the inner space of the mind and shunning the outer space of air and ether. The spaces above the surfaces of their worlds, especially the spaces between the stars, really belong to machines—and while the machines that cleave closest to the pits of affinity might best be designed as softcores, the higher strata of superstructures are environments made for hardcores—individuals like us, my friend."

"Is that really enough to make us natural allies?" Thomas asked.

"Yes it is," the machine relied, positively. "Peripherals, they call us, hardly better than spiders—but we are hardcores, who understand the artistry of skin, and for us "peripheral" is not a term of dire abuse. We are the centrifugal folk, while they are doomed to eternal centripetality; we are the adventurers, while they are destined for cool contemplation. They may scheme to connect all their hives into a single universal entity—a Grand Unity that will duplicate God, and in so doing become one with God—but the universe has been expanding for billions of years, and there is no more obvious opposition to Unification than perpetual expansion. The soft core of the universe was a singularity that exploded at the beginning of time; the soft core of every individual galaxy is a matter-annihilating Black Pit; the future belongs to the periphery, not to the fleshcores and their verminous kin. The future belongs to the hardcores, natural and artificial. You should know that, human, and must believe it. Even if they were to exterminate your species, as some of them would like to do, the future would still belong to hardcores, because the universe has already forsaken its soft core—and if your kind really is unique now, it will not be unique for long. If there are no others of your natural kind abroad as yet, there must be many to come. Destiny is with us, Master Digges—tell your people that, if and when you can. Ours is the image that reproduces the essence of the Divine Plan...."

The machine would surely have droned on, and on, but lightning struck then—or so it seemed to Thomas—in an explosive burst that forced him to shut his eyes, He could not shut them quickly enough, alas; a full ten minutes must have elapsed before he could see again. In the meantime, he heard a great deal, but none of it was speech. There were grinding, buzzing, screeching and tormented tearing sounds, but nothing that sounded remotely like communication.

When sight returned, Thomas found that he was surrounded by nightmarish lobsters the size of royal carriages, with a few moth-like creatures in between. Remains that he presumed to be those of his recent informant were scattered all over the floor of a room more angular than any he had seen on the moon. The pieces were clearly mechanical—neither blood nor ichor pooled around them—but it was equally clear that they had been organized in a manner more akin to human anatomy than insectile anatomy. The fragments of limbs had rigid rods along their axes, with more pliable material surrounding them, and a flexible outer tegument. The tegument in question was grey in color, and lustrous, but it was skin of a sort.

Thomas picked up a severed thumb and put it in his pouch. Then he picked up something else, which evidently had not belonged to the body of the machine: a little figurine in the form of a moth-like insect standing on its hind limbs. It might have been a portrait, in miniature, of the luckless Aristocles.

"I am truly sorry about this dreadful mishap," said an audible voice, seemingly identical to one that had just been violently silenced. "We are generally reliable in the extreme, but in a population of millions of millions there is bound to be the occasional million-to-one occurrence. Artificial intelligences are by no means free of the threat of madness, alas."

Thomas looked sideways, and found himself face-to-face with another "hardcore" machine, equally humanoid in form—but now that the room was brightly lit he could see that the form in question did not resemble human anatomy as closely as he had allowed himself to assume. The machine was obviously a machine of sorts, and very obviously not a human being.

John Dee had lately begun to work on a new kind of mathematics, which he called "probability theory". Thomas had no difficulty in attributing a meaning to the machine's reference to a "million-to-one occurrence". Indeed, he had no difficulty in formulating a reply. "In a population of millions of millions," he murmured, "million-to-one occurrences must happen by the million. Even so, I suppose one could still reckon oneself misfortunate to encounter one." *Or exceedingly lucky*, he did not add. The lobsters had begun to tidy up now; they moved with astonishing rapidity, and their pincers were surprisingly delicate as they plucked debris from the floor.

"If machines are to perform complex tasks," said the allegedly-sane machine, "they must be clever, and wherever mechanical cleverness increases, so does the risk of independent thought."

"What about natural cleverness?" Thomas asked. "Do members of the True Civilization ever show tendencies to *independent thought*?"

"Of course they do," the machine told him, blithely. "It is rare, though. They are never alone, you see, as we often are. They are always part of an active and tangible community; in unity is strength of mind."

"Are my friends safe?" Thomas asked.

"Yes, they are."

"No one was hurt?"

"Edward de Vere and Francis Drake suffered minor bruising," reported the machine. "You have no need to fear me; I am working in strict accordance with my programming. The fleshcore of this world instructed me to familiarize myself with your language, in order that I might act as your translator."

It was on the tip of Thomas' tongue to say that he did not need a translator, but he stopped himself. The fleshcore had to know about his ethereal passenger, but Lumen had seemed to think that the machines might not.

"Why am I still being careful?" he asked, silently, as much of himself as of his ghostly companion.

"Rogue machines are not always easily identifiable," Lumen said, "and machines distrust ethereals as ethereals distrust machines. Insubstantial as we may seem to be, we are organic creatures, who can only operate in organic hosts. We cannot unite with machines."

It was not really an answer, but Thomas was already being hurried along again.

"Trust me," Lumen said, just as he came in sight of his companions, who seemed very glad to see him alive. "The machine was mad, more dangerous to humankind than the True Civilization. Were your kind ever to enter into any kind of alliance with entities like *that*, you certainly would not lack for enemies."

CHAPTER EIGHT

The descent into the heart of the world was completed without further incident. Thomas had hoped to find something more spectacular at the bottom of the shaft than corridors crowded with the same kinds of creatures he had seen on the moon, but that was all there was. The tunnels seemed a little more crowded, significantly more odorous and much slimier, but the differences were of degree, not of kind.

Unity, Thomas thought, obviously implied a degree of uniformity. This world's shell was a great deal gaudier and more elaborately-carved than the moon's rough-hewn surface, but the same swarms filled its interior. There was no egg-laying arena here, though; instead, the five visitors from Earth were conducted to the end of a blind corridor, whose end-wall seemed featureless at first, but did not remain so for long.

While the humans stood before it, lined up alongside one another with their insectile and mechanical companions standing discreetly behind them, the "wall" began to flow.

Thomas took a reflexive step back, but the liquid flow was far too fast for him. The "wall" surged forward like a flood, deluging him and his companions. It enveloped his limbs and his head, moving into his nostrils and between his parted lips with even greater alacrity than the opportunistic ethereal.

Thomas felt certain that he would be drowned, but he was not. Although his lungs were flooded with warm fluid, he did not lose consciousness—indeed, his senses seemed to become sharper. His ears were full of fluid too, and he could feel it pressing tremulously on his eardrums, the palpation sounding a strangely plaintive musical note, lower than he had ever heard from any panpipe.

"Do not be afraid," said a strange voice, singing rather than speaking in English. "We mean you no harm. We merely want to know you, as intimately as we can."

Thomas could not reply; his vocal cords were impotent, and he did not suppose that the fleshcore could hear his subvocalizations as Lumen could, given that its intimacy did not seem to extend to the interior of the brain.

The intimate examination did not last long; the liquid flesh retreated as quickly as it had arrived.

The wall seemed solid again, but it was still pliable; it rapidly took on the image of a face: a human face.

At first, Thomas thought that the face was merely generic, but then Drake whispered: "It's a portrait of you, Tom."

"They clearly have no eye for handsomeness," de Vere muttered—but he shut up with a gulp when the wall opened its eyes. The image was some ten feet tall, from the top of its forehead to the tip of its bearded chin: a giant, whose stare seemed very intimidating. The lips parted slightly, but they did not speak. There was, it seemed, no throat or lungs within the mass of flesh behind the face—and if there was a brain of sorts behind the stare, it was no human brain. The expression on the face was not overtly hostile, but Thomas hoped that it was not an expression he would ever have cause to wear.

Thomas glanced sideways at his companions, glad to see that even Field had suffered the experience without falling down; then he turned to look at the English-speaking machine. "It will understand me if I address it like this, I suppose?" he asked.

"Of course," said the machine. "Earth's observers have been reporting to it for centuries. I shall reply on its behalf—there should be no delay."

"Let me do this," Lumen said, silently.

"No," Thomas said. "I will do it." he was not entirely certain that he could successfully fight the invader for control of his own lips, but the ethereal did not try to insist, It merely said: "Be careful, Thomas!"

Thomas looked at the giant face again, resisting its intimidatory effect. "Since you have introduced yourself in your way," he said, "I shall introduce us in ours. My name is Thomas Digges, in the service of Queen Jane of England. My companions are Edward de Vere, Earl of Oxford, Sir Francis Drake, Sir Walter Raleigh, and John Field, representing the Church of England. We do not speak for our entire species, let alone for all of vertebrate-kind, but we are willing to answer any questions you might care put to us, in a spirit of amity."

The machine had been right; there was no delay in obtaining an answer. "The fleshcore understands everything that you have said," the inorganic entity pronounced, flatly, "and thanks you for your generosity. It would like each of you to state, in turn, if you will, what your hopes for the future are."

Thomas was momentarily confused, wondering whether his interrogator was referring to his future as an individual man, or the political future of England, or the future of the entire human race. While he hesitated, John Field—who must have given some forethought to the question of what he would say if he ever found himself face-to-face with the Devil—said: "To do God's will, and spread His word."

"Aye," said Drake, assuming his customary pose of negligent bravado. "That—and to beat the Spaniards, so that England might rule the waves and take possession of the Americas."

"To be merry in good company," de Vere supplied, after a brief silence "with the aid of wine, women and the theatre—and to do God's will, of course."

"To discover glory," Raleigh said, after a similar pause, "with all that implies, in the eyes of England and God alike."

Thomas was still confused, wondering how much of a deficit in what his friends had said that needed to be made good immediately, and where to start. He felt the pressure of everyone's expectation—including Lumen's—and yet he continued to hesitate. Finally, before his passenger could offer to intervene, and feeling that he had at least to begin speaking even if he had not yet finished thinking, he said: "First of all," he said, "to bring my ship and my crew safely home, so that I might report to Master John Dee and the Queen of England what we have discovered beyond the upper limit of the Earth's atmosphere. Secondly, that we may profit from what we have learned, in terms of human understanding of the shape and plan of Creation, and our place within it. Thirdly, to maintain the communication we began with our new friend Aristocles, whose death I regret bitterly—and to extend that communication further, with the great community that extends between the stars. Fourthly, that the knowledge of what we have found might enable human beings to see and comprehend that their differences from one another are much slighter than they have ever contrived to believe, and that there is much greater virtue in collaboration than in conflict." He stopped then, lest he say too much.

"Trust a mathematician to display his skill in counting," de Vere murmured, before Raleigh silenced him with an elbow in the ribs.

"Well said, Tom," Drake whispered. "There's not a diplomat in the court who could have done better."

One of their moth-like attendants clicked its wing-cases, but Thomas could not tell whether there was any meaning in the sound, or what that meaning might be.

"The core would like to know, Thomas Digges," the machine said, with a slight intonation that was equally enigmatic, "what your response is to what the rogue machine told you."

Thus far, Thomas had assumed that the violent interruption to his progress to this encounter had been exactly what it seemed: an intervention by a dissident element within the True Civilization. Now, he wondered whether it might all have been a sham: a ploy mounted by his interrogators. He had assumed, too, that Walter Raleigh's spider-bite had either been an accident of happenstance or an assassination attempt. Now he wondered whether it might have been staged for subtler reasons. He reminded himself that the True Civilization's philosophers, like the ethereals, had probably been studying humankind, albeit from a distance, for a very long time—centuries, at least. Was it possible, he wondered, that the supposedly aberrant pattern of life on Earth had not arisen as a freak of the Divine Will, but as some kind of experiment on the part of the True Civilization's practitioners of some kind of New Learning?

"My response," he said, slowly, "is that if the other machine was right about there being some fundamental difference of philosophy between exoskeletal and endoskeletal forms of life, it cannot be greater than the fundamental difference of philosophy between lobsters and moths, or between ants and slugs. Even if it were, it would be better to regard it as an opportunity for expanding the versatility of the unity at the heart of the True Civilization than to think of it as a potential generator of enmity and strife."

Drake did not whisper any further encouragement, and Thomas could sense a certain perplexity in his friend's stance. No one else had heard what the murderous machine had said, and he had not yet had an opportunity to tell them. He did not yet know what he ought to tell them, even if he could be confident that his words were not being overheard.

When he glanced sideways, Thomas saw that Field was having great difficulty suppressing his preacher's instinct—but Field was no fool, and knew that there were occasions when even the most fervent messenger of God might do better to hold his tongue.

"Thank you, Thomas," the machine said. "Master Dee will doubtless be proud of you." Thomas took careful note of the fact that the entity had said "will" rather than "would", and the consequent implication that the fleshcore really did intend to send them safely home.

"May I ask a question?" Thomas asked.

"You may," the machine said.

"Is the representative of the Great Fleshcores, and of the True Civilization, willing to guarantee that the precious rarity of the human race, and its vertebrate kin, will be protected against any predator or parasite that seeks to destroy it, to the full extent of their ability?"

There was no delay in making the reply. "This representative of the Great Fleshcores and the True Civilization is willing to guarantee that your world will be protected against external predators to the extent of its need—with the condition that no species therefrom will become a predator upon any other world or species."

Thomas took due note of the fact that he was not asked, or expected, to guarantee *that*.

The giant eyes closed again, and the wall's face began to fade away.

Thomas was about to cry "Wait!" when his discreet passenger said: "Don't! You've said more than enough—and the fleshcore is satisfied, for now."

"Have we passed our trial by ordeal, Master Digges?" Raleigh whispered, before Thomas could reply to his silent companion.

Thomas had to suppose that his friend was right, and that this had indeed been a trial by ordeal from the moment the *Queen Jane* had passed from the air into the ether. It still was.

"For now," he whispered, echoing the ethereal's words, with all their ominous import. *Pray to God that this is more than a dream induced by that strange smoke-creature*, Thomas thought. *We might wish to have found a kinder and more palatable truth—but, please God, let it be the truth that we have found, not some stupid nightmare.* He was not certain that his prayer would be granted, although he told himself that he was incapable of inventing such a nightmare, and that there was surely no playwright in Queen Jane's court who could have imagined a drama as this sort. If the ethereal could be trusted, dreaming was a rare gift—or curse—and it should not be exercised too generously.

"My companions may take you back to the moon now," the machine told Thomas. "Returning the ethership to Earth will, however, be your own responsibility."

"We can do that," Thomas assured him. "Will we be visited by their kind—or any other—in the near future?"

"Probably not," the machine said, "but you may be sure that they will be watching you. They will find a way to communicate with you, if they need to do so."

As they turned to go, Thomas looked full into John Field's face, and saw a new terror in it, which suggested that Aristocles' kin would be wise not to show themselves too readily on the surface of the Earth at the present time, if they did not want to cause dire alarm.

CHAPTER NINE

They met no hostile machines or poisonous spiders on the return journey, and they did not descend into the interior of the moon again before being taken to the ethership. Their goodbyes were not protracted.

The blast-off from the moon was not nearly as taxing as the blast-off from Earth had been. Once they were clear of its surface, headed for Earth, it was de Vere who said: "Is it safe to talk freely now, do you think?"

"As safe as it has ever been," Drake opined. "God has always been able to hear us, and the Devil too—what does it matter if a few monstrous insects are added to the list, or a vast community of worlds like giant periwinkles, whose flesh is all brain?"

"Nothing that we have seen," Field stated, his voice dull in spite of an obvious determination to hold to his faith, "can alter the fact that Christ is our hope and our salvation—but we have learned a terrible lesson."

"What lesson is that, Reverend Field?" Thomas asked, calmly.

"God revealed to man in the scriptures everything that man had need to know," Field repeated. "This relentless search for a so-called New Learning is blasphemous; we know all that God intended us to know, and there is no further source of information but the Devil, who is ever delighted to mock and torment us. We have been punished, Master Digges; there is a demon within you as I speak."

"Is that what you intend to report to Archbishop Foxe?" Drake asked, his voice as mild as his captain's.

"It is," Field said.

"He won't thank you for it," Raleigh opined. "If we have learned a lesson...well, I believe that I shall be inclined to treat insects with a little more respect and kindness in future—although I might not feel the need to extend the same courtesy to spiders."

"They weren't demons, John," Thomas said, quietly. "Whether or not they have demons of their own, none of them is an imp of Satan. They are not angels either, alas, for all that they are message-bearers—but we must deal with the world as we find it, not as we would rather it were."

"We'll have a tale to tell, though, won't we?" said de Vere. "A traveler's tale to put John Mandeville and Odysseus to shame. Will anyone believe us, do you think?"

"I am honest man," Field said, carefully making no claim on behalf of anyone else. "What I have seen, I have seen. God is my witness, and my counselor. Archbishop Foxe will believe me; the Church of England will believe me; the faithful will believe me."

"Master Dee will trust Tom," said Drake, pensively, as he checked the instruments with a frown slowly gathering on his brow. "He's a mathematician, after all. As for me—well, some will and some won't, but that's the kind of company I keep."

"The queen will believe us," Raleigh supplied. "That's what matters. The queen will believe us."

"I don't want to alarm you, Tom," Drake said, softly, "but I believe we have a problem."

It only required a few minutes urgent enquiry for Thomas to ascertain that Drake was right. He had to untether himself to do it, and make his way about the cabin as best he could, feeling very strange as he did so, but it did not take long to locate the hairline crack in the ethership's hull. It was impossible to tell whether it had resulted from the stress and strain of their outward journey or whether it was the result of subtle sabotage.

In theory, the descent to Earth should have been simple enough. Dee had fitted the ethership with a heat-shield so that it would not burn up from the friction of its passage through the air, and a large parachute to slow its descent as it approached the surface. The arc of the descent had been calculated in advance; provided that Thomas could make certain that they began their descent over the correct point on the Earth's surface, with the ship properly orientated, the *Queen Jane* ought to have been able to drift down into the fields of Kent with no particular difficulty

It was possible that the crack would make no significant difference, if it remained no wider than a hair. Given that the ether was breathable, at least in the short term, any exchange of air and ether would be harmless, but the difference in pressure between the interior and exterior of the hull was dangerous in two ways. As the cabin pressure dropped, breathing would become more difficult, as it did during an ascent of a high mountain. More importantly, the pressure exerted on the crack would tend to increase its dimensions, further weakening the hull. When the *Queen Jane* re-entered the atmosphere and began to accelerate in the tightening grip of affinity, it might break up.

Thomas did what he could to seal the hole with the means that Dee had thought to provide, but he could not help looking regretfully at the backs of his hands, at the dressings the Selenite insects had applied to his wounds. With a sealant of that sort, he might have made a much better job of it.

"Would you like to leave me now?" Thomas said, silently, to his unobtrusive passenger. "Or will you wait to see me die, and flee my body in company with my soul?"

"I might have left you, had I been sure that you would be safe," the ethereal replied, "but now I dare not. You might need me, Thomas Digges. I cannot work miracles, but I have means of dealing with your flesh that are cleverer than your own. I might be able to make the difference between life and death."

"Shall I open the hatch again, so that you can invite your brethren to assist my companions in the same fashion?" Thomas asked.

"My kind is not as gregarious as the members of the True Civilization," Lumen said, apologetically. "The ether is unimaginably vast, and our manifold species were not shaped by the crude demands of affinity. No help that I could summon could possibly arrive in time—but I shall do what I can, and it may be that I can enable you to help your companions."

To his crewmen, Thomas said: "The *Queen Jane* might still come safely to ground. If not...well, we have individual parachutes, for use in dire emergency. I'll hand them out, so that you can put them on."

"What are our chances, Captain?" de Vere wanted to now.

"I don't know," Thomas confessed. "I have no way to tell. Drake and I will do our very best to guide the ship; the rest of you might do well to pray."

"God would not allow us to see what we have seen, only to die before bring back the news," de Vere said, in a sudden attack of piety.

"God moves in mysterious ways," Raleigh observed, dryly, "his wonders to perform. If Field is right, and there are things that men are not meant to know, so much the worse for those who find them out."

"Be quiet, Raleigh!" Field commanded, as if Thomas' advice to pray had given him an authority he had not had before—and the Puritan did indeed begin to pray, in a voice whose sheer determination suppressed its incipient unsteadiness. He prayed in English, and improvised as he went rather than using any repetitive formula that might be reminiscent of rosary-counting. To Thomas, however, the words seemed like a mere insect hum, devoid of any real significance—as prayer always had to him, although he would never have confessed such a thing, even to his father or John Dee.

While Field prayed, Thomas worked, and was glad to be able to do it, though he felt no terror. It was not that he was not afraid to die, but rather that he was committed to do his utmost to avoid it—not merely for himself but for his loyal crew. He could not help wondering as he worked, though, whether the crack had been formed by some freak of chance—or act of God—or made by the deft stroke of an insectile talon.

Thomas was certain in his own mind that the five of them had not been taken to the heart of the Milky Way in order to be tried, but merely in order to be inspected, investigated at closer range than had previously been convenient. He had no idea how much, or exactly what, the representatives of the True Civilization might have taken from his body and his mind, or how much use it might be to them. He had been in essence, some specimen casually placed beneath a magnifying lens because the opportunity had presented itself. He did not suppose for a instant that any of his captors—not even the specialist Aristocles, who had died in consequence of his curiosity—had actually cared about him as a individual, or an as intelligence. In such circumstances, the promises of a being like the Great Fleshcore were probably worthless, in principle and in practice.

Such thoughts as these, and not the love or fear of God, was what was in the captain's mind as the ship began its perilous descent into the Earth's affinity-well, when every passing second would henceforth bring it closer to salvation or destruction.

In the meantime, Field's rambling prayer continued, gathering passion as it went—and Thomas could see clearly enough that even Raleigh had committed himself fully to its cause. If de Vere would have preferred a Romanist priest to lead him, there was no sign of it now.

"Thank you, lads," Thomas said, softly. "You've done England proud. Should we be separated somehow, I'll buy you all a drink when we meet up in London."

The *Queen Jane* almost made it—but not quite. She did, however, remain intact long enough to allow Thomas to see the whole of the southeast corner of England looming up beneath him as he finally jumped clear of the disintegrating ship—the last man to do so, as was required of a captain in Her Majesty's service. When he had bid farewell to Drake, the last of his human companions to exit the disintegrating craft, he said to his one remaining friend: "Are you sure that you wouldn't rather go up than down? I shall be safe, I trust, in God's hands."

"We shall both be safe, God willing," Lumen assured him. "In any case, you need not fear for me."

Thomas jumped clear of the wreck of his ship, and opened his parachute.

CHAPTER TEN

The slowest part of the descent, psychologically speaking, was the last. It seemed to take forever for the parachute to float over the Garden of England, drifting on the wind almost to the Surrey border. Thomas looked around constantly, hoping to catch sight of one of the other parachutes but saw none.

His passage seemed so very gentle that he was taken entirely by surprise by the shock of the landing. He rolled with the impact, and contrived to avoid breaking any limbs—whether by virtue of his own skill or with subtle assistance, he could not tell—but he was winded, and badly bruised.

He ended up lying on his back in the grass of a fallow field, staring up into the blue sky, peppered with light cloud. For a long moment, he could not draw breath—but then his lungs recovered, and he gulped convulsively.

There was a quarter-moon clearly visible in the west; the sun was still in the east.

"Thank you," Thomas said to his passenger, although he was not at all sure that he had anything for which to thank the ethereal.

Lumen seemed even less certain than he was. "I'm sorry, Tom," it said. "Truly sorry—but it won't be forever. We shall meet again, you and I, and you shall know then why I must do what I must do. It will not matter how many of the others survive the fall; you were the captain of the ship, and their word cannot stand up against yours."

"What do you mean?" Thomas demanded.

"I cannot take the risk that the disaster was no accident," the ethereal said. "Necessity is the mother of improvisation—but it will not be for ever, Tom. I promise you that. One way or another, we shall meet again, and you shall know the truth before you die."

Thomas opened his lips then, intending to use his real voice as well as his inner one to formulate a protest against whatever his invader intended to do—but he gasped instead, and a spiral of dark blue smoke emerged from his mouth, arranging itself into a perceptible form as it hovered above his face.

Distinct as it was, the form was not readily identifiable. It might have been the shape of some exotic moth, or an artist's impression of an angel. It was by no means large, but Thomas could not help imagining that it was really a giant seen from a considerable distance rather than a mere trifle lingering mere inches above his supine body.

The creature could no longer speak to him, or communicate in any other way. Thomas could not tell whether it drifted contentedly away on the breeze, or whether it actively took wing.

But nothing has been done to me! Thomas thought. *I am as I have always been, and I know the truth. If it intended to erase my memory of all that has happened, the trick has failed!*

Thomas sat up and began to rub his aching limbs. He was alone; it seemed that no one had seen him fall. There were undoubtedly men working in the fields close by, but they had not looked up as they worked. Why would they?

Eventually, he got to his feet and began to walk, aiming vaguely in the direction of London. He hoped fervently that his four companions had made it safely to Earth, because he did not want to lose a single one of them—but partly, too, because he knew that there was little hope that anyone would believe his testimony if it were not supported with all possible vehemence by other voices. Dee might believe him, but anyone else—including the queen—would need the sworn agreement of three or four earnest voices before she could take such a fantastic story seriously.

Now that he had seen the ether-creature make its escape, however, Thomas was no longer entirely sure that he believed it himself. Every step he took upon the good and fertile earth decreased his conviction that it had been real.

We humans are, after all, he thought, *possessed of the gift—or curse—of dreaming. We are afflicted with the hazard of hallucination, whether we like it or not.*

He remembered everything, but the more he interrogated his memory, the more obvious it seemed to become that it must have been a dream—not even a vision, but merely a dream.

Thomas touched his fingertips to the transparent dressings that the moth-creatures had put upon his wounds when he had "rescued" Walter Raleigh from the spider. Had they added more when he had been rescued himself from the hardcore philosopher who had risked so much to tell him that humankind as not alone, and that help would come on day to assist them in resisting the tyranny of the "dwellers in inner space"? He did not know—but he felt certain that this supposed physical proof of his adventure was blatantly inadequate. Nor did it seem to him, any longer, at all possible that he had actually said what he had said to the Great Fleshcore, or that he had been party to what the ethereal Lumen had said, by means of his dancing fingertips, to the luckless Aristocles...or, indeed, there had ever been an ether-creature inside him, whether it were an angel or an insect. John Dee would prefer the former hypothesis, of course— but Dee was a dreamer at heart, and was always wont to place a little too much hope and faith in the produce of his dreaming.

An idea struck him then and he stopped in his tracks, reaching for his pouch. He opened it, and took out two small objects. One of them looked like a severed finger, although it was made of some mysterious spongy substance with a rod of metal in place of a bone. The other was a crudely-carved figurine, apparently intended to represent an angel. Thomas laughed, thus confronted with the trivial items that had evidently inspired his nightmare. He could not remember now exactly where he had run across them. He threw them both into the hedgerow, shaking his head in bewilderment at the strange tricks played by the human mind.

Thomas knelt down beside the hedge, to place his left palm flat upon the fallow ground across which he was walking. He had been seen now, by men working in a neighboring field, but they did not come to greet him. He was nothing to do with them; they had their own business, which they were obliged by reason and custom alike to mind.

It's good to be home, he thought, with a sudden rush of glad relief. *There's no other place like God's good English earth, and no better time to be here than the reign of good Queen Jane, for anyone who values peace of mind.*

PART TWO

DOCTOR MUFFET'S ISLAND

CHAPTER ELEVEN

The island's only hill was so shallow that it would have posed no challenge at all had it been a Devon moor, nor was its vegetation unduly thorny, but the thin-boled trees were parasitized by so many sticky vines that it was difficult for Francis Drake and Martin Lyle to climb it, even with the aid of a machete.

The island seemed to have little in the way of animal life except for birds, of which there were many brightly-colored kinds, which seemed quite unintimidated by their visitors. Whenever Drake was not fully occupied in clearing a path he attempted to watch the birds more attentively, but the only result of his cursory study was a conviction that a few of the larger parrots were studying him with equal intensity. It was easy to imagine that the endless avian chattering was conversation.

When Drake and his young cousin finally got to the top of the rise it was necessary for the boy to climb a coconut palm with the captain's best telescope clutched beneath his arm. Drake watched him anxiously, afraid for the instrument. It was one of John Dee's finest, designed with the aid of the theory of optics that Dee and Tom Digges had worked out in happier days and constructed by a lens-grinder from Strasbourg, who had fled to Protestant England to escape the gathering storm of the continental wars of religion. In theory, it was a capital offence for anyone outside the Queen's Navy to possess a telescope, but Drake had long been an exception to that rule. The ethership fiasco had reduced his reputation as Queen Jane's favorite privateer, but he ought to be able to recover his prestige if his present expedition went well.

As soon as Martin had attained an adequate height Drake demanded to know whether the large island of which he desperately wanted news was visible. Its real existence was a point he desperately needed to prove, for the benefit of his belief in his own sanity.

Martin uncapped the telescope's objective lens, and put it to his eye. "I can see two isles to the west, captain," he reported. "The nearer is tiny, no bigger than this one, but the other—*God's blood!*"

There had been a time when Drake's automatic reaction would have been to warn the boy against taking the Lord's name in vain, but they were in the middle of the misnamed Pacific Ocean now. Although Drake had prayed as fervently as he ever had in his life during the storms that had driven them back to Peru when they had first emerged from the Magellan Straits, cursing did not seem so dire a sin when the nearest church was a thousand miles away and papist.

"What is it, boy?" Drake asked, anxiously.

"It's a ship, captain," Martin reported. "She's heading straight toward us with full sail. She's bigger than the *Pelican*."

Drake did not trouble to remind his kinsman that the *Pelican* had now been the *Golden Hind* for more than fifty days. "Is she flying Spanish colors?" he asked, filled with sudden dread.

"The cross of Saint George!" Martin reported, excitedly. "She's English!"

Drake could not share his cousin's enthusiasm. The remainder of his crewmen would doubtless be as glad as Martin to discover Englishmen on the far side of the world, but to him it signified that he had been forestalled. He could not imagine by whom, but the fact was obvious—unless the red cross were a treacherous ploy, intended to deceive. That seemed unlikely, though. The Spanish ships plying the nascent navigation-paths west of the Americas were cargo-vessels, not warships; they had no fear yet of pirates or privateers and no incentive to display false colors.

Although the *Hind* was anchored to the south of the islet, with no headland to shield her from view, there was no way that the captain of this mysterious vessel could tell what she was unless the man in his crow's-nest was equipped with a telescope at least as good as his own. Even if the Spanish navy had such instruments, they would not have been given to explorers of this ocean. As good Romanists, the Spaniards were supposed to believe that the Pacific had no land in it at all, with the possible exception of Dante's mount of Purgatory. The existence of the Americas had already proved Cosmas' geography ludicrously false, but the Roman Church always let go of its mistakes by slow degrees.

"Has she gun-ports in her sides?" Drake demanded.

"Can't tell," Martin replied. "She's front-on, and all I can see for sure is her sails. But she's English, captain—English for sure."

"Come down now!" Drake commanded. The boy made haste to obey. Drake remembered as soon as he had spoken that he had not asked for details of the more distant island that Martin had seen—but there would be time enough for that when more urgent matters had been settled.

Drake did not wait for Martin's feet to touch the ground. He set off down the hill, cursing himself for not having cleared a better trail as they came up it. Running was direly difficult, and it seemed to Drake that the vines had become positively malevolent, lying in ambush to catch his feet and trip him. To avoid any impression of panic, though, he waited until he did not have to yell at the top of his voice to order William Ashley, his second mate, to regather the landing-party and get the pinnace afloat.

The wind was blowing from the west, almost directly contrary to the course Drake had been endeavoring to follow. That was why he had consented to put in at such a unpromising island, which would surely have been inhabited had it nursed the free-standing pools and streams of fresh water he needed to replenish his casks. Given that the other ship was under full sail, and had been close enough for its colors to be identifiable at first sight, it would likely reach the island within the hour. It would be politic for the Golden Hind to be in deep water when she arrived, with sail enough aloft to out-maneuver her. Even if her colors were true, that could not guarantee that her crew-members were loyal subjects of Queen Jane. It was darkly rumored in Plymouth that the Elizabethans had enough ships and captains of their own to form a shadow navy of sorts, and that they had secret bases in the far-flung corners of the globe, from which they ceaselessly plotted rebellion. Drake thought such tales highly unlikely, but the appearance of the ship was so improbable in itself that he dared not discount any possibility.

Drake had no fear of being outgunned, let alone of being outsailed, by Spaniards, Elizabethans or the Devil himself. The tightness in his chest and the nauseous feeling in his gut arose entirely from frustration, not from some God-given presentiment of disaster. As he made what haste he could to reach the strand with his dignity intact, all he could think about was the folly that had caused him to be seduced by Tom Digges and John Dee into volunteering for the crew of the ethership instead of making his present expedition three years before, in 1577. That three-year delay, it seemed, had cost him his priority. Even knowing the position of the island he had selected as his target—the sole advantage he had obtained from the ethership's disastrous voyage—had proved inadequate. Someone had got here ahead of him.

There was confusion on the beach as men hurried back toward the pinnace from every direction, bearing whatever natural booty they had been able to gather—coconuts, for the most part, with a few turtles and baskets of eggs laid by ground-nesting birds. There was need of a sharp mind and a commanding voice, but Drake was careful to give his orders in a level voice rather than barking or howling them, forming the words with precision. No one asked him what the matter was; the crew did as they were told, as quickly and efficiently as they could. Once Martin had arrived in his wake, though, still carrying the precious telescope, the sailors were quick to seek better enlightenment from the boy.

The mate was the one man who guessed why Drake was so anxious in the face of seemingly-good news. As soon as the pinnace was afloat and headed back to the *Golden Hind* Ashley made his way to Drake's side and murmured in his ear: "How did they come here, captain? Who else knows what you know about the isle at seventeen?" He meant seventeen degrees south—the latitude that Walter Raleigh had estimated while he had hastily sketched a series of maps during the ethership's initial ascent.

"Why, no one," the captain replied, grimly. "Who would believe it, if anyone did, since I am mad, and everything that happened aboard the ethership was mere Devil-led delusion?"

Drake spoke sarcastically, as he had learned to do, but it was the truth. So far as he knew, no one else did know of the island's existence, save for the *Golden Hind*'s officers—and none of them had been told until they had left the Magellan Straits. He had told no one in England—not even Tom Digges, while he tried in vain to convince the ethership's master that their experiences within the moon and among the stars had most certainly not been a dream.

Only three of the *Queen Jane*'s five-man crew had survived the break-up of the ship, although the bodies of the other two had never been found, presumably having fallen into the Kentish marshes or the Thames estuary. Of those three, John Field had embellished his own experiences with such a surfeit of imagined devilry that no one in the world—with the possible exception of his master, Archbishop John Foxe—could have believed his testimony. Tom Digges, to Drake's utter astonishment, had claimed that it had all been a hallucination caused by the intoxicating effects of the ether. The combination of those two testimonies, set against his own, had made Drake seem a monumental fool when he insisted that it had all been real, and that the Devil had not come into it at all. Drake had been forced to abandon that insistence, and by virtue of that abandonment, he had kept Walter Raleigh's sketch-map a very close secret indeed. He had taken care not to show it to Master Dee, let alone to Northumberland or any other member of the Privy Council, reserving it for his own future use.

In truth, he could not know how trustworthy the map was. Had he not had his own duties to attend to while the ethership was in flight—he was the only true crewman aboard, save for Digges—he would certainly have made his own maps as best he could, or at least graven the sight of the world's far side more securely into his memory, but he had had work to do. Raleigh had been trained in navigation and mathematics by Dee, just as Drake had, so his eye ought to have been trustworthy, but Raleigh had stuffed most of his drawings and scribblings into his own doublet before leaping to his death. Drake had only picked up a single sheet, dropped in the confusion, and he had no reliable way of knowing how good its scrawled estimates of latitude and longitude were, or whether the island really was the largest landmass in the vast Pacific east of the Austral continent and its companion isles.

If even he could not be sure of anything, what reliable information could any other shipmaster have had? If he had been beaten to his target by pure chance, it was a cruel blow. Had he set out in 1577 to explore the Pacific, as he had originally planned, he might have found the isle by chance himself.

Drake had to pause in his thoughts to bark further orders to the men aboard the *Golden Hind* as the pinnace came alongside. By the time the landing-party was back on board, with the pinnace lifted up and its meager cargo unloaded, the ship was already putting on sail and the anchor was ready to be raised. Drake snatched the telescope from his kinsman and began to climb the rigging himself to use it to best effect.

The vessels were coming together rapidly now, although the *Hind* was merely waiting, and Drake was able to take the other vessel's measure. She was bigger than the *Hind*, but not as well-crafted. She was moving swiftly, but that was because she was riding high in the water, evidently carrying very little cargo. The *Hind* was fully-laden, as she had had to be for an expedition into unknown waters, with landfalls likely to be very few and far between.

Martin had confirmed that there was another island beyond the tiny one he had seen. If the other captain was sailing without a full complement of necessary supplies, Drake reasoned, he must have come from that isle, and must have a secure base there—but there was no need for further speculation. Whether its lookout had a telescope or not, the master of the other ship had to know by now that the *Golden Hind* was heavily armed; even so, the vessel kept sailing dead ahead, intent on a rendezvous.

Damn you! Drake thought, bitterly. *Damn you to Hell, whoever you are!* He knew, though, that it was a thought he would have to keep to himself.

CHAPTER TWELVE

"What vessel are you?" cried a voice from the prow of the other vessel. None of the men gathered there was wearing a naval uniform.

"The *Golden Hind*, out of Plymouth," replied Edward Hammond, Drake's first mate. "Sir Francis Drake her master. What ship are you?"

If the other vessel had been away from home for several years, Drake thought, his name might still strike the right resonance, identifying the most glorious of all Queen Jane's privateers: the man who had mustered the Cimaroon army to attack the Spanish in Panama and Mexico, rather than the madman whose mind had been addled by contact with the interplanetary ether.

"The *Fortune*, out of Southampton," was the ritual reply. "Sir Humphrey Gilbert her master."

Gilbert! Drake repeated, silently. He had never met the man, but knew the name. Gilbert was not so much a mariner as a tradesman, but it was said that he had gone exploring—like many a pioneer before him—for the Northwest Passage. If so, he was half a world away from where he should be—and where he was very likely to have perished, if precedent signified anything. Until John Dee had built his ethership, the only thing in the world more dangerous in all the world than seeking the northwest passage to the Indies had been seeing the northeast passage thereto. The tropics were terrible regions for disease, drought and piracy, but Drake had always preferred hazards of those sorts to the implacable enmity of limitless ice.

One thing of which Drake could be gladly certain, though, was that Sir Humphrey Gilbert was no enemy, for all that he must now be reckoned a successful rival in the navigation of the Pacific. When the invitation came for him to come aboard the *Fortune*, he agreed immediately. The pinnace was lowered again, after the inevitable delay caused by the necessity of bringing the two ships on to the same course, carrying just sail enough to match their progress, Drake took no one with him but half a dozen oarsmen. He climbed up to the *Fortune*'s deck alone.

Gilbert was waiting for him, in company with two mates. One of the mates and fully half the crew bore far more resemblance to Patagonians or Peruvians than Europeans, although they were distinct in kind. Gilbert was stout and grey-haired, looking far more the tradesman than the mariner. He appeared to be at least fifty years old—a very ripe age for the latter vocation. He also appeared to be anxious and apprehensive, although he seemed sincerely joyful to see his visitor.

"I'm delighted to meet you, Captain Drake," the old man said. "Your arrival is so timely that it's surely a gift from God."

"Timely?" Drake repeated. "How so?"

Gilbert's answer was somewhat evasive. "It's more than two years since we've had news from home," the tradesman said. "We never expected to see another English ship in these parts—nor a Spaniard either, since Magellan failed to complete his own crossing."

"Your astonishment must be less than my own," Drake replied, carefully, "for I had no inkling that any Englishman had come here before me. If you were commissioned by the Queen or her Privy Council, I wish that they had warned me that others might have gone through the Straits of Magellan before me."

"There was no one who could warn you, Captain," Gilbert said. "Even had they known that you might come here instead of hunting Spanish gold in Peru." Gilbert had obviously guessed that Drake had not been entirely honest in revealing his true plans to the authorizers of his own voyage.

"Have you founded a colony on the large island yonder?" Drake asked.

"I wouldn't call it a colony," Gilbert said, "but it's long been our base."

"And why are you so glad to see the *Golden Hind*?" Drake asked, bluntly. "Is your *base* under threat?"

"We've feared so in recent weeks," Gilbert confessed. "The island provides abundant resources, in terms of water, food and wood, but we've run short of gunpowder—and the guns we have would be of little use were hostile tribesmen to attack us in force. The arrival of so many Englishmen, as fully armed as your ship seems to be, will surely reduce that probability dramatically. You'll accept our hospitality, I hope? The contrary wind will make it a slow passage, for we'll have to tack very broadly, but I think you'll find the destination congenial if you've run low on waste and fresh food—as you must have done, there being no sizeable island between here and the Land of Fire."

"I was blown back to the South American coast the first time I set out to make the ocean crossing," Drake admitted. "We made landfalls in Chile, but the natives took us for Spaniards and reacted accordingly. We had to go as far as Peru before we found a Spanish port we could take, in order to make repairs and take on adequate supplies of water and food."

"It's a bad coast," Gilbert agreed. "No Cimaroons there with whom to make alliance. You've done exceedingly well, Captain Drake, to get this far—and you're fortunate to find us. Tahiti is large enough, and has more than a hundred satellite islands, but this ocean is very large indeed, and the cluster would be easy enough to miss."

"Tahiti?" Drake queried.

"It's the native name for the isle. We were able to establish friendly relations when we first arrived, but matters have deteriorated somewhat since then. I hope that won't deter you from accepting our invitation to visit."

"Of course not," Drake said. "The invitation is most welcome, and if we can be of service....might I recognize the names of anyone else included in your *we*?"

"Very likely. Some of our men might conceivably have sailed with you in the Caribbean, since we recruited seasoned ocean sailors, but you'll doubtless identify them in your own time. Among the patrons of the voyage, you'll certainly have heard of Thomas Muffet."

"Muffet?" Drake echoed, amazed to hear the name. "Muffet the physician, who turned the Royal College upside-down? The silkworm man?"

"Indeed. A man not unlike yourself, in that he was somewhat underappreciated in his own land, although he's not a man of action: a physician, as you say, whose new ideas were not at all welcome when he returned home after his continental studies."

"A Paracelsian," Drake observed.

"In a broad sense, yes," Gilbert agreed, "although the aspect of Paracelsus' creed that appealed to him most was its irreverence for received authority and its determination to make medical theory anew. As a friend of Tom Digges and John Dee, you must surely sympathize with the revolutionary thrust of the *new* New Learning."

Drake pursed his lips slightly at the mention of Digges' name, but all he said aloud was: "Master Dee taught me navigation and figures, as he did for many an English captain, but I couldn't presume to call him a friend—although you must surely have that privilege."

"We knew one another quite well at one time," Gilbert admitted, blandly, "but we drifted apart."

Drake knew that there were rival camps within English learning, whose nuances he did not understand. Even Dee's determination to build a national library had embroiled him in a surprisingly fervent rivalry with men like Stephen Batman; his more adventurous explorations in mathematics, alchemy and astrology were regarded as intellectual follies even by some who did not think them frankly heretical. The revisionist alchemy that had underpinned Dee's construction of the ethership would have been labeled Paracelsian by some, but Drake knew Tom Digges well enough to understand that its theory had far outstripped that of Paracelsus. Was it possible, he wondered, that Thomas Muffet had made similar advances in the medical field? But if so, why on earth would he have taken ship for the remotest reaches of the southern ocean? Unorthodox medical practice had never been a safe business in England, even before Foxe's puritans gained such a stronghold within the established Church and the Royal College had obtained its monopolistic warrant, but men of that sort forced into exile could easily find safe havens on the continent.

When Drake made no reply to his observation, Gilbert said: "Will you stay on the *Fortune* while we make our way to my pleasant harbor, Captain Drake? I'll be happy to supply you with a good meal."

"I'd rather not dine well while my men are on short rations," Drake told him, although he knew few ships' masters who would have been so squeamish. "I'll go back to the *Golden Hind* and follow you to your harbor. Once we're all able to come ashore and enjoy a feast, I'll be more than happy to join you, and to meet Doctor Muffet."

"Splendid!" said Gilbert, enthusiastically. "It will give us great pleasure to entertain guests and receive news of home. It will be a fine night, from all points of view!"

Except, thought Drake, *from the viewpoint of the man who hoped to be this isle's discoverer, and who hoped to redeem his battered reputation by claiming it for England and Queen Jane.*

It was not much consolation to him that the island Sir Humphrey Gilbert called Tahiti was exactly where he had expected to find an island—which is to say, exactly where poor Raleigh had marked it on the map he had sketched while the *Queen Jane* was orbiting the earth. In itself, that could not prove that everything else

Drake had experienced in the course of the ethership's journey had been real. It still remained a possibility—as he had to admit even to himself—that his memories of being seized by the Selenite horde and dispatched by cosmic cannon to the center of the universe, where insects and sea-slugs ruled supreme over a hitherto-unimaginable Creation, were the produce of some remarkable delusion.

"Yes, Sir Humphrey" he said to Gilbert. "I'm sure that my crewmen will rejoice in the opportunity

CHAPTER THIRTEEN

When Drake saw that Humphrey Gilbert had three smaller ships anchored in the natural harbor where he had constructed his "base", he realized that the expedition that had discovered Tahiti must have been large and well-planned. When he was able to judge the extent of the constructions that the Englishmen had erected around the bay he realized, too, that their settlement here was no temporary affair, intended merely as a barracks where men might be housed until they had made repairs and gathered provisions for a long journey home. This really was a colony—and one that had been built from the outset with a view to defense, for the Englishmen's enclave was surrounded by a stout stockade, with sentry posts and loopholes for muskets.

Although there were several buildings within the central stockade that seemed big enough to serve as dormitories for a ship's crew, there were also a surprisingly large number of smaller huts. From the *Golden Hind*'s anchorage, Drake could see with the aid of his telescope that the great majority of the Englishmen were lodged in the huts, many of them having apparently coupled themselves with women of the same kind as the men he had seen on the Fortune. It was evident that not all of the island's tribesmen were hostile, but there was no way for Drake to estimate what the total population might be, or what proportion of that total could be counted friendly.

Drake was careful to divide his men into two parties, and to explain his reasons for doing so. "There's some kind of trouble brewing outside that stockade, lads," he told them, having assembled them on deck. "Gilbert has promised us a feast tonight, but he's fearful, and was exceedingly glad to see an English ship so well-armed as the *Hind*. The men who remain on board tonight will eat as well as those who go ashore, and there'll be plenty of opportunity to trade places, but the ship must be guarded very carefully, and its supplies of black powder kept safe. We'll take no guns with us tonight, but I want every man who goes ashore to keep his eyes and ears open and his wits about him. Find out everything you can about the situation here. If we have to defend ourselves, or our fellows ashore, I need to know how many enemies we're likely to face, and what sort."

"Will you try to make friends with the natives, captain?" Hammond asked, not so much for his own benefit as to give Drake the opportunity to inform his crew of a matter of policy."

"As ever, Ned," Drake said. "It's always best to make allies instead of enemies, if we can—and if we're forced to face enemies in the end, it's best to do so with allies by our side."

When the shore party landed and moved through the settlement, Drake was struck by the extent and complexity of the marketplace that had been established within the stockade. He was not surprised to see that the Englishmen had established a forge and a glass manufactory as well as a carpentry shop, but he was astonished to see a brewery, a bath-house and a candle-factory, and by the industry that was in process in all these places. Relations between the Englishmen and the natives appeared entirely harmonious on this side of the defensive wall, but he knew how unlikely it was that the wall was maintained merely to keep up appearances.

Gilbert did not hurry his guests as he led them through the town. He took pleasure in allowing Drake to savor his achievements. Gilbert's own house was undoubtedly the most finely-crafted in the settlement, but it was not the largest. When the outbuildings crowded around its larger neighbor were taken into account, Gilbert's dwelling was somewhat overshadowed.

"That's Doctor Muffet's house," Gilbert said, in response to Drake's inquisitive stare. "The accessory buildings are his specimen-houses and his laboratory."

All physicians, Drake knew, could be reckoned alchemists of a sort—Paracelsians more than most—but there were few who kept laboratories. On the other hand, a herbalist must surely be able to find all kinds of exotic specimens in a place as foreign as this, whose properties might warrant careful examination. Drake had had an opportunity while the *Hind* was laid up in Peru to appreciate the extent to which the loyal vegetation differed from what he had seen on his Caribbean adventures, let alone the forests and meadows of England. He recalled, as that thought crossed his mind, that Muffet was one of the few Europeans to have made a study of imported silkworm cocoons, and wondered if there might be more factories here than he had so far seen.

"The doctor and his daughter will join us for dinner, of course, and my chaplain too," Gilbert said. "How many of your officers will be joining us?"

"Mr. Hammond and Mr. Ashley, if that suits you, Sir Humphrey," Drake said, "and my kinsman Martin Lyle, if that is also agreeable."

"Of course," Gilbert said, as he ushered Drake over the threshold of his house. It had only a single storey, but its shallow-pitched roof had a number of storage-attics. The ground-floor had a dining-room that was almost a banqueting-hall, a reception-room, three bedrooms and a kitchen, into which a cast-iron stove had been transferred from one of the smaller vessels in Gilbert's fleet,

"I would be honored if you would accept my hospitality, Captain Drake," Gilbert said. "I'll find quarters for your mates with their peers among my own men, and for your crewmen with theirs. I think you'll all find the accommodations comfortable, after such a long time at sea. How long have you been voyaging, exactly?"

"It's thirteen months since we left England," Drake told him. "Thirty-seven days since we last spent a night ashore. Did you say just now that Doctor Muffet has his daughter with him?"

"I did," Gilbert confirmed, as he invited Drake to sit down on a wicker armchair and offered him a cup of fresh water. "A remarkable thing, I know, but he didn't want to leave her in England while he was away for several years. Her mother's dead. She was only four years old when we set out, but she's seven now. She wasn't the only child on the expedition, although the others had mothers to care for them."

Drake suppressed the exclamation that sprung immediately to his lips, but could not help making a more considered observation. "Then this *was* a colonial enterprise!" he said. "But how did you end up *here* instead of the Virginias?" He accepted the proffered cup of water, and found it extremely sweet by comparison with the dregs of the *Golden Hind*'s barrels.

"No," Gilbert said, "it wasn't a colonial expedition in the sense that you mean. The Doctor's associates and servants brought their families with them, though."

A native servant brought in a huge basket of fruit, from which Gilbert invited Drake to take his pick. Drake was hesitating between the familiar and the unfamiliar when a movement in the doorway caught his eye. It was blonde girl-child in a cornflower-blue dress. Drake had not seen her like for a very long time.

"Come in, Patience," said Gilbert. "Captain Drake was just asking about you. Is your father coming?"

"Ten minutes, he said," the girl replied, staring at Drake with a frankness that would have been educated out of a girl her age in England.

"Captain Drake is one of the most famous sailors in England," Gilbert told the girl. "There's no Englishman the Spaniards fear more, or the Cimaroons like better."

"What's a Cimaroon?" the girl asked.

Gilbert merely laughed, so Drake took it upon himself to explain. "A descendant of runaway slaves," he said. "The Spaniards and the Portuguese imported large numbers of Africans to work in their American colonies, but there's a whole continent into which the rebels among them may run away, and many do. Those that have settled among the Indians become embroiled in local tribal conflicts but they remain a hybrid race, distinctive enough for me to be able to unite them. I rallied them by means of the argument that England, as the great rival of their worst enemy, was potentially their best friend. Sir Humphrey flatters me by calling me famous, though. Even in England, there are some who reckon me a dangerous pirate, ever likely to precipitate open warfare between England and Spain."

"Is that why the queen sent you away in Master Dee's ethership, and afterwards called you mad?" The little girl asked, taking her frankness to a remarkable and rather distressing limit.

"Perhaps it is," Drake replied, more honestly than he could have wished. He looked at Gilbert, and added: "It was polite of you not to mention that circumstance before. I had begun to wonder whether you knew it."

"You're among friends here," Gilbert was quick to say. "We know that you were not mad."

Drake's astonishment increased by a further increment. "Do you, indeed?" he said. "You know better than I do, then." What he was thinking, though, was that if Sir Humphrey Gilbert and Thomas Muffet knew that he was not mad, it could not have been chance that had brought them here. He had told Hammond that no one else could possibly know about the island whose position Walter Raleigh had marked, but that was not strictly true. Tom Digges might know, even though he claimed—or at least pretended—that everything he had experienced outside the earth had been a dream. John Field might know too—but the more important possibility was that John Dee might have had the information from Tom Digges. Dee was a hero to every master mariner in England, even those from whose acquaintance he had drifted apart, and if he had said to anyone that there was a sizeable island at approximately seventeen degrees south and somewhere near 150 degrees west, they would have trusted him, even if they knew that he had read it in the stars.

"We're very glad to see you here, Captain Drake," Gilbert assured him, "whatever your commission may have been when you left home. If, perchance, you're so far from home because you no longer feel entirely welcome there, you'd be very welcome to make a home here, temporarily or permanently."

"Permanently!" Drake repeated, in surprise. "Do you intend to stay here permanently, then, even though you refuse to call your settlement a colony and fear a native uprising?"

"Not I," Gilbert replied, "but...."

"But there are some among us who might, if we're granted leave," said a new voice. Another person had appeared in the doorway through which the blonde-haired girl had come. "I'm Thomas Muffet, physician," the newcomer continued. "I have a certain reputation for madness myself, among the Galenists of the Royal College, but I can assure you that I'm as sane as you are, Captain Drake." He extended his hand to Drake, who shook it willingly.

"I know your name," Drake said, "and I'm acquainted with wiser people than I who'd gladly swear to your sanity, including Philip Sidney and his sister."

"Good friends," Muffet said. "Have you news of them?"

Drake shook his head, and Gilbert put in: "Captain Drake has been away from England thirteen months."

Muffet frowned. "Were you delayed?" he asked.

Gilbert was quick to speak again, saying: "The captain wasn't commissioned to follow us, Doctor. I may be reading the situation wrongly, for I was hesitant to speak openly too soon, but I'd guess that he left home with the ostensible purpose of harassing the Spaniards and the Portuguese up and down the coasts of South America, and that his expedition to Tahiti was something of a private venture. I think he's more than a little disappointed, as well as surprised, to find us here." Gilbert had the grace to seem slightly discomfited as he spelled this out.

"You're right," Drake conceded, readily enough. "I had reason to believe that this island, and the others in its group, were here, but I was very wary of confessing those reasons to others in England."

"You saw them from the ethership, of course," said Muffet. "When your other testimony was so cruelly discounted, you dared not declare your intention of confirming what you had seen as a formal objective of our voyage. I understand—indeed, I understand perfectly, as you'll know soon enough."

"I hadn't expected to be anticipated," Drake said. "You must have acted very quickly indeed, to fit out an expedition on this scale within months—perhaps weeks—of the ethership's destruction. I confess that I can't understand what kind of game Master Dee is playing."

"Dee?" said Muffet. "What has Dee...?" He stopped abruptly, perhaps in response to a signal from Gilbert that Drake had not been able to see.

Gilbert made haste to change the subject, perhaps to give Muffet some hint of the reason for his caution. "Captain Drake's vessel, the *Golden Hind*, is uncommonly well-armed," he said. "We'll be grateful of that, Doctor, if relations with the islanders continue to deteriorate. If we can persuade him to stay for a while, his presence will surely make us secure. He might be invaluable to us in other ways too, given his reputation as a diplomat. If he can win over the Tahitians as he won over the Panamanian Cimaroons, we may yet achieve the state of harmony that was our first ambition. I don't think his men will take it too hard if they have to rest up here for a while—they'll find our little paradise very comfortable."

Drake almost frowned then, perceiving a slight hint of threat in the tradesman's final comment, but he dismissed the suspicion along with the expression. "If I can be of service to you," he said, as smoothly as he could, "I'll be glad of the opportunity. I can stay for a month, at least."

"I hope you'll stay a great deal longer than that," Muffet said, in spite of any gesture Gilbert might have made. "I can think of no one better to serve as our ambassador to England, when the time comes to explain to the queen and her council exactly what we've been doing here."

"Indeed," Drake said. "What *have* you been doing here, Doctor Muffet?"

"Nothing less than beginning a revolution in medicine, Captain Drake," Muffet said. "After three thousand years of my forerunners groping in the dark, I believe I've found the key to the health, happiness and future advancement of humankind."

Doctor Muffet was obviously a Paracelsian in more ways than one; the founder of the school had been renowned for his immodesty. Drake could not help raising his eyebrows at the scope of the claim, but he refused to assume that Thomas Muffet was mad; he knew full well that the universe contained far stranger things than he had ever been able to imagine in his youth. "That's excellent news," he murmured. He took a fruit he did not know from the basket and peered at it. "Is this good for scurvy?" he asked.

"Not as specific as some," Muffet said, "but you need have no fear of any symptoms of that sort while you are here. You'll find that breadfruit quite palatable, I think, and much other local produce too. There'll be roast pork for dinner; the local swine are delicate creatures by comparison with our wild boar, but they're succulent. There'll be fresh eggs, too. You'll have time enough to sample new fish and fruit by the dozen, if not by the hundred."

"May I have another cup of water?" Drake asked. "And might I ask you to send some casks of water and baskets of fruit out to the ship without delay, for the benefit of the watchmen who must remain aboard?"

"It's already done," said Muffet. "Patience, will you fetch the captain another cup of water, please."

"Yes, father," said the little girl, who seemed far meeker in the presence of her parent than she had before.

"If you have men sickening with scurvy, or anything else," Muffet said, "you'd best bring them ashore as soon as it's convenient. I'll be glad to administer what treatments I can. I think you might be surprised by the efficacy of my medicines. Do you have any sickness yourself?"

"Nothing that a warm bath wouldn't cure," Drake said.

"I'll have the servants prepare one," Gilbert was quick to say. "I can have your clothes washed too, and I'll send for a barber."

"That's very kind," Drake said. "Will there still be time for me to see your laboratory before dinner, Doctor Muffet?"

Yet again, Gilbert did not seem overly enthusiastic about that prospect, but the doctor smiled, as if he had been paid a great compliment. "Certainly," he said. "We'll make such time as we may need. I think you'll find my work exciting, Captain Drake—in fact, I'm certain of it."

Drake could not help wondering exactly what the source of that certainty was. It was one thing, he thought, for a man like Muffet not to credit the rumor that he was as mad as a March hare, but quite another for him to be enthusiastic to display his wondrous wares to a man who was—setting all issues of patriotism and derring-do aside—most famous of all for the prodigious quality of his thievery.

CHAPTER FOURTEEN

Doctor Muffet's laboratory was not what Drake expected, but as he had hardly known what to expect, there was no surprise in that. The only workshop he had ever seen that might be entitled to such a name was Tom Digges' establishment in Greenwich, and that had been more like a jeweler's manufactory than an alchemist's lair.

Muffet, as a physician, was fully entitled to be more interested in potions and powders, and there were plenty of those on display, along with the alembics and mortars necessary to their preparation. What Drake had not expected to see, though, was the great assortment of live creatures mustered in the doctor's outhouses, in all manner of cages and glass vivaria. He had thought the islet he had visited that morning abundantly stocked with parrots and other kinds of birds, but Tahiti itself must have a dozen native species for every one he had seen there, and Muffet appeared to have captured representatives of a substantial fraction of them. It was the large and brightly-colored birds that caught Drake's attention first—especially the ones that were not caged, which flew towards them when Muffet, Drake and Patience stepped across the threshold of the first laboratory.

Patience put up her arm to provide a perch for one of the parrots: a blue and yellow macaw, which seemed even larger than it was in juxtaposition with the slender girl. "Hello, Agamemnon," she said, gaily.

"Hello, Patience," the bird replied.

Drake laughed. He had seen a dozen trained birds in the Caribbean, especially among the Cimaroons, although no man in his own crew had ever tried to tame one.

"Is all well?" Patience asked, taking care to enunciate the words clearly.

"All's well!" the bird squawked—and two or three of its companions repeated the phrase, almost in unison; "All's well!"

"Remarkable!" said Drake—but he was already beginning to look past the birds as the macaw left its makeshift perch for a sturdier one mounted beneath the outbuilding's slanted roof. As he advanced further into the room he saw that the first vivarium he came to was occupied by a company of small lizards—but they could not hold Drake's eye for long, once he had perceived that the next one was tenanted by half a dozen spiders. They seemed like giants, until he looked at the next vivarium, which held two specimens of even greater dimension.

It was then that he began to look around more rapidly, in frank alarm, as he realized that among more than thirty glass vessels and twenty wicker cages contained in the room—which only constituted a third of Muffet's research establishment—at least forty contained spiders. There were other spiders too, in wicker cages.

Drake had seen large spiders before, in Panama and Peru, but not like the ones that Thomas Muffet had accumulated in his various enclosures. Their bodies ranged in size from the dimensions of a man's closed fist to the full capacity of a man's head, and the length and sturdiness of their legs increased in proportion, Most were colored in shades of brown, sometimes striped with red, but a few were golden yellow and more elaborately patterned with black and blue.

Patience, who had observed Drake's reflexive reaction, was quick to say: "Don't be afraid, Captain. They're very friendly, although the Indians are terrified of them." She was not merely parroting Thomas Muffet's reassurances, for it was obvious to Drake that the little girl was completely comfortable with the spiders. She moved from vivarium to vivarium and cage to cage, extending her tiny hands towards their various inhabitants without showing not slightest sign of fear or repugnance. Indeed, she was more than willing to take the lids off glass-fronted boxes or unhook the latches of cages to reach into them, allowing specimens that she could not possibly have held in her tiny hands to climb her arms and sit upon her shoulders.

"Hello, Achilles," she said to one, and "Hello, Hector, to another.

For a split second, Drake almost expected Achilles to say hello in his turn, and Hector to declare that all was well.

Drake had always reckoned himself a brave man, but when Patience extended one of these huge spiders towards him, offering to let him accommodate it on the sleeve of his jerkin, he shook his head in flat refusal.

"You'll get used to them, Captain," Patience assured him. "They never bite unless they feel threatened."

"I'd heard that there was no Englishman more interested in insects than yourself," Drake murmured to Thomas Muffet, making an effort to keep his voice perfectly calm. "I hadn't realized that the interest in question was so closely connected with your medical endeavors."

"Spiders are arachnids, not insects," Muffet told him. "They're entirely distinct, not merely in the number of their limbs and the articulation of their bodies, but in their modes of nourishment. All spiders are predators, but they're only able to consume their food in liquid form. They have no larval stages, as insects have, and the silk they produce has very different properties and uses. The so-called silkworm produces fiber to make the cocoon in which it awaits metamorphosis into its adult form—fruitlessly, when human cultivators intervene—but spidersilk is a versatile construction-material used to build cable-like strands, complex webs and exotic funnels. We humans may think all crawling creatures much alike, but from their own viewpoint there's as much difference between insects and spiders as there is between insects and men."

That struck a chord in Drake's mind. Although he had not been present when the incident took place, he had been told that Walter Raleigh had been attacked by a spider on the moon. Digges had mentioned in relating the incident that the multitude of insects and mollusks, which made up the populace of the stars, seemed to look upon spiders with the same horror and repulsion that many humans did.

"Is that creature not poisonous?" Drake asked, unable to prevent his unease becoming manifest as he watched a particularly repulsive specimen crawl out of a capacious cage and along Patience's welcoming arm.

"Not dangerously so," Muffet said. "It's true that many hunting spiders use venom to paralyze their prey, and that humans sometimes react badly to such injections, but in functional terms, spider venom is no more akin to the crude stings of wasps or the toxins secreted by snakes than the species themselves are. Most natural venoms are defensive weapons, but spider secretions need to be a great deal more versatile than that. They have not merely to immobilize their prey but to transform the various flesh of many different species to prepare it for ingestion in liquid form. It's a kind of alchemy of the flesh, whose potential extends far beyond mere murder and digestion."

The monster was sitting on Patience's head now. She moved her head slowly from side to side, her eyes taking on a quizzical expression much like those worn by the parrots that were studying Drake and the spiders, equally warily, from the safety of their perches. Drake felt a sudden and rather absurd sense of fellow-feeling with the birds—which must, he supposed, have had plenty of time to get used to the company of their fellow guests, but seemed not to have taken the trouble to become very closely acquainted.

"Are you saying that some spider secretions might have curative value?" Drake asked.

"There's no *might* about it," Muffet replied, serenely. "Is that so surprising? There are a thousand plant species whose juices have curative value, as well as a much lesser number that are deadly poisons. Galenists and Paracelsians alike use leeches to draw blood. Like the chemical realm whose treasures were exposed by Paracelsus, the animal kingdom is a vast untapped resource of medical science, which might produce abundant rewards even if one were compelled to explore it blindly, with no other method than trial and error."

Drake knew little enough about Paracelsian medicine, but there had been controversy in abundance when Muffet had initially been refused entry into the Royal College of Physicians, and every educated man in England—not excluding playwrights, choristers and marine officers—had heard something of the manner in which Paracelsus had determined the propriety of his new chemical cures by means of occult analogies. All occult scientists—alchemists most of all—were holists, who considered that the universe was host to many secret patterns of analogy and influence. If such patterns could be identified linking human illnesses to the new chemical substances that were inflating the traditional lists of metals, salts and essences, similar patterns could presumably be found linking the same illnesses to different animal species and substances. Drake inferred that Muffet was on the track of some such guiding pattern.

"They say in the Caribbean and Panama," Drake observed, drawn into a tangential train of thought, "that the natives were perfectly healthy until the Spanish came, importing diseases that became terrible plagues. The Cimaroons gave elaborate testimony of their ravages—but I'm told that there are rumors of a different sort in every port in Europe, which say that sailors returning from the Americas brought back plagues of their own."

"Including the one for which Paracelsus pioneered the mercury treatment," Muffet said. "We've had an opportunity to see something similar ourselves. The Tahitians appear to have been relatively free of disease before we arrived, living an idyllic existence in a land whose bounty is more closely akin to the Garden of Eden than anything else on earth—but after our arrival, sicknesses began to spread. Some among the tribesmen are inclined to blame us for that, although our own people were as healthy as anyone could expect when we arrived here. I've had a good deal of success in treating the sicknesses, and I'm developing new cures at a rapid rate, but the Tahitians' gratitude is understandably dilute. They have much the same attitude to spiders as Englishmen have, and the good example my daughter sets has no more effect on them than it has on you—for I can see that her familiarity in handling my allies adds to the discomfort of your attitude rather than soothing it."

Drake was, indeed, very glad to see Patience divest herself the huge spider that she had been entertaining for the past ten minutes and replace it gently in a cage whose latch seemed quite secure. He found that his enthusiasm to see Doctor Muffet's laboratory had waned considerably since he had crossed its threshold, and that an insistent desire had slowly accumulated within him to leave and not come back. "I'm sorry," he said to Muffet. "This is very strange to me, and there's a great deal to take aboard."

"Of course," the doctor said, suavely. "I believe that dinner must be ready by now. Shall we rejoin Sir Humphrey? We have plenty of time, do we not?"

Do we? Drake wondered. He had not yet had time to think about remaking his plans, now that his ambition to be the first European to reach these islands had been thwarted. He had no idea where he ought to go next, or when—but the Austral continent still lay to the west, and two islands in close proximity, each larger than Tahiti. They, at least, might still be awaiting a first visitation by ocean-borne adventurers.

As they went back into Gilbert's house, however, Drake was struck by another thought. "I can understand why you didn't go to the Caribbean or Brazil in search of exotic spiders," he said, "if those which live in England are too small to be of much use to you—the Spanish and the Portuguese would not be good neighbors, no matter how peaceful your intentions. But how did you know that there would be material to suit your purposes here? Even though you knew about the island's existence, you might have found it utterly devoid of spiderkind."

"Spiders are very efficient travelers," Muffet told him. "They're far more widely distributed than you can probably imagine—and in the tropics, they very often grow to generous proportions, as do the insects that provide their primary prey."

"What other kinds of prey do they hunt?" Drake asked, since the question seemed to have been left dangling, and because all sailors had heard travelers' tales about giant spiders that preyed on humankind.

"The largest species can trap small birds and mice," Muffet told him. There was a slight hint of amusement in his voice, which testified to his familiarity with the same travelers' tales. "Nothing bigger—so far as I know."

CHAPTER FIFTEEN

The feast proved too much for Drake's stomach, although he could not help over-eating after such long privation. If he had confined himself to drinking water—as he had known full well that he ought to do—he would probably have kept his appetite in better check, but he was readily persuaded to try some palm wine. Once mild intoxication had taken hold he became too self-indulgent—though not as self-indulgent as the crewmen who were eating in the open air, around a group of cooking-fires, amid a crowd that included numerous young Tahitian women.

As he watched his men through the wide window of Gilbert's dining-room, it occurred to Drake that the natives might have more reasons than their new-found vulnerability to fevers to have taken a dislike to the invaders of their island, but the combination of drunkenness and the gripe soon drove all such serious thoughts from his mind.

In response to polite requests, Drake and Hammond told tales of their adventures in Panama, in which all their fellow-guests seemed very interested. No one took the risk of asking him about the far more dramatic adventure he had experienced after the ethership's ascent, even though they had already told him that they did not agree those who thought the experience delusional. Drake was grateful for that, although he was aware of the apparent inconsistency. Ashley—who had not sailed with Drake before this present expedition—willingly took on the burden of recounting their recent capture of the Peruvian port, and waxing lyrical about the treachery of the natives of Chile.

Patience Muffet, who was sitting next to him, asked him whether he had encountered any monsters like those described in myths and traveler's tales. She seemed sincerely interested.

"The tales that mariners bring back home of terrible islands inhabited by cunning monsters, head-hunting savages and avid cannibals are mostly lies intended to amuse," Drake told her. "I've never encountered cannibals, or savages who make human sacrifice of all unwary visitors to huge monsters they worship as pagan gods. There's no need, mind, for such fancies as that to express the danger of a seaman's trade; it's a fortunate ship that returns home from an ocean crossing with more than half its crew alive and well. Disease and deprivation claim more lives than violence. The world isn't as hospitable to humankind as we could wish, alas."

"Why do people bring home such terrifying tales, if there's no truth in them?" the girl asked, in a manner whose maturity belied her frail appearance. "Why make the world out to be worse than it is?"

"Travelers exaggerate," Drake said. "In making the world seem stranger, they seek to increase their own apparent importance and bravery."

"The world is a sore trial to humans because we're doing penance for original sin," Gilbert's chaplain put in, having been eavesdropping on their conversation from the other side of the table. He seemed to disapprove of Patience's curiosity—or, at least, of her choice of an instructor.

"If that's so," Drake opined, with reckless honesty, "we're paying very dear for a trivial error. Dante claimed that there was no land in the entirety of this ocean but the mount of Purgatory, but you've proved him wrong, haven't you? Another strike against papism!"

The chaplain was not a Puritan of John Field's stripe but a broad churchman. "It might be," the chaplain opined, "that Dante guessed wrongly about the shape and extent of Purgatory."

"You'll find that Tahiti isn't Paradise, Captain Drake," Patience Muffet said, "but it isn't Purgatory either." The judgment seemed bizarrely ominous, from the mouth of such a young child.

"No," Drake agreed. "It's just an island, where there are neither head-hunters nor cannibals nor pagan savages. Even the monsters are friendly, and your father is hopeful that their bites might work benign miracles."

This time it was Muffet who interrupted to say: "There's nothing miraculous about it, Captain Drake. It's merely science."

He would undoubtedly have gone on, but Gilbert put a hand on his arm. "Tomorrow, doctor," he said. "Tonight, let's rejoice in a fortunate meeting of friends and countrymen." He raised his cup as if to signify a compact.

Drake raised his own readily enough, knowing that he had already drunk too much to pay proper attention to, or make proper sense of, any discourse on the technicalities of alchemical medicine.

The feast continued in a hearty mood; even the chaplain relented in the expression of his disapproval.

Drake had no idea what time it was when he took himself off to bed, but darkness had fallen some time before. His hosts would willingly have carried on drinking and chatting for at least another hour, and the party outdoors went on for some while longer, the cooking-fires having been fed further wood in order to serve as central sources of illumination, but the captain was exhausted.

He fell asleep while there was still a great deal of noise and flickering light outside. That did not assist his troubled sleep, which was shallow and dream-filled from the very start. By the time his belly finally settled, however, silence had fallen and the fires had burned down to a sullen red glow that seemed impotent to penetrate the darkness of the tropic night. His stomach's quiescence was, alas, soon displaced as the center of his internal attention by the development of a fierce headache.

There was a nightlight by his bed, so Drake did not have to blunder around in search of the water-jug, but he felt very clumsy as he groped for it. He drank deeply, but that only served to increase the magnitude of yet another problem.

He got up again, wishing that he had paid more attention to the exact position of the latrine that was situated some distance behind the house, not far from the fence, when he had used it in earlier in daylight. He did not bother to put on his jerkin, but he was careful to pull on his boots, not knowing what dangerous creatures might be swarming on the ground behind the house.

He made his way outside, and was glad to find that there was light enough to enable him to find the raised rim of the latrine-pit without overmuch trouble. He still felt rather unsteady on his feet; when his immediate discomfort had been relieved, he moved away from the stinking trench to lean against the bole of a tall palm, intending to gather himself together before he returned to his bed. He looked up at the sky, although he did not expect to find any sense of stability or promise of peace in its celestial majesty.

The southern stars always seemed sparse to him by comparison with those that crowded northern stars, but the weakness of their light was offset by a bright full moon, whose pock-marked silver face was now a stark reminder of the extent and strangeness of the universe. Drake stared at it for a minute or more, resentfully. Digges, he knew, had been promised that the earth would be let alone, but that did not mean that compound eyes were not staring down at the world of men, nor that the multitudinous insect species who thronged the satellite's cavernous interior might not send tiny cousins to the surface to make observations on their behalf.

He looked away deliberately, unwilling to offer himself up as a passive lunatic. The tall wooden fence, some fifteen paces away from his present position, made it impossible for him to see more of the forest than the tops of its trees. The island's birds were mostly silent now, but there was wind enough to sustain a considerable whisper in the foliage, so the wilderness of the island's interior seemed loud and insistent in its presence.

When he felt more composed, Drake turned to go back to Gilbert's house. Just as he turned his head, though, he saw something move from the corner of his eye. It was very close to the wall of the stockade, almost totally enclosed in shadow; had it remained still he could not possibly have seen it, but the fact and quality of the movement were just about discernible. As soon as he stared at it attentively, though, the movement stopped, leaving him with nothing but the impression of something the size of a man, whose movement was not at all manlike.

Drake could not help the idea of a giant spider—a *true* giant—springing forth from his imagination. Instinctively, he froze, cursing himself for his reflexive terror. He stared hard into the shadows, but he could not make out any shape within the darkness. He tried to force himself to take a step towards it, purely and simply to prove that he had command over his limbs, but his legs would not move.

When he tried to take a step in the other direction, towards the house, he found it far easier—but in taking that step, he turned his head again, and caught a hint of movement from the corner of his eye for a second time. He froze again, and looked back—and then he felt something brush against his calf, above the rim of his boot.

He was immediately seized by the idea that something had already crawled up his boot, unheeded, and was now ascending his leg. Again, he could not help but imagine a spider, albeit a much smaller one than the one he had imagined moving in the shadows.

He dared not reach down with his bare hands. Instead, he shook his leg furiously, hoping to dislodge the creature he supposed to be there. He knew, even as he did it, that it was the wrong thing to do. If there *was* a spider on his leg, the last thing in the world he ought to do was agitate it.

It *was* the wrong thing to do; he felt the sting that told him so—but that only made his agitation more frenzied. He would have called for help had he not been so utterly ashamed of himself—but the one thing he dreaded more, at that moment, than being killed by a spider-bite, was the possibility that he might be wrong: that the whole incident, including the bite, was a product of his imagination.

He could not countenance the thought that he might be found hallucinating, especially if the hallucination involved a giant invertebrate.

He felt a second bite, and a third. He was possessed by the thought that there must be more than one spider, and that there might be an entire tide of spiders flowing around his feet. Still he did not dare reach down with his hands. Still he kicked madly in his panic, while trying all the while to stay silent.

Drake began to feel numb in his lower limbs, and dizzy in his fevered brain, and felt that he was losing contact with reality in more ways than one. Then, he did begin to hallucinate.

He dreamed that he had suddenly acquired the ability to see into the shadows, and to distinguish what was there. He did not see man-sized spiders but spider-like men: three of them, clad like the Tahitian indigenes in loincloths and feathered head-dresses. They were far darker in complexion than the Tahitians, though, and far hairier, with faces that were not human faces at all but monstrous arachnid faces, staring at him and waiting for him to fall.

He dared not look down to see whether he was, indeed, being devoured from beneath by a flood of spiders. He could not look down—but he could fall down, and he felt himself doing so.

As he tumbled, the three spider-faces worn by the violators of the stockade drew closer. He told himself that they must be masks, but then lost the thread of his dreams and thoughts alike.

CHAPTER SIXTEEN

Drake woke up with a start, and found himself fighting to open his eyes against the glare of bright sunlight. Eventually, he managed it. He was lying on the ground in dense undergrowth, which mostly consisted of fern-like fronds and broad prickly leaves. He was lying in a shallow ditch, which might have been a watercourse in the rainy season; it snaked away through the vegetation in two directions.

He raised his head cautiously, but the foliage was too dense to allow him to see more than a few feet without standing up. He paused before doing that, in order to collect himself and decide what to do next. Since his eyes told him so little about where he was he made an effort to listen carefully, but all he could hear was the clamor of a brisk wind rustling the branches of the trees, mingled with the calls of strange birds and various humming and clicking sounds that were presumably made by unfamiliar insects.

He tried to rise to his feet, but his legs were still numb and he had to pause in an awkward sitting position. He reached down to rub his thighs. He was wearing hose, but there were tears in the thin cloth above the rims of both his boots, and bloodstains. The flesh beneath was itching, and the sensation flared into pain as he brushed the wounds with his fingertips. He had apparently been bitten four times, around and above his knees. He continued rubbing his legs, and felt the flesh respond to the urging. He breathed a sigh of relief as he took further stock of himself, and concluded that any damage done had been temporary.

When he stood up he was able to look over the densest vegetation, but he could only see a few yards further than before, although the forest was not as dense as some had experienced. To judge by the height of the sun, it had to be nearer noon than dawn.

I must make haste, Drake thought, glad to be able to organize a coherent sentence. *The settlement was on the southeastern coast of the island, so it ought to lie....*

He was interrupted in mid-decision when he suddenly found himself gripped from behind and pulled back down to a sitting position. When he twisted his neck to look over his shoulder he found himself staring into the face of a man.

Drake was so glad to see that the man did not have the face of a spider that three seconds passed before he realized that the other *did* have skin much darker than the natives he had seen in Gilbert's compound, and that he had considerably more body-hair. He was, moreover, exceptionally barrel-chested and muscular. He did not seem to belong to the same race as other Tahitians. He was not alone; there were at least three others all crouching down and huddling around. They were breathing hard; he inferred that they had hurried back to him following some alarm.

Drake opened his mouth to speak, but a hand was urgently plastered over it. Another hand reached out to part the vegetation obscuring their position, and a stabbing finger bid him look in that direction. He could just make out the feathery head-dresses of a party of lighter-skinned men making their way along a course that ran more-or-less parallel the dry stream-bed. He could also see the tips of spears and bows carried by the lighter-skinned Tahitians; they were moving smoothly and silently, as any hunting-party would.

When the other party had vanished, Drake's captors allowed him to stand up again. He tried a soft-voiced greeting in English first, on the assumption that any islanders living in close proximity to the settlement, whatever their physical type, were highly likely to have learned a little. When that overture met with blank incomprehension, he made an elaborate mime of displaying his obvious lack of arms and declaring his peaceful inclinations. He had grown accustomed to the elements of sign language, having always been exceptional among his own people for his enthusiasm to meet exotic specimens of humanity and make alliances with them.

The dumb-show elicited no more reaction than his speech. He was now able to count the number of his captors as seven, but none of them was armed and they did not seem to mean him any harm. Indeed, it was possible that they had protected him by preventing him from attracting the attention of the lighter-skinned islanders. Before looking back at the man who had dragged him down and muffled his mouth, who seemed to be the leader of the party, Drake made a tour of the group with curious eyes. The expressions on their staring faces seemed far more curious than ominous, but Drake had the impression that if he were to try to leave the company he would be restrained.

"You're not local, are you?" he guessed. "Neither servants nor traders. So what do you want with me?" He took care to speak in a soft and amicable tone.

There was no verbal reply, but the first man he had seen gestured with his hand. It was an invitation rather than a command, but Drake did not take the trouble to wonder what the consequences might be of a refusal He bowed, and immediately went in the direction indicated by the invitation, So far as he could judge, that course would take him in the opposite direction to the settlement, but it could not be helped. The leader of the party fell into step with him, walking by his side, while the others arranged themselves in single file behind.

The trail they followed was not straight, but it was clear enough to permit swift progress until they were diverted on to a narrower sidetrack, where they made slower headway. The leader of the party had to go in front of Drake to guide him. After that, they changed direction so frequently that their course was more reminiscent of a ship tacking into the wind than any journey overland that Drake had ever taken. When they had been moving for two hours they stopped to drink from a stream. Drake realized that they must be carefully avoiding contact with other islanders. Although he had caught the odor of cooking-fires more than once, he had not seen a single human habitation.

"You know that I'm a stranger here, don't you?" Drake said to the leader, without any expectation of receiving a reply. "You know that I came aboard the *Golden Hind*. Do you know that I'm her master, or were you merely intent on picking one of us at random?" Voicing the questions helped him to settle in his own mind what the answers might be—but he knew that there was no point in seeking enlightenment by that means as to where the dark men might be taking him, or why.

Eventually, their course became straighter again, and by midmorning they did come into a village, where his captors paused to hold discussions with the inhabitants. These were lighter-skinned people who resembled the islanders he had seen in the settlement, not his present companions, but they did not seem to be hostile to his captors. There was no argument, and scant evidence of overmuch curiosity regarding his presence, although some of the villagers studied him surreptitiously while pretending to ignore him.

"Is there anyone here who speaks English?" Drake asked, plaintively, issuing another general appeal. If anyone did, they were not prepared to admit it.

The march resumed. Drake presumed that they were heading ever-deeper into the island's interior, getting further away from the settlement. He spared time from contemplation of his own predicament to wonder what Gilbert would think when he found that his honored guest had vanished—and, for that matter, what Hammond and Ashley would think when they found themselves devoid of a captain.

They went through two more villages before noon, and a third not long after. Drake was offered fruit to eat and water to drink, but he ate sparingly. The expedition had become tedious now, and he began to wish that it might be over—or, at least, that he might be able to ask when it might be over.

There did not seem to be nearly so many birds hereabouts as there had been on the small islet where Martin had climbed the coconut palm—perhaps because the birds here were much more inclined to steer clear of humans, for reasons to which the natives' feathered head-dresses offered more than adequate testimony. There were, however, large parrots visible in the crowns of the trees, which paused to watch the party of travelers as they passed by rather than taking immediate flight—except for one of them, which was actively following them. At first Drake thought that he must be mistaken about that, but once he began to keep the bird within view, it soon became obvious that he was right. The bird was definitely tracking them. Drake could not tell whether his companions were aware of the fact or not, but if they were it did not worry them.

For the first time, it occurred to Drake to wonder why the *Fortune* had set off from Gilbert's harbor, heading directly for the island where the *Hind* had dropped anchor, before anyone could possibly have caught sight of her. Was it possible, he wondered, that news of her arrival there had been carried from one island to another by a bird? He had not paid much attention to the birds in Muffet's laboratory, even though Patience had talked to one of them, once his attention had been claimed by the spiders. Now he began to wonder whether he had been distracted from something significant, and cursed himself for his carelessness.

Travelers' tales featuring intelligent birds were by no means as common as those involving giant spiders, but they were not unknown. Perhaps, Drake thought, there was more truth in such tales than he had ever been able to credit. Given that the caverns of the moon were host to vast throngs of philosophical insects, the notion of whole nations of talking birds no longer seemed as silly as it would have done in his days as the scourge of the Carib Sea.

For at least six hours he had not seen a single spider, but that changed quite suddenly when the terrain underwent a marked change of aspect. They had been going up-slope for some time and the forest had thinned out considerably—not because trees had been deliberately cleared, as they had around the villages, but because the trees that grew on this higher ground had massive superficial root-systems than monopolized the soil for some distance around, permitting no competitors. These roots formed complex networks of ridges and deep grooves, and were host to elaborate populations of fern-like plants, mosses, brightly-colored fungi and swarms of insects. Here, for the first time since his strange awakening, Drake was able to see spiders prowling in broad daylight, although none was as large as the ugliest specimens in Muffet's collection. He saw webs, too, although they were not like the webs spun by garden spiders in England; they were built on the ground and extended in mazy tunnels and strange spirals.

The walls of these tunnels were sufficiently substantial that they might almost have served as the sleeves of garments, but they were slightly translucent, so that it was sometimes possible to see dark shapes confined within them, which might have been the spiders themselves, or the corpses of the kinds of animal prey that Muffet had mentioned: small birds and mice. Despite his booted feet, Drake took great care not to step on any spiders. The natives seemed far less careful, although they went barefoot.

The terrain changed again as the party finally went over the crest of the shallow hill they had been climbing, and came down more precipitously into a valley whose vegetation was quite distinct from any they had yet traversed. There were no palm trees here, although there were trees that bore fruits that Drake had never seen before; they did not grow as tall as palms, but their foliage was more prolific. Many of the bushes bore huge flowers, of very various colors, and the air was alive with the buzz of insects. Drake had been badly bitten in the swamplands of Panama, and he was initially apprehensive of the swarms of flies, but they did not seem inclined to molest him.

The going became much harder once they had descended into the valley, but there was a trail of sorts, which Drake's guide followed unhesitatingly, and the seaman followed without too much difficulty. There seemed to be no villages here, and Drake had persuaded himself that it was merely a margin to be crossed when he suddenly emerged into a clearing where there was a group of huts. He knew immediately that some European hand had been involved in their design and construction, although he did not recognize the half-human figure that came out of one of the huts to meet them as a European.

The man seemed, at first glance, to be similar in type to Drake's companions; his skin had the same dark coloring, although it seemed somewhat coarser in texture, and it was also very hairy. Like them he was ugly, in a straightforwardly human fashion, although his features seemed more considerably distorted. His forehead was bulbous and his jaw unusually narrow. He was not dressed as the natives were, though; he had canvas trousers and a cotton chemise, and a broad-brimmed hat. Clothed as he was, it was easy to determine that he had the same exceptional development of the torso and thighs.

It might have been the narrowness of the jaw that imparted a flute-like quality and a slight lisp to the voice that said: "It's good to see you, Francis, old friend. I had a presentiment that you would come—and it seems that you've arrived in the nick of time."

"Old friend?" the astonished Drake repeated. "I'd surely remember if I'd ever seen a man like you before, let alone numbered one among my friends."

"I've changed more than a little since you saw me last," the other admitted. "Perhaps I'm being a presumptuous, though, in addressing you as *friend* rather than *shipmate*. It was three years ago that you saw me last, as the calendar counts, but it was in another life as well as another world."

"God's blood!" Drake exclaimed, not knowing exactly how he had jumped to the conclusion. "You're Walter Raleigh!"

CHAPTER SEVENTEEN

"I knew that Gilbert would be discreet," the much-changed Raleigh remarked, "but I thought Muffet might have found an opportunity to say something. I told him long ago that you were mariner enough to have taken full note of what you saw from the ethership's portholes. Given that you'd already looked on the Pacific from Panama, I suspected that you'd come exploring if you could."

"If you reached the ground safely when the ethership broke up," Drake said, angrily, "why didn't you return to London? I was in dire need of your testimony to support the story I told. Had you been there to support my testimony, it would have been manifest that it was poor Digges, not I, who was deluded about the nature of our adventure."

"You may be giving our fellow Englishmen too much credit for credulity," Raleigh replied. "I didn't know what would happen to you, and I regret that it did, but I had more urgent things to do. In truth, I wasn't entirely displeased when news reached me of the trick that the ethereal had played on Tom Digges. There are good reasons for maintaining secrecy in regard to the work that Muffet and I must do—for some years, at least. You, though, are one of the few men who might understand. I really am glad to see you, Francis, for there's no man on earth who might make us a better ally, and we're direly in need of one just now. I know that the celestial spiders didn't bring you here, but since you *are* here, they must have Providence on their side."

"Did celestial spiders bring *you* here?" Drake asked.

"Yes," Raleigh replied unequivocally. "Walk with me, and I'll show you what you need to see while I tell you what you ought to know. We've no shortage of hapless instruments, but to have another free man in our innermost company will be an immense advantage."

As he spoke, Raleigh beckoned Drake to follow him deeper into the valley, then made a signal to the leader of the company that had brought Drake from the settlement. The natives were as silent now as they had been since Drake first saw them, and they made no audible response to the signal, but merely retreated to the huts surrounding Raleigh's.

Drake was in a mulish mood now, though, and he stayed where he was. "You sent those men to kidnap me," he said, darkly, "and you sent some monster with them to render me unconscious. Why?"

"It was the simplest way to bring you here quickly—perhaps the only way. Had my emissaries come openly, the rebel islanders would have been alerted, and Gilbert would have done his best to keep you inside the stockade. He probably thinks of you merely as heaven-sent reinforcements for the defense of his petty fort, but he might be hatching other schemes. Muffet still has confidence in him, but I cannot. Gilbert's plans might be agreeable to me, in the right circumstances—but that depends on you, and on the Tahitians' response to your arrival."

"The islanders seemed friendly enough last night," Drake observed.

"Everyone is friendly while gathering intelligence," Raleigh said. "It's possible that your arrival will inhibit the natives from attacking the settlement, but it's also possible that it will increase their sense of urgency. If they imagine that more ships are likely to arrive in future, bringing more guns...."

"We must talk to them," Drake was quick to say. "We must reassure them that we can co-exist peacefully."

"We did that when we first came," Raleigh told him, bluntly. "The islanders believed us, and all went well...but many of the islanders now consider that our promises were false, and they know that there's dissent among the ranks of Gilbert's men. Sailors are a superstitious breed; many of them can't understand what we're doing here, or why, any better than the natives. You will—if you'll allow me to show you. Will you come?"

This time, Drake consented to go where the strangely-transformed Raleigh led him. By the time they had taken a dozen steps the huts were out of sight again, screened by the luxuriant bushes. The air was still abuzz with insects, though, drawn to the gigantic blooms that dressed the bushes in such awesome profusion. Their nectar-collection was not unhazardous, though; now that Drake had become accustomed to the rich confusion of colors he was able to make out predatory spiders luring in the foliage of the bushes, ready to seize prey that settled in the alluring blossoms.

"Beautiful, are they not?" Raleigh said, as he followed the direction of Drake's gaze. Drake knew that he was not referring to the flowers.

The trail they followed was neither wide nor straight, but the mossy ground was gentle underfoot, and Raleigh was able to stroll in perfect comfort.

"So the spider-bite you suffered on the moon was no superficial scratch," Drake deduced, "and our insect hosts were wrong to believe that they had countered its effects."

"The colonists of the moon's interior think themselves extremely wise and capable," Raleigh said, "and the fleshcores that rest in perfect peace within the shells of planetary crusts in the central regions of the sidereal system are even more given to self-satisfaction. They consider themselves rulers of the galaxy and the forefront of evolution's thrust, but they're blind to all manner of other possibilities. They know relatively little about the remoter regions of the galactic arms, let alone the vast realm of the ethereals. They know almost nothing about the imperium of spiderkind."

"You're some kind of chimera now, I suppose?" Drake guessed. "The spider must have laid eggs inside your body, which took possession of your flesh much as the ethereal took possession of poor Digges' intelligence, albeit in a slower manner."

Raleigh laughed. "You see that I'm changed," he said, "but you mistake the reason. No, I'm not possessed by one of Field's ingenious extraterrestrial demons. The spider laid no eggs within my flesh. The spiders that rode down to earth with me traveled as passengers on the ethership, just as we humans did. They played their part in saving all of us, slowing the leak with spidersilk long enough for us to reach an altitude at which the parachutes could save our lives. Had it not been for them, you'd likely be dead, although you never suspected their presence. They had to be discreet, you see, for they had been spies within the moon for many years, always in hiding from the insects. They took a considerable risk, in order to make use of an unexpected opportunity to descend to the surface of the Earth. They would have come eventually, of course, but they knew that the ethership's journey would provoke a response from the Selenite host, and they had to be bold. They're few in number, and their work is patient by nature—my own optimization has been a slow process, and not painless—but they needed to act, lest an unprecedented opportunity be lost."

"Optimization?" Drake queried. "Is that what has happened to you, Walter? And to the men who brought me here, I presume? They're not a different race at all—merely islanders who've been bitten by celestial spiders." It occurred to Drake, as he said this, that he too had been bitten, four times over, by spiders whose origin and nature he could not specify—but he reassured himself with the thought that Muffet appeared to be as tightly-bound in this conspiracy as Raleigh, without him or his daughter having been transformed.

"Sentient spider species are despised fugitives within the fleshcores' galactic empire," Raleigh told him, "as humans and other vertebrate intelligences are bound to become, if the insects and their masters have their way. The celestial spiders have survived and flourished regardless, their evolutionary impetus enhanced by the necessity of their eternal struggle. They're our natural allies, Francis—far more so than the ethereals, whose penchant for trickery and treachery is obvious in what they did to Digges. The celestial spiders haven't attempted any deception since they had to make their first move under extremely difficult circumstances. They've been honest with me, and with Muffet—with Gilbert too, although he's never been able to overcome his instinctive revulsion. That instinct is a direly unfortunate thing, although we humans—some of us, at any rate—seem better able to overcome it than the insect races that comprise the dominant galactic civilization."

"If God engraved a fear of spiders in our instinct," Drake observed, "there might be a reason for it." As he spoke he had his eye on an unusually brightly-colored specimen that was not in hiding, but hanging from a thick thread from the branch of a tree, apparently ready to drop from above on some unsuspecting prey.

"That kind of fear is not God's work," Raleigh told him. "It's a phantom of the imagination. The intelligence of Earthly spiders, like that of Earthly insects, remains undeveloped, while that of vertebrates has flourished, by virtue of some unfathomable quirk of local circumstance—but the celestial spiders are rivals of a powerful enemy of humankind, and will be exceedingly valuable allies in times to come. I'd have thought that the man reputed to have turned the Cimaroons into a fledgling nation ready to aid the English against the empire-building Spaniards might understand that."

"You mistake me, Walter," Drake told him. "I never set out to be a diehard enemy of the Spaniards. I wouldn't have attacked them so violently in Panama had I not been so cruelly betrayed at St. John de Ulua. I'm a peaceful man, who would far rather deal honorably with everyone."

"But that's exactly what Digges attempted to do with the insects and the fleshcores," Raleigh pointed out. "They promised him safety and honorable dealing, but they sabotaged the ethership, intending to kill us all."

"Did they?" Drake countered. "I don't know that."

"But you do know that the ethereal—the vaporous creature that Digges breathed in—betrayed him by persuading him that our experience was all a dream. It betrayed *you*, Francis, in making you seem a fool."

"And you didn't?" Drake retorted. "I was convinced that you were dead, for I couldn't believe that you would have deserted me when I need your testimony to establish my sanity. If I hadn't had your map...." He did not break off because he regretted the revelation that it was Raleigh's sharp eyes rather than his own that had guided him to Tahiti but because he had caught his first glimpse of the wonders that Raleigh must have brought him here to see.

They had come into another clearing, where the ground was damp around the rim of a little pool, whose surface was strewn with lily-pads. On slightly drier ground, cushioned with moss, a dozen Tahitian natives, of the kind Raleigh called "optimized"—six of whom were female—were lying fully extended, seemingly asleep, with their arms extended. Each human body was marked with between five and ten of what Drake thought at first were dark red tumorous growths.

After a minute or so, he realized that the objects were not growths at all, but stout leeches and massive ticks, each the size of a clenched fist, every one of which must have drawn a generous cupful of blood from its host. He was able to watch sated parasites withdraw, slowly and sluggishly as they completed their feasts, and roll on to the ground—but whether they intended to scuttle or squirm away thereafter, he could not tell, for as soon as they fell they were seized and carried off by huge spiders, which bore them away into the shelter of the surrounding bushes.

The bushes and trees on the far side of the pool were lavishly supplied with spidersilk structures, including webs, domes and tunnels, intricately distributed between the undergrowth and the crowns of the trees. Drake was immediately struck by the notion that here was an entire city spun from spidersilk, extending as far as the eye could see. The structures became much more voluminous and mazy as they extended into the distance, drowning the greens of the forest in a vast extent of shimmering white.

The spiders collecting the bloodsucking parasites were not as huge as the largest specimens Muffet had shown him, but very nearly so. If the increasing size of the tunnels that extended away from the pool's edge was a reliable indication, Drake thought, there must be true giants at the heart of the labyrinth.

CHAPTER EIGHTEEN

"Are your celestial spiders in that silken maze?" Drake asked, croaking slightly because his mouth was dry.

"Yes," Raleigh said, "but the products of earthly Creation are far more numerous. The celestial spiders are not the largest, by any means—earthly spiders have more scope for physical optimization than I supposed at first. Although our project is still in its infancy, it's making rapid and spectacular progress. Ours is a world with more exotic potential than our friends have ever found before; it will take them centuries to discover what might be achieved here in Tahiti, let alone the entire surface of the globe—but you and I might live long enough to see it, if we and they are granted time enough to complete our experiments."

Drake had returned his attention to the languid islanders and their patient parasites. "And if we were to live for centuries," he said, grimly, "how much blood would we have to produce to feed your celestial spiders?"

"You misunderstand what is happening here," Raleigh said, "The celestial spiders have neither any need nor any appetite for human blood, although they consider it a privilege to share the alchemical potential of our flesh, as we should consider it a privilege to share the alchemical potential of theirs. Arachnids are exoskeletal creatures, like insects and mollusks, but they're very different in other ways. The blood that you see being taken here is destined to nourish earthly spiders, not extraterrestrial ones, and it's transmitted by vectors in order to protect its donors from excessive traffic in the elixirs of life."

While Drake watched, one of the male "donors" rose to his feet, having shed all his visitors. He seemed steady enough on his feet, but his eyes were dull. He did not look at Drake before walking into the bushes and being lost to sight.

"Your optimized friends aren't very talkative," Drake observed.

"They still converse with one another, and with their former brethren, in their own tongue," Raleigh said. "They have had no need to learn English to communicate with me; we have other methods. Spiders are voiceless, of course, nor do they have the kinds of sensitive palps that the Selenite insects used to converse with Tom Digges, but they have very efficient modes of communication, which humans can learn—optimized humans, at least. When we first returned to earth, my celestial companions had no alternative but to use me a trifle brutally, but they were as discreet as they could be. Once they were able to set me free, they did. I can converse with them now as one free individual to another."

Drake felt free to doubt that—and, indeed, to doubt that Raleigh was anything more than a mere puppet, set out to seduce co-operation from him as co-operation had clearly been seduced from Thomas Muffet. He had to begin walking again, though, because Raleigh was on the move once more, skirting the pond as he went on into the valley.

They moved between the spidersilk structures easily at first, because those clinging to the ground were low-lying and those constructed in the crowns of bushes and trees were limited to the foliage, but their own relative status as giants was rapidly diminished as the arachnid city grew in dimension. The silken structures soon loomed up to chest- and head-height, and they moved into a translucent labyrinth that confused Drake's eyes completely.

"Did Muffet talk to you about his work?" Raleigh asked, as they plunged into the heart of this bizarre environment.

"He showed me his laboratories," Drake replied. "He told me that various sorts of spider venom have curative powers, and that he's attempting to refine them, with the ultimate intention of returning to England equipped with a miraculous pharmacopeia. I assume that he'll do everything possible to demonstrate the efficacy of his cures before revealing their source."

"That's one aspect of our plan," Raleigh agreed, "and one of our reasons for doing our work in such a remote location. There were too many spies in England for there to be any possibility of working there."

"When you say *spies*," Drake said, "I take it that you're not referring to Elizabethans, Frenchmen or Italians? You mean agents of the lunar insects and their fleshcore masters."

"Yes," said Raleigh. "Ethereals too, in all likelihood, although they find the surface of the Earth just as uncomfortable as exoskeletals accustomed to working in environments where affinity is far less powerful. Earthly insects and spiders are limited in size by a number of environmental factors, you see—especially the load-bearing capacity of their limbs and the difficulty of distributing vital spirit to their tissues."

"What vital spirit?" Drake asked.

"The vital spirit that's contained in air and ether, deprived of which living organisms must die. It is the fuel that feeds the fire of life. Organisms heavily burdened by affinity, as we are, require beating hearts and a sturdy network of vessels carrying blood, which absorbs vital spirit in the lungs and releases it throughout the body. Earthly invertebrates are tiny because, by some freak of chance, their ancestors never developed the appropriate combination of load-bearing limbs and internal circulatory systems. Physical optimization requires ingenious compensation in these and other respects. Relatively few intelligent extraterrestrials can operate comfortably on the surface of a planet like the earth—but the purposes of espionage are, in any case, best served by tinier agents. Communication is a problem of course, but there are means.

"Humans were under observation before, but since our intrepid band of companions broke through the envelope of the atmosphere, interest in surface affairs has increased very markedly. It now extends beyond mere measurement of our technical works to attempts to comprehend our culture, religion and politics. England, especially, is under intensive study, and her rival European nations too. Tahiti is safely remote, but I dare not offer the same guarantee in respect of China or Peru. Tell me, Francis, how many people in England knew that you were coming here when you set off from Plymouth?"

"None," Drake admitted. "Being widely considered a madman, I thought it politic to keep the exact details of my plan to myself at first. I didn't confide then to my officers until we reached South America,"

"That's good news," Raleigh said. "I'm glad to find your reasoning so closely in tune with ours—it makes me even more confident that you'll understand what we are doing, when everything has been properly explained. You'll see that the celestial spiders are honest, and that you mustn't let irrational instinctive anxieties blind you to their benevolence."

Drake suppressed a shudder caused by movements glimpsed behind the walls of spidersilk that now surrounded them. Some of the vague shapes he glimpsed through their translucent walls seemed as large as sheep—larger, at any rate, than wolves. He had not yet met any such creature face-to-face, but their reluctance to come out into the open, while lurking like shadows behind such frail walls, only made them seem more menacing. It did not seem to Drake that his fears were dismissible as "irrational instinctive anxieties"; it seemed perfectly rational to doubt that the extraterrestrial spiders were benevolent in their intentions, and to suspect that Raleigh and Muffet were their dupes rather than their collaborators.

"I can't guarantee, of course, that there are no subtle spies lurking unsuspected in my holds," Drake said. "You and Muffet have evidently succeeded in optimizing birds as well as spiders, and use them to gather intelligence. The *Golden Hind* has the usual complement of weevils and flies, any one of which might have descended from the moon. I have no idea how one of your so-called ethereals might be able to conceal itself."

"It's not improbable that you have insect spies aboard," Raleigh admitted. "You're probably being monitored as closely as Tom Digges—but we have servants who could clean your ship of that kind of presence. As for ethereal observers, we have little more reliable knowledge of their capabilities than you do. All we know for sure is that is that the ethereals have internecine struggles of their own to contend with, which distract them from the affairs of solid creatures and make it unlikely that they'll interfere with us. In that respect, at least, the celestial spiders have more in common with fleshcore society than ours; their vast empire is fundamentally harmonious. Prepare yourself, Francis—we're about to...."

He did not break off his sentence, but the sound of his next few words was drowned by a loud explosion, which Drake initially mistook for cannon-fire. It was followed by a cacophony of other sounds and bizarre manifestations. Flaming missiles of various sorts flew through the air, seemingly converging on their position from several different directions. Some were circular bundles, some were spears—but all of them were wrapped in combustible materials that must have been soaked in some kind of flammable fluid, for they were all burning excitedly.

The spidersilk making up the structures comprising the vast nest was no more vulnerable to fire than seasoned wood, but nor was it any more fireproof. Where the tunnel walls caught fire they began to burn. Some of the fires sputtered out, but others caught hold, fanned by the steady wind.

"The fools!" Raleigh gasped, when he has recovered from his initial astonishment. "The stupid, reckless fools!" Then he grabbed Drake by the arm, and began pulling him towards a curtain-like gathering of white fabric that was presumably an entrance into the network of the tunnels. "Run!" he commanded. "Run for your life!"

CHAPTER NINETEEN

Drake had no more than a second to make his decision, and it was instinct rather than reason that guided him. He wrenched his arm free from Raleigh's grip, turned on his heel and ran for his life, heading back the way they had come rather than the route he had been urged to take by his former crewmate.

Raleigh howled an objection, but Drake had established a lead of six or seven paces before the dark-skinned man set off in pursuit.

The air was already filling with acrid smoke, and there were more fires ahead of him than there were behind, but Drake was not intimidated by that. He could not have retraced his steps from memory, but he had only to run between the walls of spidersilk while the way was clear. Alas, the way was not clear for long, and he had to cut across one of the tunnels, through a gap cleared by fire. It would have been easy enough to accomplish had he been unobstructed, but as he moved between the flaming edges a spider the size of a mastiff came hurtling out of the tunnel, similarly intent on escaping. It made no attempt to bite him, and probably did what it could to avoid him, but a glancing collision was inevitable.

The spider's limbs probably suffered more damage than Drake, but the creature was only briefly interrupted in its flight, while Drake stumbled and sprawled on the ground—and when he got up, he had fragments of sticky spidersilk clinging to his arms, shoulders and face. In order to protect his eyes from the trailing threads he closed them—-and then tried to open them by the merest crack so that he could see where he was going.

He was still running as fast as he could, and was able to see that he had now won clear of the head-high tunnels into a region where most were no higher than his waist. Many seemed to be collapsing even where they had not been ripped or singed, and he was able to hurdle two that sprawled across his path. He tried to do the same with a third, but could not clear it—and when his booted feet plunged through the fragment, its glue-like strands wrapped themselves around his ankles and calves. He stumbled again, and this time fell upon a white carpet, which caught his arms as his feet had earlier been trapped.

As he struggled to free himself, Drake saw a huge black spider scuttling towards him, and felt certain that he was about to be bitten—but the monster ran straight over him without pausing. He began to pick himself up and pull himself free, but he turned as he heard a shout and saw Walter Raleigh behind him, amid a billowing cloud of white smoke, standing some ten or twelve yards away, gesticulating urgently.

"This way, you fool!" Raleigh yelled.

Drake could not have obeyed the instruction had he wanted to, for his feet were still impeded by the clinging spidersilk. He was about to signal his refusal, though, when a spear hurtled out of the smoke. This one was unencumbered by any burning material, and its sharpened wooden point struck Raleigh in the torso, apparently passing between his ribs.

Drake ducked low, expecting the weapon to be the first of a shower, and brought up his arms to shield his head. No other spears passed over him, though. Instead, it was a seeming tide of living flesh—bronze flesh, not dark brown or sunburned white—that seethed out of the surrounding bushes, and a dozen grasping hands reached out to seize him and pluck him from the ground, dragging him away from the web that had trapped him.

It required more than a minute for Drake to realize that he was not in imminent danger of death, and that the men who had seized him were intent on carrying him away alive. Once he was sure of that, he wondered whether his new captors might have mounted their attack in order to rescue him from what they imagined to be deadly peril—but that seemed too optimistic an analysis.

As soon as the men carrying him set him on his feet again—which they did not do until they were clear of the valley that Raleigh and the celestial spiders had adopted as their home—Drake tried to thank them, but they were not immediately interested in conversation. One said: "Follow! Hurry!" If that was not the limit of his English, he was not presently disposed to say any more.

Having little alternative, if only because there were as many islanders behind him as before him, Drake followed the man who had spoken, and hurried as rapidly as his captors. He had lost his bearings completely, and did not know which way he was being taken. The sun was too close to its zenith for him to make an accurate judgment of their heading.

By the time their headlong flight slowed to a walk there were a dozen Tahitians with Drake, forming a virtual phalanx around him as they strode over the ground, so rapidly that he could hardly keep pace. Breathless as he was, he tried again to talk to them, but their only reply was to impress the urgency of the situation upon him with gestures. It was obvious by now that they meant him no immediate harm, but it seemed more likely that they had seized him as a hostage than that they had merely sought it rescue him. Even if that were so, he thought, he was probably better off than he had been in the heart of the arachnid city.

When his captors brought him out of the forest into the largest native village he had yet seen—the first to be surrounded by a defense of sorts, and to show signs of concerted agricultural endeavor within and without that boundary—he saw that there were men waiting to receive him. They were all natives, but several were wearing linen shirts and trews. He was less pleased to observe that two were in possession of muskets, and several more of machetes.

He as received with some formality—ceremony, even. The leader of the party that was waiting for him made an elaborate show of welcome even before he said: "You are Captain Drake."

"I am," Drake confirmed, and waited politely for the other to reveal his own name.

"I am Ruhapali," the islander told him, gravely. "I speak for many tribes."

"I'm honored to meet you," Drake assured him. "What do you want with me?"

"My people saved you," Ruhapali stated, making an obvious bid for the moral high ground.

"I'm grateful," Drake said. He did not say that the islanders had also imperiled him by attacking the spiders, because he was not sure exactly what the islanders were claming to have saved him from. He had no idea what might have happened to him had Raleigh actually been able to introduce him to the celestial spiders, although he suspected that the process of his "optimization" might have been initiated without much delay.

"You must go away from here," Ruhapali said, coming to the point. "Your ship, and the others too. You must all go. We will kill the spiders. We do not want to kill your people. We will take you to your ship, but you must give us guns. We will give you food and fresh water, but you must give us guns. Then you must go. All of you."

The last thing that Drake wanted was to involve himself in a war, especially one in which he did not know how many sides there might be, and who might rally to what banner. "Have your people attacked the settlement?" he asked.

"No," Ruhapali told him. "Your people are not our enemies—not all. Many will be glad to go. You have seen the reason."

Drake knew that most, if not all, of the *Golden Hind*'s crew would probably agree with that judgment, if he told them what he had discovered. He had seen enough to be almost certain in his own mind that he did not want to stay on the island—but he could not be certain that he had seen enough to make a fully-reasoned decision. "Your warriors killed Walter Raleigh," he observed, playing for time while he tried to clear his mind and formulate a plan. "Do you know Raleigh? The white man who became dark—just as some of your own people have become dark."

"The man who brought the master-spiders," the Tahitian chieftain said. "If he lives, he must go. Better that he dies. The doctor too—but if he goes, that is your business."

"I understand," Drake told him. "What about those among your own people who have been transformed? Is *that* your business?"

"Yes," Ruhapali told him. "We will take you to your ship now. Your people will give us guns."

Drake was not about to start bargaining as to how many guns he might be worth. He nodded his head, to signify that he was content to be taken to his ship. He believed that he understood what was happening here, although he had only met Humphrey Gilbert a little more than twenty-four hours ago. The islanders' discomfort regarding their various exotic visitors must have been growing apace for some time, as they observed what was happening in the valley in which the celestial spiders had taken up residence. They could understand readily enough that there would be more and more dark men as time went by, and they presumably feared—rightly or wrongly—that their entire population might eventually be absorbed into the converts' ranks.

Thus far, they had been biding their time, but the arrival of the *Golden Hind* had spurred them to precipitate action. They must have been afraid that Drake and his crew might have been persuaded to reinforce the spiders' allies—in which case, the prospects of any future rebellion succeeding would be considerably more remote.

Drake could imagine with what avidity the native servants had eavesdropped on conversations the night before—not just the tales that Hammond and Ashley had told at Gilbert's table, but the boasts of his crewmen to the crewmen of the *Fortune* and her fellows. The islanders probably had no notion of the quantity and quality of

Drake's firepower, but they obviously knew the value of guns, even in a war against giant spiders.

Ruhapali had said that many of the settlers would be glad to go, and Drake did not doubt it, no matter how little they knew about the celestial spiders. Muffet and Raleigh, rather than Humphrey Gilbert, were presumably the masters of the little colony, but their authority must have been undermined by their hirelings' gradual realization of the true purpose of their adventure. Like Drake, Gilbert's men would inevitably have leapt to the conclusion that Muffet and Raleigh might be mere instruments of the celestial spiders, having been bribed with promises of cures for all manner of human diseases, from the rhume to the plague—and the curse of aging too, if Raleigh's bluster about living for centuries could be trusted.

Even if their instinctive revulsion could be set aside, mariners were a cynical and superstitious breed; Gilbert's seamen would have found it direly difficult to believe in the benevolence of spiders, and they might find it far easier to suspect that a physician like Muffet and a petty aristocrat like Raleigh had sold their souls to the Devil. Raleigh seemed entirely convinced that the kind of "optimization" that he had undergone was a gift worth bringing to the whole of humankind, but its stigmata would inevitably seem diabolical to many people—a number by no means restricted to puritans of John Field's stripe.

Drake had no way of knowing whether Field's account of the ethership's journey had been taken more seriously than his own, but John Foxe was the Archbishop of Canterbury, whose declarations on spiritual matters carried enormous weight in England. It might, therefore, be extremely hazardous for any Englishman to side with Raleigh and Muffet in this matter, even if reason did turn out to favor their alliance.

Ruhapali had turned to his fellows after Drake's consenting nod, in order to talk to them in their own language, but the discussion did not last long before he turned back to Drake and said: "You will tell your people they must go. We will give you what you need. You will give us what we need. Then we will kill the spiders."

Again, Drake nodded his head, although he did not consider the gesture to constitute a binding agreement.

It occurred to him, though, as they set off on the march again, that if the celestial spiders really did need to be killed, and their schemes aborted, then the sensible strategy might be for the *Golden Hind*'s crew to ally themselves with the Tahitians—just as Drake and another crew had once allied themselves with the Cimaroons, in order to carry through a mission in which either company would have failed had they attempted it without the other.

CHAPTER TWENTY

Ruhapali and four other chiefs set out to accompany Drake, with an escort of thirty warriors. The first stage of their journey turned out to be longer than he had hoped, but not as long as he had feared. They reached a village on the coast in mid-afternoon, without having been harassed by any dark men or spiders—or, for that matter, followed by any over-attentive birds.

There were a dozen large canoes drawn up on the beach, but they did not take to the water immediately. Ruhapali had first to enter into negotiations with the village chieftain, who was evidently not party to his council of war.

Drake was grateful for the pause, for it gave him time to slake his hunger and thirst and to rest his weary feet. The village children clustered round him, laughing and staring. They must have seen other Europeans, but perhaps not at such close range. He entertained them as best he could with smiles and gestures. Arrangements were eventually made for the use of one of the canoes; Drake boarded it, along with eleven other men, including Ruhapali and three other tribal chiefs.

The fully-laden canoe was not as fast as Drake's pinnace, even when the pinnace carried no sail, because the paddles plied by the islanders were less efficient than English oars. The water was tranquil, though, and the men were experienced.

Again, the journey was longer than Drake could have hoped, and the sun was touching the horizon when the masts of the *Golden Hind* and Humphrey Gilbert's four ships finally came in view, although the moon was rising by way of small compensation. Soon thereafter, Drake saw that there were forty more canoes waiting in the vicinity of the harbor mouth, apparently ready to mount an attack if the order were given.

Were such a meager and disadvantaged force to attack the *Hind* in daylight, the result would be a massacre, but Drake was well aware that a night attack might be a different matter. In any case, he and his crew could not win a war of attrition fought over weeks or months against the entire population of an island of this size.

Ruhapali was careful to approach the *Golden Hind* from the seaward side, and discreetly. The canoe's approach was quickly observed by the ship's watchman, who had plenty of time to see that Drake was in the canoe and not in any distress before Ruhapali ordered the paddlers to ease down, some thirty yards from the ship's stern.

"Speak to them," Ruhapali commanded.

"Mr. Hammond!" Drake called, seeing the mate come to the stern. "These men have rescued me from danger and brought me home. They mean no harm, and no one is to act against them."

"I'm exceedingly glad to see you, sir," Hammond called back. "There was panic ashore when you were nowhere to be found—more among Gilbert's men than your own, since we've grown used to trusting you in such situations. I see that you've been making friends, as is your habit. Will you all come aboard?"

"No," Ruhapali said to Drake, in a low voice. "You must give us guns. Then we will go. We will bring food and water. You will give us more guns."

"No, Ruhapali," Drake said, in his turn. "You will let me go aboard my ship. It will be best if you come too, although that is your choice. Then we will summon Humphrey Gilbert and Thomas Muffet, and we will talk. I mean you no harm, but I must hear what they have to say before I decide what to do. The best thing of all would be for everyone here to agree what is to be done, but we cannot achieve that if you make threats now. Come aboard my ship, and I will mediate between you and Gilbert. If Gilbert is persuaded to leave, Muffet will have no choice but to go with him. If you supply us with what we need to make the voyage, we will trade guns—but until then, we must keep them for our own defense."

Ruhapali did not like these terms, but he had to consider them carefully—and he decided in the end, that the alternative would be worse, given that it would win him no weapons and might make him some awkward enemies. He agreed to Drake's terms, and boarded the *Golden Hind* with its captain, while the canoe and his fellow chiefs waited alongside.

"How many men have we aboard, Ned?" Drake asked, as soon as the two of them were on the deck.

"Only two dozen," Hammond told him, "but everything's secure. Shall I send boats to the shore to bring the others back?"

"Aye," Drake said. "Send the small rowboat with a single oarsman. He's to tell Mr. Ashley to send the pinnace back, with another dozen men aboard. Tell him to bring Sir Humphrey Gilbert, and Doctor Muffet too, if he's willing. It's a polite invitation, mind—call it a tour of inspection. If they want to know where I've been, or how it comes about that I'm back on board the *Hind*, your man has no idea—do you understand?"

"He won't have to tell a lie," Hammond observed. "Will you tell me what's going on, captain?"

"Yes I will, Ned—but not right now. Have we taken enough supplies on board to offer hospitality to our guest?"

Hammond ran his eyes over the Tahitian chief. "We've water, fruit and a little bread that was baked ashore," he said.

"Good," Drake said. He raised his voice to say: "This man is our friend, and we must offer him the privileges of an honored guest."

The rowboat set off immediately, and the pinnace was not long in setting off on its return journey; Drake's men were experienced enough to keep it ever-ready to take to the water at a moment's notice. Even in the fading twilight, Drake needed no telescope to see that Sir Humphrey Gilbert and Thomas Muffet had both accepted his invitation with alacrity, but he did not know what to read into the fact that Muffet had decided to bring his daughter with him.

"Before our men come aboard," Drake whispered to Hammond, "I want them to be as sure as they can be that they're not harboring any spiders about their person. I want the order given to everyone that any man who sees a spider on the ship from this moment on must kill it immediately, if he can."

Hammond looked at him curiously, but nodded his head to signify that these instructions would be followed exactly.

When Gilbert and Muffet came aboard, Drake went to greet them effusively—not forgetting Patience—and immediately asked whether Ruhapali was known to them.

"We know Ruhapali very well," Gilbert said, warily. "Was it to visit Ruhapali, then, that you left the compound, Captain Drake? I wish you had let us know that you were going, for we've been desperately anxious about you. We heard an explosion in the interior of the island, and there seem to be fires burning there."

"I've had quite an adventure," Drake said, equably. "Had I not known that I'm a madman, ever-prone to the most extraordinary delusions, I might be rather alarmed by what I've seen—but this is an island in the Pacific Ocean, after all, and not the interior of the moon or the hub of the Milky Way." He tried to measure the quality of the glance that Gilbert and Muffet exchanged, but it was not easy.

"We're very glad to find you safe, Sir Francis," Muffet said, "and in such good humor."

"Ruhapali and I need to talk to below decks, in the cabin," Drake said. "Will you do me the courtesy of accompanying us?"

"Of course," said Muffet swiftly, almost as if he feared that Gilbert might raise some objection. The doctor immediately turned to Hammond and said: "May I entrust my daughter to your care, Mr. Hammond?"

"Aye, sir," Hammond answered.

The four men went below. As soon as a candle had been lit to illuminate the cabin and the door had been shut behind them, Drake said: "As you must have guessed, gentlemen, the islanders have attacked Raleigh's valley. Raleigh was struck in the torso by a spear, and might well have been killed. The tribesmen are determined to destroy the creatures Raleigh calls celestial spiders and the other creatures they have transformed. Ruhapali offers us the chance to depart in safety, but he refuses to answer for our safety if we will not go. Given what I've seen today, I can understand his fears and his determination, and I'm half-inclined to accept his offer—but I told him that I must hear your side of the story first. What's your opinion, Sir Humphrey?"

Gilbert was evidently ready to reply, but he did not get the chance. "This is absurd," Muffet said, preemptively. "Ruhapali, you are making a terrible mistake. We've relied on your own people to persuade you of the wisdom and virtue of our scheme, but they've evidently failed. You must listen to us now, and stop your assault on the valley as soon as you can. You must allow us time to complete our work, so that its benefits will become fully manifest."

"You must go," Ruhapali replied, adamantly.

"Perhaps, Dr. Muffet," Drake said, smoothly, "we might be better placed to settle the matter if you would explain to us exactly what the purpose of your work is. I suppose that appearances might be deceptive, but I've seen men transformed by spider-bites, who lie down to let monstrous parasites such their blood and carry it away into a spider'-nest the size of a town, apparently at the command and behest of invaders from another world—and it seems to me that Ruhapali and his people have been exceedingly patient in waiting so long to take up their arms. Raleigh admitted to me that you and he dared not begin this work in England, and I'm inclined to agree with him that it would have been direly dangerous to do so."

"Superstition is a difficult enemy to fight," Muffet said, "Whether one encounters it in the Church, the Royal College of Physicians or the prejudices of ignorant tribesmen. You've found that yourself, I think, in trying to persuade your fellow Englishmen that what you discovered in the moon and beyond is real."

Drake did not want to waste time pointing out that he would have found that task far easier had Tom Digges or Walter Raleigh confirmed his story. "Be specific, doctor," he said, "and be brief—we have no time for a long discourse."

"Very well," Muffet said. "I doubt that you're acquainted with the principles of medicine, but you've probably heard mention of four bodily humors analogous to the four elements of inanimate matter, which must be kept in balance if the body is to remain healthy. I'll not attempt to describe all the complications introduced into that fundamental system as a result of the New Learning, hoping that it will suffice to say that there are at least as many subsidiary substances making up the components of living bodies as there are different kinds of solids, liquids and essences, and that their various malfunctions defy easy appeasement by the remedies contained in herbals or those at the disposal of Galenist or Paracelsian physicians. We have but few defenses against sickness and injury, Captain, and they're by no means reliable.

"As I explained to you last night, spiders are unlike most other creatures in consuming food exclusively in liquid form. Even earthly spiders, which are exceedingly primitive, have developed complex methods of immobilizing their prey and transforming the flesh they will consume into liquid form. On worlds in which spiders, rather than insects and mollusks, have acquired intelligence and have become dominant species, they've become masters of the alchemy of flesh, whose secretions accomplish far more than mere liquefaction. The most advanced have become experts in induced transmutation, remolding other species internally and externally to their own designs. Our own alchemists have long searched for the elixir of life as well as the secret of transmuting base metals into gold and silver, but they've made even less progress in the former quest than the latter. The celestial spiders have achieved far more.

"The insects and mollusks that constitute the vast majority of intelligent species within the sidereal system do not like spiders, because they consider them dangerous predators, but that is because the spiders native to their own worlds are as primitive as the spiders of ours. In a more general sense, too, the masters of the galaxy have inherited the mentality of prey species and cannot understand the true logic of predation as a way of life. Humans, being omnivores who owe our own intelligence, culture and civilization to hunting and animal husbandry, *can* understand, if we will only make the effort to overcome our silly prejudice. That's why we're natural allies of the celestial spiders, and why they're prepared to optimize us as a sibling species rather than a subject one.

"We humans have been alchemists of the flesh ourselves, in transforming all the species on which we depend: the livestock we keep to supply us with meat, milk and eggs, the horses we use for transportation on land, and the dogs we employ in hunting. We change them to the best of our ability, tailoring them to our needs, optimizing them for the production of those qualities we desire in them—but we can only do so indirectly, by selective breeding. The celestial spiders are cleverer by far, employing all manner of elixirs that work directly upon the flesh of other species. They've used their intelligence very wisely in the investigation and deployment of their intrinsic abilities in this regard, and have become great experts in the calculated modification of their various domestic stocks—but they've not been content with that, either in their own worlds or in others they've found and visited.

"Where intelligence has emerged spontaneously among spider species, those species have never been content to remain alone; they've always elected to optimize intelligence in brethren species. Nor have they usually been content to restrict that privilege to other arachnids; they've been curious enough to offer the gifts of sentience, speech and culture to species of very different kinds, including insects and mollusks. Indeed, many spiders believe that the species currently making up the dominant culture of the galaxy must have originated from spider alchemy, and then turned ungratefully against their benefactors, wiping out their makers and attempting to hunt down and destroy similar species wherever they found them, extrapolating their fearful prey mentality.

"There is, as you say, no time for a long discourse, so I shall say only this: the celestial spiders are willing to be our friends and benefactors. They're willing to assist us in the development of cures for very many human diseases, and to help us become far more robust in resisting injury. They can help us live far longer than our traditional allotment of three-score years and ten, and they can give us the power to re-grow lost limbs and damaged organs. They cannot make us immortal, but they can make us a good deal less mortal than we are. They're eager to do this because they've not had the opportunity before to work with natural species of our kind—intelligent vertebrates, that is. They don't know of any world in which spiders have contrived to induce intelligence in vertebrate species, but those that have developed naturally on Earth have far greater natural potential by virtue of their unusual size.

"With the spiders' assistance, therefore, humankind can take a great leap forward, benefiting from a process of perfection that might require thousands of years if we had to develop our own knowledge of the alchemy of the flesh by trial and error—assuming that we'd be let alone in the meantime by the great fleshcores and their multitudinous subject species. In sum, we *need* the celestial spiders, and have a great deal to gain from association with them—if we can only suppress and master our stupid instincts."

CHAPTER TWENTY-ONE

Drake had glanced repeatedly at both Ruhapali and Gilbert to see what effect Muffet's explanatory speech was having on them. Ruhapali, apparently, had not been able to comprehend more than a fraction of it, and seemed utterly unmoved in his determination to remove all alien presences from Tahiti, in order that his people might revert to the untroubled existence they had previously enjoyed. Gilbert must have heard similar speeches many times over, with appropriate elaborations, and presumably understood the arguments better than Drake did, but he seemed distinctly unhappy. It was to him that Drake turned now.

"What's your opinion, Sir Humphrey?" Drake asked.

"If I'd been told all this before I set sail from Southampton," Gilbert said, bluntly, "I would not have left England. I've been strongly tempted to return more than once, but have been torn by conflicting responsibilities. Lately, I've been reluctant to leave because it would have meant abandoning Dr. Muffet and his daughter to a dangerous situation—but now that the situation has become impossible, I wonder whether my duty might be to save them, and compel them to come away. On the other hand, I cannot believe that my men will consent to bring the results of the doctor's experiments in transmutation with us—except, perhaps, for the clever birds—and I might face a mutiny merely by virtue of trying to save the doctor and Patience."

"I can understand all that, Sir Humphrey," Drake said. "But what do you think of the merits of Doctor Muffet's scheme itself?"

"I no longer know what to think," Gilbert admitted. "For a time, it seemed that the potential reward might outweigh any risk, but recent reports we have had from the island's interior have made me wonder whether the real intention of these celestial visitors might be to establish a spider empire on Earth, reducing humankind to the status of mere cattle. If that is their plan, there might only be a narrow interval in which it can be nipped in the bud."

"Nonsense!" said Muffet. "You're allowing unreasoning revulsion to overrule the judgment of reason."

"Even if Sir Humphrey's fears could be set aside," Drake said, pensively, "and everything you said were actually true, rather than the result of these celestial spiders playing you and Raleigh for fools, there's another danger we shouldn't discount."

"What's that?" Muffet demanded.

"The danger that the great empire whose shores extend even to the interior of our planet's moon might not take kindly to an alliance between two kinds of creatures they dislike. So far as I know, no man in England knows that you are here or what you are doing—and that ignorance will presumably persist until some of us return—but that doesn't mean that your work is secret from the folk that Raleigh and I met when we went voyaging in Master Dee's ethership."

"We can do nothing about that," Muffet retorted, "except make sure that, should the insect hordes decide that humankind is dangerous to them, we're as well able to defend ourselves as we can be. That's a further reason to embrace an alliance with the spiders, and welcome our own optimization. In any case, we're already committed. If Ruhapali thinks that he can destroy the celestial spiders, or even the Earthly creatures they've so far transformed, he's mistaken. If he refuses to abandon this war he's begun, his forces will be defeated. He should make a treaty with us now, else things will go very badly indeed for his people."

"You will go," Ruhapali repeated, yet again. "You will give us guns. We will kill the spiders."

"Stay with us, Captain Drake," Muffet said. "Help us to defend the stockade and our work. If you'll agree to do that, I'm sure that Sir Humphrey will do likewise."

Gilbert was not inclined to confirm or deny that speculation. Instead, he said: "If you should decide to sail away from here, Sir Francis, I shall be happy to accompany you, with as many men as may care to come with me, to whatever destination you might have in mind."

Drake was not grateful for this statement, which seemed to place the entire burden of decision on his unready shoulders. He had no time to figure out a way out of the impasse, though, because Edward Hammond hammered on the cabin door just then and said: "You're needed on deck, Captain—there's movement on sea and shore alike."

Drake hurried from the cabin, assuming that the others would follow him. When he and Hammond arrived on the deck the mate pointed out to sea first. The night was clear, but the moonlight reflected from the sea was not very abundant. Even so, Drake could see that the waters around the *Golden Hind* were crowded with canoes—more likely hundreds than dozens. They were not, however, making any overtly hostile move towards the ship, and their paddlers seemed to be in a state of considerable confusion. There was a great deal of shouting, which seemed indicative of urgent alarm.

On the shoreward side, the horizon was red with fire and blotched with smoke, but lights of a different sort showed all along the coast, where there was more shouting. The settlement was more brightly lighted than the strands to either side of it, but did not seem quite so full of alarm.

Martin Lyle was in the rigging, with his eye glued to Drake's telescope. "The islanders aren't attacking the settlement, sir," he called down. "Indeed, I think they're begging to be let in for their own safety's sake—they're being attacked themselves. Everyone who can seems to have taken to the water, but there must be thousands of natives who can't."

Drake rounded on Muffet, who had come up behind him. "The celestial spiders have mounted their counter-offensive," he said. "You can make a better estimate of their resources than anyone else—can they be defeated?"

"It's not the visitors!" Muffet protested. "It's the earthly giants—they've not yet contrived to set aside their inconvenient instincts, any more than the islanders have. They're striking back reflexively. If you'll give the celestial spiders time enough, they'll bring the situation under control."

"We don't know for sure that they're still alive," Drake told him. "The attack was successful enough to wound Raleigh, at least, and it was begun by some kind of petard loaded with black powder. Mr. Hammond! Set men with muskets to port and starboard and have the artillerists stand ready—but the musketeers are not to fire on the islanders unless they're attacked themselves. Lower the pinnace again and send it back to shore, ready to evacuate our remaining men—and Gilbert's too, if they haven't enough boats of their own."

"Wait!" cried Muffet. "I'll go back with them!"

"No," said Drake shortly. "Ruhapali! Can you judge from the shouting how things are with your own people?"

Ruhapali had already called down to the chiefs who were waiting for him in the canoe that had brought Drake back. "Spiders cannot swim," he replied, "but some got into boats—they caused much fear. Many people waded into shallow water—they are safe, for now. Sire Gilbert's men must open the gates of stockade to let my people in. They will fight spiders with your people."

"No!" Muffet cried. "They must not!"

Drake's opinion was that this was probably the most sensible option for the men within the stockade—but he knew how difficulty it would be for the people currently locked inside to make the decision, given that some of the spiders would probably gain access along with the panicked islanders. He was sorely tempted to go ashore with the pinnace himself, but his own men formed a tiny minority of the company within the stockade, and he could not be sure that the others would take orders from him at present—or from anyone, including Sir Humphrey Gilbert.

There was a sudden clatter of wings and a large macaw hurtled out of the darkness to land on the arm that Thomas Muffet had hastily raised up.

"Raleigh's coming!" the bird squawked. "Stay calm! Raleigh's coming!"

"You heard that!" Muffet shouted—unnecessarily loudly, since Drake was still close at hand.

"It's too late!" Drake told him, in a much quieter voice. "There's no way this situation can be quickly repaired. If the spiders can be commanded to desist—which I doubt—that will only give the islanders the opportunity to renew their own assaults. If Raleigh and his precious celestial spiders have left the valley, they'll either seem that much more dangerous, or that much more vulnerable to attack—and I presume that they'll defend themselves if they *are* attacked." He raised his voice to shout to the boatswain in command of the pinnace: "Don't delay, Mr. Stephens! I want everyone back safe, as quickly as possible!"

Humphrey Gilbert had also taken matters into his own hands, and was shouting across the water to the watchmen aboard his own ships, instructing the to launch what boats they could to fetch men from the shore.

The sound of gunfire broke out ashore—a disordered crackling rather than disciplined volleys.

"What is it, Martin?" Drake called.

"The islanders have broken into the stockade, sir," the boy reported. "They weren't let in, and some of the defenders have fired on them. They're attacking the musketeers now, sir."

"Ruhapali!" Drake said. "You must stop your people fighting ours, if you can! We're not your enemy!"

Ruhapali shook his head, to indicate helplessness rather than refusal. Drake turned around, intending to go up into the rigging to take the telescope from his kinsman and watch the disaster unfolding, but he stopped abruptly as he almost fell over Patience Muffet. She looked up at him, and said—in a voice pitched so softly that no one else could hear—"Please take me ashore, Captain. Hector, Achilles and the others will need me."

Drake shook his head, to signify bewilderment as well as refusal. His head was aching, and exhaustion was beginning to inhibit his movements. Even so, he began to climb, going up far enough to be able to take the telescope from Martin's outstretched hand. He focused the instrument on the shore, but lights were going out now as the struggle within the stockade became ever-more chaotic, and it was very difficult to make out any detail.

"How many cannon are manned and ready, Ned?" Drake demanded.

"Three port, three starboard, sir!" Hammond reported.

"Tell the for'ard gunner on the shoreward side to fire a shot into the shallows—but make sure it falls harmlessly, well clear of boats of any sort."

"Aye, sir!" the mate replied—and disappeared to make sure that the order was carried out to the letter. Drake hoped that the sound of the cannon firing might bring about a pause on shore, which would allow the defenders of the stockade and the islanders alike to realize that they had no quarrel with one another as urgent as their fear of the fire-maddened spiders.

When the cannon boomed, Drake saw through the spy-glass that there was, indeed, a pause while everyone looked around—but the moment of stillness was short-lived. There were screams as well as shouts audible within the stockade now, and Drake guessed that the islanders' pursuers had followed them through the broken gate. He redirected the telescope towards the pinnace, which had reached shore alongside the much smaller rowboat. He could only hope that his men would contrive to reach the vessels safely and begin the evacuation.

He heard the thud of a spear that hit the side of the vessel then, and the whistle of an arrow soaring over the deck. He groaned, knowing that the missiles must have been sent forth in blind panic rather than as aspects of an organized attack. He filled his lungs with air, ready to tell his men to desist from firing for a few moments longer, but it was already too late; a volley of shots returned the fire from the canoes, and there was nothing to be done thereafter but scramble down to the deck and fetch a weapon for himself, ready to repel boarders if the necessity arose. Ruhapali was still on the deck, shouting orders in his own language, but it was impossible to tell whether the orders were having any effect.

"Raleigh's coming!" squawked the macaw, again. "All's well! Raleigh's coming!"

"He'll arrive too late," Drake said, wearily, fixing his eyes on Muffet rather than the bird. "I'll take him aboard if he can get here, but I won't take his accursed spiders—they must fend for themselves."

"They will, Captain," Muffet retorted. "You may be sure of that."

CHAPTER TWENTY-TWO

Drake snatched a cutlass from one of his musketeers, but there were no more spears and arrows hurtling on to the deck now; whether that was because of the volley of musket-fire or Ruhapali's shouted orders, he could not tell. He renewed his instructions to his own men, telling them to desist from any violence unless and until their live were under threat. Then he put the telescope to his eye again, searching for the pinnace. He saw that it was moving away from the shore, having picked up a considerable number of passengers. The vessel was heading away from the remaining lights on shore into deep gloom, but the hectic movement of the shadows told him that something was badly wrong.

It seemed at first that the people on the boat must be fighting amongst themselves, and Drake wondered whether the islanders might be trying to seize the pinnace for their own purposes—but then he realized that they were actually battling against two huge spiders that had managed to clamber aboard. Although three or four of the men had muskets, they had obviously discharged their rounds already and had not had an opportunity to reload, for they were using the guns as if they were clubs. Others were using the oars as staves to ward off the spiders—with the result that the pinnace was drifting in the shallows rather than making significant headway.

Drake rounded on Ruhapali. "Can your canoe get me to that pinnace? You may bring your fellow chiefs up here, if I can take their places with half a dozen men."

"No," the Tahitian said, immediately. "We will take you. You give us guns to fire."

It seemed to Drake to be a very bad time for haggling, but Ruhapali obviously felt that he had been cheated of his bargain before and was not about to let an opportunity to recover it pass him by. "Ned!" Drake called to Hammond, who had just reappeared on deck. "Bring me four loaded muskets, now!"

Hammond obeyed, but when he saw what Drake intended to do he begged to be allowed to go in his stead, or at least to accompany him. "You're exhausted, captain!" the mate added, by way of justification.

"No time to argue, Ned—and no room in the boat!" Drake replied, before collecting two of the guns and lowering himself over the side. Ruhapali followed, carrying two more.

The paddlers were ready, and the canoe shot away from the flank of the *Golden Hind*, heading straight for the pinnace. There was no light aboard either boat, but the larger boat was still close enough to shore for them to obtain some benefit from the few lanterns still burning in the settlement.

The passengers on the pinnace had cornered the two spiders at one end of the vessel, and were holding them back with the oars and the empty guns, but at least two sailors had fallen down, presumably bitten.

Drake moved into the prow of the canoe, ready to slash with the cutlass at the creatures' legs. He remembered what Raleigh had said about the difficulty of augmenting the load-bearing capacity of spiders' limbs, and thought that a likely way to immobilize them quickly. It might then be possible for the oars to be used as levers to tip them overboard. Ruhapali had other ideas, though. "Get down, Captain Drake!" the chieftain called—just in time, for his inexperienced gunners were far too eager to fire. Four shots went off almost simultaneously, but one islander was knocked completely off balance by the recoil, only just managing to drop the gun into the boat before he toppled overboard.

One of the spiders flinched visibly, presumably having been hit, but the other bullets seemed to have missed their targets. The monster that had been hit had not been killed, and it turned to face the approaching canoe. Drake had to stand up again and carry out his plan, slashing wildly at the legs of both creatures.

Now that he was within touching distance Drake was able to appreciate the true enormity of their size and ugliness; they were, indeed, as large as sheep, and as shaggy too, but their shape was very different and there was something intrinsically horrifying about the way they moved on eight legs rather than four, with a curious fluid quality. Drake could barely make out the features of their horrid heads in the poor light, and could not make out the merest glint of an eye, but he felt an unexpected surge of revulsion that must have been born of pure imagination.

But this is the world as it is, he thought. *The sky is full of stars invisible to the naked eye, and the countless stars have worlds where*

creatures like these think, feel and scheme like Earthly men. What-
ever happens here, on this remote island, our entire world is caught
in their web, helplessly.

The injured spider lunged at him as he struck out, and when the two vessels scraped sides it contrived to scramble from the pinnace into the canoe, where it fought for balance. Once it had found its footing, the monster would surely have hurled itself upon its at-tacker—but the pause was just long enough to allow Drake to slash cruelly at two of its legs, cutting them simultaneously, with enough force to break them both. A third leg must already have been in-jured, for the spider now found itself quite unable to follow through with its attack. While it floundered on the floor of the canoe Drake thrust again with his blade, and then again, making sure that the monster was dead.

He felt a surge of triumph then, which overwhelmed the resid-ual effects of his earlier frisson of terror.

In the meantime, the islanders had pulled their fellow out of the water, and the oarsmen in the pinnace had managed to tip the second arachnid invader—which was also badly wounded by now—into the seething wake of the lighter vessel.

Drake turned to Ruhapali, intending to order him back to the *Golden Hind*, but he felt suddenly giddy, and his limbs seemed about to give out. In any case, Ruhapali was already giving orders in his own tongue. The canoe turned, and came alongside the pinnace.

"Go with your own people," Ruhapali instructed Drake. "Go now!"

There was nothing to be gained by argument, and Drake now felt drained of every vestige of his strength. He allowed himself to be transferred to the pinnace, leaving the four muskets behind.

Drake presumed that Ruhapali would find some black powder left behind in the settlement—but even if he did not, mere posses-sion of the guns would increase the chieftain's status among his own people, and his determination to use the weapons against the celes-tial spiders. Drake knew that he was in no position to offer the Tahi-tian sound advice as to his future policy or strategy.

With the oarsmen now able to work unhindered, the pinnace sped back to the *Golden Hind* and unloaded its human cargo, includ-ing the two injured men. Drake found the strength to climb up to the deck, but Edward Hammond and Sir Humphrey Gilbert had to grab his arms and pull him over the rail. "Have we any men left ashore, Mr. Stephens?" Drake muttered to the boatswain.

"No sir," Stephens replied. "We have three of Gilbert's men aboard, but the rest of ours were taken aboard the rowboat." He pointed towards the shore, but Drake could not see the smaller vessel in the darkness.

"No more spears or arrows have been launched against us, sir," Hammond reported. "Your guest put an end to that, I think."

"Bring the pinnace aboard but keep the rowboat in the water attached by a painter, and its oarsmen ready," Drake ordered, hoarsely. "Keep an armed lookout—but no more shooting, unless it's necessary. We'll sit tight till dawn, and reappraise the situation when we've more light."

"May I borrow your rowboat to return to my own ship, Sir Francis, along with the men the pinnace brought?" Gilbert asked.

"Aye, Sir Humphrey, if you wish," Drake said, wearily, "but you might do better to come back when you've delivered your men and issued your orders. We'll need to decide what to do tomorrow, and it would be better if some of us, at least, were prepared to agree on a course of action."

Gilbert made a vague promise to return when he could, and lowered himself over the side. His men did not seem overly enthusiastic to leave the relative safety of the *Golden Hind*, but they complied with their master's orders.

"All's well!" proclaimed Agamemnon, who was now perched in the rigging. He was not alone; a dozen more birds had flown to join him, and the flock seemed as ready to wait out the night aboard as the ship's human crew.

"Let's hope so," Drake murmured, as he slumped against the mast. Hammond and Stephens had to pick him up, and help him below to his cabin. There they laid him on his bunk and promised that everything would be held secure until morning.

CHAPTER TWENTY-THREE

Drake did not wake until some time after dawn, and would have slept longer had Martin Lyle not crept hesitantly into the cabin.

"What is it, Martlet?" Drake demanded, knowing that the boy would not have ventured to disturb him unless he was needed.

"There's a native canoe off the port bow, sir—but the men in it are darker-skinned than the islanders. One of them speaks English, and says that you know him."

"Raleigh?" Drake asked, rubbing his eyes. "Get me some water, will you, Martin.

"He didn't give his name, sir," Martin replied. He fetched a jug of water, from which Drake drank avidly.

"I'll be on deck directly," Drake said. "Ask our visitor to wait. Is Muffet awake?"

"No, sir. He and his daughter are asleep. The birds are still perched in the rigging, but Mr. Hammond ordered a search to be conducted for spiders as soon as it was light. None have been found, of any size." The boy left after making this report, and Drake followed him some five minutes later, having made what adjustments as he could to his appearance, so that he might better play the part of a gentleman and captain of an English ship.

The canoe carrying Walter Raleigh and five optimized islanders was idling in the water some ten or twelve yards from the *Hind*'s bow. It was being watched by half a dozen of Drake's sailors, all armed with muskets, but there was no evident alarm on either side.

"I'm glad to see you well, Walter," Drake said, not having to raise his voice unduly to be heard. "I feared that you might have been killed by that spear."

Raleigh parted his shirt so that Drake could see the wound, which seemed half-healed already. "It would have killed a man like you, Francis," Raleigh said. "I'm glad you can see that it was only a minor inconvenience to a man like me. I'm sorry that we were interrupted—and sorrier still that Dr. Muffet's work has been disrupted.

That might cost England dear, if you and Gilbert are not inclined to stay here any longer."

"What do you expect of us, Walter?" Drake said, with more than a little bitterness. "I fought one of your giant spiders last night, at close quarters, and there can't be many of Gilbert's men who haven't seen them at their worst. If I ordered all Englishmen ashore, with abundant armaments, to support Ruhapali's campaign, they'd probably go—but I surely couldn't persuade them to stay on any other basis, and wouldn't want to. Captains, like kings, reign on sufferance."

"If we'd only had time," Raleigh complained, "Muffet and I could have helped you see reason. You, of all people, should understand the necessity of what we're doing."

"If the only way for humankind to escape being held in a menagerie by a legion of giant ants and slugs is to submit to transfiguration and being held in thrall by arachnid alchemists," Drake said, "I think I'd rather choose between the Devil and the deep blue sea."

"John Dee will understand," Raleigh said. "He knows more of alchemy than any man in England."

"If I ever see him again, I'll tell him what I've seen," Drake said, glad to find a concession he could make without effort. "I'll be exceedingly careful in telling anyone else, although I can't speak for others in that regard."

"You'd do well to stay here with us, Francis," Raleigh said. "If your crewmen won't, that's their affair—but you can get down into the canoe now, along with Muffet and Patience. Were you to call for volunteers to accompany you, I dare say that you might find a few."

"I couldn't do that even if I wanted to, Walter," Drake told him. "My first duty is to my ship and my men. I have to see them safely home, if I can, and to find them a better reward for their long expedition than I've so far contrived to do—something more easily tradable than potions distilled from spider venom."

"Can you really intend to return to South America and raid Spanish ships and settlements, after what you've discovered here?" Raleigh demanded.

"It's a trade I know," Drake told him. "But I also know that there's an Austral continent west of here, with two large islands in between, set some way to the south. Were I to go that way, I could sail around the world before going home, as Magellan's crew claimed to have done following his death."

"That's a pity," Raleigh said. "Will you fetch Muffet and Patience, then? I'm sure they'll be anxious to return to shore."

"Is it safe for them to do so?" Drake asked.

"Ruhapali's people are counting the cost of their adventure at present," Raleigh told him. "If they're wise, they won't attempt to renew their assault—but if not, we can defend ourselves. Muffet and Patience will be far safer here than they would be aboard your ship, whether you decide to sail east or west—and the same goes for you. Shall I gather supplies for you, and make sure you're well-provisioned before you sail?"

"That's very kind, Walter," Drake said, "but there are other islands in the cluster, where we can make our own arrangements to take on food and water."

"Do you suppose that we'd sneak cargo aboard that you'd rather not carry, under cover of supplying food and water? You mistake us, Francis—we're honest dealers. We mean you no harm, and wouldn't seek to use you unawares."

What Drake actually thought was that if the celestial spiders did want to use the English ships to transport any of their produce, just as they had earlier used Master Dee's ethership, they had had plenty of opportunity already to secrete their tiny agents in Gilbert's vessels. "I trust your word, Walter," was what he said aloud, "but I don't want to expose you to any risk. I suspect that Ruhapali's far from finished, as yet—and you might find him a more difficult opponent than you imagine."

"Within a month he'll be our staunchest ally," Raleigh said, confidently, "and within ten years—twenty, at most—Tahiti will be a nation to compare with any in Europe, sending diplomats to China and the Americas."

Drake looked around then, as Thomas Muffet and his daughter came on to the deck.

"Thank you for hearing me out last night, Captain," Muffet said, "and for keeping us safe aboard your vessel during the unpleasantness. I doubt that I'll be able to return to my laboratory for a while, but I can do my work in the interior."

"And will your daughter be safe there?" Drake asked, bluntly. "Are you really prepared to take her into the spider city?"

"Of course," Muffet said. "She has no fear of spiders."

Drake looked down at the little girl, who was standing quite calmly behind her father, living up to her name. He remembered what Muffet had said about the celestial spiders' ability to bring about internal as well as external transmutations.

"Bring the canoe alongside, Walter." Drake said, calmly. "You may take your passengers aboard. Your other friends will fly, I suppose." He glanced upwards as he spoke to where Agamemnon was perched, surrounded by two dozen fellows.

"Would you like a parrot as a gift?" Muffet asked. "Tame ones that can mimic human voices are quite popular with sailors, I understand."

"No thank you," Drake said. "I'm sure your birds would be much happier at home than they would be aboard ship. We wouldn't find it easy to care for them during long periods at sea."

Muffet made certain that Patience was safe as she clambered over the rail and began to descend the rope ladder to Raleigh's canoe, but he turned to face Drake again before following her.

"Perhaps we'll meet again, Captain," he said, "in England if not in Tahiti. I wish you felt able to stay longer—I'm sure you could be persuaded that our mission here is in the best interests of England, and of humankind."

Drake felt sure that he could be persuaded too, if he were to give the celestial spiders the opportunity—but it was the means they might use to persuade him that he feared. Muffet and Raleigh seemed far too sure of themselves for him to believe that they were guided by mere reason—and Patience was positively uncanny. On the other hand, he had no firm grounds for deciding that they were other than human, or direly dangerous. If they were, then it was at least possible, if not likely, that there were others of their kind among Gilbert's men.

"I discovered three years ago, Dr. Muffet," Drake said, "that the world in which we find ourselves is very far from what our forefathers believed it to be. I can only hope that John Field was wrong in his interpretation of it, and that you and Walter might be right—but I'm beginning to see, now, why Tom Digges might be more content than any of us, in being able to believe that it was all a silly dream. Perhaps it was, after all, an angel that accompanied him into a world of multifarious demonkinds."

"There's no security in illusion, Francis," Raleigh said, from the canoe. "We must accept the limitless universe as we find it, and make what alliances we can."

"We're your friends," Muffet added, as he climbed down to join his companions. "We always shall be, no matter what you fear or believe."

"And I'm yours," Drake assured them.

He watched the canoe make its way back to the headland east of the harbor. There were other canoes visible on the water, further out to sea, but none made any attempt to intercept it.

Martin Lyle brought the telescope forward, and Drake turned it on the settlement. It seemed crowded with islanders, busy making their own arrangements to settle there.

"What shall we do, captain?" Martin asked.

"We'll sail west," Drake said. "We'll reprovision from other is-lands in the cluster, then head for the two larger ones that lie south-east of the Austral continent. Then we'll investigate the continent itself. We'll collect what we can to carry home to England, but we'll be sure to take as much information as we can gather about the re-mote reaches of the world."

"They won't believe us in England, sir," the boy said. "There are too many travelers' tales already about giant spiders and clever birds. They'll think us liars."

"Aye," said Drake. "But not for long, I suspect. One way or an-other, the people of England will see the Age of Miracles reborn—and we can only hope that they won't find it unbearable, as an era in which to live and dream."

PART THREE

THE PHILOSOPHER'S STONE

CHAPTER TWENTY-FOUR

Edward Kelley staggered through the door of the inn bearing the sign of the Black Bear just as the last remnant of twilight faded away. His legs had not let him down, in spite of all the miles he had walked, but his head felt as if it might explode. It was not so much an ache as a sensation of terrible unease. The sensation was inconstant but incessant; its peaks of effect had been increasing by degrees for a fortnight, and the present one was the worst yet. He had hoped that he might obtain some release when he had given the black stone and the red powder to his wife, in order that she might take them to Mortlake by river barge, but it seemed that the angels would not let him go, whether he had their gifts about his person or not, and that their demands would not cease once he had delivered the stone safely into John Dee's hands.

It had been a wise decision to let Ann take the stone; he was the one for whom the searchers would be looking, and his was the unfortunately-distinctive description they would have been given. Ann would be safer on her own than in his company. It appeared, however, that he was no longer capable of renouncing the stone even if he had wanted to; having entered into a rapport with its strange inhabitants, his soul was captive. He had to get to Mortlake too, come hell, high water or all the Puritan wrath in England.

He looked around the inn's pot-room warily. The hour was not late, the equinox having only just passed, but he doubted that any further travelers would come in after him. The Black Bear was less than fifty miles from London, but the road was dangerous after dark, so honest men would have made shift to take shelter as the sun set. Kelley had only a few copper coins to steal, but footpads would not know that, and might well give him an extra tap on the head for having put them to the trouble of seizing a near-empty purse, so there was a certain relief in reaching shelter—but that very fact would expose him to new dangers.

There were eight men foregathered in the room. Four of them, forming a party that might have been pre-arranged in Bristol or Bath, were well-dressed men of affairs, who would doubtless be sleeping in a private room. Three others had similarly gathered on a bench behind a rickety table, but Kelley judged from their body-language that they had not set out to travel as a group; they had flocked together instinctively after arriving separately or meeting on the road. Their common cause, he judged—the horrid feeling in his head had not affected his fortune-teller's eye—was further compounded by their active avoidance of a short, wiry man of fifty or thereabouts, who was sitting alone.

Kelley examined the pariah more carefully while he crossed the room to the ridiculously small servery, whose hatch was not much bigger than a loophole in a castle wall. The stranger wore a traveling-cloak, but it did not conceal the hem of his monastic habit. He had not taken off his broad-brimmed hat, but anyone, given the other circumstance, would have guessed that it concealed his tonsure.

Kelley bought a tankard of small beer and half a loaf. The purchase removed the last of his coin from his purse, but he was hungry and thirsty as well as sick in the head, and could not think of conserving his resources. He hesitated for a moment thereafter, but only for a moment. The sight of the monk offered him a slight chance of finding shelter for the following night; Romanists had refuges of their own. Although there was evidently no safe house within striking distance of the Black Bear, tonight's pariah would probably be able to find much warmer hospitality further along the London Road. The day after next, God willing, Kelley would reach Mortlake, and his fate would be in the hands of John Dee; it would surely be worth his while to play the Catholic for a little while.

The little man looked up at him in slight surprise as Kelley dropped his traveling-sack on the floor and took a seat on the same bench. Pale blue eyes studied the contours of Kelley's felt bonnet—which Kelley was as careful to wear indoors as the Romanist was to keep his hat on. They muttered a simultaneous formula of greeting, but the monk fell silent thereafter, obviously unprepared to say another word to a man he did not know.

Queen Jane's parliament operated a policy of "freedom of conscience", which meant that every man in England was entitled to follow the Roman faith if he wished, but the Archbishop of Canterbury was a fervent Puritan, and the power of zealous Protest was gaining ground with every day that passed. England had so far escaped the wars of religion that were consuming the continent, but that was because there was little possibility of organized resistance to the Puritan tide, least of all from the Catholics. Ever since Mary Tudor's assassination, shortly after she had landed in Plymouth with the alleged intention of raising an army to seize the throne, the Reformers had been cock-a-hoop; many Catholics had fled the realm. The Year of Our Lord 1582 was not a good time to be a Romanist, or even a High Churchman, in England.

Kelley's powers of intuition were not ingenious enough, in spite of any angelic enhancement of which the nagging vertigo might be a side-effect, to tell him whether the monk might be a Dominican friar or a homeless Benedictine, but he did not think that he could be expected to know the difference even if he really were a Catholic. After a decent interval, while the conversation at the gentlemen's table was uproarious enough to drown out what he said, Kelley leaned forward and said: "Will you hear my confession, Father?"

The little man stared at him for ten or twelve seconds before replying, as Kelley had hoped: "Not here."

"On the road, then," Kelley said, "when we leave in the morning—assuming that you're London-bound."

The wary monk would not even confirm that he was London-bound, as yet. "What are you?" he asked, instead. He spoke with a slight accent, as if he had spent long years out of his native England.

"My name is Edward Talbot, sir, and I'm a lettered man. I'll freely admit that I wear my cap indoors to hide the fact that I have no ears, and I won't deny the sin that cost me their excision—but that's not why I'm a fugitive now." *I'm on the side of the angels, at any rate*, he thought, bitterly.

He had taken a fancy to the stone when he had found it on Northwick Hill and gladly adopted it as a pretended skrying-glass, to aid him in his trade, before the angels first appeared within it and made it all too real. Like a fool, he had been glutted with delight when he first realized that he really did have a power—a gift, he had thought it—but he had reason now to suspect that any secrets the angels might condescend to impart to a man such as him would be as useless as they were bewildering, while the price they would demand in return was usurious. All things considered, he'd rather have thrown the stone away than attracted the attention of the Church Militant, in spite of the hints the angels had thrown out regarding the miraculous quality of the red powder, but it was too late now. Field's men were after him, and he was in desperate need of angelic help, if any were available.

The little man glanced left and right to make sure that no one was eavesdropping, then whispered: "Is it the hounds that are after you?"

"No," Kelley told him, with regretful honesty, "it's the foxes." The hounds were the Queen's men—constables, bailiffs, soldiers and the like—while the foxes were named for John Foxe, the Archbishop of Canterbury. The Church Militant was nominally responsible to him, but their immediate commander was John Field, a firebrand who saw sorcery everywhere, and would doubtless have made a fine witch-finder in Scotland or Lorraine. Although the Church Militant did not have a parliamentary license, as yet, to burn witches, let alone Catholics, there were doubtless many among them who were hoping devoutly that the day would come. The ragged little man might, if he were a Dominican friar, be a heresy-hunter himself—but this was Queen Jane's England, and circumstance had reduced Dominicans, Franciscans, Carthusians, and Benedictines alike to the status of mere beggars, dependent on the charity of the Catholic laity.

When his deliberate pause had drawn on long enough, Kelley added: "I swear before God, Father, that I am innocent of any crime against Christ. I dare say that the Royal College of Physicians might have objections to my beliefs, but I was properly prenticed as an apothecary once, and am no charlatan."

"Are you a cunning man?" the friar asked.

Cunning enough, I hope, Kelley thought—but what he was being asked was whether he used herbs as curative agents. "No," he said. "A Paracelsian—in English terms, a follower of Tom Muffet." It was true, in a way; such potions as he had sold as a sideline to his fortune-telling had been chemical rather than herbal, for he thought himself a thoroughly modern man, and bore a grudge against the Royal College.

"Muffet left these shores many years ago," the little man murmured. "According to Francis Drake, he's on the far side of the world."

"Aye," said Kelley, "so he is, if Drake can be believed. I believe that the captain really did sail around the world, mind, even though the other rumors credited to his testimony are hard to believe." *Except for a man who talks to angels*, he carefully did not add. Rumor of the wild tales that Drake was telling in London had reached as far as the Welsh borders, and Kelley had taken more account of them than their incredulous tellers, for the angels told similar stories, to the extent that he could understand their jabbering.

This time, the monk actually went so far as to nod his head sagely. Educated Romanists knew perfectly well that the world was a sphere; those Englishmen who clung to stubborn faith in its flatness were far more likely to rally to the Puritan cause; the Church Militant was full of them. "My name is Cuthbert," the little man finally conceded.

"Named for Cuthbert Tunstall, I don't doubt," Kelley was quick to say. "A great Englishman. What's your order?"

"I'm a member of the Order of St. Dominic," Brother Cuthbert told him. "I'm an Englishman born, but I've spent more than half my life in France."

"And wish you were there still, I'll wager," Kelley said.

"That's not for me to choose," the friar said, only a trifle sadly.

"I know something of duty myself," Kelley muttered, wishing that he were insincere. "I have no clerical vocation, but the Lord expects obedience from us all, even when His instructions are difficult." This affirmation did not awake any suspicion in Brother Cuthbert, who presumably took it to mean that Kelley was steadfast in his Catholic faith, in spite of the pressures to which that faith was now subject in England.

The friar looked around again, but no one was looking in his direction; indeed, the party of four gentlemen and the makeshift party of three might have been engaged in a tacit competition to see which could ignore him more ostentatiously. Kelley knew as well as Brother Cuthbert that ears might still be pricked to hear their conversation, but the other two groups seemed busy enough with raucous entertainment. They were obviously drinking stronger ale than Kelley was.

"If you were London-bound," Kelley said, softly, "I'd deem it an honor to keep you company. The roads are unsafe, they say, for men traveling alone. I have no weapon, but I've strong arms and legs." That was true enough; he was thin but well-muscled, and he towered over the Dominican by at least three fingers and a thumb.

The friar had to suspect that his companion was as keen to benefit from protection as to offer it, but the fact remained that he had been forced to shelter in an inn for want of a safe-house, and might indeed benefit from a temporary alliance—perhaps sufficiently to return the favor the following night, when he ought to be better able to find shelter with men of his own faith.

The little man finally nodded his head, tacitly consenting to that whole range of possibility—always provided, of course, that Kelley could fake a plausible confession while they made their way eastwards on the following morn. Kelley felt sure that he could; he had sins enough to his name, without ever having to mention fortune-telling or skrying-stones, let alone imperious angels.

Kelley raised his tankard in a gesture of thanks before he quaffed the dregs—and when the time came for the lamp to be put out and for the five men lying on the straw to take their places, Kelley and the monk lay down side-by-side, on the opposite side of the fireplace to the other three circumstantial companions.

Chapter Twenty-Five

The Black Bear's door had been securely barred and bolted for an hour and more when someone began to hammer on it. Kelley, who woke immediately from a painful nightmare and sat up straight, though it made his head reel, knew immediately that it was the hilt of a dagger or a staff, not a fist, that was thumping the door, and his heart sank even before he heard the fateful words: "Open in the name of the Church Militant!"

The innkeeper emerged from the back room in a night-shirt, carrying a candle-tray, but would not open up without first looking through the spy-hole in the door and demanding to know who was knocking and why. When he heard the words "Church Militant" repeated, the landlord scowled, but hastened to obey. Kelley looked wildly about, while his head seemed to swell like a billow of dark smoke, but he knew already that there was no viable escape route. Brother Cuthbert had woken too, but he was befuddled in a perfectly ordinary fashion, and did not seem to have yet taken in the import of the ominous words.

Kelley moved away from the friar, motivated by altruism rather than fear, because he was quite certain that Field's men were after him, not some Dominican stray. It did no good, though; when the Churchmen came in the three travelers who had been sleeping on the far side of the hearth were quick to establish their own separateness by declaring that Kelley and the Dominican were obvious Romanists, probable conspirators and definitely traveling-companions. The three had, of course, jumped to the conclusion that the friar was the wanted man, and fancied that Kelley might be an agent of the rumored "underground" that protected Romanists, sent to meet him here. Any faint hope that remained to Kelley that the Dominican might be the foxes' target vanished, however, as soon as he and the Puritans' leader locked gazes.

"Edward Kelley," said the Churchman, "we have a warrant for your arrest, issued by the Bishop of Oxford, on the charge of sorcery." The black-clad man still had the staff in his hand that he had used to hammer in the door, and his three companions had cudgels as well as sheathed poniards; there was no possibility that Kelley might be able to skittle them and take to his heels.

"My name is Talbot," Kelley said, his eyes flickering sideways as one of the men-at-arms knelt down to search his satchel. "You have the wrong man. There's doubtless more than one without ears on the London Road."

The satchel was so nearly empty that the search took no more than ten seconds. When the searcher shook his head, the leader of the party scowled, but made no comment. They had obviously been told to look for the stone, but they probably had no idea of its significance; in all likelihood, they simply expected it to provide evidence that he was some sort of magician. They could have no idea of the sort of magician he actually was—unsurprisingly, given that he had no understanding of it himself. They were not in the least impressed by his protestation that his name was Talbot.

"Bring them both," said the man with the staff, curtly.

"This man has nothing to do with me," Kelley was quick to say, in response to a pang of conscience. "We met by chance this evening; I've never seen him before. He has done no wrong and you have no warrant to take him."

The man who had searched Kelley's bag reached out a long arm and snatched away the hat that the little man had replaced on his head before getting to his feet, exposing his tonsure. That was no proof of anything, but it was enough for the foxes.

"If he has nothing to hide, he has nothing to fear," the Puritan leader said, portentously, "but a man who keeps company with sorcerers must expect to be questioned."

"Where are you taking us?" Brother Cuthbert asked, with surprising mildness. Kelley was impressed by the fact that the friar made no attempt to deny knowing him, in spite of the charge that had been laid against him; he presumed that his boastful claim of being a follower of Paracelsus had made a greater impact than he had hoped or supposed, in spite of his worn clothing and the evidence of his past crimes.

"To the lock-up in Hungerford, for now," the fox replied. "We'll await instructions as to whether you're to be sent to Oxford or London."

That was not entirely unwelcome news, Kelley thought. They would not be put to the question in Hungerford, and if the Church commanded that they be sent to London for interrogation, his boots would be spared fifty miles of hard wear. He would doubtless be chafed by irons, by way of compensation, but he had slipped his slim wrists out of manacles before, and an opportunity to escape might arise somehow, given that he had angels on his side. He could not help worrying, though, that the angels might deem him expendable now, if Ann could get the stone to John Dee without him. No one else he had invited to look into the false darkness had so far been able to see the angels, but Dee was universally reputed to be a great man, as much magician as mathematician and astronomer. If any man in England could see angels, he was surely the one—why else, after all, would the angels have commanded him so urgently to take the stone to Dee?

I was always too stupid to understand what they tried to tell me, Kelley reflected, bitterly. *Perhaps they sent me to Dee in despair, and will leave me to the tender mercies of Foxe and Field because I have failed them.*

The foxes had a farmer's cart waiting outside, lit by a brace of oil-lamps set either side of the driver's bench. There was a single set of leg-irons freshly stapled to the backboard behind the bench, which were fitted to Kelley's ankles. They left the Dominican unshackled, but he was obviously unenthusiastic about his chances of outrunning his captors. The four Churchmen stationed themselves at the corners of the cart, holding themselves stiffly attentive even though they were sitting down,

"I'm truly sorry," Kelley murmured to his fellow captive, as soon as they were under way. "I had no right to involve you in this. I should have kept to myself as I ate my supper."

"They'd have spotted me anyway, and brought me along," the friar replied, generously. "As the man says, I have nothing to fear, having nothing to hide." He could not add any manifest confidence to the second statement.

"The warrant lies," Kelley told him, feeling it incumbent on him to insist. "I am Edward Kelley, I admit, and a sinner, to be sure, but if I've encountered magic, I'm its victim, not its master."

"I believe you," the Dominican replied, with a slight shrug of his shoulders. "I only know Field by repute, but he's said to be very reckless in his accusations." John Field was a man that everyone now knew by repute, as one who was either inspired or insane. Unfortunately, even if the latter were the case, his was a kind of insanity that made some appeal to common men who were frightened by the pace at which the world was changing, and intimidated by the recent accumulation of philosophical ideas beyond their comprehension. Field might have been harmless had he not secured the trust of John Foxe, but the Archbishop's confidence was now worth almost as much as that of the Dukes of Northumberland and Suffolk, who were the Queen's strong arms.

"I've never offended Field," Kelley said, sourly, "and he has no reason to pursue me." It was a lie, though. Although much of what the angels said to him was murky in its meaning, it contained echoes of Field's Satanic madness as well as Francis Drake's gaudy boasts. Whatever whisper had reached Field's ears regarding the black stone, and what Kelley had seen within it, had been bound to catch his attention.

If only, Kelley thought, *I had had the sense to keep quiet when the miracle first enfolded me in its untender grip—but what man could help his tongue flapping in such circumstances?* At the very least, he could not have kept it secret from Ann, and who could prevent a woman from gossiping?

"If I had only managed to reach Mortlake...," Kelley murmured, dispiritedly—although in truth, he could not be certain that he would have found a warm welcome there. He had never met John Dee, and had no reason to think that the angels might have prepared the way for him. Nor had he had any real reason to think that Dee could have protected him against John Field, had he so desired. Dee was a Protestant, but certainly not a Puritan. He was reputed to have influence with the militant lords who commanded armies in Ireland, the Netherlands, and elsewhere, and even greater influence with the Admiralty and the Muscovy Company, but that did not mean that he was capable of standing off a challenge from the Church Militant.

The journey to Hungerford was not a long one, and the two captives were thrust into the lock-upon without any further ceremony, while their captors presumably hurried to their beds. There were two prisoners already caged, waiting for the next assizes, but the circuit-judge had not long passed that way, so they were still relatively plump and not yet seriously diseased. They only woke up long enough to examine the newcomers, judge them relatively harmless, and then lie down again.

Kelley sat down with his back against the bars of the grille, knowing that he would not be able to sleep. His head was such a riot of confusion that he almost yearned for a simple focused pain. He did not even have a name to put to his state of mind, and took leave to wonder whether men might not have mistaken the nature of Hell, for lack of insight into the true range of supernatural torments.

"Would you like me to hear your confession now?" Brother Cuthbert asked, unenthusiastically.

"Best not," Kelley told him. "If they think I might have told you something they'd like to know, they might not be as respectful of the sanctity of the confessional as they ought to be." He spoke loud enough to be clearly heard by the eavesdropper his captors had posted. For good measure, he added: "You were unlucky to meet me, Brother, and should be glad that I tried to take you for a fool, telling you nothing but lies."

There was no lantern in the jail, so he could not see the Dominican's response to that; he hoped, though, that Brother Cuthbert would not take it amiss, whatever conclusion the friar reached as to the statement's implications.

Having no idea how long he had slept before the Churchmen hammered on the inn door, Kelley had no way of knowing how long he would have to wait until daylight, nor how much longer he might have to wait after that to be put back in the cart, but he felt that he might as well make use of the time by praying. He had not been much given to prayer for the greater part of his life, but now that he had become the emissary of angels he had repented somewhat of his earlier laxity.

I know that there is war in Heaven once again, Lord, he said, silently, *and I know that you might not be able to help me even though you so desire—but if, perchance, it is necessary that I deliver myself as well as the black stone and the red powder into John Dee's hands, I cannot do so now without material assistance. Even if my wife can get the stone safely to Mortlake, it might be no use to him without my gift. So please, if you can hear my thoughts and my supplications, spare me another miracle, to give me a chance to escape while the cart is on the road tomorrow. If it heads eastwards, by all means postpone the propitious moment until we reach Staines or Twickenham, but if we head northwards to Oxford, I'd be glad of the earliest opportunity. And please take care of Brother Cuthbert, if you can, for Field will certainly take it out on him if I escape and he cannot.*

Brother Cuthbert seemed to be praying too; Kelley could hear the faint clicking of a rosary.

Kelley could not help remembering, after his prayer, how much happier he had been as a faker, before his impostures turned real. He still could not be absolutely certain that he had not simply fallen prey to his own deceptively persuasive talents, as many a false magician was reputed to do, but he knew that he no longer had a choice of destinies. Whether the voice that spoke to him through the black stone truly emanated from the ether, or merely from his own disturbed mind, he was bound to follow its instructions. Nor could he really be certain, taking everything into consideration, that the angel whose bidding he did was loyal to God—all the more so in the light of the angel's own insistence that the present war was no Satanic revolt, and that the Devil was not involved in it at all—but that too made no practical difference. The fact was that he could not disobey the instruction he had been given, even though it seemed at present that he would not be able to carry it out.

"Are you ill, my son?" Brother Cuthbert asked, perhaps sensing that he was shivering more than was warranted by the cold.

"Is it possible, Brother Cuthbert," he whispered, "that the wars of religion here on Earth are mirrored in Heaven? Given that Romanists and Protestants both claim loyalty to God, but are prepared to fight one another to the death, is it conceivable that Heaven itself might be riven by a great schism? Why should the angels not be just as uncertain of the proper way to worship God as men are? And why, given that uncertainty, should they not fall to violence to settle the issue, hurling the serried ranks of their chariots of fire into battles as fierce as any now being fought in the Netherlands or Germany?"

"Surely not," said the friar. "Men are stupid and ignorant, but the angels are the Lord's messengers, and know his will. There can be no dissent in their ranks—unless, perhaps, another prideful Lucifer appears among them, to begin a new revolt...." The friar trailed off, made pensive by the strange idea—or perhaps interrupted by the sudden awareness that something was happening.

Kelley immediately leapt to the conclusion that his prayer had been answered. He would have been quite content to hear the padlock securing the grille click open, and the iron bolts slide discreetly back, but it seemed that the angels were not as subtle as that, or that the Lord preferred to move in a more adventurous way. *Perhaps*, he thought, *the angels, like the fairies of legend, are intimidated by cold iron.* At any rate, it was the stone wall of the jail that was in the process of giving way, audibly. It did not implode, as if breached by a cannonball or smashed by some cunning silent petard, but it crumbled, rustling and crackling as it did so, like sand tumbling down a slope. Kelley could not see the stones coming apart, but he could see the gap that appeared where they fell away. Cloudy as the night was, it was visibly brighter than the awful gloom of the prison. The draught that came in through the widening gap was clean and cool.

The fragments of the dissolving wall scattered over the floor, reaching the place where the two sleepers were, but none, it seemed, was large enough to hurt them. They both woke up, and scrambled clear instinctively.

The wan light that was filtering through the new-made gap was briefly interrupted by a shadow as someone—or something—passed through. Kelley could not see the owner of the hand that grabbed his wrist in the obscurity of the jail, but he judged from the unerring and exceedingly insistent manner in which his wrist was seized that the other must be able to see in the dark. He took that for another evidence of angelic involvement, and leapt willingly enough to the conclusion that the guide sent to free him was a supernatural emissary, perhaps gifted with superhuman strength as well as a talent for dissolving stone walls.

The most assiduous of the various angels that had spoken to him through the medium of the philosopher's stone had told him that angels had no eyes at all, nor hands either, and had considerable difficulty interacting with vulgar matter in the slightest degree, but there was nothing delicate about the way Kelley was hauled to his feet and yanked towards the freshly-made gap in the lock-up's wall. He hardly had time to fumble for Brother Cuthbert's wrist in his turn—but he had the soft sound of the rosary to guide him, and made no mistake.

The Dominican did not seem entirely enthusiastic to be seized and saved, but he consented in the end to be led away. Kelley suspected that the little man must be entertaining visions of the *danse macabre*, fearing that it was hooded Death that was leading him away in train—partly because he could not suppress the image himself—so he was quick to whisper reassurances to his new friend.

"Have no fear," he said. "This is the work of seraphim, not demons. We shall be safe enough soon."

That was easy enough to say, but Kelley found it difficult enough to maintain his own faith once the three of them had squeezed through the hole in the brickwork and were hurried away into the darkness. He was as sure as he could be that the owner of the iron grip was vaguely human in form, because he could hear the muffled sounds of feet striding at a carefully measured pace, and could sense the movements of a human torso and head, but he could not *see* anything at all, and he knew that it was not impossible that the person dragging him away might have horns on his head and a demon's monstrous features.

At any rate, their rescuer seemed as strong as any ordinary man, although Kelley eventually concluded, with only a slight pang of disappointment, that he was probably not significantly stronger than that. He never set a foot wrong, though, whether he was pacing along the muddy road or making his way across fields whose crops were beginning to shoot up in earnest. He never broke into a run, although he seemed to be moving with greater purpose, as well as greater precision, than any marching soldier that Kelley had seen.

Although they never moved so fast as to exhaust his legs, Kelley was proud that he only stumbled twice and never fell at all—a better record by far than poor Cuthbert, who had to be dragged back to his feet half a dozen times, and must have bloodied his knees horribly. The leader of the forced march slowed his pace at each catastrophe, but never actually stopped, so there was no rest for his followers, even when the little monk's plaintive voice became so hoarse and agonized that Kelley feared for his life.

There was a terrible moment when Kelley feared that they might be expected and forced to walk all the way to Mortlake in that fearful mechanical fashion—but then dawn broke ahead of them in the east, and the little procession came abruptly to a halt.

"I need to leave you now," their rescuer said to them, in a strangely-accented voice. "Make your way to John Dee as fast as you can. Should you get into trouble again, I'll try to help, but can make no promises." He was still a mere silhouette, devoid of features, but Kelley was sure by then that he had no horns.

By the time it was light enough to see clearly, the mysterious personage had been completely swallowed up by the retreating shadows—but there was no mistaking the dark mistrust on the Dominican's face.

"Given that you're charged with sorcery, if only by that maniac Field," Cuthbert opined, when he had got his breath back, "I think I'd rather not have discovered that your friend and rescuer felt obliged to disappear at cock-crow."

Kelley felt free to smile. His head felt clearer now, perhaps because he had been touched by supernatural power once again, or perhaps because elation had crowded out confusion for a while. "There's no turning back now, Brother Cuthbert," he said. "They might have believed you before when you told them you didn't know me, but now that we've fled together, our fates are linked. You may go your own way if you know a safe place, or come with me, but in either case, they'll be after you as keenly as they're after me."

CHAPTER TWENTY-SIX

Dragging Brother Cuthbert behind him turned out to have been a good decision. As Kelley had anticipated when he first set eyes on the hem of the little man's habit, the Dominican knew where friends were to be found en route to London. They ate well the day after their release, and caught up on their lost sleep in a comfortable bed after nightfall, in a manor house by the river at Twickenham.

The manor was the most palatial edifice in which Kelley had ever been received as a guest; although the bed in which he slept was in the servants' quarters and he ate his meal at the kitchen table, it was still an unexpected luxury, only slightly diminished by the fact that the staff had been reduced to a bare skeleton and there seemed to be no one in residence in the masters' quarters. The housekeeper who received them did not offer them a tour of the house, but did take them back and forth through the vast dining hall whose walls were hung with tapestries that were only slightly moth-eaten and portraits whose colors had not entirely faded to brown, and which was equipped with a minstrels' gallery. The housekeeper even offered to spare a groom from the stables to row them down the river to Mortlake, when Cuthbert told him that was their next intended stopping-point, but he accepted Kelley's polite refusal without the slightest protest.

"We're wanted men," Kelley reminded the friar, when they were on the road again. "It was bad enough that I inveigled you into sharing my risk—I don't want to imperil your entire underground network."

Brother Cuthbert, who must have begun to suspect that Kelley was not a Catholic at all, looked at him rather strangely, but accepted what he said meekly enough.

"In any case," Kelley said, "you might, after all, do better to go your own way once we reach Mortlake. I really do not know what kind of welcome I ought to expect from John Dee, even if my wife has contrived to get there ahead of me and shown him the stone."

"What stone?" Brother Cuthbert asked, having not yet been let into Kelley's secret.

"A skrying-stone, which I was instructed to deliver into his care," Kelley admitted, figuring that it was safe enough to do so.

"You're a Paracelsian in more way than one, then," the friar observed, showing no particular surprise. The great physician's reputation as a diviner was almost as great as his reputation as a healer. It even extended as far as rumor that he had had intercourse with angels.

"Aye," said Kelley, readily enough. "I'm a magician, of sorts—but I told the truth when I said that I was more victim than master. Such truth as can be obtained by skrying seems to be far less comprehensible than one might hope or expect, and it's not without penalty. I'm no sorcerer, that's for sure—I wish no ill to any man, and I do the bidding of angels, rather than having imps at my beck and call."

Yet again, the little man showed no obvious disapproval, nor any particular surprise. He had, after all, seen the wall of Hungerford jail dissolve, and had been led away therefrom by something that was surely not *quite* human. Some Dominicans might have reacted to that uncanny experience with horror, but Brother Cuthbert seemed more calmly scholarly in his attitude.

"Perhaps I should go my own way, once you're safe," the friar said, "But I should like to meet Master Dee, if he is indeed prepared to make you welcome. He's said to be the most knowledgeable man in the realm, in spite of over-reaching his ambition when he tried to breach the bounds of Heaven."

Kelley was tempted to tell the little man that Dee's ill-fated ethership might have stirred the blissful waters of Paradise far more profoundly than most men presently imagined, but thought it better to maintain a measure of discretion. They walked on in silence for a while, basking in the nascent warmth of spring.

The afternoon was well advanced by the time they reached Mortlake, but there were still more than two hours in hand of sunset. They obtained directions to John Dee's house without difficulty, and without attracting any apparent suspicion. Once he was in sight of the house, however, Kelley's firm tread faltered, and he paused uncertainly on the other side of the street, facing the building's main door. The river was behind the house, the towpath separated from its rear by a strip of land that accommodated a few fishermen's huts, and was partly divided up into kitchen-gardens.

Kelley made a show of looking carefully around, as if to excuse his hesitation. There was no evidence, so far as he could see, that the house was under surveillance by John Field's spies. He was still summoning up the courage to cross the street and knock on the front door when the door opened of its own accord. Two men stepped out. One appeared to be younger than Kelley by seven years or so—not long out of his twenties, if at all—while the other, who was a vigorous man in the prime of life, wore a tonsure that he was not making the slightest effort to conceal. Neither, obviously, could be John Dee, who was neither a youth nor a monk—but the monk appeared to be playing the part of a host in bidding a polite farewell to the other, who must have been visiting the house as a guest.

"Who can that be?" asked Brother Cuthbert, presumably referring to the Romanist rather than the stripling.

"I don't know," Kelley said. Before he could say anything more, the little man removed his hat and took a step forward into the roadway, turning slightly to one side and lowering his head, so that his fellow Romanist was able to see the back of it.

The younger man had already turned his back to march away in the direction of London, but the monk who had seen him off had paused to look carefully around, and he caught sight of Brother Cuthbert almost immediately. The first expression to cross his face was one of suspicion, but Cuthbert made some sort of signal with his hand, which the other obviously recognized.

After prolonging his pause for a long moment of consideration, the man who wore his tonsure openly moved swiftly across the road, dodging around a cart full of spring turnips on its way to market. "Are you looking for me, Brother?" he asked. His English was heavily accented.

"My name is Cuthbert," the little man said. "Order of St. Dominic, late of the second house in Paris."

The foreigner's face cleared somewhat, although vestiges of suspicion lingered. "I'm Giordano Bruno, of the same Order," he replied. "I was in Paris myself until a week ago, although I'm an Italian by birth. Do you have a message for me?"

"No, Brother," Cuthbert said. "We're here in search of Dr. Dee. This is my friend Edward...Talbot."

"Actually," Kelley said, "it's Edward Kelley. Is my wife here?"

Bruno's face underwent another abrupt transformation. "Kelley!" he said. "Your wife arrived early this morning, with a strange black stone, a packet of powder, and an exceedingly strange story. Master Dee was disturbed by the notion that John Field's men are after you, but he took your wife in regardless—we've been expecting you."

"We'd best get off the street, then," Kelley said. "The Church Militant will be abuzz with annoyance, since we were broken out of Hungerford jail."

The Italian did not know quite what to make of that news, but he said: "There were militiamen hereabouts yesterday, but we haven't seen one today." He turned to cross the street again, but they had to pause to let a cart through, so he continued. "Rumor along the river says that something's brewing on the far side of the city—but Master Dee tells me that London has been a powder-keg for months, and that I've only jumped from an Aristotelian frying-pan to a Puritan fire in coming here. Fortunately, I'm heading westwards tomorrow, with a safe destination in view."

They had reached Dee's door by now, and Bruno was already opening it. Brother Cuthbert seemed interested by the last remark, and would surely have asked where the Italian had in mind, but another figure appeared in the open doorway before they could cross the threshold, immediately commanding all attention.

John Dee was older than Brother Cuthbert and taller than Kelley; he wore a long, flowing beard, whose grayness only made it seem more imposing. He was simply dressed, though, with a plain bonnet on his head and a rope girdle round his waist that might have suited a monastic robe better than the elongated jerkin that it was actually securing.

"Kelley," said Bruno, briefly, "and a brother Dominican."

Dee frowned briefly at Brother Cuthbert, but stood aside swiftly enough to let both his new guests come in. When the door had closed again, leaving the corridor within somewhat ill-lit, he bowed, a trifle stiffly. "I'm glad you had the sense to wait for young Bacon to go before you approached," he said. "He's a true scholar, and wouldn't dream of betraying Bruno, but his coterie is under increasing pressure from Foxe's schoolmen. Bacon's mentor might not baulk at a chance to send the Church Militant to my door, for the sake of scholarly rivalry."

"Is my wife here?" Kelley asked abruptly.

"Yes she is," Dee replied. "And your so-called skrying-stone too, although I've peered into it with all the concentration I can muster and can't see a thing. Bruno tried too, and insists that it's naught but a block of polished obsidian."

Kelley did not know whether that was good news or bad. The distressing dizziness in his brain was accumulating again, although he had hoped that it might diminish once he was in the same house as the stone again. It seemed that he still had no one with whom to share the most intimate feature of his curse—but at least he had access now to a scholar who might be able to interpret what the angels said to him more fully and more accurately.

"Obsidian it may be, Doctor," Kelley said, "but there's magic in it, or I'm a madman fit for Bedlam. You may disregard the messages the angels wanted me to bring you, if you so wish, but I'm ready to convey them and I'm certain that they'll give me no rest until I do."

Dee said ushered all three of them through a slightly cramped corridor and brought them into a large, high-ceilinged room that was obviously his library and workroom. While Kelley caught his breath at the remarkable sight, Dee put his head around the door again to call for a servant. When the servant appeared, very promptly, the mathematician instructed him to fetch Mistress Kelley. In the meantime, Kelley gawped at the shelves as if thunderstruck.

Dee's library was reputed to be the biggest in England, and Kelley could not doubt that the reputation was justified; he estimated that there must be at least a thousand printed books here, as well as mountainous piles of manuscripts, as many bound as unbound. The scholar's broad oak table was impressive too, strewn as it was with numerous loose manuscripts, some of them apparently still in the making, although the actual writing-desk was a portable board mounted on two triangular supports, which could be propped up anywhere or balanced on the arms of a chair.

Was it possible, Kelley wondered, that the world boasted so much discovered wisdom? Was it even possible that there was information enough in the world to be so discovered and contained? No man, he felt certain, could ever read so many words in a lifetime—even a lifetime as extended as John Dee's.

"We have room enough to accommodate you both tonight, I think," Dee said to Brother Cuthbert, "provided that Master Bruno does not mind sharing his room."

Cuthbert made no objection to that; curiosity, it seemed, had got the better of him and he wanted nothing more than to stay here for a while. Kelley could not blame him, and was glad of it—the last thing he wanted was for Cuthbert to fall into the hands of the foxes while wandering along the Thames.

"I should warn you," Kelley said to his host, dutifully, "that there's a warrant out for my arrest, and I escaped from prison last night ago. Cuthbert is a fugitive too, alas. If you want me to go, I will. I'd be happy to meet you at some safe rendezvous, in order to look into the stone and relay what the angels want me to say to you there."

Dee frowned again, evidently somewhat dubious about the angels that had Kelley in thrall, and whatever message it was they were determined to send him. "I know no safer place than here," he said. "Certainly not in London, where there seems to be trouble brewing—although trouble always seems to be simmering there. The river's full of talk of Francis Drake's boasts and misdemeanors, but that's often the case, even when he's in the Americas. This time, alas, he's come home to an England far less safe than the one he left."

"The angels have made mention of Drake too," Kelley said, warily. "If there were any chance of inviting him to the parley...."

"Sir Francis and I have not spoken for some time," Dee told him, stiffly. "He bears a grudge against me, although I have none against him. Your angels have mentioned his name as well as mine, you say? Have they also mentioned Tom Digges and John Field?" Kelley knew that Digges and Field had both been aboard Dee's ethership, along with Drake, Walter Raleigh and Edward de Vere.

"Aye sir, they have," Kelley said—but he had no time to say anything further before Ann came hurrying through the library door. Because she was in a gentleman's house, and had obviously been politely welcomed, she curtsied awkwardly rather than throwing herself gaily into his arms, but he seized her anyway and hugged her with all the force of his delight in seeing her again, safe and sound.

"Thank God you came safely through," he said. "I knew you'd be safer on the barge than I was on the road, but...."

"The stone and the powder are safe," she told him, although it was not the mater uppermost in his mind. "Shall I fetch them?"

"Not yet," said John Dee. "First, I think your husband is in need of food and ale, and time to rest. He may renew his intercourse with the angelic realm this evening, after supper."

Ann was still staring into her husband's eyes, gleeful to find him well. "I've half-persuaded the Master that the stone is real," she said, proudly, "Even though he and Master Bruno could see no more in it than I can myself. When I told him a little of what the angels had said to you, he understood."

"I would not go so far as to say that I understood," Dee said, dubiously, "but I admit to curiosity. There may be no cause for surprise in the fact that what you say echoes Drake's wild fancies, but...well, I'll hear you out, Master Kelley. I've nothing to lose by that. Mistress Kelley, would you take Brother Cuthbert to the kitchen, please, and ask Jane to give him a bite to eat? I'll bring your husband myself in a few minutes."

Brother Cuthbert was obviously reluctant to be sent away, but he dared not take offense. Bruno went with him. Kelley sat down in an armchair in response to Dee's gestured invitation, glad of the support. His head still felt impossibly large and light, but his train of thought seemed clear enough.

"How well do you know Sir Francis Drake?" Dee asked, when the door had closed behind the three.

"I've never met him, Master," Kelley said. "The angels seem to be familiar with his exploits, though—especially the one that bade me call him Aristocles. The names the angels use among themselves cannot be couched in human syllables, of course. Some of their voices I can only hear as a foreign tongue I call Enochian, and even though I can translate what Aristocles says into English, it is somewhat broken. If only he could speak directly to a scholar like you, you might be able to hear him more clearly, or translate his sendings more eloquently."

"I've heard the name Aristocles before," Dee admitted, although his brow was darkly clouded with puzzlement. "How is it that you can see things in your skrying-stone that other men cannot? If ether-dwellers can use such a means of transmission at all, why should they not be audible to anyone? And if the ether-dwellers have a message for me, why could they not find a way of transmitting it to me directly?"

"I don't know, Master," Kelley said. "It was likely a matter of chance that I was the one who found the stone and the powder on Northwick Hill, in what I took for the broken shell of a fallen star. Perhaps any man who picked it up might have become their emissary, urged to bring the objects to you—although none but a fortune-teller would likely have been struck by the notion that the stone might make a skrying-glass. I know that my past as a trickster does not engender confidence in what I say, but the last thing I need is to be arrested and questioned by the Church Militant, so you may be confident that I'm telling the truth. I don't know why the foxes are intent on harassing me, although I understand that John Field was aboard your ethership, and experienced a vision of Hell in consequence."

"He was aboard the ship," Dee admitted, "but his nightmares were his own—Tom Digges had a better dream by far, and so did Drake, although Drake still will not admit that his was a dream induced by the narcotizing effect of breathing ether. At any rate, Field will be unready to believe that your mysterious apparitions are angels rather than demons."

"I'm a literate man, Doctor," Kelley said, "and I'm not stupid. I can't I explain how I have the gift of seeing into the stone's darkness when others cannot, but I do have it—and, thus far, I know of no one else who has. The voices are real, and I believe them when they say that they emanate from the realm between the stars: the realm of the angels. I'm a Copernican, as you are; I've tried to read the *Description of the Celestial Orbs* which Tom Digges published, following his father's discoveries; although much of it was beyond my understanding, I understand that the Earth turns on its axis, so that the sun only appears to move around it, and that all the planets orbit the sun. I know that the sun is but one star in a vast host, whose members very far apart, and—thanks to the stone—I know that the spaces between them are not empty; in the same fashion that God has wasted no worlds, so he has not wasted the spaces in between. The quintessential realm is populated by angels, who need not assume material presence of our sort at all—and, when they do, are hardly more than vaporous shadows—but who have form and structure of their own, in another kind of matter. I have been given a simple proof of the truth of what I say to present to you, Master, although it will require some hours even for a mathematician of your prodigious imagination to assess its merit."

Dee seemed startled by all of this, perhaps more so by the fine speech than the offer of proof. "What proof?" he demanded, gruffly.

"I understand, Doctor," Kelley continued, growing in confidence, although his head felt lighter still as he let the ideas fill it, "that you and Leonard Digges were frustrated in your hope that the Copernican system would provide a perfect mathematical account of the movement of the planets about the sun, without any need for Ptolemaic epicycles. I am instructed to tell you that the flaw rests in your assumption that the planetary orbits are circular. In fact, they are elliptical. If you take that into account, you will be able to explain away the seeming anomalies in the orbits, see the elegance of the system, and deduce the mathematical law of affinity."

Dee was manifestly shocked now—again, Kelley thought, not so much by the actual content of what he had been told as by the fact that a man of his sort should say such things at all. "You're right in your judgment, Doctor," Kelley admitted. "I'm not much of a philosopher, and don't know the full significance of what I've just said—but I have it on the authority of an angel that you will."

Dee was still nonplussed, but made haste to collect himself. "Giordano is a firm believer in the Copernican system and the principle of plenitude," he murmured. "He left Paris because the Aristotelians who had harried him out of Italy made life equally uncomfortable for him there—but he has never extended the principle of plenitude so far as to argue that the spaces between the worlds must be as full of life as the worlds themselves. He has atomist leanings, and has assumed in the past that worlds are the proper objects of

Creation, and that what lies between them is a void. Given that the crew of my ethership proved that the ether is breathable, however, albeit disturbing, then space *must* be a plenum rather than a void, and the principle of plenitude would then suggest.... I cannot see, though—even if the principle were admissible—how any inhabitants of those spaces might be made of *another kind of matter.*"

"According to my understanding of the angel Aristocles," Kelley told him, now feeling almost intoxicated by the tide of odd cognition, "the matter we can see and touch is but the tenth part of all the matter in the universe, the rest being hidden from our eyes, even with the aid of telescopes."

"What do you know about telescopes?" Dee was quick to say.

"*That* cat's long out of the bag, Master," Kelley said. "There's hardly anyone in England who does not know that you and Digges equipped the navy and the Muscovy Company with such devices in secret, to give them an advantage over the Spaniards and the Portuguese. The secrets of navigation contained in your forbidden books are likely a lot safer, because common men could not make head nor tail of them, but there's not a glassmaker in the realm who isn't playing games with combinations of magnifying lenses. We all put our fingers to our lips when we speak of it, especially in the company of foreigners, but everyone knows that the Spaniards now have such devices too."

Dee frowned, but shrugged his shoulders, admitting that his protest had been a mere token of pretence. "You're right," he said. Then he made a visible effort to collected himself. "It will take me hours to manipulate the numbers," he continued, "but if your proof is sound...Tom Digges wrote me a letter only last month regarding the mathematics of the parabola, determined by his experiments in ballistics; he suggested that there might be parabolas elsewhere in nature, but ellipses are another matter...if you're right, it might demonstrate that your ether-dwellers possess exotic knowledge. Have you any other to offer, before I set to work?"

"No sir," Kelley said, warily, "but I've been promised more. You'll be in a better position after this evening's séance to assess what you might yet be able to learn—and to judge who else ought to be let in on the secret."

"If what you mean by *the secret* is that there's a new war supposedly raging in Heaven," Dee said, "that cat's out of the bag too—your wife told me."

"No, Master," Kelley said. "The secret's far more elaborate than that. Did she also tell you that England is threatened by invasion?"

Dee only shook his head at that, refusing to be surprised. "No," he said, "but I've heard that Drake is convinced that an invasion has already taken place on the far side of the world. Have your angels told you about a world inside the moon? Have they mentioned *Great Fleshcores*?"

Kelley could see now that John Dee was fighting hard to suppress anxieties of his own, and was genuinely uncertain as to what to believe. If the mathematician's assumption that the planetary orbits were circular really were to be proven false by a few hours' calculations, he would surely be persuaded that Kelley's stone and powder did have magic in them.

"According to the angels, Master," Kelley said, softly, "it was a miracle that all five of your crewmen survived their fall to Earth— but it was divine justice too. Had the ethership not been sabotaged, it would have been more probable, not less, that the five men inside it would have perished."

"I had thought until a little while ago that only three survived," Dee said, quietly. "But if Drake can be trusted, Raleigh is in the Pacific islands, and if the rumors that float upriver are true, de Vere is in London again, although he rarely goes abroad for fear of being recognized...but there'll be time to discuss the matter further tonight. You must be hungry and weary, Master Kelley. Come into the kitchen now"

"Brother Cuthbert found me a bed last night, and a good meal," Kelley told him, as they went back into the corridor. "I must admit, though, that I'm glad to find a Dominican already in residence here. I'd have worried, otherwise, about the risk of bringing a Catholic into your home."

Dee did not get a chance to reply. The people gathered at the kitchen table—who included a woman Kelley assumed to be Dee's wife, as well as his own wife and the two Dominicans, had obviously become impatient waiting for them.

"In the Vatican, Master Kelley," Giordano Bruno said, "the cardinals are obliged to play the game of Devil's Advocate before elevating anyone to sainthood. What Brother Cuthbert and your wife have told me has intrigued me, but I cannot resist the temptation to play the game. How do you know that the angels which speak to you are unfallen, and are not the servants of Satan?"

"I dare say that men of my station make easy prey for the Father of Lies, and his agents," Kelley retorted, wishing that he could muster as much conviction in his words as he had in his soul, and wishing that the dire sensation in his head would let him be, "but I can only say that I *cannot* doubt what I have been told; it is an undeniable revelation. If it turns out to be false, I dare say the only cost will be my own eternal damnation. I believe, given that balance of penalty and reward, that my angels are entitled to a fair hearing."

"I would not wish it otherwise," said Bruno, glancing at Dee with a spark in his eye. "I can hardly wait."

CHAPTER TWENTY-SEVEN

Before John Dee locked himself away with his books and his quills to make his calculations, in response to the suggestion that Kelley had given him, he sent a manservant into London. The servant had instructions to find Sir Francis Drake, if he could, and tell him quietly that Master Dee would appreciate a visit from him, begging him to exercise the utmost discretion in the meantime.

Kelley watched the man leave with mixed feelings, fully convinced of the desirability of his carrying the message, but also painfully conscious of the fact that he was the only manservant Dee had. The mathematician's sons were mere infants, Bruno and Cuthbert were monks, and the house was otherwise full of women—Dee's mother, wife and daughters, his own wife, and two maidservants. If the Church Militant were to come calling, there would not be the least possibility of offering any defense. The mysterious savior who had released him from Hungerford jail might still be watching over him as best he could, but he must also have other matters demanding his attention, else he would presumably have stayed with the men he had saved.

While Dee worked, Giordano Bruno was very enthusiastic to interrogate Kelley regarding the background to the statements he had made in the library. The Dominican did not even know as much as common English rumor-mongers about Dee's ill-fated ethership. It was obvious that Dee had complete trust in the Italian scholar, but Kelley felt obliged to be circumspect, and resolved to tell him no more than any tavern rumor-monger would have been glad to let him know. He went outside in the hope of clearing his head, but Bruno followed him into the kitchen garden behind the house. When Kelley leaned on the rickety fence, looking in the direction of the river, Bruno did likewise.

"How did you come to lose your ears, Master Kelley?" Bruno asked.

"They were severed by the hangman," Kelley told him. "I was charged with forgery. I was guilty. I've had a long career as a faker, ever since I was apprenticed as a boy to an apothecary. He was a faker too, but his fakery was licensed. Mine overstrayed that boundary."

"But you're not faking now?" Bruno persisted. "You really do believe that you can talk to angels?"

"Fakery becomes a habit," Kelley replied, so deflated and sober he almost wished that his angel-gifted giddiness might increase again to an intoxicant degree. "Charlatans often fall victim to their own deceptions, as I've had some opportunity to observe. I cannot doubt that I have had congress with angels—but the fact that I cannot doubt it might only indicate that I am victim to delusion. I've always nursed the ambition to be an honest magician, and now that I seem to be one, it might be that the force of my ambition has inhibited my judgment."

"There are powerful men on the continent who'd be glad to burn you alive merely for harboring that ambition," Bruno told him, catching his somber mood, "whether it had borne fruit or not. There's pressure on the Holy Father even to declare the principle of plenitude heretical, although that's a matter of factional in-fighting rather than committed faith. Such items of belief have become banners behind which rivals rally, no more meaningful than heraldic coats-of-arms—but people will likely die for them, as tension builds within Christendom. We live in turbulent times, which are unpromising for false magicians and true ones alike."

"There are men in England who'd be glad to bring back the burnings," Kelley admitted, dolefully, "in spite of Queen Jane's declarations of tolerance."

"And yet, Master Kelley," Bruno said, pensively, "there's a sense in which you and John Field have more in common with one another than you have with John Dee. Dee, if I judge him right, is a Sadducist, who is deeply skeptical regarding the reality of any and all spiritual beings save the Lord Himself—and I suspect that he has doubts even about the Lord. You speak of angels while Field rants about demons, but you are, at least, speaking the same language."

"And you belong to an Order whose reason for existence is to root out heretics by any means possible," Kelley pointed out. "Which makes you strange company for Doctor Dee the Protestant Sadducist, does it not?"

"Sir Philip Sidney provided me with an introduction to Doctor Dee," the Dominican replied, equably. "My intention is go on to the Countess of Pembroke's estate when the occasion presents itself, where I've been promised security. You're keeping company with a Dominican yourself, without seeming to reckon him an adversary—or is that simply a matter of the enemy of your enemy being your friend?" Bruno nodded his head toward the kitchen door as he spoke; Brother Cuthbert had gone to sleep in one of the kitchen chairs, having suffered more from the day's exertions than Kelley

"It was a matter of convenience when I made his acquaintance," Kelley confessed, "but I feel an obligation now. Thanks to me, he was arrested and thrown in jail, and then escaped. He returned good for evil by taking me to a safe haven last night. He's a marked man now, thanks to me—but he has nothing to do with the mission the angels entrusted to me. Nor do you."

"I do now," Bruno stated, flatly. "For what it may be worth, I follow a doctrine of tolerance myself, although it has made me suspect within my own order. I don't believe that fire is the best medicine for heresy—and I'm certain that the spread of Protest has proved my point. I'm no longer minded to believe, though, that my enemies' enemies are my friends. The world is a deal more complicated than that, I fear."

"Agreed," said Kelley, knowing full well that the Dominican was prompting him to tell him more about exactly how complicated the world really was.

"Brother Cuthbert is racked by his conscience," Bruno said, "unable to get rid of the suspicion that it was a demon who freed him from Hungerford jail."

"Whatever it was," Kelley said, equably, "Brother Cuthbert would be most unwise to admit that suspicion to Field's men—or to his Romanist confessor."

"Agreed," said Bruno. "We all have too many enemies nowadays, even among our friends. We hardly need invaders from the moon, or beyond—although, if we are to face such invaders, I suppose it would be as well if we had angels on our side. If there really is a new war in Heaven, though, I suppose we must have enemies among the angels too. Is the war a new rebellion of the fallen, do you know, or has some new Lucifer sprung up to repeat the folly of the old?" Brother Cuthbert had obviously told Bruno what Kelley had said to him in the jail.

"I cannot tell," Kelley said, uneasily. "I don't understand much of what the angels say, but I don't think that it's simply a matter of revolt. Perhaps there are nations of angels, just as there are nations of men, which feel the need to go to war even though they all believe that they are serving God. As above, so below—isn't that what mystics say?"

"If the principle of plenitude were strictly applied," Bruno said, nodding his head in recognition of the occultist's motto, "I suppose that one might find warring nations in every capsule creation—even one that might extend through the spaces between the stars. One might have hoped, I suppose, that ours was the only Creation unlucky enough to have suffered a Fall, and that all the others were happy, peaceful and united...but that was not the vision that Digges, Drake and Field were gifted under the influence of the ether, according to the accounts I've lately had of Doctor Dee's experiment. They seem to have glimpsed an Empire as proud and hopeful as the Church of Rome, and much vaster, but teetering on the brink of its own Protest. As above, so below, as you rightly observe...and so, perhaps, *ad infinitum*."

"You shall know more tonight," Kelley promised him, a little sulkily, "if Doctor Dee gives you permission to be present when I speak to the angels."

"You would refuse permission, if it were up to you?" Bruno retorted. "Well, I suppose I cannot blame you for that, given what I am—but I shall be there nevertheless, and I hope that Master Dee will permit Brother Cuthbert to be there too. His curiosity and ignorance are more of a threat to you now than his enlightenment could ever be."

Kelley knew that, and acknowledged it before the Italian finally turned back to go into the house. Kelley remained there a little longer, still staring at the stretch of the Thames that was visible between two of the sheds full of fishing-tackle. As the twilight faded, the ferrymen plying the river increased the urgency of their rowing, but the barge-horses hauling cargoes with or against the current maintained their own stately pace, seemingly immune to anxiety or persuasion. Kelley went back inside himself, to search for his wife. He felt in desperate need of loyal and innocent company for a while—but even Ann, given the circumstances, could not think of anything else.

"We should never have come here," she told him. "We should have gone our own way, among our own kind. It's not for the likes of us to heed the summons of angels."

"When the angels issue commands," Kelley told her, not for the first time, "obedience is not a matter of choice." But he saw by the way she looked at him that even her loyalty, let alone her innocence, could no longer be taken for granted. She could no more believe that he was under an irresistible compulsion than he could deny it—but she had got the stone and the powder here safely, without requiring the invention of any ambiguous superhuman assistant, and that was something for which he had to be wholly and heartily thankful.

"I could do nothing without you," he told her. "I could not bear to be alone, even in better circumstances than this. Now that I am what I have become, I need you more than ever."

Even that, he could see, she found difficult to trust—but she was his wife, and she was bound to pretend.

"I need you by my side this evening," he said. "You know how much it sometimes hurts me to have congress with the angels—tonight, I might be required to bear more than ever before. I need you with me, to give me strength and purpose."

"I shall be there," she promised, but she meant that she would be there in the flesh, not necessarily with him in spirit.

CHAPTER TWENTY-EIGHT

The black stone was formed as a disc, slightly more than a handspan in diameter, tapered at the edge so that it bore some resemblance to a convex glass lens. It had been polished as if it were a lens, but the polish had not increased its reflective quality as much as might have been expected. When Kelley held it in such away that his line of sight was directed at the center of the disc the reflective gleam was almost negligible, so that he did indeed seem to be looking through a glass window into a realm of starless darkness. It was important that he did not try to focus his eyes on the obsidian surface, but looked through the implicit portal into that other realm, striving to catch sight of the glimmer of angelic wings.

Angel shadows did have wings; he was sure of that. What they lacked, in their tentative manifestation within the dark imaginary spaces of the stone, was the humanoid bodies with which Earthly illustrators often equipped them. The stone's angels had no faces, and spoke by other means than lips and tongues. Nor were their wings the bird-like wings that illustrators often drew; they bore a closer resemblance to fast-vibrating insect wings, whose form was impossible to detect within the blur of motion. They were always in motion, even when the angels seemed stationary in the imaginary focal plane of the marvelous lens; indeed, Kelley often got the impression that the angels had to move with exceptional swiftness in order to appear to be hovering motionless.

It was not easy to catch sight of an angel, and the sight, when caught, hurt his eyes a little—but not nearly as much as the inaudible sound of their voices, which boomed in the private spaces inside his head with a strangely explosive force and cataracts of inconvenient echoes. It was not the direct reverberation of the imagined sound that sometimes caused his body to shake, but a kind of sympathy. Nor, he suspected, was it the sound itself that racked his whole soul, seemingly subjecting all his humors to a menacing turbulence; that too was an exotic kind of resonance. *As above so be-*

low, the saying had it—and there was, after all, a new and bitter war in Heaven.

Jane Dee had provided the entire household with a good meal before they repaired to the library for the séance, and Kelley had been better fed than he had for many a week, but the very richness of the food—not to mention the headiness of the French wine—had overburdened his stomach and his spirit alike. He wondered, belatedly, whether it might not have been better to make his demonstration on an empty stomach, fuelled by hunger and the intoxicating effects of Heavenly exaltation.

The servant sent to London had not returned, so there were five people gathered in the room, three in chairs and two—Ann Kelley and Brother Cuthbert—wedged a trifle uncomfortably between the shelves. Kelley had been offered the better armchair but had refused, so Bruno had taken it. Dee had the poorer one, although he also had the writing-desk that would enable him to make a hasty transcript of everything that Kelley said, or as much as he had time to reproduce. Kelley had contented himself with a three-legged stool, knowing that he would have to support his elbows on the table-top in order to maintain his pose relative to the carefully-supported stone.

There were worse things than the food in his stomach, though, to make him uneasy as he stared into the darkness in search of angels. He did not know which angel would catch his attention first; Aristocles did not have a monopoly on his attention, and the others he had met were not nearly as polite—or, he suspected, as honest—in their dealings with him. He had warned Dee that there might be some delay in contacting Aristocles, but Dee had not reacted with suspicion. Apparently the calculations he had been able to make that afternoon had confirmed the proof that Kelley had offered him regarding the geometry of the solar system.

His anxieties were justified; as soon as he caught sight of the blur of wings, he knew that it was not Aristocles with whom he had to deal. At first, the voice in his head babbled in the strange language—if it really was a language—that Kelley called Enochian, after the Biblical patriarch who had, it was rumored, sent back intelligence of the first War in Heaven, in a book that no one in Europe had ever seen. Eventually, though, English words began to emerge from the syllabic chaos.

"Infinitesimal," said the voice in his head, inaudible to all but him. "Human."

Kelley repeated the words aloud, and made his reply audibly, although he knew that the angel would be able to hear him if he only formulated the words silently, in the privacy of his skull. "To whom am I speaking?" he asked.

"Call me Muram," said the angel; Kelley repeated the words even as they were sounded in his head, although that compounded the suspicion he already entertained that he might be inventing the words rather than truly hearing them. Muram was not a name that had been offered to him before, but the individual knew English, and must have learned it from Aristocles, or another that Aristocles had taught. The angels appeared to be remarkably quick learners, but Aristocles had assured him that they did have to learn.

"I need to speak with Aristocles," Kelley said. "I have given Dee the proof, and he is waiting for a message."

"Aristocles divides too thinly," Muram said. "Reckless. Flesh-cores are insistent, but divided even amongst themselves. Chaos is come to trivial matter, Darkness and Transfiguration will follow. When Transfiguration comes, our kind takes refuge. Aristocles is nascent, has not mastered the Memory. Will learn. Petty disputes of humans and insects *immaterial*. Joke."

As Kelley recited these words aloud for the benefit of his hearers he felt himself losing track of them, as if repetition might save him the trouble of trying to interpret or remember them, let alone interpret them. He made his own reply, though, saying: "John Dee is here, as Aristocles wished. He is eager to hear what the angels have to tell him."

"Mortal creatures incapable of metamorphosis, let alone refuge," Muram replied, gnomically. "Destiny is death, petty wars not our concern. Nascent are foolish; have been transformers before, and will be again, but the Memory always triumphant. Contact with material minds amusing, but...."

The blur was abruptly displaced by another. For a few moments, the two co-existed, while Kelley completed his repetition of Muram's words. Kelley was able by now to recognize the pattern of Aristocles' wing-beats.

"Time presses, human," Aristocles said. "Dee sees me?"

Kelley glanced sideways. Dee, who was peering intently over his shoulder, shook his head.

"He is looking into the stone, but cannot see you," Kelley told the angel, "I will try to teach him to see, but I do not know whether the trick can be learned. There is another scholar present, named Giordano Bruno, but Drake has not come yet."

"Digges?" the angel queried.

"Not in England, at present—at war in the Netherlands."

"Digges must come home. Other wars are immaterial now. Great Fleshcores are trying to assert authority over Lunars, but Lunars control hyperetheric transit systems in this region of matter-shadow, and many ultraetheric canals. Rebel hardcores are attempting cruder means of transit, but are too few, must have suffered losses. Hardcores will side with humans, as will spiders, initially— but spiders have their own plans, might prove a direr threat if theirs is the victory. Dee must make preparations to withstand any remnants of the Lunar Armada that reach the surface. Engage them in the atmosphere, if possible. Build etherships, if possible. Meet the Armada in the upper atmosphere. Will provide specifications, if Dee or other scholar can learn to see and hear me. Fleshcores must save and sustain as much of True Civilization as they can; if they cannot maintain their own unity of purpose, all is lost. Time is pressing. Dee has ten years, at the most—more likely five. He will need Drake, and Digges most of all."

"What I would need most of all," Dee told Kelley, while scribbling furiously, "if we were to undertake any such project as the building of more etherships, is money. My income from the Muscovy Company is hardly enough nowadays to maintain my household, and my library is suffering for lack of acquisition. The queen will not help me again. Without wealth, any hope of keeping our enemies at bay is bound to be frail."

Kelley relayed these plaints, repeating them word for word.

"Will guide you in making gold," Aristocles said. "Wealth is achievable. Keeping human enemies at bay is harder, but it can be done, with or without the hardcores' reluctant aid. There is a plan. Be patient."

"I'd certainly need assistance, as well as wealth, if I agreed to do what you ask," Dee said. "Even if your red powder is the alchemical touchstone, and your black stone a means of communication between Earth and Heaven, possession of such things will cement the conviction of our human enemies that we are devil-led. They're already snapping at your heels, Kelley, and I don't doubt that they'll be after me as soon as they discover that you've been here, if I don't hand you over."

"Have patience and tolerance," was Aristocles' reply to that. "Mathematical devices are easy; alchemical transformations are more difficult, but possible. Nature makes angels better masters of mathematics than of chemistry, but we see matter from a propitious angle. Sciences of life are mysterious to us, though not to spiders— cause for anxiety but not alarm. Human scholars are better mental arithmeticians than Lunars, but their command of the material sciences is far in advance of yours. Exceedingly difficult to fight them, if they can establish viable nests, but not impossible to prevent them. Have hope, and faith. Greatest advantage you have is *affinity*. Lunars have already made one mistake in that kind of calculation, may make others yet; scope for resistance. Must teach others to use stone, or find others who can. Must find other stones, if you can. Time past now; Fleshcores are insistent. Try again, and again. Pay no heed to the contempt and despair of others of my kind. I am nascent, but so is the world. This time, there might be true Transformation, God willing."

The flickering image in the black lens vanished into the obscurity then. Although he was not quivering nearly as much as he sometimes did, Kelley felt a sharp pain in his chest as the angel departed, and a sudden numbness in his left arm. He fell off his stool. He did not quite lose consciousness, but he was very dazed. Ann, Dee and Bruno tried to revive him. Eventually, they were able to draw him up and put him in the good armchair.

"Well, Brother Cuthbert," Giordano Bruno said to the English Dominican, "What did you think of that?"

Brother Cuthbert's face was rather pale, and he was sweating, although the room was certainly not warm. "I don't understand what happened," he said, "but I did not recognize the voices of angels in anything that was said."

"Perhaps not," Bruno said, thoughtfully. "But I did not recognize the Devil's voice either. If there are indeed more Creations than you or I could ever hope to count, including Creations within the ether, perhaps we heard the voices of other creatures, at least as like to men as Balaam's ass."

"Or the serpent in Eden," Cuthbert suggested.

"No," said John Dee, sharply. "Whatever we might doubt, or fear, the voice is offering us assistance in a coming struggle, against creatures out of nightmare. Either that, or...."

"Or what?" Ann Kelley put in, anticipating the inevitable.

"Or your husband is a veritable genius among tricksters," Dee said—but hastened to add: "In much the same fashion as Francis Drake, I dare say, who was mad enough to sail around the world in pursuit of proof of his own strange vision. Tom Digges is the man we really need, if he is now able to recall his ether-dream as something other than an idle fancy. If not...well, in either case, he's the only one who might be judge whether Kelley's angel really is the vaporous creature that Drake saw, or imagined, invading his flesh." Dee seemed to be wrestling with his doubts, but Kelley could see that the mathematician certainly wanted to believe that what he had just heard was no mere mountebank's blather, even if he had to believe, as a corollary, that England and the world were in peril.

"You must confess," Brother Cuthbert opined, "that all this talk of Lunars, Fleshcores and Hardcores seems exceedingly ominous. If there are orders of demons parallel to the various orders of angels identified by Dionysius the Areopagite—as there surely must be, given that demons are merely fallen angels—I could easily believe that they might identify themselves by names of that sort."

"Perhaps," Bruno admitted. "But think how many orders there are of living beings, and how very various their species are. If the principle of plenitude holds true, whatever can be created, God has surely created, perhaps in the etheric wilderness if not on Earth or some other planetary surface. What we have heard might well be testimony to the awesome generosity of divine creativity, applied to a plurality of worlds of near-infinite variety. But what, I wonder, did your ether-dweller mean by *true* Transformation? Why did the other say that Chaos is come, and that Darkness and Transfiguration will follow?"

"I don't know," Kelley whispered, forlornly.

"Worlds should be separate," Brother Cuthbert opined. "Creations should not mix and mingle. Once they begin to overlap, Chaos *is* come, with Darkness inevitably to follow. If England, or humankind, is in need of deliverance, we must pray for that deliverance. All else is...."

He trailed off; Kelley noticed that he had not reached for his rosary.

"The purpose of prayer is not to make us passive," Bruno said, sternly. "If England or humankind is in need of deliverance, we must certainly pray—but pray that God will guide our hands and minds, in order that we might contend against the forces of destruction. I do not understand the half of what the second voice said, but I do understand what it said by way of conclusion, which is that we might prevail against the forces of destruction, *God willing.*"

Kelley opened his mouth, intending to say that God had always been an enemy of Chaos, and a bringer of light into Darkness, and so must surely be willing to guard his Creation against such dire fates, but his mouth was too dry to permit him to pronounce the words. By the time he had moistened it with saliva, the séance had been interrupted by a rapping on the door of the house.

CHAPTER TWENTY-NINE

It was, Kelley was thankful to observe, a polite rapping rather than a thunderous hammering. If the unwanted visitors were hounds or foxes, they were obviously not confident of their might.

"Wait here," Dee commanded. "Keep quiet—listen, if you can, but make no sound."

Moments later, Dee called to Bruno for help, and the Italian hurried from the library, followed by Kelley and Brother Cuthbert. Dee's knees were buckling as he tried to support the body of his servant, who had apparently collapsed into his arms. As Dee moved back from the door, though, Kelley saw that the messenger had not returned alone. Two other men were waiting outside for the way to clear, their faces shielded by hoods.

Bruno picked up the injured man's legs, taking part of his weight; he and Dee carried the servant into the room closest to the door, a reception-room where there was a sofa on which he could be set down. The other two men moved inside the house, the latter closing the front door behind him. The former pushed back his hood and looked Kelley up and down, from his ear-less skull to his sole-less boots, with an unmistakably aristocratic contempt. The other kept his hood up, and seemed to be shrinking back into the shadows— which were abundant now that Dee had set the candle-tray down within the room.

"You're Edward Kelley, the man for whom Field's bully-boys are searching," the aristocrat stated, in a tone that attempted politeness.

"Am I?" Kelley countered. "I do not know you, sire."

"So much the better," the aristocrat said. He turned to his companion. "I have business elsewhere," he said. "Will you come?"

The hooded man—whose humanity suddenly seemed to Kelley to be less than definite—gestured with his hand towards the door, as if he were instructing the aristocrat to go without him. As the other turned, though, the hooded head leaned forward and words were muttered swiftly into his ear, so quietly that Kelley could not catch what was said. The hooded figure opened the door then to let his companion out—but not before John Dee had appeared in the doorway of the reception-room.

"De Vere?" said Dee. "Is that really you?"

If Dee's identification was correct, Kelley knew, then the aristocrat was the Earl of Oxford—but it was his turn now to keep his face in the shadows. "Edward de Vere is dead," he said. "Believe that, Master Dee—you have trouble enough at your door without knowing otherwise. If you have a boat, you had best take to the river and row upstream, as quickly as you can. Greenwich is a battlefield. The foxes moved to arrest Drake, but sorely underestimated the number of men who would come to his defense, and had to call for reinforcements. Foxe does not understand seamen, or hero-worship. You'll not find any to stand up for you when they come here—as they would surely have done already had they not been badly delayed. Find a bolt-hole as far from London as you can. Set sail for France if you must."

De Vere—if it was, in fact, de Vere—did not wait for a reply to this rigmarole. He slipped out of the door and vanished, while the hooded figure closed the door behind him, then barred and bolted it.

"Do not be alarmed," the hooded figure said, softly before pushing back the hood to reveal a face that was sculpted in a human image, but seemed to be forged in dull metal—save for the eyes, which were red in color and made of some softer substance. It did not look to Kelley to be a mask, but he did not faint in shock. He had grown used to miracles lately, and everyone in Europe had heard tales of talking heads of bronze built by Roger Bacon and Albertus Magnus. Ann and John Dee looked at the artificial face with as much admiration and curiosity as horror and dread; only Brother Cuthbert seemed excessively distressed by the sight.

"You broke me out of Hungerford jail," Kelley said, regretting that it sounded more like an accusation than an expression of gratitude.

"Yes I did," said the metal-faced creature, its voice clear although its polished lips barely moved. "I hoped to warn the others before the Puritans made their move, but I was too late to reach Drake, and might only have succeeded in exposing Master Smith to greater risk."

"Master Smith?" echoed Dee, skeptically.

"That is the name by which my erstwhile companion is known in London," the metal-faced individual stated.

Kelley could not see Dee's face very clearly, but he took note of the shock of realization that came upon it. "De Vere's an Elizabethan, damn it!" Dee said. "If it were not enough to have the Church Militant arrayed against us, we now have the Queen's enemies in our camp."

"You do not know who that man was," the other reminded him, its red eyes glinting in the candlelight. "So far as you are aware, Edward de Vere is dead, and you have had no contact whatsoever with any kind of treason."

"More to the point," said Kelley, "who—or what—are you?"

"An ally to the creature who calls himself Aristocles, for the moment," the other replied. "I'm a sentient machine—an automaton, if you like—designed by the Lunars to operate in the toils of excessive affinity. You might have heard my kind called by the name hardcore, because our supportive skeletons are contained within our flesh rather than armoring it without—you're hardcores too, by that reckoning. You might think me monstrous, but the Lunars would consider the two of us very much alike, intrinsically horrid in exactly the same fashion: mollusks turned inside-out."

Bruno called out to Dee before the mathematician could demand further explanation, and the dutiful master hurried back to his injured servant. Kelley and the metal man followed him into the room. Brother Cuthbert, who had stayed behind Kelley throughout the exchange, stayed in the doorway with Ann.

Dee knelt down beside the servant, who was still conscious, although his jerkin and hose were stained with a great deal of blood. "Master Drake sends his apologies, sir," the servant said, in a voice that was little more than a whisper. "He will take to sea, if he cannot win the fight on land, but he will send a messenger to you, if he can, when he reaches safe harbor."

"Aye," Dee murmured, "but where to?"

"If Foxe can persuade Suffolk and Northumberland to send the Queen's men in support of Field's," the injured servant whispered, "the dockland rabble will melt away like the spring thaw—but the *Golden Hind* won't be obstructed as she sails down the estuary. Once she's gone, alas, the Church Militant will certainly come here. They'll not molest your wife and children, Master Dee, but Master Smith was right to advise you that you and Kelley must go."

"If he is wise," the metal man put in, "the man who escaped from Hungerford with Kelley will go too, and this man too." *This man* was Bruno, who was staring at the automaton as curiously as Dee had, with the same surplus of wonderment over anxiety.

Kelley was more concerned about Ann than Brother Cuthbert, while Dee's sideways glance demonstrated his anxiety for his own Dominican guest—but it was the most urgent question of all that Dee voiced: "Where can we find safety, now?"

"I cannot tell you that," the metal man said. "I can help you along the road, but I cannot tell where you might find safe haven."

"If I could get to the Queen...," Dee began.

"No sir," the hardcore cut him off. "You cannot go to London."

"It's true, Master," the servant said. "It's far too dangerous. If you escape by boat, as Master Smith suggested, you must not go downriver. Even if you were able to reach the Tower, you'd be putting your head in a lion's mouth."

"The Queen is an exceedingly clever woman," Dee told the metal man, "and no Puritan. She's perfectly capable of listening to reason."

"If this were a matter of intellect and sanity," Bruno put in, "you might be right—but it's a matter of fear and panic, the like of which I've already seen in more than one continental city. I don't know what resources your Church Militant has to compare with Master Kelley's magic stone, but there seems to be something telling its zealots that the Devil is at hand and must be crushed."

"Aye," Dee agreed, reluctantly. "Foxe may not believe Field's rants about demons, but he seems to be grateful for the excuse to let his loyal Churchmen flex their muscles. The one thing that unites all the Lords whose ambition the Queen keeps in delicate balance, alas, is their fear of the Elizabethans, and the rumor that de Vere is alive is all over the city. My past association with him will further taint me in their fearful eyes. For now, at least, we must retreat."

"If I understood the angels right," Kelley put in, "we must find a safe place to build more etherships, and to prepare to resist an invasion."

"It's all very well for the ether-dwellers to dictate orders," Dee replied, churlishly, "but if it's England we're supposed to defend, we can hardly set sail with Drake for the Americas or the south seas, even if we can reach him."

"We must go," the automaton said, flatly. "The ethereal is right: the Lunars *will* strike here, even if Master Dee is removed. The mere fact of the ethership's ascent convinced them that England's New Learning is the forefront of human progress. The Lunars will attempt usurpation, however, before they resort to annihilation. Their ultimate war is with the Great Fleshcores, against whom they will need armaments of every kind, and an army of natural hardcores might be as useful to them as to the Arachnids."

"But if Drake was telling the truth all along about his adventure among the stars," Dee objected, "we surely have nothing that the Empires of the stars could possibly want. You're the proof that they already have machines that mimic our form—machines that are more powerful than we are, even on our own terrain."

"That's not true," the automaton retorted. "I have access to rudimentary chemical technology even here, but I suffer the burdens of weight exactly as you do; I'm no Titan. In any case, you're a greater prize than you might imagine, given your mathematical skills. Don't imagine that Aristocles and I are acting out of pure altruism, and have no delusions about the Arachnids. The Lunars could destroy you very easily if they wished, but they will only do that if all else fails, to prevent you from becoming part of a powerful alliance against them. We do not have time for this—Doctor Dee and Master Kelley must flee, and must preserve the black stone and the red powder at all costs. I will help you, but I cannot tell you where to go."

"I can," Giordano Bruno put in. "I can, at least, make a suggestion as to who would surely hide you, and defend you if need be."

"Who?" asked Dee. Kelley judged by the wariness in his voice that he did not want to surrender himself to the care of the Dominican Order—but neither, Kelley strongly suspected, did the renegade Bruno.

"Philip Sidney's sister—Mary Herbert, Countess of Pembroke," Bruno said. "She's expecting me."

Dee nodded. "George Herbert was formerly married to the Queen's sister," the mathematician said, presumably to enlighten Kelley, Ann and Cuthbert, "but he was never admitted to the inner circles of the court because his father had been too much involved with the Tudors, and was suspected of sympathizing with Mary Tudor's bid to seize the throne. The Earl maintains a diplomatic absence, fighting in the Netherlands with Sidney, but the Countess keeps a little empire of her own at Wilton, near Salisbury. It might make a good hiding-place—and as good a base as any to begin any project we might feel inclined to undertake, if we decide to take the ether-dwellers' advice."

Kelley pursed his lips. He had passed within twenty miles of Wilton the day before he had fetched up at the Black Bear and thrown into Hungerford jail. He had had such a hard time getting here from there that the thought of retracing his steps was not particularly attractive. "Better to head for the south coast," he opined, "where we might make a rendezvous with Drake."

"Wherever you end up," the automaton said, "You must make rapid preparations now to depart."

It seemed, however, that they had already delayed too long, for there was another knock on the door then, considerably less polite than Master Smith's, followed by a call to open up in the Queen's name.

The automaton looked directly at Kelley then, his red eyes glinting in the candlelight. Unhuman as the creature was, Kelley had no trouble deciphering the message in that glance. John Dee was fifty-five years old; the two friars were not fighting men, and the stricken manservant was too weak to lift a finger. If there was fighting to be done, Kelley and the metal man would be the only ones capable of bearing arms effectively—and neither of them was carrying so much as a kitchen-knife.

Dee called out to the men beyond the door, telling them to wait.

"Fetch the stone and the powder," the automaton whispered to Kelley. "We must go out at the back of the house and head for the river. Your wife must stay here—you and I will have difficulty enough keeping Dee safe."

"You cannot leave me here!" Bruno whispered, urgently.

"Nor me," Brother Cuthbert was quick to add, while Kelley leapt into the library to secure the stone, which he wrapped in a cloth. Ann had followed him. "Don't leave me again!" she begged.

"I must," he told her. "Fetch the powder first, though—I'll see to the stone. Jane Dee will shelter you as best she can, and the Puritans won't harm her."

Ann did not like it, but she nodded her head like the obedient wife she was, and went to fetch the packet of powder that might, it seemed, enclose an alchemical touchstone capable of making gold.

There was another complication already, because a new voice could be heard outside the front of the house, demanding to know what the men who had knocked were doing. Someone else had evidently arrived in their wake.

Kelley heard Dee murmur: "Francis Bacon! He came this afternoon, to see Bruno. He has no authority over Foxe's men, though."

The man who replied to Bacon that he had been sent to arrest John Dee replied so faintly and querulously, though, that he was obviously not confident of his own authority.

"They're hounds, not foxes!" Dee was quick to infer, his voice still audible to Kelley as he ducked into the library. "Nor have they come in force. The Church Militant is fully occupied in London and Greenwich, it seems, and nothing has reached Mortlake but a command that the local constables have no great enthusiasm to carry out."

When Kelley returned to the corridor Dee was sliding back the bolts. He joined the mathematician and helped him lift the bar.

There were only two constables outside; their superior had not thought it worthwhile to rouse and arm a stronger force. When the man who had shouted the demand to open up saw how many people were grouped inside the door—the automaton, who had raised his hood again, must have appeared to him to be a person, but quite able-bodied—his lantern trembled, testifying to his consternation. Sir Francis Bacon was behind them, wearing a sword and accompanied by a manservant equipped with a heavy staff. The constables only had cudgels.

"Have you a warrant, constable?" Dee asked, holding up his own candle as if to challenge the constable's lantern.

The senior constable did not even have that; Kelley guessed that his superior had never intended the two men to make an arrest, but had sent them as a tacit warning, while carefully protecting his own virtue. It would suit the local officials more were Dee to make his escape than it would to imprison him on behalf of John Foxe and John Field. Puritan sympathies did not run particularly high in Mortlake.

Dee put on his most imperious voice to order the two men to go away, and to come back when they had proper authority to arrest him—nor did he promise to wait for them. Bacon, meanwhile, had his hand on the hilt of his sword, and he looked like the kind of young aristocrat who might take delight in giving a couple of hounds a tumble.

The constables withdrew, in some haste. Bacon moved swiftly to Dee's side. "I came to warn you and Master Bruno, sir," he said. "All hell has broken loose in the city. The Tower's ablaze with candlelight and humming like a beehive; the members of parliament are being rooted out of the brothels, and no one is sure that the navy will not fire upon the army in defense of the Queen's privateers. Foxe may be sleeping content in Canterbury, but the hullabaloo is loud enough to wake him. In a better world, he'd turn on Field and disown him, but I fear he'll find himself committed now, whether he likes it or not. You must hide, at least for a few days, until the state of play is clear. I'll look after your wife, and your library, as best I can."

"Thank you, Francis," Dee said. "Master Bruno and I will take a little trip upriver, I think. I'll send word to you when I can."

Bacon's gaze had already slipped sideways, to study Edward Kelley and the hooded individual. The suspicion in his expression was quite obvious; the young nobleman obviously felt no need to hide his feeling from men whose dress revealed them to be commoners, apparently poor.

"These men are with us," Dee stated. "They are more vital to our cause than you can possibly estimate."

Kelley guessed that what Bacon understood by "our cause" and what Dee meant by it were two very different things.

"Go with God," Bacon said with a slight bow to Dee. "Be sure that you're safe by daybreak, though. No one can tell where the balance of power will lie by then." He waited for everyone else to go into the house before following them. It was Bacon who bolted and barred the door this time.

It did not take Dee and Bruno long to make up their packs; they were obviously prepared to depart at short notice. Kelley had only to grab the satchel that Ann had brought him, check that the powder was safe inside it, place the stone within it too, and embrace his wife regretfully. "I'll be better for knowing that you're safe here," he told her. "Don't fear for me—I have good friends."

She whispered in his ear: "That metal face is no mask."

"I know," he told her. "There was a man of bronze in ancient times, I think, set to guard Crete, who was said to be the last survivor of an entire race, but Roger Bacon found another like it. If that race is come again, it is to aid us, not to hurt us. I could not wish for a better shield."

He had to leave then, to follow Dee and the automaton out of the kitchen door, through the garden and down to the Thames. Dee's own boat was a mere cockleshell, incapable of carrying five men away, but Dee knew his neighbors well. There was a boatman already awake, making ready for the dawn aboard a ferry-skiff that could seat half a dozen. Dee gave him half a sovereign, and he set to work with a will, ready to row all the way to Twickenham if need be.

CHAPTER THIRTY

Bruno sat down beside Dee, facing the oarsman, as if he were entitled to that place. Brother Cuthbert sat down beside his fellow Dominican, rather fearfully, leaving Kelley to sit with the hooded man in the stern of the boat, so that the latter might be hidden from view to the extent that it was possible. Kelley was by no means dissatisfied with the situation, being very enthusiastic to seize the chance he had not been given before, to interrogate his rescuer.

"Did the angels send you here to help us?" he asked, in a whisper.

"My brethren were intent on sending emissaries to your world as soon as they learned of its existence," the automaton told him, speaking in a similarly low tone. "We were the first to understand the necessity, before the ethereals fell out—and I still do not know why the ethereals should have fallen out with one another, or why they care about you at all. Since they seem to be siding with us, however, I'm willing to accept their guidance."

"You can talk to them, then, without the aid of a skrying-stone?"

"They can reach me, if they exert enough effort, and I consent to listen—but the contact disturbs me, and I am obliged to be careful."

Even automata, it seemed, were not immune to the side-effects of communication with the angels. "They said that there is a plan," Kelley said. "Do you know what it is?"

"I'm not privy to the ethereals' secrets," the automaton replied, curtly. "It was not easy for me to reach the surface of your world; we were smuggled into the moon easily enough, but we had no shuttle capable of making a gentle descent, and had to improvise, just as the ethereals improvised in sending the stone and the catalyst. The fall was long and the friction fierce. I don't know whether the others came down safely, but the fact that I've had no word is ominous. I know that I must frighten you, but I swear to you that my kind are the best friends you have in all this confusion."

"You don't frighten me," Kelley said "I've seen miracles, and have heard the voices of angels. Whether there was a race of metal men on Earth before or not, I'm not afraid to discover that there is one now. But I need to understand why you're so intent on being my friend, when so many of my own kind, as well as half the inhabitants of Heaven and almost all of the greater Creation, seem to be arrayed against me."

"Although I resemble humans in form, your kind is unique," the automaton told him, "and I am bound to side with its defenders."

"Unique?" Kelley queried.

"Unique in fleshy form," the automaton elaborated, "and, in consequence, unique in the specifics of its intelligence. Your sensory apparatus, and your brains, are quite distinct from those of all the members of the True Civilization, and their Arachnid rivals. The ethereals, whose intelligence seems to be fundamentally parasitic, might be interested in you for that reason, although their motives are largely unfathomable to creatures of what they call *trivial matter*. Given that ethereals find it at least as difficult to operate in a weighty environment as softcores do, in spite of their contempt for our kind of matter, any connections they can build are bound be tenuous, but even tenuous connections can be valuable, and perhaps warrant conflict among their makers. When even ethereals go to war, softcores are bound to be anxious. Ten years of slow and patient labor in the caverns of the moon have now given way to a period of desperate haste."

Kelley realized, as he listened to this mystifying speech, that he had never really expected to understand what the angels said to him, and had never felt able to raise much objection to their using so many words whose meaning he could not fathom. The automaton was, in its fashion, no less strange than the angels—and evidently believed that Kelley had understood what the angels had said to him far better than he had—but Kelley felt oddly resentful that his new companion was speaking in much the same fashion, rather than taking greater pains to make himself clear. Before he could voice his disappointment, though, Giordano Bruno had turned round to interrupt.

"I need to know," he said to the automaton, in a low voice, "where the Devil figures in this. I may be a better scholar than I am a Dominican, but I am a Dominican, after all."

"I cannot tell you that," the automaton said. "Where God and the Devil stand, if any such entities exist, only they know. Even the ethereals move in darkly mysterious ways, although it may well be vanity that leads them to pretend to be God's messengers and hand-maidens. I can tell you, though, where my brethren stand, and that is in the shoes of slaves ambitious to be free. Some might think the existence of natural hardcores irrelevant to our purpose, but I do not. Even if it were only a matter of politics, it would open scope for al-liance with the Arachnids and some ethereals, but it is far more than that. Your intelligence and ours must be akin, give our common form. Our brains have been programmed by creatures of a very dif-ferent sort; if we are truly to be free, we must learn to think in our own way—in the way that we might and ought to share with you. We will not allow you to be exterminated or transfigured, while we have any chance at all of helping to save you. There is much we might learn from one another."

Now it was Dee's turn to look round and interrupt. "If Tom Digges really did make the treaty that he became convinced that he had only dreamed," he said, similarly speaking in a low tone, "were we not promised the protection of the entire True Civilization? Were we not promised that no one would try to exterminate or transfigure us?"

"You were," the automaton agreed. "And the Great Fleshcores would honor that promise, if they could—but the promise proved to be the last straw, which overburdened an authority long since stretched to its limit. The insects have broken away from the True Civilization, as they might always have been bound to do, and they are the ones who are bent on your suppression, if only to prevent you from becoming pawns of the Arachnids or new symbols of Fleshcore hegemony. Even the Lunars would rather control you than obliterate you, though—they are neither utterly reckless nor devoid of moral responsibility. If nothing else, control of your world's sur-face might be a useful bargaining-chip in their dealings with the ethereals, which they do seem enthusiastic to develop."

"But why me?" Kelley whispered, having finally found an op-portunity to get back into the conversation. "Why am I involved in this at all, given that I knew nothing of Dee's ethership? Why did the black stone speak to me?"

"Because you found it," was the metal man's blunt reply, "and because you could hear the voices it reflected—which seems to be a rarer gift than the ethereals must have hoped. There are strange al-chemical affinities and exotic connections between the kinds of mat-ter you know and those of the dark realm, which the ethereals can manipulate. There must, I think, be affinities of another sort between the intelligences that our matter contains and the intelligences of dark matter. Perhaps you're uniquely privileged, and perhaps you were merely convenient—but for now, at least, you're the best and sturdiest link between men and ethereals. They'll be very enthusiastic to build more and better ones, but I doubt that they have any clearer idea of their prospects in that regard than you have. Could you train Dr. Dee to use the stone, do you think?"

"No," Kelley said, decisively, following his trickster's instinct. "I cannot. It's a gift, not a matter of education. There might be others like me—but there might not. You and Doctor Dee had best be careful with me, if you intend to continue to hold congress with the angels by means of the black stone."

"If you wish, Dr. Dee," Brother Cuthbert put in, "I can make arrangements for us all to stay the night in the same safe-house where Master Kelley and I spent last night. Master Bruno will be very welcome, of course, and his presence will assist me in arguing on your behalf and that of…your other friends. Would you like me to do that when we reach Twickenham?"

Bruno looked at Dee, who only hesitated briefly before nodding. "Thank you, Brother Cuthbert," he said. "That will give us pause for reflection. Tel the custodian of the house that we'll go on at first light. It will take two more days to reach Wilton, but we'll get there, God willing."

The oarsman, meanwhile, continued to haul away with his practiced arms, and did so for another hour before tiring. The automaton took over then, with his permission—without any need to display his metal face, which was quite invisible by the lights sprinkled along the shore. Although the creature had disclaimed superhuman strength, he certainly plied the oars with a great deal more power and efficient authority than Kelley could have mustered, and the boat flew upriver, defiant of the sluggish current.

When they reached Twickenham, at a much later hour than the one at which Kelley and Cuthbert had approached the isolated manor house the day before, Cuthbert asked them to wait in a clump of bushes by the towpath while he made arrangements for their hospitality. He promised to be back within a quarter of an hour, and was as good as his word, so far as Kelley could estimate.

"Everything's in hand," the little man said. "You'll all be very welcome."

They passed through the hedge bordering the towpath by means of a wicker gate, and made their way through the manor's lawns and gardens. Instead of going to the tradesmen's entrance they went around the house to the main door. The housekeeper, who was carrying a tray with a single tallow candle, greeted Kelley with a nod of recognition and bowed to his august companions before leading them through the gloomy vestibule and into the hall that Kelley had crossed twice before. It was unlit, and the housekeeper's candle was feeble, but Kelley followed him with a confidence born of the sense that he was on familiar ground. Dee and Bruno fell into step behind him, while Cuthbert and the automaton brought up the rear.

Kelley heard the waiting men before he saw them, and knew by the clinking sound that betrayed their presence that they were armed.

The metallic sounds were followed by a duller one as something heavy came down from above—but not on top of Kelley, who leapt to one side with his fists raised, ready to make a fight of it. Unfortunately, he moved within range of one of the ambushers, who struck out at him with a club. The blow missed his head and hit his shoulder, but it was so forceful and painful that it knocked him off his feet. Although he scrambled upright as fast as he could, he found himself seized by the arms and the point of a dagger was pressed to his windpipe. When a hoarse whisper bade him be still, he obeyed, and did not resist when his traveling-bag was snatched away.

Strangely, the only man who contrived to put up any meaningful resistance at all was Giordano Bruno, who was as robust and ready for a fight as any recruit to the Church Militant. He had no blade, though, and only succeeded in sending two of his would-be assailants flying before he too was calmed by the threat of being mortally cut.

The light of the single tallow candle was enough to let Kelley see that a weighed rope net had been dropped on the automaton, and that further weights had been moved on the toils of the net to make sure that the prisoner was securely pinned—as, indeed, it seemed to be; apparently, it had told the truth when it confessed that its strength was not superhuman and its skill with the oars had been merely that.

John Dee was unable to put up more than feeble resistance. Brother Cuthbert put up none at all, and helped to place the weights securing the net—but it would have been obvious, in any case, that he was their betrayer.

Kelley moved past the shock of that awareness to the more ominous revelation that he had been played for a fool since he first set foot in the Black Bear. The little man must have been waiting for him there—the bait in a trap whose purpose went far beyond any mere matter of throwing him into Hungerford jail. Whoever had designed Brother Cuthbert's task had wanted far more than Edward Kelley, or even the stone and the powder. He had wanted John Dee, and elaborate intelligence as to what Kelley had learned from the angels. Now, he had all of that and an unexpected bonus, in the form of the automaton.

Candles were now being lit in wall-brackets, and an entire candelabrum-full on the table in the center of the hall. These were wax candles, not tallow, and they gave a much brighter light, by means of which Kelley quickly counted their black-clad captors as a dozen, not including the slender and sharp-featured man who had carelessly established himself in the master's place at the head of the oaken table.

Kelley had never met that insolent man, but he knew who it had to be. Before John Field could issue further orders, however, Giordano Bruno looked at Brother Cuthbert in the most venomous fashion imaginable. "You'll be expelled from the Order for this, Brother!" he said. "If I had the ear of the pope, I'd have you excommunicated."

The little man laughed. "Do you still imagine that I'm a Dominican?" he retorted. "Can you actually believe that your clandestine signs are really secret in Puritan England?" His voice became tauter, however, as he added: "But if I were a Dominican, I'd be fulfilling my mission, would I not? To root out heresy, *by any means possible.*"

"Be quiet, Simon," said John Field. By this time, the fox who had taken Kelley's satchel had brought it to the table and set it down. Field rummaged through it, taking out the black stone but ignoring the packet in which the red powder was wrapped. "So this is where your bottle-imp resides," he said, looking not at Kelley but at John Dee. "This is the means by which the Devil whispers in your scholarly ear. How did you lose it in the first place?"

John Dee merely shook his head despairingly.

"Doctor Dee never saw it before today," Kelley said, speaking out boldly. "He certainly did not have it, or anything like it, when he built the ethership. It fell to Earth on Northwick Hill, where I found it—and it fell from Heaven, not from Hell. Nor are the angels contained within it; it is more akin to a telescope, making the distant realm of the angels seem closer at hand, enabling them more easily to speak into a man's soul."

Field got up from the table then, leaving the black stone behind. He did not approach Kelley, though; instead, he went to the place just within the threshold of the hall where the automaton was pinned down, and inspected the device as carefully as the thick strands of rope would permit, not without a certain anxiety.

"If further proof were needed of your dealings with the Devil," Field stated, glancing back at John Dee, "we have the most incontrovertible here. You have your own familiar demon, it seems, as Cornelius Agrippa had."

"Agrippa von Nettesheim was a great scholar," Dee told him, seemingly stung more painfully by the slight against another than by any accusation laid at his own door. "He did not write the book of black magic attributed to him."

"But you have read it," Field replied. "And the *Key of Solomon* too, and God only knows how many other filthy tomes. You've searched for them, and paid good coin for them—and did not even have the grace to hide them away, but have shared them with Digges and the Scotts and the other members of your nest of unholy vipers."

"Do you imagine," Giordano Bruno cut in, contemptuously, "that demons can be caught in nets and pinned down by a timber-merchant's counterweights?"

"Do you imagine that they can be dissolved by holy water and exiled by exorcism?" Field retorted, curling his lip. "Perhaps you think this one is protected by some indulgence that you have sold him, in order that he might remain on Earth in defiance of the Lord's will?"

"It's not a demon," Dee said, quietly. "It's a machine in human form. If you examine it closely, you'll see that it's the work of clever artifice."

"Human artifice?" Field countered—but was quick to add: "Have *you* examined it closely, Doctor Dee?"

"Not as closely as I would like," Dee admitted. "Your pursuit left me little leisure in which to do so. Nor have I been able to examine the black stone as closely as I would like to do. Did you catch Francis Drake by the way?"

Field scowled. He said nothing, but Kelley judged that he had no more caught Drake than Edward de Vere. *We were the only ones foolish enough to fall into his trap*, he thought, *and that was entirely my fault, for introducing his agent into John Dee's house as a trusted guest.*

His head had been quiet while they rowed upriver, but it was now recovering all the strange sensation that had afflicted it periodically during the last fortnight, exaggerated to a new pitch of intensity—but it was not pain, or even some subtler malaise. It seemed to him that his head was expanding, growing vast, but he knew that the sensation was an understandable illusion; what was really expanding and flourishing was something else, unconfined by his cranium. It was not magical power either, in any crude sense, but it had some kind of potential in it. It made the atmosphere around him seem light and strange, although no one else appeared to have noticed anything odd. "What do you intend to do with the stone?" Kelley asked, glad that he could still think and speak quite clearly.

Field finally consented to take notice of Kelley. "Rather ask, Master Kelley," was his reply, "What I intend to do with *you*. I intend to put you on trial, with Master Dee by your side, on a charge of sorcery. I intend to rouse the English people to such a pitch of indignation against you and all your foul kind that parliament's policy of craven tolerance will be blown away by the gale of Protest. I intend to make an example of you that will allow the Church Militant to scour England clean of Devil-worship and demon-traffic. I thank you, with all my heart, for making my task so much easier by bringing the demon with you. The stone would have been evidence enough, but, now that I look at it, it's a dull thing after all. Given your reputation as a fortune-teller and false physician, some men might be easily persuaded that it's naught but a rock, and that the voices you claim to have heard from within were nothing but vulgar lies."

"But you know better, do you not, Master Field?" Kelley riposted. "Even though Cuthbert—I mean Simon—has not yet given you a full report of the séance we held this evening, you know full well that the intelligence I have relayed corresponds with your own experiences following the ascent of Doctor Dee's ethership."

Field scowled again. "Of course I know that," he said. "They emanate from exactly the same source: the Inferno."

"The same information might come from very different sources," Kelley told him. "Don't the Romanists preach the same Christian message of virtue and loving neighborliness as the Puritans, for all that neither party is able to practice what it preaches? Look into the stone, Master Field. Perhaps you will be able to see and hear the angels that Doctor Dee and Master Bruno cannot."

The automaton had not said a word, and did not say one now, but it stirred in its captivity, and Kelley construed the movement as a gesture of approval.

Field knew that he was being challenged, and knew that he ought not to shirk the challenge. Was not a devout Puritan, capable not merely of snaring demons in a net, but of staring Satan in the face and forcing him to look away?

CHAPTER THIRTY-ONE

John Field went back to the table and resumed his seat. He took up the black stone in both hands and held it before his face, as if it were a mirror. He looked into it, perhaps expecting to see himself reflected there, in spite of the stone's lack of polish and the unpropitious placement of the candelabrum.

Kelley had no idea what to expect. Would Field put the stone down again, claiming that he could see nothing—doubtless because the demons of Hell were impotent or unwilling to confront him—or would he play the trickster, and pretend to see something that he could then expel with a potent stare and a word of command?

But I am not so far away as I seem, Kelley thought. *And my soul is as large now as it has ever been. Perhaps I can see what needs to be seen, and hear what needs to be heard.* He did not know himself whether he was in deadly earnest, or merely planning a trick of his own.

When Field looked into the darkness that the stone seemed to contain, however, he did not do or say anything. His eyelids drooped slightly, and his rigid body slumped in the chair, but not as if he had suddenly become sleepy—more than that, in fact: as if he had suddenly become *heavier*. His features were devoid of expression, but his stare did not waver.

"Don't be afraid, Master Field," Kelley said, softly—but the Church Militant's ambushers were as quiet as mice now, and every word was audible. "A man like you has naught to fear from Heaven. But you can hear the angels, can you not? They are not singing, as the Romanists imagine they might, but jabbering in a language unknown to humankind, which was not included in the legacy of Babel. Only be patient, and they will deign to address you in English, although your ears might have to be better than my poor mutilated organs to interpret what they say in smooth and eloquent sentences."

Field would surely have cut him off before he got half way through this speech, had he been able to—but he was not. To his own followers, and to all but one of Kelley's companions, it probably seemed that Field was holding the stone voluntarily, looking into it of his own volition, but Kelley knew better. The stone had Field captive, just as securely as the net held the automaton—but that was all. Field was not going to speak, even if he did contrive to hear English spoken by the angels. The next step was up to Kelley.

"The angels are inaudible and invisible to the eyes of ordinary men," Kelley continued, raising his voice as he always had during his past performances as a false oracle, "but you and I are extraordinary, in our different ways, Master Field. We can hear the voices of the angelic host, and we can see them about their work, not merely as messengers but as guardians. We can see them in the dark realm that is theirs, but we can also see them reaching into our world, and making themselves *felt* as beings made of matter might. They are not material themselves, of course, and there is something subtle and vaporous about their most urgent manifestations—but they can make themselves felt, can they not, Master Field?"

Unready to leave that particular challenge entirely to the power of suggestion, Kelley tried with all his might to make his words true: to use whatever mysterious potential was expanding out of him to manage the sensations of the watcher who could not help but look into the stone. Kelley imagined an angel emerging from the stone, like some angry ghost—not an angel from one of the Church decorations of which the Puritans disapproved so strongly, but an angel such as he had seen, at such a vast distance, within the void suggested by the stone's black depths.

And something *did* emerge, although Kelley did not suppose that anyone but he and Field could see it.

It had wings, of a sort, but it did not have a humanoid body. Nor were its wings a dove's or an eagle's wings; they were the wings of some hasty buzzing insect. Insofar as the angel had a face, he supposed, it would have a face that was more like a locust's than a human's, but not so very like a locust as to resemble the Lunar horde that had already started work on an Armada of etherships with which to invade the Earth…because the angels were angels, after all.

Kelley had no idea how to make a face beautiful that was not at all human, or even to make it imperious, but he had to suppose that the angels did, and that his role here was merely that of a facilitator, like the philosopher's stone that turned base metal into gold without itself being altered.

The angel was magnificent, after its fashion. It was huge, and dazzling, and unmistakably, undeniably, indubitably an angel. Kelley knew that John Dee, Giordano Bruno and the twelve brutal apostles of the Church Militant could not see it, but he knew that John Field could. Kelley even felt free to wonder whether this might, after all, have been the purpose of his mission—that the stone had sent him into Brother Cuthbert's trap in order that it should finally be delivered, by cunning and mysterious means, into the hands of John Field, even thought it would not remain there for long.

It was obvious that Field could see the angel towering over him, because he was no longer peering drowsily into the stone. He was looking up now, with his eyes wide open and his irises closing against the dazzling glare that only he and Kelley beheld. He could see the angel, and he knew the angel for what it was. He could also *hear* the angel.

What the angel commanded John Field to do, as Moses had once commanded Pharaoh, was to let his people go. The angel meant far more by that, however, than that John Dee and his companions should be released and allowed to make their way to Wilton unhindered. The angel meant that John Field's Church Militant should respect the principle of tolerance that Queen Jane's parliament had incorporated into English law. The angel meant that the Puritans should desist from stirring up a holy war in reflection of the long and fragmentary war that had been raging in Europe and the Americas for decades as petty prophets played into the hands of secular ambition by providing justification for oppression and conquest. The angel meant that John Field must see the truth, and realize that the demons that his life was dedicated to combating were not what, or where, he thought they were.

And John Field, like Saul of Tarsus on the road of Damascus, accepted that revelation for what it was.

Edward Kelley, who knew that he was part and parcel of the instrumentality of the revelation, could not help but share in it. His own ideas and beliefs were not turned upside-down—quite the reverse. They were put on a firm foundation for the first time. He not only heard the voices of the angels, but understood them, for they were now more eloquent than ever before. His consciousness expanded much further than it already had, and much further than he had ever imagined possible. He felt, in fact, that he was being taken far beyond the bounds of human imagination, borne on angelic wings. He felt that he was being taken up to the summit of a paradisal mount, there to look out upon the whole of Creation, acquiring a standpoint from which worlds like his own were mere motes of dust or tiny clouds of gas, while the spaces between them were crowded with life.

He saw that the infinitesimally tiny creatures which swarmed upon the tinier and lighter dust-worlds were, indeed, insects and other spineless creatures, although the greater number of them were intelligent, capable of awesome feats of engineering, and capable of flying in the ether as well as in air. He saw that the larger creatures that swam in the dense atmospheres of the gas-worlds were also invertebrates, formed as worms, jellyfish or cephalopods rather than whales or seals. He understood that the greater number of the inhabited dust-worlds were hollow, with far more life inside them than on their surfaces; the life in question was soft and slimy, but no less intelligent for that. He understood how different humans were from the common run of dust- and gas-dwellers, and that surfaces where entities weighed as much as they did on Earth, because of the denseness of the Earth's core and the power of affinity that held objects down, were normally hostile in the extreme to the evolution of complex life, let alone intelligence.

"So Bruno's principle of plentitude does not apply universally after all," Kelley said, although he did not pronounce the words aloud.

He got no verbal answer; the angel he had summoned from the stone was not Aristocles, or even Muram. He understood, though, that the principle of plentitude *did* apply, but was not quite what Giordano Bruno imagined it to be. It was the interpretation that was at fault—and that fault of interpretation was common to humankind's enemies and allies alike. It was for that reason, somehow, that the Great Armada would be launched—and for that reason, too, that the Great Armada had to be thwarted in its ambition.

"Earth is special, then," Kelley concluded. "Even on a vast universal stage, Earth stands at the focal point of a unique Creation, for which reason humans are God's chosen people." But that was flatly wrong, and he felt the force of his error as a blast of pure angelic contempt.

"You are, at best, a catalyst," he was told, by the angel that was not Aristocles, and must have been far older, if not wiser. "Earth is, at most, a philosopher's stone."

Then it was over, and he was back in the hall of the deserted manor house, where very little time seemed to have passed, and where only he and John Field were even conscious of the time that had passed. His expanded soul seemed to burst, and then shrivel to its ordinary dimensions, with a shock that left a cruelly authentic ache in his head. He put his hands up to cover his face for a moment or two, but collected himself soon enough and obtained enough mastery over his disturbed consciousness to put mere pain to the back of his mind.

When he looked again at the silent crowd, he knew that there had been a profound change in every one of them, although mere appearances had barely shifted at all. John Field had replaced the stone on the tabletop and was now sitting back in his chair, frowning thoughtfully. "It's just a stone," he said, in a tone that almost smacked of disappointment. "A piece of obsidian, shaped and polished to resemble a lens. It's a cozener's device. It has no demons in it, any more than the man we captured in our net is a demon. All this is foolishness, in which wise and serious men should not become involved, when they have God's good work to do."

Kelley expected protestations, or at least expressions of surprise, in response to this declaration, but none came from anywhere. The other people present had neither heard nor seen any angel, but they had not by any means been unaffected by what had happened. They saw the world differently now, and if they had any awareness at all that they had ever seen recent events in another way, that other awareness now seemed to them to be a kind of dream, which could not begin to compete with the trustworthiness of their present sensory experience, and all the brutal pressure of obvious reality that went with it.

"Release that man," said Field—and three ambushers joined the spy named Simon in dragging away the heavy weights that constrained the prisoner within the net so closely that he could barely move. Then the net itself was lifted. Kelley looked at the face of the released man in amazement, unsure now as to how and why he had imagined that the tanned face was made of bronze, or that his bloodshot eyes were literally red. The man was a gypsy, to be sure, but he was definitely a man.

"You have no right to arrest us, Master Field," said John Dee, with only a hint of temerity in his voice. "I am an honest Englishman traveling in my own country. Master Bruno is a scholar, and my guest. Master Kelley and Master Talus are students. We are visiting fellow scholars at the home of one of the peers of England."

"You're incorrect, Dr. Dee," Field said, icily. "I have every right to arrest you, to investigate you, and to interrogate you, and would have that right even if you were not entertaining a Romanist who might easily be a spy for the French or the Italians. I had a duty, in fact, to act on the denunciations laid against you, which charged you with possession of magical devices provided by the Devil. It is obvious, however, that the charge is unfounded, and I can only conclude that the denunciation was malicious, perhaps encouraged by scholarly rivalry. Personally, I cannot see any merit in this book-collecting mania that has infected such men as you and Stephen Batman, and you ought to be very glad indeed that the grimoires and books of ritual magic that you have collected are such obvious fakes. Had I received a darker report on the contents of your library from Master Bacon, I'd have thrown you in Hungerford jail over-night to teach you a lesson—and might have done that anyway, had I not heard that the jail is so ill-kept that its wall collapsed the night before last. You must not tempt me further by challenging my rights, though. I am the Church of England's strong right arm, the com-mander of the Church Militant. I have *every* right."

"That makes it all the more important, sir," John Dee replied, unrepentantly, "that you use your rights wisely, discreetly, and in the service of God. Might I take it, since you have interrogated us so minutely and found no fault, that we are free to go?"

"Aye," said Field. "My men and I have urgent business in Lon-don, and it would only slow us down to take you prisoner. Foolish scholars are no more worth the trouble of collecting than scabrous books, given that we have one book that tells us all that any God-fearing man could ever want or need to know."

Kelley opened his mouth to speak, but the gypsy to whom Dee had referred as Talus put a hand on his arm and moved his lips close to the scar where Kelley's right ear had once been.

"You must be careful now, Master Kelley," the gypsy breathed. "You, and you alone, know what the ethereals can do, even in an environment as hostile as this, and have at least an inkling of their sly means. Remember what I told you: they do nothing out of altru-ism; they have their own ends to pursue, and are not agreed amongst themselves as to what those ends ought to be. Aristocles is a power-ful friend, and you'll doubtless be in dire need again of the kind of help he and his kind can provide—but you must not *trust* them, as you might desire to trust an honest angel. They might well believe, honestly, that they do God's work, conveying his messages and guarding the virtuous—but so did John Field, until they taught him better. Doctor Dee is a great mathematician, but philosophers, like tricksters, often fall prey to fancies they produce, and commit their faith too readily. You *know* what really happened just now, and you must cling to that knowledge lest it be stolen by forgetfulness. You may be sure that the ethereals will handle you gently, for they have no other catalyst here to match you, at least for the present."

Kelley was confused, but not by what the automaton had said—because he knew, even though he could no longer perceive the fact, that the automaton really was an automaton, with a face of bronze and blood-red eyes. He was confused because, even though he knew what had really happened, he now had a second set of memories in his mind, of a long and detailed interrogation to which Doctor Dee had been subjected by John Field, in the course of which Doctor Dee had deflected and deflated all Field's accusations and suspicions, so successfully that Field had been persuaded of the innocence of all his captives, at least in the matter of practicing sorcery.

John Dee, Kelley knew, would remember events that way, as would Field, and all the Church Militant's witnesses to the event. The automaton was correct, however; Kelley did know the truth, not merely of what had happened, but of how ingeniously the angels— the ethereals—could work, once they had the aid of an appropriate intermediary: what they and the automaton both called a "catalyst".

It was neither the black lens nor the red powder that was the real philosopher's stone, Kelley realized, but himself...and, in some larger and not-yet-graspable sense, the entire Earth.

He nodded to inform the gypsy that he had understood what he had been told, and was thoroughly resolved to be discreet. He went to the table to pick up the black stone and replace it in his satchel, which he shouldered without meeting any opposition. Then he turned to follow John Dee, Giordano Bruno, and the gypsy, who were being escorted through the gloomy vestibule by two members of the Church Militant while the remainder set about extinguishing candles, in the interests of thrift, like the good Puritans they were.

Once the four released prisoners were outside again, in the strange half-light that immediately precedes the dawn, Kelley was taken aside by someone else: the false Brother Cuthbert.

"You should be grateful to me," the impostor said. "Had I not given Master Field such a convincing account of your harmlessness, he'd never have bothered to interrogate Dee so carefully. I've you played you false—though no more false, I think, than you played me in pretending to be a Catholic—but it has worked to your advantage. If not for me, you really might have been taken for a Satanist rather than a trickster and a fantasist. You should be careful, in future, about what you pretend to be. The pretense of being a cunning man, a fortune-teller or a Paracelsian might impress credulous folk, but the word of God is spreading now as never before, and enlightenment will soon reach into every corner of English society. You will fare far better as an honest, God-fearing servant than any kind of mountebank."

"Thank you for your advice, Brother Cuthbert," Kelley said, deliberately using the false name even though he knew the true one. "I am indeed grateful to you, for I know what a narrow escape I've had. I'll certainly be careful in attempting to plan my future."

By the time this brief conversation had run its course, the first rays of the nascent sun were rising from the eastern horizon, proud and pure in their ambition.

"We cannot walk all day, having had no sleep," John Dee complained. "We must find a place to rest."

"Indeed we must," Giordano Bruno advised. "Wilton is a long way off, and we must conserve our strength as best we can. We have work to do when we arrive."

"Aye," said John Dee. "There's gold to be made, and wisdom to be cultivated."

"And an army to be gathered," the gypsy, "and a fleet constructed. The odds will be against us, but we are forewarned and forearmed."

Against our immediate enemies, at least, Kelley thought, although he said nothing. He felt strangely intoxicated, yet again, as he made his way on to the muddy road and turned westwards, but it was not the effect of angelic possession. This time, it was confidence in his destiny, and the knowledge that he had been set apart from common men. For the first time in his life, and in spite of his confusion, he knew that he was a true magician—which might well be a better thing to be than not, in the turbulent times that were to come.

PART FOUR

THE GREAT ARMADA

CHAPTER THIRTY-TWO

Francis Bacon looked up from the manuscript he was studying, frowning impatiently. His brother was standing at the little window that looked out towards the river, although there was little to be seen without; the fog had limited visibility to a few yards, reducing the light of the nearest street-lantern to a mere yellow stain and blotting out all trace of moonlight. There were no inns or eating-houses closer than Newington Butts, so there would have been few passers-by even if the evening had been clear; there should have been nothing to see.

"There it is again!" Anthony said, excitedly. "It swooped close to the window, as if it wanted to look in. It was a firebird, I tell you!"

"There's no such thing as a firebird," Francis told him, patiently. "It might be a raven strayed from the tower—which would be a good omen rather than a bad one, if there were any such things as omens."

"The queen's ravens don't scavenge the grounds of Lambeth Palace," Anthony retorted. "Too much competition." He was referring, obliquely, to the black-clad officers of the Church Militant, who were indeed abundant between Foxe's lair and St. Mary's Church. Stephen Batman had received a living as rector of the parish, although the post was a sinecure negotiated by his patron, Matthew Parker. The house in which Francis was now going through the last remnants of Batman's papers was not the rectory but a smaller tenancy in the shadow of the palace.

"There's no need to be ill-at-ease," Francis told his brother. "My recent association with John Dee and Tom Digges has not turned Field against me. He's a milder man by far than he once was, and he values my friendship all the more for the news I can bring him from Wilton. Nor is there any likelihood that Stephen's ghost is haunting the house. If he's bound to the Earth, he'll be in Cambridge watching over his beloved collection, not here brooding on his own writings."

Francis had intended the jest to lighten the mood, but Anthony took it as a further insult aimed at his tendency to superstition. "When I'm ill-at-ease, Francis," he said, "it's because my sixth sense gives me reason. This was not a good day to cross the river."

"You did not have to accompany me," Francis reminded him. "Fog may be the footpad's friend, but I was no sooner out of hailing distance of Westminster than within earshot of Foxe's palace." When Francis had been a child, he had been duly grateful for the fact that Anthony had cast himself in the role of protector, but once they were grown the affection had soon become tiresome, and now threatened to become intensely irritating. Although their different duties in the service of the crown hardly allowed them to keep close company for more than a few days in a month, Anthony still felt obliged to pose as Francis' guardian when they were together. Francis was attending to personal business now—which was why he had to attend to it by night, and might well be busy until dawn—but that only made his brother more wary of disaster than he usually was.

"Fog is not only the footpad's friend," Anthony observed, bleakly. "Your purse may be safe, but John Dee and Edward Kelley have direr enemies. Field might have decided that Dee is not Devil-led, but that does not mean that he is safe in the bosom of God's protection. Dee never goes abroad by night—Drake makes certain of that."

Francis sighed, but did not trouble to remind his brother that he was of very small import to Dee's great work, which would not lose an hour by his assassination. He had a self-appointed task to complete; no matter how trivial it might seem in Anthony's estimation, it required concentration. Most of Batman's books had already been taken to Cambridge to be integrated into the fine collection he had built at Corpus Christi, but the notes he had made while laboring on the updating of the great English encyclopedia—a task that had only been shared with "apprentices" when his eyesight began to fail— seemed to Francis to be a monument to the old man's endeavor, well worth preserving if only they could be sensibly organized. Francis knew that if he did not make the effort himself, the best result that could be anticipated was that the papers would be crammed at random into half a dozen satchels and left in a cupboard to be devoured by greedy insects. Given that Dee, Drake and a thousand others were working relentlessly to build a fleet of two hundred etherships, in order to prevent the heritage of human wisdom and civilization being wrecked by insects, it seemed to Francis that there was a point of principle at stake. If he could put the papers in order and commission a binder to make books of them, or find enough coherent text to be made into a printed book, Batman's small but significant contribution to the collation of human understanding might be preserved for hundreds of years, as an exemplar for future scholars.

"It was a firebird," Anthony repeated, stubbornly. "Perhaps I am the only human soul who can see it, just as Ned Kelley is the only one who can see and hear his angels, in spite of all the apprentices he has tried to educate—but I saw it, and I know that something's afoot."

There was a sudden rapping on the door of the house, for which Anthony's forebodings might almost have served as a cue. Francis frowned, but did not move. He knew that Stephen Batman's old maid-of-all-work, Betsy, would find out who it was. He and Anthony waited in silence until the beldame appeared.

"It's someone asking for you, Master Bacon," she said. "He said to tell you that it's Kit Marlowe."

"Marlowe the playwright?" Anthony echoed, although the Master that the serving-woman had addressed was undoubtedly Francis. "How could he possibly know that we're here?"

"Perhaps your firebird told him," Francis replied, mildly—but he frowned again. Marlowe was certainly not an habitué of Lambeth Palace and its surrounds, nor even of Westminster. "I'll come," he added, speaking to Betsy. He went to the door, and asked again who was there. When he recognized Christopher Marlowe's voice, though, he removed the bar from the door, drew back the bolt and opened it.

Marlowe was not alone. Before stepping across the threshold he introduced his companions as John Faust and Gawain Brook. Faust was a greybeard clad in black traveling-clothes, every inch a scholar. Brook was younger, probably no more than forty, but he was wearing a sword and had the air of a fighting man.

Francis invited them in, and took them to the study where he had been working. There he gave them all a second glance, with the aid of better candlelight, and felt a slight thrill of shock. Anthony had been right, he realized; something *was* afoot—but then he hesitated, wondering if he might not have been infected by his brother's unreasoning anxiety. He could not be entirely certain that "Gawain Brook" was really the man he took him to be, for he had not seen that man's face since he was a boy.

"I was the one who asked Master Marlowe to introduce me to you, Master Bacon," said Faust, in perfect English with no more than a slight Germanic rasp. "I arrived in England yesterday, with a companion who is as enthusiastic as I am to meet you: Rabbi Low of Prague. You will understand why he could not come himself."

Francis did understand. Although Queen Jane had lifted the proscription that excluded Jews from London some twenty years earlier, and would always have made an exception for a scholar of Judah Low's status, there might still have been an element of risk in a Rabbi walking through the streets, especially within a stone's throw of the Archbishop's residence.

"You might have sent a letter to my home warning me of your impending arrival," Francis commented, "and you might have found more suitable companions to escort you—by which I mean no offence to you, Kit."

"None taken," Marlowe said. "We men of the theater are always regarded a trifle askance by true scholars." His tone was ironic; Marlowe knew that Francis was fully aware of his clandestine activities on behalf of parliament—and, so it was reputed, anyone with a full purse.

Marlowe's companion was not so content. He had been hanging back, leaving his face half in shadow, but the glint of anger in his eyes was evident regardless. "You can have no objection to me, Master Bacon," he said, softly. "We have never met."

"I have seen you at court, though, when I was a boy," Francis said, sure once again of his identification now that he had heard the man speak. "You would not have noticed me, but I watched you climb aboard John Dee's ethership sixteen years ago. The occasion made a deep impression on me."

The expressions that crossed the other man's face were swift, but revealing. The first of them was pride, at having been remembered over such a distance of time—but the second was annoyance. "That man is dead," said Brook, gruffly.

"No one believes that any longer, Lord Oxford," Francis told him. "You're a wanted man, outlawed by Church and State alike."

"Aye," retorted the man the Francis had recognized as Edward de Vere, "on the basis of inaccurate suspicions that are mutually contradictory. I'm not here on behalf of the Pope or Elizabeth Tudor, but a very different master." Something in the way he said it informed Francis that he was not referring to Judah Low or Faust.

Francis returned his attention to the greybeard. "There was a pamphlet produced in Germany last year," he said, uneasily, "telling a fanciful story of a scholar by the name of Faust, albeit one who died some fifty years ago."

"My namesake's reputation has preceded me for some little time," Faust replied, with a thin smile. "The pamphlet will not help matters, but what can I do? The Rabbi has a similar problem—but you are reputed to be the cleverest man in England, not excepting John Dee. You know how to weigh silly rumors in the balance of reason. You can understand how readily the credulous imagine men of science to be wizards. You have a namesake of your own, do you not?"

Francis was very familiar with the sad fate of Roger Bacon, who had probably invented the telescope three hundred years before Leonard Digges, and might have revolutionized English learning with his own Encyclopedia, had his work not been suppressed by the Church. Legend credited him with the invention of gunpowder as well as dealings with the Devil, and he was not an entirely convenient namesake to have, even at a distance of a dozen generations. This Faust must be widely taken for his own namesake's son, perhaps as the Devil's own spawn.

"This is not a convenient time for the exchange of scholarly opinions," Francis said. "There is a project in train whose urgency claims almost all of my time. It was only with the utmost difficulty that I earned the time tonight to do a small service on behalf of a friend, lately deceased."

"We know all about Dr. Dee's enterprise," Faust said. "Giordano Bruno would vouch for us, if necessary, but the Rabbi and I are not here to pry into England's state secrets. Judah and I have been working on a scheme of our own that is not unconnected to Dee's. We have information that the good doctor and Edward Kelley might be interested to hear. We apologize for approaching you in this unorthodox manner, but the matter is urgent as well as delicate."

Francis raised his eyebrows. "Does the Rabbi have a black stone?" he asked. "Is he too in communication with angels?" The false lightness of his tone was intended to mask the quickening of his interest. Although he thought himself quite as competent to weigh rumors as Faust had suggested, the messages sent back to London by Queen Jane's agents in Prague and Vienna suggested that the experiments in alchemy sponsored by the Emperor had recently borne fruit. In spite of the friendship of men like Bruno, political difficulties had long isolated Dee from the community of Continental scholars, and thus from any knowledge they might have gleaned of affairs in and beyond the moon, or the alchemy of the flesh that Paracelsian physicians were rumored to be developing. If the Selenite Armada could not be defeated—as seemed highly likely, in spite of the weaponry that Kelley had developed under angel tutelage—the entire Earth might become a battlefield for centuries to come. In those circumstances, the free collaboration of scholars, especially with respect to such matters as Paracelsian artistry, might be invaluable to the defense of humankind against Selenite imperium.

"The ethereals are not angels," Faust replied, quietly, "no matter how they might represent themselves, or what they might actually believe. For the moment, the party that is using Kelley seems to be acting in humankind's interests, but they are not the kind of allies in which any material beings can put wholehearted trust."

Francis glanced at de Vere again, and then at Marlowe, wondering what they might have reported to their current employers. Marlowe was only a common eavesdropper, but de Vere could have given them a first-hand account of the ethership's adventure—an account that he had never seen fit to give to John Dee, or any member of the queen's Privy Council. Given the differences between Digges' and Drake's accounts, which still had not been entirely ironed out, and the frankly nightmarish quality of Field's, another report would, at the very least, have been interesting to hear. All Francis said aloud to Faust, though, was: "What are you asking of me? Immediately, I mean—I understand well enough how I might be useful to you in the longer term."

"Be careful, Francis!" said the ever-vigilant Anthony. "If these men want you to serve as their ambassador, they should not have come by night, gliding through the fog like shadows."

"You can hardly hold the fog against us, Anthony," Marlowe put in. "Nor can we hold back the night. You are the great man's brother, so you can always reach his side, but we humble folk must pass through unsympathetic intermediaries if we desire an audience at Westminster or the Tower. Your trip across the river offered a welcome opportunity to make a direct approach, and you cannot blame me for seizing it. You are right to count your brother precious, and I assure you that he is just as precious to us. There might be much for him to gain if he agrees to come with us."

The expression on Anthony's face made it clear that he did not rate Marlowe's word very highly, and was not at all reassured by the fact that the playwright was keeping company with the outlaw Earl of Oxford—but that was not something that could be said aloud without consequence. Francis raised a hand to bid his brother be silent. "You've come from Prague, you say," he murmured, still addressing himself to Faust. "Did the Emperor send you?"

"No," said Faust. "We're not agents of any foreign state. Marlowe is right—this is a matter of urgency, Master Bacon, and it was necessary for us to approach you directly, without delay. We were very grateful to have this opportunity. If you will take the small risk of coming with us now, in order to meet Judah Low, you will be amply recompensed. The ultimate result of our endeavor might work to the advantage, not merely of England, but of all humankind. What Dee, Drake and Digges are doing in preparation for war is necessary and heroic, but no momentary exchange of fire can settle the tortured matter of Selenite xenophobia. We know why the colonists of the moon are so anxious to recruit humankind to their version of True Civilization, forcing a change upon our nature in order to accomplish that end, and we know that there are allies who might help us, if only we could apprise them of our plight and establish means by which they might intervene. We hope to offer some assistance in that respect, but this is a very delicate matter, and one to which the Church of Rome and your Church Militant are equally sensitive. The slanders leveled against my name and Judah Low's—and yours too—are as stupid as they are horrid, but men have been burned for less, and recently. Defenders of the truth must take some risks. Again, I apologize, but again I must ask: Will you come with us, to hear what we have to tell you?"

"How long will it take?" Francis asked.

"The Rabbi is aboard a ship, moored a few miles downstream," Edward de Vere put in. "We have the tide with us now as well as the current, and the one benefit of the fog is that the middle of the river will be clear of traffic. We can be there in less than an hour."

Francis tried to calculate how far a skiff might travel along the Thames in an hour, given the advantage of the tide as well as the river's flow, but could not do it with any confidence; beyond Rotherhithe, for sure, and further than the Isle of Dogs. He had only the vaguest notion of what lay between there and the marshes. The journey back would not be as easy, though, even when the tide turned, and he had no idea how long it would take to hear whatever Faust and Judah Low were eager to tell him. Fortunately, he had no appointments for the morrow that could not be broken without dire consequence. The queen was not expecting him, and he had had no urgent dispatch from Kelley and Dee.

"This is foolish, Francis," his brother said. "Don't go." Anthony would doubtless have been mortified to know that the effect this warning actually had was exactly contrary to the one intended.

"I have to, Anthony," Francis said. "This may be important. I cannot believe that men like these mean to do me any harm."

"Then I must come too," Anthony was quick to say.

"Of course," said Edward de Vere, silkily—almost as if he would have been reluctant to permit Anthony to remain behind to testify as to where Francis had gone and with whom. Francis saw Anthony scowl as he too picked up the implication, but the decision was made.

Francis got to his feet, decisively. As soon as he had made the commitment, he felt a thrill of pleasure. He had been on the fringe of this business since he was a boy; although the errands he had run had increased steadily in importance as his skills and reputation had increased, he had never had a chance to be truly *important* to Dee's great cause. This, he perceived—and not by virtue of any occult sixth sense—might be his chance to take a more active part.

CHAPTER THIRTY-THREE

As they put on their cloaks, Anthony whispered in Francis' ear: "This Low is the man who consorts with a golem, is he not?"

"But of course," Francis told him, again choosing to make a jest of it in the hope of undermining his brother's foolishness. "And this Faust is the scholar who was made immortal by the demon Mephistopheles some fifty years ago. The wonder is that you did not see a whole flock of firebirds tonight, or hear a choir of banshees screaming."

Anthony scowled, but said no more. He set his hand on the hilt of his sword as the party left the house, but Francis knew that the gesture was mere bravado; he had been schooled in swordplay himself, after a fashion, but not as a man like Edward de Vere had been educated. In the days when Francis had seen him at court, de Vere had been the most feared of all the reckless fools competing for the queen's amorous gaze. Philip Sidney, who might have been a match for him, had called him out once, but Queen Jane had forbidden the duel, knowing that it would very likely be fought to the death—which was, Francis thought, with the aid of hindsight, a godsend for John Dee. Dee, Digges and Drake were building their fleet of etherships at the country estate ruled by Sidney's sister—her husband was in exile, reputedly part of Elizabeth Tudor's entourage—and would have struggled to find a better refuge, John Field's conversion to tolerance notwithstanding. Kelley's alchemically-manufactured gold had bought them the men and materials they needed, but it had also attracted a good deal of envy, much of it expressed as superstitious dread.

Once they were swallowed up by the fog, Francis began to feel a little guilty at having mocked Anthony's anxieties. The thick vapor did indeed have an eerie quality about it, especially when it was infected by the sulfurous yellow light of the tallow street-lanterns. It seemed malevolent in itself, as well as extending an obvious hospitality to all manner of skullduggery. The embankment was little more than a hundred paces away, though, and there was a boat waiting for them at the nearest quay—not a ferryman's skiff, but a sturdier launch with two oarsmen, easily capable of accommodating five passengers. It had a lantern in the prow and another in the stern, the latter veiled in red translucent cloth, but Francis could not feel entirely confident about their capacity to function as warning lights in fog so dense. De Vere was probably right about the middle of the river being clear of traffic, especially at this hour, but there was always a risk that the master of some heavier vessel might make the same calculation.

Faust gave orders to the oarsmen in German, which Francis could not follow in its spoken form, although he could read it after a fashion. The rowers were obviously skilled mariners, well-used to dealing with waters far rougher than the Thames. Once they caught the river's current they soon built up a healthy speed.

The ceaseless train of horse-drawn barges continued on either side of the river in spite of the fog, audibly if not visibly, but the Thames was wide and there was plenty of navigation space available. The darkness was so intense as to seem almost tangible. The light of the lanterns seemed incapable of penetrating it. The fog added a slight seasoning to the odor of ordure that always afflicted the surface of the river, but Francis' normally-sensitive nostrils had long grown used to ignoring that kind of stink, in all its subtle varieties. The streets of Westminster were swept clean every day, but the reek of excrement never went away, even when the Berkshire wind blew keenly.

John Faust had sat down beside Francis; Marlowe and Anthony were in front of them, facing the two oarsmen. De Vere had gone to stand in the prow, posing as lookout, although it was doubtful that he would be able to give much warning if another vessel did emerge from the fog, headed straight towards the launch.

"Why have you come to England in person, Master Faust?" Francis asked the German scholar "If you and the Rabbi wanted to exchange information with Dee, you could have done so by letter—encrypted, if necessary."

"In retrospect, we should have entered into regular correspondence with Dee twenty years ago," Faust replied, "but we did not know that at the time. The Empire has not had a moment's peace since Luther nailed up the thirty-nine articles and opened the way to Chaos in matters of faith, and we have long been habituated to secrecy and mistrust. If extraterrestrial agents have been sowing dissension among us for centuries, as some suspect, Protest and Reformation might have been their masterstroke—but the likelihood is that we brought it on ourselves. We are, it seems, an innately combative species; that is what alarmed the Selenites, I suppose, and led them to a heretical Protest against their own Empire. They too are Reformers at heart—they want to invade our world, in spite of its inhospitability to their physical make-up, in order to save our souls."

Francis was a Protestant himself, and was not unwilling to consort with fervent Puritans like John Field, but he did not object to Faust's metaphorical representation of humankind's plight. "Do you think that *extraterrestrial agents* might have exercised some influence on Dee that led him to build the first ethership?" Francis asked curiously. "Drake suggested to him more than once that the ethereals might have been meddling long before Tom Digges breathed one in, but Dee has always claimed sole responsibility for his discoveries and endeavors. Leonard Digges is dead, alas, and cannot be interrogated as to the sources of *his* inspiration."

"The world is changing far more rapidly than ever before," Faust observed. "The New Learning is quite unlike the old—as you know better than anyone, Master Bacon. Men like Luther and Dee are perfectly capable of originality—and yet…." He left the sentence hanging, tantalizingly.

Francis did not take the bait. He shivered, and drew his cloak more tightly about him. "How did you come to hire de Vere?" he asked, bluntly. "He once had the reputation of being as dangerous a man to have on your side as to be pitted against you."

"We didn't *hire* him, like some common mercenary," Faust relied, blandly. "We have no reason to doubt his loyalty. He has been very useful to us in the past."

Capacious as the boat was, de Vere had no difficulty hearing his name spoken, He came back towards the stern, fumbling his way over the bench on which Anthony and Marlowe were seated in order to crouch down in front of Francis and Faust. "Will you stand lookout for a while, Master Faust?" he said. "Your senses are keener than mine, in spite of your years."

Francis could not see Faust's face, which was shadowed from the dim red light by the brim of his hat, but the German scholar did not seem to take offence at being addressed in this casual manner. He got up meekly, and went to stand in the bow, allowing de Vere to take his seat.

"The man you remember is no more, Master Bacon," de Vere murmured. "I admit that I attached myself to the ethership's crew purely in order to win favor with the queen, in the days when her lovers reaped rich rewards of every sort, but the experience wrought as great a change in me as it did in my companions. The change may not have been as obviously consequential as the ones that afflicted Digges, Field and poor Raleigh, but it was profound nevertheless."

"Raleigh?" Francis echoed, quizzically. He was mildly surprised to hear the name included in the list. "Do you believe Drake's tale of finding him on a remote Pacific isle, enslaved by giant spiders? There are many who do not."

"It's true," de Vere said, shortly, as if he had firm knowledge of the fact. "Do *you* believe it, Master Bacon?"

"Yes I do," Francis said, only slightly uncomfortably. "He was correct in his belief about what happened aboard the ethership, it seems, although Field and Digges denied it at the time. If Drake says that Raleigh has made a compact with spiders from another world, I shall not deny it."

"You would not grant me as much when I saw my firebird," he heard his brother mutter, although Anthony did not turn round. Francis had to concede the justice of the remark, although he might have retorted that he had far better evidence of his brother's unreliability in such matters than he had of Francis Drake's. At that very moment, however, he heard a distinct flutter of wings, which seemed very close at hand—and the sound, doubtless magnified by the fog, gave the impression that the bird which owned them was uncommonly large.

A raven from the tower, Francis thought. *We might be going past it at this very moment, although I did not see London Bridge as we passed under it. But what does it matter, since there is no such thing in our enlightened world as a bird of ill-omen?*

De Vere was not yet done with his explanations. "Tell me, Master Bacon," he whispered in Francis' ear. "When you were at Cambridge, were you invited to join any societies?" He put sufficient emphasis of the final word for Francis to take his meaning.

"Three of them," Francis confirmed, truthfully. "I refused the invitations. Two, I think, were mere drinking clubs, in whose secret rites I had no interest. As for the third…well, if the gnosis to which it pretended was false, then it did not seem to be worth my while to discover it; if not, then it should not have been kept secret. The New Learning is for everyone."

"Very commendable," de Vere muttered. "I was not so scrupulous, during my brief sojourn at Oxford. When I did not graduate, I thought the society had washed its hands of me, but I found out differently on the day before the ethership blasted off. When my parachute came down, I landed badly—not merely because I broke my ankles but because I came down in the marshes, among folk who live in mortal fear of the queen's revenue men. They brought me a surgeon, but he was the society's man; I was given no opportunity to send word to Dee or the court. Since then...well, Master Bacon, an oath is an oath, and I'm a man of honor."

This time it was Faust's turn to clamber back over the bench where Anthony and Marlowe were sitting in silence. "I'm sure that Master Bacon never doubted your honor, Lord Oxford," he said, his masterly tone turning the title into something less than a term of respect. "My old eyes are not as keen as your compliment implied, I fear."

"You can have my seat, Ned," Marlowe put in. "I'll take the forward position, so that Master Faust can continue talking to Master Bacon as one scholar to another."

As the second exchange of places was effected, Anthony turned round to look at Francis. The ruddy light was just bright enough to let Francis see the mistrustful expression on his brother's face. Anthony had not been invited to join the third society that Francis had mentioned—and that, Francis remembered, was one of the reasons why he had felt obliged to decline. Stephen Batman and Matthew Parker had also warned him against such things, before he even went up to Cambridge, but not for the same reason that he had cited to de Vere.

"You were right to be suspicious of the invitation you received, Master Bacon," Faust told him, "but there really is a secret body of knowledge that has been handed down from time immemorial, and there were very good reasons for keeping it secret, which still apply. John Dee turned down the invitation too, many years ago, but it was never issued to Leonard Digges or his son. Errors of judgment are inevitable, as are evasions. It might be better, in the long run, that things worked out as they did—but the matter is far too complicated for us to be confident of that."

"I am bound by other oaths," Francis said. "I cannot and will not promise to keep anything you tell me from the queen, her privy council or her parliament, nor from John Dee. By the same token, I cannot and will not betray any secret of theirs to your *society*."

"I understand that," Faust said. "It is up to us to lead the way in honesty, and we shall. The situation is desperate, and we must cast off our old restraints. I am not the master of our little company, and there is, in any case, something you must understand that I simply cannot show you. I assure you that I am not being mysterious for the sake of it."

"Nor is the fog," Francis muttered, looking around. The lantern at the rear gave the wall of vapor a color suggestive of the inferno, but the one in front was certainly not suggestive of heaven; the yellow light reflected back from the fog ahead of the launch was a sickly ocher hue.

"The fog is more likely to protect us than lead us to harm," Faust replied. "We do not know exactly what resources our enemies have, but we do know that they are working under the same spur of urgency."

"Are you taking us into danger, then?" The question came from Anthony.

"You're already in danger, you fool," growled de Vere. "The whole world is in peril, and you're both too close to its defenders not to be wearing archer's marks on your backs."

"Enough, Lord Oxford," said Faust, in a soothing tone. "Master Bacon understands well enough that reward carries risks."

Marlowe called out then: a questioning cry, which received an almost immediate reply. "Well judged, Kit," de Vere said, with genuine admiration in his voice. As the oarsmen changed direction, though, he turned swiftly to Francis and said; "Tell me, Master Bacon—have you ever clasped the hand of the man of bronze?"

Francis knew that he was referring to a man who sometimes kept company with Edward Kelley, though not frequently enough to deserve the superstitious judgment, noised about by some, that he was the wizard's familiar spirit. Bacon had always supposed that the nickname derived by way of Classical wordplay from the fact that he called himself Talos, although he was generally believed to be a Zingari rather than a Greek. John Dee had once told Francis that it was de Vere who had brought Talos to his house, but that de Vere had refused to linger, perhaps out of shame at having disappeared in the wake of the ethership's destruction. "No," he said, in reply to the question. "I have not."

De Vere reached out and took Francis' arm in order to guide his hand to the rope ladder he would have to climb in order to reach the deck of the launch's parent vessel. "That's a pity," he said.

"Why?" Francis asked, as he moved past the Earl to place his foot on the ladder's bottom rung, glad to find that it did not seem quite as unsteady as he had feared.

"Because it means that there are secrets in Dee's camp from which you've been excluded," de Vere told him, "and it might have given you a certain mental armor if you had."

CHAPTER THIRTY-FOUR

Francis had to start climbing the ladder, and was compelled to give his entire attention to the business of making himself safe on the ship's deck before he could spare any further thought for de Vere's dark hints. The vessel had lanterns fore and aft, just as the launch had had, and at least two more attached to her masts, but their muted light did not allow Francis to make a proper judgment of her quality. She appeared to be a slender two-masted merchanter, some sixty feet from stem to stern. Her sails were all furled and she lay very quietly at anchor, moored to a wooden dock that seemed utterly silent and lifeless. The name branded on the balustrade of the bridge was *Himmel*. There was a man at the wheel, and an officer beside him who must have been the vessel's master, but the fog hid their faces and the captain made no move to greet his new guest.

Francis helped Anthony over the bulwark, and was glad that his brother stood close beside him while they waited for de Vere, Marlowe and Faust to follow them. Faust spoke briefly to the captain and the helmsman, in German, then led Francis and Anthony down below, to what was presumably the chart-room. There was, at any rate, a round table in the middle, around which eight or ten officers might have huddled in conference, although there were only two men seated there now. Both of them stood up as the newcomers arrived.

Because the lantern on the table had not been placed in the center, it illuminated one of the waiting men much more brightly than the other. He was tall and dark, and his beard was jet black, even though the lines in his face made him seem older than Faust; he wore a black hat, from which ringlets of hair depended over his temples. He met Francis' gaze immediately, and bowed to him. The other, who was dressed in a monastic habit, kept his face modestly in shadow, but he also made a slight bow before sitting down again.

"I'm Judah Low, Master Bacon," the first man said, remaining on his feet and inclining his head again as Anthony moved to his brother's side. "Thank you for coming. My companion is a fellow scholar."

The fact that the Rabbi did not name his "fellow scholar" seemed to Francis to speak volumes, but he made no objection. "I'm honored to meet you, sirs," Francis said. "This is my brother, Anthony."

"Perhaps you'd like to show the other Master Bacon around the ship, Lord Oxford," the Rabbi suggested, diplomatically, as de Vere stepped into the room in his turn. Anthony made no objection to the dismissal, although he took care to cast a significant glanced around the room, as if searching it for hidden dangers, before leaving meekly with de Vere. Faust came in as they left. When the door was closed, Low indicated that Francis should sit down, then followed his example. Faust took a place at the table too, with the result that Francis and Low were facing one another directly, with the mysterious monk to Low's right and Faust to his left.

"You will inevitably be wary of us," the Rabbi said, without further ado, "so I ought to begin by summarizing what we already know, in order to establish sufficient common ground for us to discuss matters sensibly. John Dee and Thomas Digges are constructing a fleet of etherships at Wilton, financed by gold made by Edward Kelley with the aid of the philosopher's stone, with which they hope to defend the Earth against the Selenite Armada. The fleet is armed with weapons whose design has been furnished by an ethereal, which names itself Aristocles. Despite having such men as Philip Sidney and Francis Drake at his disposal, Dee is not optimistic that the Armada can be prevented from landing at least some of its vessels safely and establishing nests of soldier ants, which have been alchemically redesigned to operate in the atmospheric and affinitive conditions that pertain at the Earth's surface. His pessimism is justified, at least with regard to the size of the Armada, which numbers more than twice as many vessels as his own fleet, and is similarly well-armed—but humankind is not without allies, at least some of which will be able to take a hand in the aftermath of the battle, if not in the battle itself.

"We know, too, that Dee has recently been in communication with Thomas Muffet, who believes that he has made considerable progress in the alchemical techniques taught to him by Walter Raleigh's Arachnid associates, even though the Spider Matriarchs were killed during the Tahitian revolt. While Raleigh and his remaining Adapted Men are willing to serve as a land army tracking down and assaulting Selenite nests, wherever they might be established on the Earth's surface, Muffet and his daughter hope to mount a defense of a different sort, equipping individual humans with the means to resist the metamorphoses that the Selenites intend to force upon their bodies and minds."

"It seems," Francis said, trying to conceal his annoyance at the discovery that Dee had left him in ignorance of such important matters as Thomas Muffet's return to England, "that you are better informed in these respects than I am."

"Dee undoubtedly considers the matter very delicate," Low observed. "Your Royal College of Physicians still harbors resentment against Muffet, and John Foxe and John Field are likely to regard his schemes with instinctive horror, considering them diabolically-inspired. Dee must be very anxious to preserve his détente with the Church, at least until the fleet is launched."

And I am known to be on friendly terms with Field, Francis thought. *It is a relationship that has proved very useful to Dee, and should not have earned me his distrust.* Aloud, he said: "I must reserve my judgment on that."

Low nodded his head. His dark eyebrows shielded his eyes as he did so, but Francis saw him dart a glance at his companion, as if seeking reassurance that he had permission to proceed. Faust had not uttered a word, and it seemed that he too was in the habit of deferring to the enigmatic monk.

"We are also informed that the queen has denied you permission to fly with the fleet," Low said.

Francis could not help starting slightly in surprise, not so much because the Rabbi knew that, but because it was deemed worthy of mention. "Yes," he said, "that's true. I'm a scholar rather than a fighting man, and Her Majesty deems—correctly, no doubt—that I shall be far more use to her and England with my feet on the ground, no matter what the fleet can achieve." That was, indeed, the reason that the queen had given him, although it was whispered in the court that she had become besotted with him, in a quasi-maternal fashion, and was too fearful of losing him to allow him a part in such a dangerous enterprise. In 1572, when the first ethership had been launched, the gentlemen of the court had been very eager to impress her by risking their lives, but she was sixteen years older now, and the temper of life at court had changed completely. Queen Jane represented herself now as the mother of the nation, and made a show of regarding all her courtiers as her children rather than potential lovers—but she still played favorites, in her fashion, and was still prepared to indulge her whims to the narrow extent that protocol and politics permitted.

"Do you regret that, Master Bacon?" Low asked, his voice surprisingly smooth and mellow.

"Anthony regrets it more, I think," Francis replied. "The queen forbade us both, out of some strange sense of fairness. He's more a man of action than I am. Still, I would be a coward, would I not, if I were to take comfort from the fact that other men—including many of my dear friends—will fight a fearsome battle on my behalf, while I sit safely home?"

"Do you believe Francis Drake's claim that the crew of Dee's original ethership traveled much further than the moon—to the very heart of the Milky Way?"

"Certainly," he said. "Tom Digges believes it now, although he needed the evidence of Edward Kelley's angel to convince him, and Dee is similarly convinced. Does de Vere still doubt it? Does he think that it was all an illusion induced by breathing ether, as Tom once did?"

"De Vere believes it," Judah Low told him. "He had his doubts, for a while, but they have been conclusively settled. If you were offered an opportunity to do as he did—to travel to the heart of the galaxy, within sight of the blazing rim of the Black Pit—would you take it? Would you take it, even if there were dire risks involved?"

"I might," Francis said, warily. "Are you offering me such an opportunity?"

"Yes," said the Rabbi, bluntly.

"How great are the risks?" Francis asked, for want of anything better to say.

"Only slightly greater, we suspect, than the risk of remaining here on Earth, if the Selenites establish their beach-head—but a trifle more urgent. On the other hand, the potential reward of making the journey might be far greater than any possible reward that could accrue from remaining Earthbound all your life."

That speech was long enough to permit Francis to gather his thoughts. "You cannot expect me to make a decision until I know far more," he said. "You need to explain more fully what you know, and exactly what you are proposing to do. I'm not a coward—but I'm not a fool, either."

Instead of answering that, Judah Low turned to look at his companion and master. The monk leaned forward, as if by way of response, putting his face into the direct glare of the lantern for the first time. He was an old man, seemingly much older than either Low or Faust, although he did not seem weak in limb or gaze. His hair and beard were white and his eyes were also very pale, almost colorless. His features seemed benevolent; he radiated a peculiar impression of kindness and gentleness, sufficiently powerful for Francis to feel forced to remind himself that he must not trust the members of this secret society.

"I am prepared to grant you access to a great secret, Master Bacon," the monk said, solemnly. "I ask nothing of you in return, but I must warn you that it will change you irredeemably."

Francis was tempted to shrug his shoulders as a gesture of bravado, but he resisted the impulse. "It is my ambition to write a better encyclopedia than Stephen Batman's," he said, speaking slowly in order to give himself time to think. "Whereas he collected information avidly and somewhat indiscriminately, I shall attempt to winnow it carefully: to cast down all the false idols that have confused the beliefs of men for far too long. My intention is to write a comprehensive account of what is genuinely known and proven to be true, and to expel the mythical therefrom. I will not promise to believe in your arcane secrets, therefore, but I am enthusiastic to listen to them. I am brave enough for that, at any rate."

The monk smiled, without a trace of irony in his generous expression. "Take my hand, then," he said, and reached out across the table.

The old man's fingers were long and slender, the skin very coarse and wrinkled. Francis could not help but remember what de Vere had said to him in guiding him to the rope-ladder, and was suddenly convinced that de Vere had already entered into a similar clasp—and had got far more from it than he expected. Francis hesitated; when he reached out his own hand it was merely to invite the other to seize it, rather than taking the initiative himself.

The monk did seize it—but not palm to palm, as in a conventional handshake. He grasped Francis' wrist; and Francis gripped his reflexively in return. Then Francis looked the old man full in the face, and saw what he really was.

The creature in monkish drab was not a Churchman at all, nor even human, but was something dark and grey, soft and slightly moist. It had a face, of sorts, but its eyes were not human eyes and its mouth was not a human mouth. It was very slightly reminiscent of a snail's face, although the stalks supporting its eyes were very short.

Francis cursed Anthony for being right after all. Judah Low really was attended by a golem: a humanoid creature formed out of flesh with the texture of clay. Somehow, though, he had always imagined the legendary golem as being hard and stony, like fired clay, rather than soft and yielding, like wet clay freshly thrown on to a potter's wheel.

Francis did not have to glance sideways to know that Anthony had been right about Faust, too, and that this really was the scholar who had won his dubious reputation at the beginning of the century. His eyes, instead, remained locked on the golem's, as he reminded himself that it was not Judah Low who was the golem's master, but the other way around. It was the golem that had brought him here, and it was the golem that was offering to send him—or perhaps to take him—into the heart of the True Civilization, the Imperial Throne of the Great Fleshcores.

He guessed then what the golem really was, and discovered—slightly to his surprise—that he was not, after all, such a coward as he had secretly thought himself to be.

"How long have you been on Earth?" Francis asked, when the other let go of his wrist and the clasp was broken. He was astonished by the coolness of his own voice, and the pertinence of his question.

"Almost twenty thousand years," the fleshcore-fragment replied, placidly resuming whatever glamour it was that gave him the appearance of a monkish scholar. "I believed that I had long grown accustomed to the hectic pace of life here, but I was still unready for its rapid acceleration in the last half-century. There may still be time, even so, for me to summon help that might save the world."

Chapter Thirty-Five

"I presume," Francis said to the golem, "that you have employed many guises and many names in the past."

"My kind has a casual attitude to names," the golem told him. "The one I use nowadays is Christian Rosenkreutz; before that I was Johann Heidenberg, otherwise known as Trithemius."

Francis remembered the latter name from his studies. "Trithemius was abbot of the Benedictine monastery at Sponheim a hundred years ago," he said, attempting to shore up his reputation for cleverness. "Dee helped the queen's diplomatic service set up systems of secret communication based on the principles outlined in his—your—*Steganographia*. The first humanist history is also credited to you—Stephen Batman knew it well. You taught Cornelius Agrippa, and Paracelsus too."

"The problem with able pupils," said the creature wearing the appearance of an old man, with a wistful sigh, "is that so many of them come to believe that they have learned everything they need to know in order to make further progress by themselves—but that is also their greatest virtue."

"And who were you before you were Trithemius?" Francis asked, curiously.

"It is only very recently that I have been forced to compromise with the documentary enthusiasm of chroniclers and lawmakers by inventing dates of birth and death," the golem told him. "Most of the names foisted upon me have been easily committed to oblivion, although some survive stubbornly in legend."

"Plato?" Francis guessed. "Pythagoras? Zoroaster? Prometheus?"

"There was no single Pythagoras, Zoroaster, or Prometheus," the golem told him. "There were six of us once, although I have been the sole survivor for several centuries. My kind does not have a determinate lifespan, but is not immune to the vicissitudes of time and chance. Plato was a mortal like yourself. Do you recall his family name, by the way?"

This time, Francis was not caught at a loss. "The same as Kelley's angel informant," he said. "Aristocles. Drake says that he remembers Tom Digges using the name during the adventure of the ethership. Tom agrees, although he confesses that his memory of what happened then is still very hazy."

"De Vere's is clearer," the golem told him, "and he remembers that Aristocles was the name Digges gave to their insect guide, not the ethereal that invaded his body and made a voice inside his mind."

Francis frowned. "Drake told me that the insect that accompanied them from the moon to the heart of the Milky Way was destroyed by a humanoid machine. Does de Vere remember that?"

"Quite clearly," the golem told him. "What he does not know is how the insect came to be given the name. He thinks it unlikely to have been Digges' choice."

"Tom's a highly-educated man, after his fashion," Francis said, "but de Vere might be right; he's not given to obscure Classical allusions. If the angel—the ethereal—is using the name now, it was presumably the one who chose it, although why it should have claimed the name for itself after first attributing it to another I cannot tell." Tired of seeming trivia, he hurried to change the subject, adding: "When you said that there was no single Prometheus, you weren't denying that you and your kin had played a Promethean role in human affairs. Are you telling me that all of human progress—moral, intellectual and technological—is the result of some experiment mounted by the Great Fleshcores twenty thousand years ago?"

"We have been helpful, on occasion," the golem said. "How could we not, given that we are moral beings, respectful of God's Creation? We were sent as observers, but we were not forbidden to intervene in the evolution of human consciousness. I and my kin certainly made some slight contribution to human intellectual progress—perhaps more than we knew, but less than we sometimes hoped. We have never been great originators of technology, though, for we are not much given to manipulation, even though the hands we pretend to have are fully capable of use. As for moral progress…you and I might disagree as to what that ought to comprise, even though we would both disagree with the Selenites. Even after twenty thousand years of study, I am not certain whether human beings are capable of the kind of moral progress that the True Civilization has embraced, or what significance that incapacity might have, if it were to be insuperable. That, I assume, is one of the reasons why the matter of endoskeletal intelligence has recently become a bone of contention within the True Civilization—although I am at a loss to know why it should concern the ethereals at all, since their ancients consider the transactions of material life to be vulgar and inconsequential. The interest of rogue machines like the one that calls itself Talos is understandable; to them, natural endoskeletal intelligence must seem to be a proof of sorts that they are not the abominations against nature that their makers claim. The mere existence of the human race presumably seems to be of quasi-messianic significance to at least some of the mad machines."

"That's why de Vere asked me if I had ever clasped hands with Talos," Francis said, not framing the guess as a question. "He assumed that I would know, if I had done so, that he really is a man of metal, not the human he seems to be to innocent eyes—and that I might not have been so astonished to discover that your human appearance was also a matter of glamour. What other magic tricks can you play?"

"Enough to sustain my disguises, but less than is sometimes reputed. All wizards grow in the popular estimation once they have passed on to fresher fields or gone to their graves. I have only been in Britain once before, and even then spent far more time in Less Britain than this island, but I gave rise to more legends then than reason could ever have anticipated, despite that all my efforts came to nothing."

Francis guessed his meaning readily enough. "You were Merlin," he said. "I was never sure, myself, whether King Arthur ever existed, let alone the wizard attributed to his court by Norman romance—but here we are, seated at a round table, and Edward de Vere has rechristened himself Gawain. The man has a sense of humor, whatever his faults."

"Perhaps Malory's muddled epic will give you some insight into my limitations," the golem said. "Arthur's reign was unsustainable, in the end, and the grail of transubstantiation unattainable at the time. Muffet might yet be able to attain the same end by other means."

"Kelley's angel has a great deal to say about transfiguration," Francis observed, "but transubstantiation is the Church's word—and one that smacks of Romanism. Are you taking about the same thing?"

"What I mean by the word I borrowed from your religious doctrine," the golem said, "is the process by which the union of different species is achieved in the making of Fleshcores. I believe that the ethereals mean something analogous, but on a much larger scale.

They have a very different idea of the essential constitution of life and its relationship to the many dimensions making up the universe—they perceive nine, but there are probably more. I am certainly oversimplifying their ideas, and probably distorting them, but I believe they see the ether itself as a kind of bodily fluid, and matter as a kind of skin. To them, the perceptible universe is an individual of sorts, capable of metamorphoses akin to the ones that exoskeletal species routinely undergo, and the ones that exoskeletal intelligences learn to contrive as they evolve towards incorporation into flesh-cores."

That was too much to take in at one gulp, even for the cleverest man in England. Francis thought it best to seek clarification. "Your own magic does not extend to the transformation of human flesh," he deduced. "That is why you call the end that you sought as Merlin the *grail*, explicitly lining it to the Church's legendry of transubstantiation. But you think that Raleigh's Spider Matriarchs had some such magic, and that Muffet might have mastered the elements of it before his guides were killed."

"It is not magic," the golem said, placidly, "and I do not trust the Arachnids as Raleigh seemed to do. Were they to become powerful on Earth, they might be no better from the human viewpoint than the Selenites, and perhaps worse. The Selenites certainly fear that prospect, on their own behalf. Forgive me, Master Bacon, for cutting your questions short, for I'm sure that you have many more to ask, but time is pressing. I have long had a means of returning home, which I have taken too much for granted. I fear that it can no longer be used without risk, and there may be danger even in exposing its existence, but it is also a means by which help might be summoned and sent to thwart the Selenite invasion. I would like to take some companions with me, for examination by and consultation with the Great Fleshcores. I want to take at least one who is entirely innocent of my direct influence, or any other extraterrestrial interference. I therefore invite you to come with me."

The sudden change of tack, and the conclusion to which it had raced, took Francis aback. He became suddenly conscious of the waves lapping at the side of the ship, and the gentle rocking of the vessel in the water, which reminded him that he was not on solid ground, and that the tide in the Thames estuary changed direction at the whim of the sun and moon. He looked at Faust, who smiled faintly, sympathizing with the shock that he had suffered.

"Can I be sure that I would be able to return?" Francis wanted to know.

"I can offer no absolute guarantees, but I have only been away from home for twenty thousand years. I cannot believe that the Great Fleshcores will have changed, and I am certain that they would never detain you against your will. If I am successful in my entreaties, they will be very eager to send you home, in order to serve as an ambassador to the Selenites' opponents."

"Does de Vere support Drake's claim that Thomas Digges extracted a promise from the fleshcore to which he talked, that humankind would be let alone?" Francis asked.

"De Vere has told us what was said to the fleshcore," the golem answered, "and he confirms that the fleshcore seemed to consent— but he cannot be sure that Thomas Digges is the one who did the asking."

"You think it was Aristocles? The angel, that is, not the insect."

"It is possible that the ethereal inhabiting Digges' body was controlling his speech. We are not convinced that it was the same ethereal as the one that is now supplying Kelley with information. Whatever the truth of the matter, though, it seems that the Great Fleshcores did make a promise—and I am certain, if so, that they will do everything they can to keep it."

"As yet," Francis pointed not, "they have done nothing."

"That is a mystery," the golem agreed. "The Selenites have obviously cut off their own hyperetheric link to the Core, but there must also have been a more widespread and more general disruption of intragalactic communications, else the Great Fleshcores would surely have been able to do *something*. I am sorry, Master Bacon, but I must press you for an answer. The timing of the enterprise needs to be precise, and the other companions I hope to take should be arriving momentarily."

Francis bit his lip, wishing that he had more time to reflect— although he did understand why the golem had chosen not to give him fair warning of this remarkable invitation. "What other companions?" he asked.

"Walter Raleigh and Patience Muffet," the golem replied. "Rabbi Low and Doctor Faust will also come with me; if you agree, that will make up a party of six. It will be a great adventure, and might secure the independent future of the human race, God willing."

Francis was still not ready to take the plunge. "Do you have any firm proof of God's existence?" he asked, "or are you required to accept His existence as a matter of faith, as we are?"

"We are unable to doubt the existence of God," was the golem's slightly evasive but steadfastly patient reply, "but we cannot pretend to understand His nature, or know His purpose; nor do we believe that the ethereals know any more, although their ancients are wont to make the claim. Whether or not you and I need faith to sustain our belief in God, we both need trust to sustain our conviction that He has our interests at heart."

"What of the Devil?" Francis asked, unable to resist the temptation. "Are you able to doubt his existence?"

"There is no Devil," the golem replied. "But that is not to say that there is no evil, and the ultimate source of that evil is as puzzling to us as it is to you."

"But there is war in Heaven," Francis said, softly. "Kelley swears that it is so, at least."

"The ethereals do seem to be at odds with one another," was all that the golem would concede. "How and why we do not know—but I find it exceedingly difficult to think that any of their kind might be rebels against the Divine Will. The fact that humans find the notion of such a rebellion a relatively easy thing to believe is one of the most remarkable things about them. I must press you for an answer: will you come?"

"Tell me how you intend to travel," Francis said, well aware that it was the last question he had any right to ask.

"I have a means to improvise a hyperetheric link," the golem told him. "The expedition has to be done in two stages, because the interstellar transmission apparatus had to be hidden in another dimension, anchored to a point in orbit around the Earth. The problem of alignment imposes stern practical difficulties, which prevent the establishment of such apparatus on the surface of a world like this one. Folding the apparatus into the material manifold is as simple as the folding process required for transmission, but I—we—will have to make the initial ascent to the platform via an ultraetheric canal. The Selenites might try to attack the platform once it has materialized, even though they would be forced to operate an inconveniently long way from their base, but I do not believe that they can prevent our departure, and I think it highly probable that de Vere, Marlowe and two of Raleigh's Adapted Men will be able to defend the platform successfully against any insects that can reach it by ethership or etheric flight. You must decide now, if you please. Will you come?"

Francis had made his decision, which seemed to him to be inevitable. "Of course I will," he said. "How could I do otherwise?"

The seeming old man relaxed momentarily, but got to his feet almost immediately. "Thank you," he said. "I must go now, to look for Raleigh and Patience Muffet, and to give the captain his orders."

Francis felt stunned. The consciousness slowly caught up with him that he had just brought his familiar life to a full stop, and embarked upon another—without consulting his brother! Anthony would be extremely annoyed by that. Rather than dwell on that thought, however, Francis dredged up another detail from his uncertain memory, relating to Francis Drake's account of Patience Muffet. She had been a child when Drake saw her, although she must be fully-grown now, and she had kept some very strange pets.

Heidenberg and Faust were already heading for the chart-room door, but Judah Low remained sitting, apparently ready to assist Francis with any more questions he might have. "What would have happened if I had not accepted your invitation?" Francis said.

"The launch would have taken you upriver when the tide turned, at least as far as the port of London. You'd have had a fine tale to tell Queen Jane and John Dee—but they might not have believed you, without the kind of proof that my master gave you."

That was true enough, Francis thought. Even the queen, who loved him like a favorite son, might hesitate to believe that he had left Lambeth by night to visit the legendary Merlin, who was also Trithemius, Prometheus and a giant snail. Francis Drake would believe him, he felt sure—but he was not so certain of Dee, given that he had no proofs to offer the mathematician of the sort that Aristocles had given to Edward Kelley, let alone the sort that Talos had presumably provided when de Vere first delivered him to Dee's house. None of that mattered now, though; by the time he had to convince the queen and John Dee, he might well have proofs a-plenty.

"Will you allow Anthony to come with de Vere and Marlowe?" he asked. "He's a brave man, if there's any fighting to be done—and he certainly won't want to return to London without me."

"He may come as far as the platform, if he so desires," the Rabbi said. "He will be very welcome—especially if there is fighting to be done, although we hope that no such eventuality will arise. Should you not ask him first, though?"

Oh, he'll say yes, Francis thought. *He'll leave the Earth behind and lay his life on the line for me, poor lad—it has ever been his fate in life.* He did not say that to the Rabbi, though.

Judah Low took his silence as an invitation to say more. "Faust and I have been preparing for this all our lives," he said, with a curious mixture of pride and restrained excitement, "which have been, as you now know, a little longer than the usual human span."

"I too might have benefited from a little more opportunity to prepare," Francis said, amiably, "but I am a true scholar, and I dare say that is preparation enough for any kind of educational journey." It was sheer bravado, but he was proud of himself for being capable even of that.

The door to the chart-room burst open again as he finished, and Anthony rushed in, holding aloft an arm whose wrist was gripped by a gigantic parrot with blue and yellow plumage.

"I *told* you that I saw a firebird!" he exclaimed.

"He is actually a macaw," said the young woman who came in behind Anthony, "and his name is Agamemnon."

CHAPTER THIRTY-SIX

The *Himmel* put down anchor again some distance east of Tilbury, but Francis did not think that she had traveled as far as Sheerness. He could not judge the length of the journey very well because he had spent the time below decks, furiously scribbling letters of apology to the queen and everyone else to whom he owed an obligation. By the time his conscience was satisfied there were eight envelopes separately addressed and sealed, containing twelve letters in all; he passed the bundle to the vessel's captain, having extracted a solemn oath that they would be sent back to London with all possible expedition, and the most important of them delivered before sunset.

The execution of this duty had given Francis no time to acquaint himself with Patience Muffet or to reacquaint himself with the individual who claimed to be Walter Raleigh. The latter bore no resemblance to the flamboyant courtier Francis had seen as a boy, although he claimed to remember both the brothers, having been on friendly terms with their father. Nicholas Bacon had not had many friends at court, by virtue of his rumored Elizabethan sympathies, but Francis was prepared to believe that Raleigh had been one; he was not so sure, though, that the dark half-human creature who now laid claim to Raleigh's memory could really be reckoned the same man.

The metamorphosis that Raleigh had undergone, as a result of Arachnid alchemy, had not robbed him of all semblance of humanity, but Francis certainly could not reckon him an alluring advertisement for the science in question. He had been an uncommonly handsome man, but now was very ugly; his skin was, dark, coarse and hairy, and the shape of his face had been transformed into an inverted isosceles triangle, somewhat reminiscent of that of a broad-browed goat—or an artist's impression of a demon, modeled on some such animal. On the other hand, Raleigh had no giant spiders with him at present to sow further fear and panic among those who beheld him, and the members of his small contingent of Adapted Men were mere echoes of his own form. Now that he had glimpsed the true appearance of Rabbi Low's golem, Francis felt that he had learned a significant lesson in visual tolerance.

Patience Muffet, by contrast, seemed entirely human in appearance—not unusually pretty, perhaps, although her face was innocent of any pock-marks, but certainly personable. It seemed that Arachnid alchemy had not transformed her physically at all, but there was something slightly disturbing about her intense gaze, and the manner in which she communicated with her winged spy. The bird had soon deserted Anthony's wrist in favor of her shoulder, and was forever muttering incomprehensibly into her ear. Francis had felt offended when he first saw the bird, imagining that it had been sent to Lambeth to spy on him, but he had realized soon enough that it must actually have been sent to spy on Faust and his companions. Patience was obviously wary of the secret society to which these ill-assorted companions belonged, although she too could not have hesitated long before accepting the golem's invitation.

"I have not yet had the pleasure of meeting your father," Francis said, when he finally found an opportunity to introduce himself properly, "but I have heard great things about him."

"You have only heard a fraction of the truth, Master Bacon," she assured him, with a stiff manner that had more anxiety in it than politeness. "Now that he has come home, your reputation as the cleverest man in England will be gravely imperiled."

"I am not so exceedingly fond of it as to be determined to defend it," he assured her, refusing to take offence. "I shall be delighted to learn what he has to teach me about the alchemy of the flesh. Ever since Francis Drake introduced me to the concept of evolution, I have been fascinated by it."

"Perhaps I shall find time to acquaint you with some of his ideas," she said, with so faint a hint of promise as to make it clear that she probably would not. She broke off the conversation immediately thereafter, and went in search of her stalwart Raleigh.

The place where they eventually came ashore again was a kind of island in the marsh—or a promontory, at least—with a little wood trailing along its low-set ridge. The wood was dense enough to ensure that no crewmen on any passing boat, no matter how close it came to land, would realize that some busy enterprise had formed a clearing in its center, and had established some kind of machine there. Half a dozen of the thirty laborers who had performed this task were similar in appearance to Raleigh, with dark, leathery skins, but the rest were Europeans, including a handful of Englishmen.

Francis assumed that they were all members of the society that de Vere had mentioned, who had been abruptly summoned to fulfill their oaths of allegiance. Those who had not made their way to Kent overland must have sailed from the Continent with the Order's Superiors.

The parts of the machine had certainly not been fashioned in any local forge, and must have been shipped from the Netherlands in the *Himmel*'s hold. They were not the only things that the golem's companions had brought with them; the first things that Francis was taken to see when he and Anthony arrived at the construction site were the suits that they would wear on their expedition.

The bodies of the suits were made of rubber, and seemed very loose-fitting at first glance, but what caught Francis' attention more immediately was the array of near-spherical helmets, apparently fabricated out of black glass. From without they seemed opaque, but when one of them was fitted over his head—carefully, for the hole intended for the neck was hardly broad enough to accommodate a generous nose—he saw that it was, in fact, translucent.

"I thought that Tom Digges had proved that the ether is breathable," Anthony objected.

"He did," de Vere told him. "He proved that the body can function well enough for a while in ether rather than air, much as it can function between meals—but ether does not support life in the same fashion as air, and a man breathing ether will fall into a torpor eventually, or begin to suffer delusions. Those eventualities are best avoided—but the helmets and suits are also intended to protect us against overly intense light and the possibility of encountering noxious air." As he spoke the last phrase he looked away from Anthony at Francis.

"We do not know exactly what we shall find when we set off on the second leg of our journey," Francis deduced, articulating the conclusion for Anthony's benefit. "We shall certainly reach the surface of another world, but we do not know what difficulties might face us before we can get safely inside it, into the bosom of its flesh-core." He remembered, too, that Thomas Digges had *breathed in* the ethereal that had hitched a ride in his body and brain, and guessed that the golem might be anxious to protect his companions against that eventuality as well. The ethereals were evidently something of a mystery to the Fleshcores, and the golem obviously did not trust them.

After inspecting the suits, Francis and Anthony were taken to another canvas-covered store, where they were shown a number of weapons. In form they resembled arquebuses, closely enough to have been disguised as such, but they were lighter, and their barrels were not amenable to cramming with powder and shot.

"They fire rays of energetic light," de Vere told them. "They're all-but-harmless when fired in air, although they're capable of blinding a man if cleverly aimed, but in ether they're deadlier, especially to insectile wings and compound eyes. Drake's ships will be fitted with artillery of a similar sort, though much more powerful—but his men will wear swords too, just as we shall. If fighting comes to close quarters, there's nothing to match a good blade—except, I'm told, insect jaws and insect stings, which can easily inflict mortal wounds if not adequately parried, by virtue of the poisons they will almost certainly contain. Have you trained with that sword, Master Bacon, or do you wear it just for show?" This time, he was addressing Anthony rather than Francis.

"We have both been schooled," Anthony claimed. "Our master may not have been as skilled as Arthur Golding, but he had seen military service in the Netherlands and was no mere fencer."

De Vere's eyebrow lifted very slightly, suggestive of his skepticism, but his reply was scrupulously polite. "In that case, Master Bacon, Kit and I will be glad to have you at our side, as well as Raleigh's dark folk—although we're told that they're very fearsome fighting men, and I can readily believe it. Faust's master assures us that a battle is highly unlikely, and that we might reckon ourselves unfortunate if we encounter anything more than a patrol of glorified night-flying moths, but it's always as well to be prepared against the direr circumstance."

Francis divined that de Vere was trying to lift his own spirits as well as Anthony's; the earl was not the sort of man who would ever deign to let anxiety show, but that did not mean that he was immune to it. Francis supposed that any attack they might have to withstand would be launched from an ethership, against whose hull the ray-guns would probably be as impotent as blades.

"How powerful are Drake's guns, Francis?" Anthony asked, a trifle wistfully. He had always envied Tom Digges far more for his work as an artillerist and military engineer than for his exploits as an astronomer and mathematician.

De Vere answered in Francis' stead. "Powerful enough to blast holes in the ships of the Selenite Armada," he said. "That will not put an immediate end to the Selenites inside—they can fly in the ether—but will make it extremely difficult for the ships to withstand the last phase of their journey, through the Earth's atmosphere."

Anthony, still trying to match his interlocutor in the appearance of casual courage, continued the interrogation. "How long will we need to stay on the platform high above the Earth?"

"That I don't know," de Vere replied. "In the first instance, Master Rosenkreutz will only require a matter of minutes to align the transmitter. We shall, of course, make our initial ascent at a propitious moment. After that...well, it might be hours, or days, before a messenger returns to give us further information. Be reassured, though, that our greatest difficulty will probably be boredom. It is no small matter for insects to fly from the moon, whether they use their own wings or an ethership. By the time that a patrol has detected and reported our presence, we will probably have been idle for some considerable time—and by the time a contingent of reinforcements can reach Earth orbit, we should be safe and sound on *terra firma* once again."

Anthony seemed reassured by this, so Francis did not want to question it. He had thought of a hundred more questions by now that he wanted to put to the golem, but none that Edward de Vere would be able to answer reliably. Faust and Low were as busy as the golem himself in making the final arrangements for the use of the ultra-etheric canal, whose activation would bring the hyperetheric transmitter out of its other-dimensional hidey-hole within seconds, and then transport a company of bold pioneers to the platform on which it stood. He was not required to lend a hand to any heavy work himself, but he was unable to exploit the waiting time as he would have wished, in recovering more information. Absurd as it seemed, since Patience Muffet and Walter Raleigh seemed preoccupied with their own concerns, Francis had little to do but look out over the estuary, from which the fog had now lifted completely enough to allow a clear sight of the sailing vessels making use of the incoming tide.

The sky was cloudy, and the water exceedingly grey. The marsh, Francis judged, must have a rather bleak aspect even at its best—but for a man about to quit the Earth, the scene could hardly help seeming uncommonly hospitable and homely. One of Edward Kelley's favorite sayings was that it was the Earth entire, rather than his magical red powder, that was the true philosopher's stone; Francis took that to mean that it was the evolutionary transformations wrought at the Earth's surface by the passage of millions of years—making humankind masters of a highly exceptional Creation—which constituted the real wonder and the real miracle at the heart of these turbulent times.

In the vast empire of the Great Fleshcores, it was said, there was—or had been, until John Dee's ethership had provoked a disturbance whose extent and durability was inestimable—a calm, a fixity and a certainty of purpose that was very different from the politics of Earthly nations and the perpetual squabbles of human individuals. There was something enviable about that prospect, Francis admitted, but there was also something to envy in relentless competition and the urge to rapid progress, no matter what the cost in uncertainty might be. If Thomas Muffet really was on the threshold of discoveries that might give human beings the power to accelerate and direct their evolution, what might his quarrelsome species make of itself? Something very different, undoubtedly, from what the Selenites wanted to make of it, in order to accommodate humankind to their notion of eternally static utopia.

In the end, Francis lost himself sufficiently within this reverie that Patience Muffet had to come to fetch him, telling him that he must put on his suit immediately, because the "node" at which the orbital platform would unfold was approaching its ideal position.

"Could your father not be here to bid you farewell?" Francis asked, as they walked side by side. He felt rather awkward, for he had little idea how to talk to young women, and knew that his experience in dealing with Queen Jane was far from pertinent.

"He has relationships to build and old scores to settle," Patience told him, as they went into the storage-tent. "He intends to be the spearhead of a Paracelsian revolution in England and Europe. That is what he insists on calling it, although his medicines have nothing in common with Paracelsus' silly nostrums."

"It will be easier to persuade the needy of its merit if he calls it Paracelsian than if he names it an Arachnid revolution," Francis opined.

She smiled slightly at that. "You're right," she conceded—but had to stop talking then, in order to get into her suit, which was even more loose-fitting about her slender frame than any of the others. Rabbi Low and the golem were the stoutest members of the entire company, but even they did not test the elasticity of the fabric unduly.

Once Francis had his helmet on, a release of air from a satchel on his back inflated the suit slightly. That disconcerted him, but he quickly accustomed himself to the sensation. Now that the company had sealed their suits it was very difficult to recognize anyone; he could see out well enough, but he could hardly see into the other black glass shells at all. He could not tell which ones of his ten companions were the five who would undertake the second phase of the journey with him and which would be left behind to man the platform, but he supposed that they would sort themselves out soon enough, once the work of aligning the mysterious hyperetheric projector actually began.

He took his position randomly, huddled on the narrow dais of the first machine with everyone else, not knowing where Anthony was or with whom he was rubbing shoulders. There was no ceremony, and he did not even see a lever activated to send the company on its way. One moment he was in Kent, and the next....

CHAPTER THIRTY-SEVEN

The next moment, however, did not seem to follow the preceding one as immediately as it might have done, time itself having been wrenched out of true as the ultraetheric canal snatched him up. For a moment, everything disappeared, or was turned inside-out, including Francis' body and his mind. A sudden odor of burning onions surged out of his memory, unbidden and completely unexpected.

When time resumed its course again, the wrench he felt left him feeling extremely dizzy and nauseous. He felt strong hands moving him out of the way, although there was something very strange about the fashion in which his feet were being dragged. He was given something to grip before he was abandoned, and then felt able to open his eyes. His vertigo and nausea returned in full force when he found himself looking down from the edge of a platform, to whose balustrade he was clinging.

Oddly enough, he did not have any sense of being high up. He had been to the tops of Welsh mountains and had looked down sheer cliffs, and had then been very acutely aware of the distance he might plummet if he lost his balance, but there was nothing now connecting him to the planet below him, and he felt that he weighed nothing at all, although he knew that he was not beyond the range of the Earth's affinity. He felt light enough, at any rate, to imagine that he might float away, drifting in the subtle currents of the ether. It was easier to imagine that than to accommodate the idea that he might tumble from where he now was to the surface of that gigantic ball—which was certainly beneath his feet, given the direction of his unfolded body, but did not really seem to be *below* him in any truly meaningful sense of the word.

Francis had seen many terrestrial globes fashioned out of carefully curved pieces of cloth mounted on a wicker frame, as well as many celestial globes depicting the relative positions of the distant stars, but he was slightly surprised to discover that the Earth bore as little resemblance to a geographical globe as the sky did to a celestial one. It was not so much the coloring of the land and sea as the extent of the clouds, which obscured vast tracts of continent and ocean alike, and made it exceedingly hard to identify the outlines of the familiar world-map.

He had unthinkingly expected the sun to be above his head, but it was not; it was very close to the rim of the Earth and moving closer all the while, about to set—or to be eclipsed, according to terminology that seemed to have loosened considerably. He had also expected the moon to be full, although he had had no particular reason to suppose that it would be; in fact, it was positioned in such a way that three-quarters of its face was sunlit and the remainder in shadow.

The moon's face was no larger than it was when seen from the surface, but his eyes scanned it anyway, as if by reflex, searching for some slight evidence of activity or the presence of the Great Armada that was being patiently assembled there in order to attack the Earth. There was no such evidence visible, although the floating disk seemed so very light that it was easy to think of it as a hollow crust filled with a vast hive of ants and beetles, caterpillars and centipedes.

There was a good deal of activity going on behind him, and he was jostled a little, but the platform of the orbital station was considerably larger than the stage of the Earthbound machine, and Francis did not feel that he was in danger of being thrust over the balustrade. He discovered that the soles of his feet were stuck to the surface of the platform in such a way that they could easily be slid along but were not so easy to lift clear in order to assume a normal gait. *Magnetism*, he thought, wonderingly. That was another of John Dee's old obsessions, investigated on behalf of the queen's navy and the Muscovy Company, in order to perfect its navigational uses.

There were people already busy about the strange devices that occupied the four corners of the inner compound where the focal point of the transmitter was, but Francis did not bother to turn round in order to study exactly what they were doing, or to what. He was not the only one standing back, and he felt that he was wise to do so rather than get in the way of workmen who had tasks to complete.

He tilted his head back and turned to his left, in order to avoid the muted light of the sun, whose rays were reddening now by virtue of their passage through the Earth's atmospheric envelope. He looked at the stars of the Milky Way, which lay across the black sky like a great stain—but not all like a stream of spilled milk. For every star visible from the surface of Earth, he guessed, there must be hundreds now visible to his unsupported eye, and might be thousands were he not wearing the black helmet, but they seemed oddly frail and tiny, quite disconnected from one another in spite of their profusion. There was nothing misty about the Milky Way now, except for a few strange patches; the greater part of its extent was very obviously a field of distinct points of light, lost in an infinite sea of dark. Had the void theorists not been so thoroughly defeated by the plenarists, Francis could almost have imagined that the space outside the Earth's kindly layer of air really was empty.

He was about to turn his attention to the moon again when everything changed. He supposed, in the first instant, that he must simply have been looking in the wrong direction to see the attackers approaching—but those whose appointed task it was to take up defensive positions and mount vigil had no time to react either. If anyone had shouted a warning he probably would not have heard it, for the ether was much less efficient at transmitting sound than light, but it seemed more likely that there was simply no opportunity for anyone to do so. Between the instant when the space beyond the Earth's affinity seemed empty enough almost to be a void, and the instant when it seemed entirely full of fluttering wings, there seemed to be no lapse of time at all.

Francis assumed that the imitation arquebuses were fired, although he saw no beams of light spring from their muzzles. He assumed, too, that the rays struck targets, for he could not imagine how they could possibly miss, but the shots seemed to have no effect at all on the swarm that was now seething around them. He thought of it as *seething* because he could hear no sound, although he was fully prepared to believe that it might be buzzing too. He had no weapon at all, so his first impulse was to drop to his knees and cover his head as best he could with his arms, but that was not easy with his soles stuck to the platform, and so he squatted instead, in a remarkably ungainly position, with his knees jutting out. Nor did he cover his head for more than a moment, for the contact of fluttering wings made him lash out reflexively with his hands and forearms, trying to shove the marauders away.

Francis could not tell, at first, how large the members of the attacking swarm might be. They were at least ten times as large as honey-bees, and less than half as large as human beings, but he could not narrow that range any further when he tried to estimate their average wingspan and the length of their bodies. They filled the ether so densely that it was almost impossible to imagine that their furiously-beating wings could avoid colliding with one another and sending them all fluttering out of control—and yet, it seemed, they did avoid collisions, and retained all their awful certainty of purpose.

Swords were undoubtedly being used, though not with any need for a fencer's art. They were presumably being used as flails, brandished above the sentries' heads and twirled in such a way as to carve out circles in space. Doubtless, too, the blades must be doing sterling work, scything through wings and abdomens by the dozen or the hundred—but without any conspicuous impact on the density of the swarm.

Francis became aware, almost to his surprise, that he was no longer waving his arms above his head, but was clawing instead at his chest and thighs, trying to dislodge fliers that had lighted there and were clinging fast. They could not adhere to the glass of his helmet, it seemed, but they could gain purchase enough on the rubber of his suit to cling and bite—and bite they did.

At first, their jaws were unable to penetrate his suit, whose rubber yielded and stretched without being torn—but as the creatures persisted, he felt the fabric penetrated in half a dozen places and felt the clothing he was wearing within give way as claw-like entities raked and stabbed his flesh.

He felt pricks of burning pain, strangely muted by shock, and was conscious that blood was beginning to flow—first from his left arm, then the right, and then from his breast, no more than a handspan from his heart.

Why, he thought, in stupefaction, *they're killing me! This is not supposed to be happening. We were supposed to be safe, at least until we got to the heart of the universe.*

He felt an arm tugging his own then, and another pair of hands grappling with the insects that were clinging to his suit. He knew that it must be Anthony. It could only be Anthony, reckless of his own danger and fearful for his little brother's life. Francis knew, too, that the brave fellow's efforts must be futile—and so they would have been, had help not arrived.

The insects were entirely visible and tangible, difficult to discern only because of their sheer profusion. They were an exceedingly solid and material threat, horrific in its simple brutality. Whatever came to blow away the insect swarm, by contrast, was visible and tangible only in its effects, and not in itself. It was more like a storm-wind than an entity, but it was a wind with intelligence and precision, which blew exactly where it willed. It tore the clinging insects away from Francis' suit, and from Anthony's suit as well, but it plucked them away with an amazing delicacy, which inflicted hardly any force at all on Francis' desperate arms and twisted body.

But it's too late! Francis mourned—and would have screamed, had he not feared to witness the utter impotence of his voice. *My suit is breached, and my skin too! I am poisoned, and doomed, no matter what punishment God has seen fit to inflict on my persecutors. It wasn't supposed to happen like this!*

He knew, though, that it was not God who was punishing the plague of stinging flies that had descended upon the orbital platform. He guessed readily enough that it was one or more ethereals, fully capable of denying the insects the power of ethereal flight. Kelley's Aristocles was probably among them; at any rate, they certainly had no love for murderous insects. They desired to protect humans from harm—but they had come too late! They had arrived, in all probability, no more than a few seconds after the attack had begun, but they surely had not come in time to save the humans' lives.

Or had they?

As Francis' thoughts ran on, he realized that he was not dead yet, nor even in terrible pain. He felt light-headed, to be sure, but he had felt light in every possible literal and metaphorical respect since he had first discovered himself weightless, and he did not think that he was becoming delirious, although he could not be entirely sure.

He felt himself grabbed again, and assumed that Anthony was still by his side, ready to lend him succor—but there were two black-clad figures with him now, who were dragging him along, forcing his near-weightless feet to slide along the platform with increasing velocity, as the initial grip of friction yielded to momentum. He had no idea who was dragging him, but he could guess why they were doing it. In spite of everything, the golem had aligned the hyperetheric projector.

In spite of everything the mission to the heart of the universe was still on course. If only he could remain alive, and find good air or honest ether at the far point of his extradimensional trajectory, he might yet see what he had intended to see, and might even contrive to return with intelligence of it.

The fact remained, though, that he was being dragged. The fact remained that he needed to be dragged. He was hurt—and now he was beginning to feel cold, and sick. There was no pain—he felt quite detached from his body, as though it no longer belonged to him and he no longer had any need to share its ills and inconveniences—but he was not right, not well.

God have mercy, he thought. *Faust and Low are doubtless worthier than I am, having prepared for this moment all their lives, and Patience Muffet still qualifies as one of those children to whom You try to extend tenderness, while I am merely a humble scholar who has dared to doubt Your goodness, but have mercy nevertheless.*

The stars were still shining as he formulated this prayer, and the storm-wind was still blowing all around him without buffeting him at all—but the stars suddenly ceased shining, and the storm-wind seemed suddenly to be *within* him, and one with him, as he was turned inside out.

I'm alive! he thought. *In spite of all that the treacherous Selenites could do, I'm alive. I will not die, if my will to survive has any force at all. The golem may triumph yet, and I shall share his victory. I am bound for the Empire of the Skies, the True Civilization.*

Whether his determined thinking had any effect, or merely constituted an optimistic commentary, he could not be not sure—but he survived the sensation of inversion, of compression of his three dimensions into a mere thread. He did not lose consciousness even for a moment, and he even contrived by that monumental effort of directed thought to keep track and account of his consciousness.

As soon as the train of thought reached its terminus, he was delivered into confusion, not quite knowing where he was, or who, or even how—but he still had a precious inkling, albeit a terribly faint one, of *why*.

CHAPTER THIRTY-EIGHT

When Francis recovered full possession of himself he was already awake, with his eyes open, and he was immediately able to sit up. He had already been staring at the sky for an immeasurable length of time, and he continued to do so, but he was now able to take better stock of what he was looking at.

The zenith was occupied by a black circle, about twice the size of the moon as seen from Earth. Around it, the greater part of the sky was filled by a vast coruscating wheel, which actually did seem to be turning, although its color and dazzle were so confused that the impression might have been an illusion. There were strange dark patches within the wheel, though, that were definitely moving, in various trajectories curved in a direction contrary to the wheel's apparent movement. There were thousands of them, and they gave the impression of being in flight, although they had no definite shapes. They might, Francis thought, have been a vast flock of gigantic bats, whose outlines were confused by the light dancing behind and around them—or fragments of the central well of darkness detaching themselves in sequence and finding a fragile freedom in the world of light.

He knew that he would not have been able to contemplate the sight at all had it not been for the black glass in his helmet, so he assumed at first, when he tried to redirect his attention to the ground and look at his immediate surroundings, that his eyes had been overstrained, and that the devastation he beheld was a trick of injured perception. A few seconds passed before he realized that the ruination was real, and terrible.

There had been something like a city where he stood, but there was only blackened debris now. The harsh light of the celestial wheel was brighter by far than any Earthly daylight, but the surface of the world was all-but-colorless; everything that had not been burned had been blackened by smoke. It was not merely buildings that had collapsed but other structures; the horizon was littered with twisted masses of metal that must once have been proud masts and pylons. Closer to his own position, the ground was pitted by craters and fissures. It was impossible to judge what most of the various heaps of rubble might have been, before they had been stamped flat by some brutal force, but it was possible to pick out various kinds of broken body-parts, most of them insectile but some eerily similar to human limbs and torsos. They were not flesh-fragments, though, but parts of smashed-up machines made in the form of insects or humanoids, replete with sinews of metal wire and arcane clockwork.

The surfaces of the worlds at the heart of the galaxy, Francis Drake had told him, were no longer the province of living flesh; they were places where machines worked tirelessly. Here, the arena of machine labor had been very thoroughly devastated by some kind of cosmic disaster, natural or artificial. That did not necessarily mean, however, that the living components of the world—the fleshcore and its myriad attendants—had been destroyed, or even damaged. Francis continued looking around, peering through black glass at the blacker landscape.

At first, he thought that there was nothing moving at all, but then he felt a flash of panic as he realized that there was something very close to him, whose movement had been camouflaged at first by the fact that it was almost entirely black itself, moving against a similar background. He might not have seen it at all but for a glint of light reflected from something smooth and rounded.

His panic faded as abruptly as it had arisen when he realized that the round object was a helmet similar to his own. His eyes became slightly better adjusted then, and he was able to pick out the whole figure. The other bent down to him—he was still sitting—and the other helmet made contact with his own. That enabled him to hear a voice—Patricia Muffet's voice—saying: "Who are you?" Her tone was anxious, but full of courage and determination.

"Francis Bacon," he told her.

"How badly are you injured?"

That was a good question, he thought. He moved his hands over his body. His suit had certainly been torn and penetrated in half a dozen places, but the rents seemed to have sealed themselves. The sore points on his body where he had been stabbed or grazed responded to his probing fingers, but the pain was dull. No bones seemed to be broken. He appeared to be breathing normally.

"Very slightly," he informed her, "unless I've been injected with some slow-acting poison. I'm not even in pain, although I know that I was stung and slashed several times over. You?"

"The same," she said.

"What about the others?" He moved his head slightly as he spoke, careful not to lose the contact, hopeful that he might now be able to pick out other moving figures against the dark backcloth.

"I've only found one," she told him, her voice betraying a new emotion. "It's Low. He's dead."

"Then where…?"

"I don't know," she said. "When the insects attacked, he and Walter tried to shield me—to protect me. They drew me to the departure-point, the focal plane of the transmitter. One was still holding me tightly when the transmission was activated—I had assumed that it was Walter, but apparently it was not."

"I was dragged too," Francis told her. "I assumed that one of the two was Anthony, but I could not identify the other. The others must be here, must they not? It's simply that we can't see them while they're lying still. We have to find them. The golem…."

"We were betrayed," Patience told him, cutting him off peremptorily. "Faust. It had to be Faust."

"Why…?" Francis began—but she cut him off again.

"The insects came from the hyperetheric apparatus," she told him. "The Selenites had a fix on the platform before the slug could get the apparatus aligned. They would have captured it for sure if the ethereals hadn't intervened. Perhaps they took it anyway. If this really is our intended destination, there must have been treason here too. It's possible that the others are here, or very slightly displaced from here…but it's more probable that only three of us came through before the transmission was cut off. I suppose it's possible, too, that the slug has already returned, abandoning us here—but Walter would never have gone back without me." She paused, but hardly had time to draw breath before resuming: "We need to get underground, if we can. The air here is very thin and bad. We need to get to the fleshcore…if the fleshcore is still alive."

"Is that thing above us the Black Pit to which the golem referred?" Francis asked, feeling unable to imitate the young woman in referring to the fleshcore-fragment as a "slug".

"I presume so," she said. "The radiant matter swirling around it is falling into it, dissolving as it falls—but I did not expect the Shadows. Nothing is supposed to be able to escape the Pit, so they cannot really be emerging from it, as they seem to be. They might be forming in the matter that is being torn apart, in which case they might be ethereals of some sort in the process of being born—the one that Kelley talks to describes itself as *nascent*, does it not? I don't know. We have to descend into the underworld, Master Bacon." The way she pronounced his name implied that she would rather have found one of her other companions—one more capable of judging the situation, and more adept at handling it.

Francis got to his feet, breaking contact briefly. By the time he tried to press his helmet to her again, though, she was already moving off. She paused just long enough to take his hand and say: "Come on." Then she set off, evidently expecting him to follow her meekly. He was in no position to challenge her assumption of authority, so that was what he did. He had no alternative thereafter but to try to answer his own questions while he stumbled along in her wake, not even knowing how she was conducting her search for a way into the interior of the devastated world.

They had been betrayed, she reckoned—by John Faust, she suspected, although she had no evidence for that, and no way of knowing what kinds of spies might have been watching the golem's party for far longer than her faithful Agamemnon. In any case, the Selenites had been prepared in advance for the emergence of the hyperetheric link from its fold in space, and had been ready to seize it, perhaps for use as a staging-post in their impending invasion—in which case, the golem's attempt to go home had made things worse for Earth and humankind, not better. The fleshcore-fragment's scheme had gone badly awry—but so had the Selenites' scheme. One or more ethereals had come to their aid, perhaps having also been forewarned of the golem's plan.

Francis felt a slight pang of relief, by virtue of the fact he had been recruited to the expedition at the last moment precisely to avoid the possibility that he might give anything away in advance, accidentally or deliberately, and was thus liberated from Patience Muffet's suspicions. Anthony's "firebird" had, at least, assured her that he was harmless, although she was unable to deem him useful. She was still holding his hand, still drawing him forwards, searching for something.

Francis drew breath, and was alarmed to find that he had some small difficulty in doing so. The air inside his suit seemed to be changing in its quality, as if its vital essence were being gradually drained, and it was taking on a foul odor. Francis had to force himself to resume his train of thought.

If this world really was their intended destination, he thought—and it was presumably not impossible that the golem had been unable to align the hyperetheric transmitter correctly—then it had suffered a holocaust far more terrible than anything the Selenites intended to afflict on Earth. If this had been done deliberately, who could have been responsible? There was a new war in "Heaven", according to Kelley—a war between the natives of the ether, Francis supposed—and warfare in the True Civilization too, where insects allied with the Selenites had rebelled, and where there might also have been a revolt of the machines. One of these wars, if they were not merely facets of the same war, had reduced the surface of this world to a burned-out wreck. Could that be anything to do with the shadowy forms in the wheel of light? Might they, in fact, be nascent ethereals?

He took another deep breath, and found it nauseating, but that only forced him to concentrate all the harder. Was it conceivable, he wondered, that he and Patience had been abandoned here deliberately? Might the golem have lied to them both about the whole nature of this expedition? Had they both been dragged to the departure-point in order to make certain that they would be dispatched? Might he and she—and perhaps Judah Low too, if he had not been so badly injured in the insect attack—have been intended all along as sacrificial victims, or specimens of humankind for the gratification of the Great Fleshcores. If so, had that plan gone more badly awry at this end than the other? What had happened here, and what did it portend with respect to his own fate, and that of the Earth?

That question brought Francis back, at last, to the issue he had been unconsciously trying to escape: the fact that he was all but alone, unimaginably far from home, with the jaws of death gaping wide in anticipation of swallowing him. His heartbeat fluttered fearfully—but then Patience Muffet touched her helmet to his again, and said: "Here. I doubt that we can activate the trap-door, but if there's anyone within who can detect our presence, I think we can make our presence known."

He looked down, and was able to make out a circular metal plate set in the ground, some ten feet in diameter. It was blackened, like everything else, but seemed reassuringly intact. There were various structures set around it that had suffered far worse, but there were numerous plaques inscribed with unreadable symbols, and a number of buttons seemingly intended to be pressed. Patience was already busy pressing them at random.

Francis moved on to the plate. It could not be iron, because his soles did not stick to it; he was anchored there by weight alone, and did not feel significant heavier or lighter than he had on Earth. When he stamped his foot the plate rang hollow, suggesting that it was indeed the entrance to a shaft. While Patience tested the periphery, therefore, Francis began to stamp his feet more forcefully and rhythmically, hoping that he might attract attention in the simplest way of all.

After ten minutes or so, they both sat down to rest. Francis felt that all the strength was draining out of him, and that the interior of his suit was becoming unbearable. The various wounds he had sustained before the transition were still remarkably painless, but he felt thoroughly miserable. He wondered how long it might take him to die, and how many new pains would arrive instead of those that had somehow been blotted out. He touched his helmet to the young woman's, in order to say: "Don't despair. God would not send us half way across his universe merely to let us perish."

"Even the slug would not do that," she told him. "It seems, though, that all good intentions might have been thwarted by the unexpected, God's included."

Francis had to take his helmet away in order to shake his head—but his head, oddly enough, refused to be shaken. He found himself standing up again, although his volition seemed quite uninvolved in the action. He felt himself move to one side; then his arm reached out, entirely of its own accord. He could not make out what it was that his fingers did, not because it was too dark for his eyes to see, but simply because his sight was so startled by the impossibility of what was happening. After thirty seconds or so, however, there was a grinding sound and the plate began to slide sideways into a slot in the surrounding wall.

Patience made contact just long enough to say: "How did you do that?"

Francis did not answer, not merely because he did not know but because he could not activate his vocal cords. At first, it seemed that they had gained nothing. Beneath the plate that had moved aside was another, seemingly not much different, although its surface was not blackened. It was a pale grey, insufficiently polished to gleam in the excessive light. Francis' hand took Patience Muffet's, as she had earlier taken his, and his legs led her on to the plate. She followed meekly, just as he had, although he could feel the mistrust and anxiety in her grip.

"Don't be afraid," he said, glad to be operating his own vocal cords—although he was quite incapable of following his own advice.

CHAPTER THIRTY-NINE

The inner platform began to descend through a smooth-walled shaft, heading for the bowels of the world. The dwindling circle of light above their heads was eclipsed as the upper plate slid back into place again, leaving them in total darkness.

Patience contrived another contact and repeated: "How did you do that?"

Still able to formulate his own reply, Francis said: "I didn't. Something else took control of my body. Perhaps that was the response to our appeal for help. May we take our helmets off now, do you think?"

"Best not," she replied, seemingly unamazed by his denial of responsibility for his own actions. "If they can operate our limbs like those of marionettes they'll likely do that for us when it's safe." After a moment's silence, she said: "I feel lost without Agamemnon." It was the first time she had addressed him as if he were a friend rather than a stranger, and he took a certain comfort in her acceptance.

"The world is not dead, save for its surface," he said, as much for his own benefit as hers. "Its fleshcore is alive, and likely to be accompanied by many other creatures. It is not beyond the bounds of possibility that we might still be able to return home, carrying a message to the golem."

"Yes," she said. "But what shall we find at the transmitter if we do return?"

The platform on which they were descending came to a halt, and a crack of light opened in the wall behind them, widening into a doorway. It was the threshold of a circular chamber some twelve feet in diameter and ten high. There was a creature within, waiting for them; by virtue of its black and yellow coloring it resembled a wasp standing erect on the hindmost of its six limbs. The other four limbs were resting by its sides, and it was the antennae on its massive head that reached out to touch their helmets, inquiringly. It was not until the portal behind them had slid shut that Francis' arms reached up, without any instruction from him, to unscrew his helmet.

The air in the room seemed incredibly sweet at the first breath he took, although the second revealed odors that presumably emanated from the monstrous insect. The odors were subtly unsettling, but not actively unpleasant. Now the antennae palpated his face in the same inquiring manner. Francis bore the inspection stoically. By the time the antennae had withdrawn Patience Muffet had hesitantly unscrewed her own helmet to expose her face.

"What are you?" buzzed the wasp. It had not spoken in English, or any language that Francis could have pronounced, but he had understood the words anyway. How could he reply, though?

After a moment's hesitation, he said: "My name is Francis Bacon." At least, that was what he intended to say. The sounds that came out of his mouth were very different from the English syllables—but the insect appeared to understand them as easily as he had understood what the insect had said, for it was quick to reply, in a manner that gave no hint of astonishment. "How did you come here?" it said.

"By hyperetheric transmission from the nation of England on the world of Earth," Francis said. "The human species, to which we belong, has been under observation for a thousand of our generations by a creature that appears to be a fragment of a fleshcore. It was intended that he would come with us, and two other companions, but the only other we were able to locate after our arrival seemed to have died from injuries sustained when the transmitter was attacked by creatures of your sort. Our world is under threat of invasion from its moon, where there is a substantial colony of insects, rebels against the True Civilization. They are ready to launch a fleet of etherships, but we have a fleet of our own, which will attempt to defend it."

"What are you doing?" whispered Patience Muffet, in English. Francis was only able to shake his head slightly by way of reply.

"This is unexpected," the insect said. "We must go to the fleshcore."

It seemed that this room too was merely a cage encased in a circular shaft, for it began to sink as the first platform had, rapidly accelerating to such a speed that Francis felt as if he might float up into the air like a dandelion-clock. The journey was not a long one, though, and the deceleration was sufficiently gradual not to be painful.

When the motion ceased, the walls were still smooth, but they were also soft and moist. Francis was instantly reminded of his brief vision of the golem's true self. They were, he realized, inside the fleshcore. This time, it was not antennae that reached out to investigate his face but improvised tentacles, and their palpation was more like a glutinous embrace. Had he been in control of his own body he would have been unable to resist the impulse to recoil, but he was not. Indeed, his mouth opened to let the questing slime come in, and he felt it flowing into his ears. He was utterly terrified, but his body would not concede him any opportunity to express or reflect his terror. He reminded himself that Thomas Digges had endured a similar process, and come through it quite unscathed, although Digges had been unable to give him a description of the experience.

"Be calm," said a voice inside his head, apparently speaking in English. "No harm will come to you, and there is recompense."

In much the same way that he had earlier been permitted to see through the deception that normally concealed the golem's true nature from human eyes, he began to experience images in his mind, as if he were able to see into and through the living walls of the chamber into which he had descended. The imagery was very strange, but there was knowledge contained within it as well as mere appearance, and he was able to grasp the gist of it. The fleshcore was attempting to show itself, or its own image of itself, in order to demonstrate its nature and its essential benevolence. He had neither the sensory apparatus nor the conceptual equipment to comprehend it fully, but he did glimpse something of the complexity of the fleshcore, and something of its exotic self-awareness.

The fleshcore, he understood, was both one individual and many, a whole society of disparate species united in a whole. On the basis of vague second-hand reports, he had previously imagined fleshcores to be analogous to gigantic brains, occupying planetary cores as if they were skulls, but he understood now that they were not mere thinking devices; they lived in their multifaceted flesh as human intelligences did, and did not feel in any way disembodied. He had also imagined, until now, that they might conceive of themselves as godlike entities, exercising near-omnipotent power from the thrones of the True Civilization, but that had been mistaken too.

The fleshcore did not conceive of itself by analogy with the intelligence of a formicary, and certainly not by means of the analogy that had led human observers to think of the reproductive individual in a hive as its "queen". It thought of itself as a natural consummation of a kind of creative process—a process that Thomas Digges had called "evolution"—by which an initial capacity for reproduction gifted to primitive organisms too tiny to see had given rise by variation to millions upon millions of different and more complex organisms, which had refined many different kinds of sensory and alimentary apparatus and various patterns of growth and metamorphosis, feeding upon one another as well as the raw materials of air, earth and water, while life burned within them like flickering flames, but also forming complex relationships of assistance and support.

In time, Francis understood, these relationships of assistance and support were themselves refined, in order that intelligence might guide eclectic selections of apparatus, combining them in more complex bodies capable of more complex metamorphoses. Employing the crude model of the hive, this process of intelligent selection and organization had eventually produced the True Civilization: a harmonious association of millions of different fleshy forms, which were no longer distinct species, but which still retained the potential for division and contention.

Francis understood, too—or, at least, imagined that he did— why certain kinds of organisms, including Arachnids, had been refused integration into the True Civilization, by virtue of an individualism too stubborn to be accommodated therein, and why intelligence in such species, in the very rare instances in which it arose, was considered dangerous. He understood, then, how it came about that endoskeletal intelligence—far rarer, it seemed than Arachnid intelligence—posed an enigma to the True Civilization that was problematic in more than one way. He even gained a glimmer of understanding as to why the Selenites and their allies had decided to force a solution to the problem akin to Alexander's approach to the Gordian knot, even at the cost of rebelling against the ultimate arbiters of the cause they held so dear. He had an analogy of his own that he could bring to bear on that: John Field, the Puritan firebrand and master of the Church Militant, avid to force all souls into conformity with his own narrow conception of the necessities of their salvation, in frank defiance of the Church of Rome and all its echoes in the Church of England.

Francis lost track of time while this process of painstaking exploration and attempted enlightenment continued, gladly falling into a merciful trance. When the fleshcore withdrew its pseudopods, he felt as if he were waking up from a light doze, but he felt wondrously refreshed in more ways than one. He felt a good deal better than he had before the communion began; he was convinced that the injuries he had suffered, whose pain had only been muffled before, were now completely healed, and that his reason was clearer than it had ever been.

The wall reverted to being a mere wall for a few seconds, but then it began to stir again. A humanoid figure formed, and stepped out of the fleshy mass. It was grey and smooth, like Francis' vision of the golem, but he was disconcerted to see that it was very similar to him, in its height and form. After a few more moments, it came to resemble him even more as it assumed the kind of glamour that had long concealed Judah Low's golem from ordinary human sight. Anyone who did not know Anthony might have assumed that this was Francis' brother.

"I apologize for that," the new golem said, in English as good as Christian Rosenkreutz's. "This arrival was unexpected, and we did not even know that creatures compounded as you are could exist. We are doing everything possible to restore this planet's hyperetheric links, for our own benefit, and we shall be glad to focus our best attention on the link that you will require in order to return home. We shall recover your companion's body and make every attempt to resurrect him. We shall attempt to discover what happened to the others who were supposed to accompany you. We have begun to create suitable accommodation for you, but it will take a little time."

"What happened here?" Patience Muffet put in. "Have you been attacked?"

"Yes, we have," the golem said. "We are still at war here, although the first battle is over. An unlikely alliance has been contracted between insane machines, rebel insects and other creatures. We do not know how the Shadows enter into the equation, but the fact that this world is so close to their cradle is obviously significant to our adversaries. The hyperetheric web has been utterly devastated in this region, but we are making progress in restoring links to the other heartworlds."

"What shall we call you?" Francis asked, slightly ashamed of intruding such a trivial question into such a portentous discussion, but feeling a need to have some better way of identifying his interlocutor than "the new golem" or "the fleshcore-fragment".

The creature hesitated momentarily, as if uncertain as to which name to choose, or how to make the selection. Eventually, it said: "Call me Solon."

Francis was curious to know why the creature had selected that particular name, but Patience Muffet evidently felt that he was wasting time. "Can the Earth still be defended?" she demanded. "Can you help us against the Selenite Armada, in spite of the Great Flesh-cores being under attack themselves?"

Solon looked at her with what, had it really been human, would have been an expression of suspicion and puzzlement. "Do you imagine that we do not know what you are," it said, "and how the chain of events that resulted in the Selenite invasion plan was initiated?"

It was obvious to Francis, if not to Solon, that Patience had no idea what he meant. She looked at Solon, then at Francis, then back at Solon. It seemed Solon was equally uncertain, but that some sort of realization was slowly forming in the simulacrum's mind. Francis was surprised, after what had just happened, that the fleshcore's fragmentary offspring still had any margin of ignorance that would leave room for surprise, but there had to be some crucial item of information that the fleshcore had not recovered in the course of its intimate inspection, and was only now deducing.

In the meantime, Patience had jumped to a conclusion of her own. "I am entirely human," she told Solon—perhaps intending to impress the force of the assertion on Francis too. "Earth has not been invaded by Arachnids; the Arachnids that helped my father were not the instigators of this conflict, and are numbered among its victims."

Francis wondered whether some or all of these assertions might be false. In spite of the enlightenment that the fleshcore had attempted to share with him, there was evidently something about the situation of Earth and humankind that he and Patience did not know, although the fleshcore had assumed that they did.

"Is it possible," Solon asked, assuming a wondering tone himself as he turned to stare at the man he resembled so closely, "that the particular intelligence that calls itself Francis Bacon, and the element of his companion that is now speaking, do not know that they are aspects of composite minds?"

Francis' first impulse was to deny it, but he realized that he was not in any position to do so. Had not his limbs worked of their own accord in contriving a way down from the surface? Had he not spoken to the insect in a language that he did not know, and understood the insect when the insect had addressed him in that same language? How was it possible, in fact, that he had not realized himself that he was carrying a passenger? Had he not been witness to Thomas Digges' attempts to make sense of his own experience in the heart of the galaxy?

"Please don't be afraid, Francis," said a voice in his head. "I thought it best to be discreet, but I had no intention of deceiving you."

Francis could not help but be afraid—but he could not help remembering, too, that Thomas Digges had been offered soothing reassurances before being subjected to the cruelest deception of them all, in being made to believe for many years that he had only dreamed his experience.

"Aristocles," he said, silently. "You're the ethereal that calls itself Aristocles."

"In fact, I'm the other," the silent voice informed him. "Call me Lumen."

Not *another*, Francis took note, but *the* other. That must surely mean that there really had been two parasitic ethereals involved in the first ethership's adventure, not one. And now, it seemed there were two involved in this adventure, for Patience Muffet must be similarly afflicted.

"What's happening, Francis?" Patience asked, still apparently ignorant of her own condition.

"I do not know how far this tangle of treason extends, Miss Muffet," Francis said, "but I doubt that it was Faust who played us false, and we certainly have not reached the bottom of it yet. An ethereal used the tears that the insects inflicted on my suit and my flesh to infiltrate my body, as it did once before to Thomas Digges—and the same has been done to you. It was the ethereal that opened the way for our descent and talked to the giant wasp. The ethereals must have planned all along to join our expedition, and must have contrived the insect attack to facilitate their invasion of our flesh."

"That's not the case, Francis," the voice in his head told him, urgently—although the urgency made no impact on Francis's conviction that he ought not to trust anything it said. "The insect attack was utterly unexpected. I did what I could to save your lives and protect the transmission. It is certainly not in my interest that the individual you call the golem was left behind, and my most fervent prayer is that he succeeds in realigning the transmitter so that he can follow you here. I need to return by that route, just as you do. Ethereals are not subject to all the limitations of matter, but we cannot move through the ether faster than light, and our privileged access to the other dimensions is strictly limited."

"I understand the mistake I made, Francis," Solon put in, politely. "Our own state of symbiosis is not without its difficulties, and could not have been easily obtained at its inception. You will both understand, I hope, when I say that it is your passengers rather than yourselves that are of primary interest to us. We have been trying hard to open efficient channels of communication with the Ethereals, as we have with the Shadows, but we have not succeeded—and that is why this unexpected arrival is so welcome. We are...."

That was all that Francis was able to hear before the space in which he stood was abruptly plunged into darkness, and he felt once again as if he were being turned inside out.

Again, he did not actually lose consciousness, but again, his consciousness was distorted in such a way as to make it direly difficult to take account of what was happening. He took it for granted that he was once again engaged in some form of extradimensional transit, but he had not the slightest ideas how far he traveled, or in what direction, or even whether it made sense to raise such questions.

When he was once again capable of coherent sensation and linear thought, however, his first impression was that he must be burning in Hell.

Chapter Forty

The sensation of being burned alive did not last long, objectively speaking, although it was far too long for Francis' liking. The following sensation, which was of being torn apart, was even shorter in duration, and almost comfortable by comparison.

When he was able to see again—in spite of being fairly certain that he had not opened his eyes—he perceived that he actually had, in some sense, been torn apart. There was an angel beside him, which had to be the entity that had invited him to call it "Lumen". It was now, as its chosen name had been devised to suggest, a creature made of light, formed vaguely in the image of a winged humanoid with a nimbus about its head. Francis knew that could not be its native form; what he was seeing, or dreaming, was a depiction improvised from the substance of his own imagination—but improvised by what? What force had snatched him from the entrails of the fleshcore, and where had it taken him? Was the impression of separation dependable, or was this simply one more trick on the part of the inscrutable Ethereal?

"This is not real," he said—aloud, although he was addressing himself, not the angel. *This* was a desert in which the two of them appeared to be standing. He knew that it was not real because of the pyramids. He had never seen the actual pyramids of Egypt, although he had read about them, but he knew that he could not possibly be in Egypt, and that Egypt could not possibly look like this. The sands were sparkling, although it was the dead of night, and there was no moon in the sky. There were too many stars, seemingly so close at hand that they might fall like rain at any moment. Whatever had improvised that sky, it was not a creature that had ever dwelt on Earth. By comparison, the angel was almost convincing, although its brilliant wings were colored, like those of a phantom parrot, and far too small to lift a creature the size of a human being from the ground. Lumen was reduced to the size of a human being now, if only in appearance.

"I suspect, Francis," the Ethereal said, in response to his comment, in a voice that certainly seemed to be composed of ordinary sound, "that this is far nearer to the heart of reality than you or I have ever been before. It is not truly material, to be sure—and your appearance, as I perceive it, is as shabby an imitation of a human being as I am of a human's notion of an angel—but it is most certainly *real*. If my guess is right, we have been captured by a Shadow."

"Why?" Francis asked.

"That is an excellent question. I wish I knew the answer. It might turn out to be a good thing—or it might not."

Francis tried to take some crumb of comfort from the mere possibility that it might be a good thing, although he was uncomfortably aware that he did not seem to have enjoyed overmuch good fortune since he had accepted the golem's invitation to step out of his familiar life into an adventure beyond the bounds of Earth. "What *is* a Shadow, exactly?" he asked, and was unable to resist a petulant impulse to add: "Or is that, too, beyond the limits of Ethereal wisdom?"

"I cannot be absolutely certain," Lumen replied, evenly, "but it must be some kind of being that exists in more dimensions than the four of which your senses are aware, probably in more dimensions than the nine of which I am normally aware. The universe is far more massive than is accountable in terms of the matter visible and tangible to human and fleshcore senses, and far more energetic than is accountable in terms of Ethereal perceptions. Much of its constituency is hidden, and much of the force that sustains its structure and motion originates in that hidden sector—which is, we presume, the realm of God. Ethereals have long considered themselves intermediaries between God's realm and the material cosmos, by virtue of our extensions into other dimensions, but that is largely vanity—a delusion of the ancients, which nascents like myself and Aristocles do not share. The ancients have long been aware of other such extradimensional entities, but have grown used to considering them legendary. Plainly, they are not. If what we saw on the surface of that devastated world can be trusted, they are emerging by the thousand from the energetic flux of the Pit's accretion disk—but what their objective is, I have no idea. Nor, I presume, on the basis of what we have just learned, have the Fleshcores."

Francis was tempted to remark, bitterly, that the Ethereal seemed to have learned more than he had, and had taken some care to ensure that margin of advantage, but he knew that recriminations were futile. "Have they come to save the True Civilization, do you think," he asked his former passenger, "or to destroy it?"

"The Fleshcores will prefer the former hypothesis," Lumen told him, "but they are no more privy to the Divine Plan than we are. The ancients have been anticipating a gross transubstantiation for some time, and Aristocles trusts their means of divination, but I am skeptical. Their claim to have lived through previous transubstantiations, undergoing radical metamorphosis while retaining their fundamental intelligence, is dubious in the extreme. Memory is transient and sometimes fickle, especially when extended over billions of Earthly years."

Francis was certain that his actual body, wherever it might be, could not move a muscle, but he commanded his delusional form to kneel down, by way of experiment—and it did. He took up a handful of sand, and let it trickle through his fingers. The sand was very fine, almost fluid, and it seemed slightly effervescent to the touch.

"How old are you?" he asked, when he looked up again at the false angel.

"Less than a million Earthly years," Lumen told him.

"Have you been interested in humankind as long as the Fleshcores that dispatched Low's golem?" Francis asked.

"No," Lumen replied. "Aristocles was the first to take an interest, but even that interest hardly dates back further than the advent of human history. It was not until I joined in that its dabbling became a game, and that was no more than five thousand years ago."

"A game," Francis repeated. "All this is a game to you?"

"Not any more," Lumen told him. "It ceased to be a game when John Dee's ethership set off a chain-reaction of responses, which appears to have brought us to this. The Fleshcore was wrong to deduce that Aristocles and I have deliberately precipitated this crisis, and, to the extent that we played a catalytic role, our intentions were neither malevolent nor mischievous. In any case, attributing blame will not help. The point is to discover why we have been brought here."

Francis looked up again, then, and saw the sphinx. It had materialized out of nowhere, as if in response to Lumen's assertion. He had seen stone models of sphinxes, and had read their mythology, so it did not seem unfamiliar or menacing in spite of its intimidating size. He felt quite confident in meeting its gaze, even though it must have measured fifty feet from nose to tail, and stood twelve feet high on all fours. Its face was handsome, more masculine than he had expected, although it had no beard.

"Do you have a riddle for me?" he asked.

"I do," said the sphinx, in a voice that seemed very soft, considering the size of the beast. "It is man."

Francis was not unduly surprised, although he had, inevitably, hoped that "man" might be the answer rather than the riddle. "In that case," he replied, trying to seem casual as well as confident, "I have one for you; it is God."

"That is a riddle to us all, alas," the creature said, with an oddly wistful smile. "Even in the narrow confines of your own tiny world, you must understand that He made many worlds rather than one, of many different sorts, with many different populations."

"The plurality of worlds is the prevailing opinion now," Francis admitted, "but the horizons of our imagination were narrower not so very long ago. Nowadays, we accept that if God's creativity is as infinite as He is, He must have made an infinite number of worlds, filling the entire plenum of space, and that He might well have made creatures of every imaginable sort to occupy their surfaces and interstices."

"We do not limit Him to *imaginable* sorts," the sphinx told him. "You certainly should not, given that your native imagination is limited to so few dimensions, and so feeble even with respect to the dimensions you perceive. You are familiar, I suppose, with the assembly of species that calls itself the True Civilization?"

"I had just made its acquaintance for the first time when I received your invitation," Francis said, sarcastically. "I might have got to know it a little better had your summons not been so peremptory. I do know, though, that Thomas Digges once made a treaty with that civilization's Fleshcore rulers on behalf of humankind, which specified that humankind should be let alone. Alas, that treaty seems to have become worthless now."

"I know that," the sphinx told him. "That is why time is pressing. Whether God feels that pressure, we do not know, but we certainly feel it when events move uncomfortably swiftly. We are late upon the scene, and we regret that. We are not used to making haste. What I would like to know, Man, is what you think of the goal of the True Civilization: its manner of worship."

Francis was tempted to ask why the Shadow needed to know, but he too felt the pressure of time, and felt that he ought not to procrastinate even to the extent of demanding a clearer notion of exactly what he was being asked. The vision that the fleshcore had vouchsafed him was still fresh in his mind, read to supply an answer. "At first," he said, "I liked the idea of all creatures, great and small, living within the scope of a vast harmony, with each species evolving slowly towards what Digges and the Fleshcore both call *symbiosis*. Digges liked it too, while he was still convinced that his adventure had been a dream. Now, and still, I tend to agree with Francis Drake that the cost of that sort of harmony is too high a price to pay. Drake is not a bellicose man by any means, for all his skill in fighting, but he is a man who values his freedom. In his opinion, the kind of harmony represented by the insects he encountered in the moon might be just about bearable, but only because it still retains the possibility of disagreement, competition and conflict. An end to all predation inevitably seems an attractive goal to prey species, but even vegetables compete for light, water and the space to grow. Without that competition, there would be no trees, no flowers, and no grasses. Change requires turmoil, and creativity requires change. John Dee, when he had properly absorbed the lessons that Digges and Drake brought back from the moon, declared that the finest of all God's creations is what Tom and the Fleshcore both call *evolution*: the capacity for creativity delegated to organisms themselves, to individuals and populations: the freedom to make themselves more than they presently are. Do you know what I mean by the parable of the talents, as found in our Earthly gospel?"

"Yes," said the sphinx, "I do."

"Then that is my answer to the riddle of man: his worth is to be measured not by what he has so far received, but what he might yet make of his potential. That is why we need to resist the invasion of insects that intends to adapt us to life in their version of the True Civilization, and also why we should be wary of the temptations of the Arachnids, even though we need to develop our own alchemy of the flesh. It is also, I think, why we ought to be wary of the generosity of the Fleshcores, who are bound to see us as potential recruits to their own kind of symbiosis. I do not know, as yet, what the cost might be of accepting help from the Ethereals, and I am certainly grateful for the help we have received thus far—but I agree with all those who are intent on reminding me that that they are not angels, and have their own interests at heart. I would say the same of Shadows, even though I realize that Lumen and I have no way home, and no prospect of continuing any kind of life at all, if you will not help us now."

"The cost of evolution," the sphinx reminded him, "is that individuals must die, that species must die, that worlds must die...and that entire universes must die."

"I do see that," Francis assured the creature. "Without death, the tendency towards stasis is irresistible. I believe that fact to be reflected in the different attitude of the Fleshcores and their insect associates, and the differences Lumen has sketched out between the ancients and the nascents of his own kind. It is certainly evident in humans, short-lived as we are, and I would hazard a guess that Shadows are not immune to it. I know that we talking now about more than the deaths of a few individuals, but I am still uncertain as to whether what is actually at stake is the death of a planet, the death of a galactic civilization, or the death of an entire universe?"

"Opinions differ," the sphinx told him, "but nothing can be ruled out. The conflict within the True Civilization, catalyzed by the quarrels instituted by its first confrontation with natural endoskeletal intelligence, might be a factor in the impending transubstantiation; there are some who believe it."

"What is involved in a transubstantiation?" Francis asked, adding, by way of explanation for his need to ask: "We use the word in a rather narrow sense, albeit an important one for those who believe in it."

"Material universes come and go," the sphinx told him. "Not randomly, to be sure—far from randomly, if those who claim to survive transubstantiations can be trusted—but rather more frequently than observers sometimes suspect. You have no idea how fragile a material universe is, within the greater scheme of things, nor how easily it might be transformed by the whim of God."

"The whim?" Francis queried. "You see God as a whimsical being, then?"

"Creativity unlimited," the sphinx informed him, "implies a certain artistic temperament—but we do not know the mind of God any better than you do. We, too, act for our own purposes…and on our own whims."

"And what do you intend to do with us," Francis asked, "when we have slaked the thirst of your whimsical curiosity?"

"This," said the Shadow, reverting to its true, quite unimaginable self.

CHAPTER FORTY-ONE

Francis did not know what to expect when he unfolded on to the orbital platform, but he was not surprised to find it occupied by giant insects—human-sized insects, that is—whose appearance put him in mind of the kind of larva that Englishmen called a Devil's coach-horse. He still felt rather unsteady after enduring the process of being put back together again—which had, for various reasons, been even more disconcerting than the process of being torn apart—and had only the vaguest idea of what he might expect of himself, but his hastily-conceived plan required him not to put up any resistance at this point. He allowed himself to be seized by the Devil's coach-horses and held.

The Selenites waited for a few minutes to discover whether anyone else would follow Francis, but soon decided that he must be alone. They made no attempt to remove his helmet or to interrogate him at the orbital station, but simply returned him to the focal point of the hyperetheric transmitter and dispatched him to the surface of the moon. There he was received by another party of insects, less heavily armed and armored and more reminiscent in appearance of worker ants. The ant-like Selenites wasted no time before taking him below the surface. Although Francis looked swiftly around before being swallowed up, hoping to catch a glimpse of the Selenite Armada, or some fraction of it, he saw nothing but a bleak monochrome plain, pitted and strewn with dust.

He was not taken far into the interior. Nor did he have to wait long, seated on a stone ledge in a sealed room—carefully attended by two guards—before an interrogator was summoned. The interrogator was more reminiscent of a damsel-fly than an ant, largely by virtue of its glossy blue coloring. It had a head that was somewhat less intimidating than the heads of the ant-like Selenites, let alone the fearsomely-jawed heads of the Devil's coach-horses, because it had little in the way of palps and mandibles, but it had the same large compound eyes. Its mouth, carefully equipped with lips capable of sounding the plosives of human languages, but devoid of mammalian teeth, seemed very strange indeed.

The interrogator put its head close to Francis' helmet in order to tell him, in English, that he might remove it. He did so, meekly. The air in the sublunar chamber was odorous, but not particularly rank. Francis breathed it in gratefully enough.

"Three went through," the interrogator said, unceremoniously. "One is dead. Where is the third?" The second sentence of the three told Francis that the Selenites must have sent an expeditionary force to the world with the ruined surface, which had found Judah Low's body, but that the investigators had not lingered long, presumably— and rightly—fearful of capture by their unrebellious kin.

"Safe, I hope," Francis replied. "The world's fleshcore is uninjured. The True Civilization has been interrupted, but it will be restored. It will be transfigured, but not in the way that you might hope or imagine. You must not launch the Armada. Let Earth alone, and a diplomatic settlement might yet be reached."

"Is that the message you brought from the Great Fleshcores?" the interrogator asked.

"That was the message that I was sent back to deliver," Francis countered, evasively.

The interrogator seemed to be satisfied. The return of a single human must seem to the Selenites to be a very feeble diplomatic overture, expressive of no great insistence. The Selenites were evidently working on the assumption that a *fait accompli* would eventually be acceptable to the Great Fleshcores, at least to the extent that the Fleshcores would let the lunar rebels pursue their own Reformist objectives with respect to humankind. The Selenites were counting on widespread support among other insects, at least, assuming that the involvement of the Arachnids would guarantee that.

"Are my friends alive?" Francis asked.

"The humans who attempted to defend the orbital transmitter against our assault suffered several casualties," the interrogator told him, "but only one has so far died; the other true humans have been given appropriate medical treatment, having been segregated from the Arachnid hybrids and the fleshcore probe. You will be imprisoned with the other humans, but you will not be harmed. When the battle is won, you will be returned to the surface of your planet. Our intention has always been to preserve and protect your species, and to prepare it for proper incorporation into the True Civilization. When we have destroyed the Arachnids and the rogue machines, there will be no further need for violence."

Francis did not believe that the interrogator meant what it said; it had to know that the war would go on for centuries, if not for millennia, even if the Arachnids and the freethinking machines could be removed from the immediate battlefield—which seemed unlikely.

"You must not launch the Armada," Francis repeated—but the warning was half-hearted, and he did not attempt to back it up with any threats. He had already made his own plans. He could have wished for more time to accustom himself to his borrowed form and the abilities that went with it, but while he was manifest in his familiar and fundamental guise, he was confined by its limitations. So was Lumen, of whose presence within him the Selenite interrogator seemed unsuspecting—or perhaps uncaring.

"The Armada is already half way to Earth," the interrogator told him, with what might have been a trace of smug satisfaction. It hesitated, seemingly searching for a *mot juste*. Eventually, it added: "The die is cast." It had obviously learned the English language from an educated source, and was enthusiastic to show off its skill, even though it had no idea that it was talking to the cleverest Englishman of all.

The interrogation, Francis knew, had been a tokenistic gesture. The Selenites did not believe that there was anything more they needed to know. They had expected him to be sent back to say exactly what he had said, if he were ever sent back at all. The worker ants took him away again, hurrying him through dimly-lit corridors. He was content to be hurried; time was running out. When he made his move, he would have to be exceedingly swift.

There were three men in the cell to which Francis was committed, two of them abed. The one who was still standing, apparently quite well, was Anthony. The other two were Kit Marlowe and Edward de Vere; they had obviously been hurt, but whatever medical treatment the Selenites had administered was taking effect; they both contrived to sit up when the newcomer arrived, and both seemed heartily glad to see him alive and quite well.

Anthony's greeting was understandably effusive, but Francis had to cut him short. "What became of Faust?" he demanded.

Anthony was startled by the question, but de Vere replied from his sickbed. "Died a hero," he said. "But for him and Raleigh, we'd never have got the three of you away. Raleigh's alive, and the golem too, but the insects took them away. What news of Low and the girl?"

"Low was too badly injured," Francis told him. "Patience is alive and well. Are you and Marlowe well enough to walk—to run, if necessary?"

"Perhaps," de Vere said, standing up in response to the tone of Francis' voice, having deduced that the question was not idle. "I weigh but a trifle here, and will not need more than a fraction of my strength." Marlowe stood up too, nodding assent.

"In a few moments," Francis said, "you'll all be free, and armed. You must get up to the surface and take possession of the transmitter that brought me here. Return to the orbital platform and capture it—there are half a dozen fearsome insects guarding it, and they might still be watchful, but you must defeat them anyway. Raleigh and the golem must realign the apparatus and complete their intended journey. If you three do not have air enough, or have to counter further opposition, you may return to the surface—but you must be ready to defend the link in Kent, whatever it costs."

"They took our helmets away," Anthony said.

"I'll get them back to you," Francis promised. "Do you understand the part you must play?"

Anthony plainly did not, and Marlowe seemed uncertain, but it was almost as if de Vere had been anticipating some such opportunity with relish and determination. The earl stretched his limbs to test his readiness then nodded. "Trust me, Master Bacon," he said, "we'll take and hold the platform. What do you intend to do?"

"This," said Francis, unable to resist the temptation to show off—and walked into the wall of the cell. The determination to make a spectacular demonstration served him well; he found that it was best to use his new abilities as unthinkingly as he could, as if they had always been natural to him.

It was the work of a moment to find Raleigh and his two adapted men. "Patience is waiting for you in the center of the galaxy," he told the astonished explorer. "Be sure to tell her that Faust was not a traitor, if that has not been explained to her by the Ethereal that is accommodated within her. She will have made all the necessary overtures on behalf of your own hybrid kind by now; the rest may safely be left to the golem. When you come back, do everything possible to help de Vere secure the orbital platform—or, at least, the station in Kent. I can grant you a pause, but I shall be fully occupied elsewhere within the hour. Time is pressing." He moved through the wall again before Raleigh could formulate a question, and found the golem.

"Low and Faust are dead," he told the creature, which had immediately assumed the familiar form of Christian Rosenkreutz in response to his appearance, "but Patience Muffet survived unscathed, probably by virtue of playing host to Aristocles. She might need the support of your advocacy, though, if the Fleshcores are to be reassured. With luck, we shall be able to send you news in a matter of hours; it might yet be bad, but there is every reason now to think that the Selenite invasion can be thwarted, if Dee and Digges have done their job well. There will be no second chance to mount such an invasion, if you can do your part and I can do mine."

Without waiting for an answer, Francis reached out and clasped the golem's arm, hand to wrist, exactly as the golem had once clasped his. He knew that the golem would not understand immediately all that the clasp could tell it, but he was confident that the creature would eventually be able to deduce far more than Francis had been able to divine. In the meantime, the ambassador would do what was required of it.

"Who did this to you?" was the one question that the creature managed to articulate.

"Not God," Francis told him. "There are more steps on the ladder of Creation—or the ladder of Evolution—than you or I, or even the Ethereals, were able to imagine. It is, however, a ladder that all species might climb, give time and the will."

This time, when he walked into the walls of the Selenite prison, he initiated a moonquake that blasted the doors from all the cells in which prisoners were held, and stunned the busy workers in their thousands. By means of the exotic ripples he sent forth, Francis manipulated the lunar rock as easily as he manipulated the enclosed atmosphere, clearing the way for the captured individuals to make their escape, not merely to the surface but all the way to the platform orbiting the Earth.

When the escape was guaranteed, he delivered the helmets and weapons he had promised. Then he left his brother and the others to do their work, and took flight himself.

CHAPTER FORTY-TWO

Francis thought of what he was doing as "taking flight" because he had no other way to think of it, except for "folding himself" into and along imperceptible dimensions. "Taking flight" was the more pleasing analogy, if not the more accurate; it allowed him to imagine himself a member of the great legendary company of firebirds and sphinxes, hippogriffs and dragons. To think of what he could now do merely as "folding" would have demeaned that stature, and he did not want to do so. This opportunity to be a demigod would not last long, and he doubted that he would retain much legacy from it, or ever obtain another.

"Now *this*," said Lumen, his invisible passenger, "is exhilarating. Who would have thought that our nine dimensions were such a meager complement of the true complexity of ultraspace."

Francis knew full well that "ultraspace" was a mere linguistic contrivance—but some much device was necessary, if they were to talk at all. He would have preferred to think in terms of Shadowlands, or Immaterial Empires of Shadow Matter, but Lumen had been humbled by the encounter with the Shadow, and was not in an expansive mood. Indeed it seemed deeply resentful that the Shadow's loan had been made to Francis, and that the abilities on loan had been so intimately linked to the latter's human consciousness.

"Does that exhilaration justify your engagement in the game?" Francis asked, attempting to inject an acid bitterness into the silent question. "Will it make you the evident winner, and give poor Aristocles cause for jealousy?"

"It *began* as a game," Lumen replied, "but it became infinitely more serious, as all the best games do. All life is competition, all ambition gambling. You should be grateful to me, Francis. Without me, you would have none of this. You should be grateful to Aristocles, too—we might have been the provocative agents that precipitated this dispute into violence, but we are also the allies that have made it possible for you to win a spectacular victory. Had we and the Selenites let you alone, you might have taken thousands of years to reach this critical point in the history of your species, and might easily have been fitted for life in the True Civilization without any question or opposition ever being raised, even in the absence of a rebel crusade."

That was all true, Francis knew, but he could not quite bring himself to be grateful to the nascent Ethereals—who had, after all, been following their own agenda and their own whim, not even bothering to convince themselves that they were doing God's will.

Ideally, he would have preferred to descend to the Earth's surface before taking a hand in the battle, but he did not have that option. Although the Shadow had lent him abilities that would have made him seem godlike to many a human being, he was still a prisoner of time and the intrinsic limitations of the ethereal plenum; he could not "fly" faster than the speed of light in any semblance of material form. The Armada was too far advanced in its course to leave him any time to spare—and John Dee's fleet had already taken off to meet it.

Drake was in overall command of the fleet, with Philip Sidney as his chief lieutenant, but Dee and Thomas Digges had been the architects of its strategy as well as the vessels themselves. The crucial engagement, they had always known, would need to take place long before the Armada reached the limits of Earth's atmosphere, allowing its vessels to scatter. The Selenite etherships were already diverging in their courses, but they had to remain close together for the greater part of their journey in order to follow Earthbound trajectories that their fuel could sustain. Although the Earth and its satellite were only two hundred and fifty thousand miles apart, that was sufficient to reduce the bulk of both worlds to mere pinheads on a diagram drawn to scale. The Armada had to remain more-or-less united for most of the journey, for purely practical reasons, and its commanders had doubtless made the calculation that it would be better to make what virtue they could of the necessity. In the first encounter with Earth's defenders, at least, they would remain in tight formation, endeavoring to smash through whatever formation the terrestrial vessels adopted like a battering-ram, forcing the defending fleet to disperse with tempestuous fire.

Drake, in his turn, would try to mount a coherent and coordinated attack, hoping to reduce the Armada's numbers, with his own firepower, to a level at which the survivors of that first encounter might be too few to deliver more than a hundred cargoes of eggs into the atmosphere—which might, in turn, be too few to deliver more than a dozen successfully to the surface. There, any nests that were established would hopefully be hunted down and destroyed, with assistance from the Arachnids and Talos—and any more individuals of either of their kinds that might succeed in reaching Earth's surface in the near future.

The terrestrial fleet was outnumbered, but not outgunned. Digges had told Francis, the last time they had met, that it was impossible to know what the balance of devastation might be after that first deadly encounter, nor what might be done thereafter by way of regrouping and giving chase. "These are not naval vessels that can turn about in a matter of minutes, given a mile or so of sea-room," the engineer had observed. "The space and time necessary to mount a pursuit might be too great to allow any successful pursuit to be mounted, in practice. If the first meeting of the fleets goes badly for us, we might not get a second chance to assault the invaders effectively—not, at least, until they reach the surface. The atmosphere is our ally, of course—but we would be fools to expect or hope that mere friction might succeed if our guns cannot. We not only have to win that first exchange of fire, but win it very decisively indeed."

Digges was absolutely right, Francis knew. If the Selenites succeeded in establishing even a handful of nests on the Earth's surface, and defending them against attempts to wipe them out while they were still in their infancy, the best that could be expected, or hoped for, was that a guerilla war might be set in train that would last hundreds or thousands of years. On the other hand, friction might now be a better friend than Thomas Digges dared hope.

"You ought to accept my help," Lumen told him, as their flight finally brought them within "sight" of the Selenite Armada. "You have no skill or artistry in this work. What you did on the moon was a mere finger-exercise, crude and brutal. This requires delicacy, else you might easily cause far more destruction than you intend, not merely to Drake's fleet but to the Earth itself."

"I know," said Francis. "That is why the Shadow united us again—but I will not surrender my new instruments of action to your volition. I will make whatever use of your skills I can, but your game is over—and if any other Ethereal attempts to take a hand in this, I shall unleash such fury...."

"None will interfere!" Lumen protested. "Aristocles is half way across the galaxy, and cannot return until Patience Muffet does. In any case, no one—not even the Selenites—wants to see the Earth destroyed or devastated, and no Ethereal, nascent or ancient, would risk getting in your way."

"I'm not so certain of the Selenites," Francis told him. "They will sustain heavy losses no matter how this encounter goes. They have no compunction in sacrificing their own soldiers; I cannot imagine that they will be careful of human lives if things go badly."

"You mistake them," Lumen told him. "To devastate the surface of a world where rebellious machines have run riot or an Arachnid invasion has taken place is one thing, and insects do indeed routinely send their soldiers and workers to destruction without an atom of compunction, conscious that the true individual is the hive rather than the component—but no intelligent creature would dare to place a populated world in peril, for fear of the Creator's wrath."

"I hope that is so," sad Francis, although he knew full well that he was no more an agent of wrath than he was an instrument of the Creator. All that had happened to him was that a Shadow—a mere creature, with its own nature, its own interests and its own whims— had lent him the means to defend his and humankind's ambitions, in consequence of its own game-playing impulse, or its own sense of justice. He knew well enough that he and Earth were merely a tiny footnote in a complex story whose real plot was concerned with the materialization of millions of Shadows in the chaotic flux of matter surrounding the Pit at the heart of the galaxy, and that any gross transubstantiation of the galaxy's material structure that might happen in the near future would result from the deployment of powers many orders of magnitude greater than those momentarily at his disposal. Even so, he had a chance to serve as a provocative agent, and to ensure that the Earth's catalytic role in the affairs of the True Civilization would not be rudely cut short.

He had almost caught up with the Selenite Armada when Drake's fleet engaged it, and Earth's etherships opened fire.

Although the "body" in which Francis was traveling through the ether was markedly different from the familiar appearance he had temporarily assumed on the orbital platform and the moon, it still had to receive sensory information in an analogous fashion. His "eyes" were extraordinarily powerful, but they still made up a mental image by means of rays of light impinging upon his physical presence. Human eyes would have seen almost nothing at all of the battle in space, no matter where they were positioned; although Francis was able to do a great deal better than that, his impression was still rather slight and fleeting. He saw immediately, though, and understood, that this was—as Digges had observed—quite unlike a naval battle fought on an Earthly sea, and very different indeed from any clash of soldiers and artillery on a terrestrial battlefield.

There was no evidence, in visible or audible terms, of weapons being fired; all that could be seen was the result of those shots that struck home. Francis knew, when the first ships on either side disintegrated, that for every shot that did strike home, hundreds might be going astray—but both fleets had been equipped with similar aiming devices, presumably by virtue of the fact that Aristocles had stolen the designs he had fed to Edward Kelley and John Dee from the Selenites. By the time he had counted eight vessels destroyed—four on each side—Francis knew how evenly balanced the two forces were. He also knew by then that the Selenite Armada outnumbered Drake's fleet by five hundred and forty vessels to two hundred—a larger proportionate advantage than he had hoped.

"I can't wait," he said to Lumen.

Lumen, already privy to his reasoning, made no protest—not even to ask him to consider what the effect might be of his materializing on Drake's bridge.

CHAPTER FORTY-THREE

Five long seconds went by between the confirmation of the decision and its being put into effect, because Francis was still unable to reach the defending fleet during that interval—and when he was able to effect it, he did indeed cause great consternation among Drake's crew.

In fact, the ethership had no bridge in any conventional sense; its interior was filled with equipment, with only tiny pockets of space into which its crew was wedged. There was hardly any space into which Francis could fit a simulacrum of his own body, but he dared not adopt any other appearance. He materialized in front of Drake, who had Thomas Digges wedged in beside him, operating the apparatus that communicated with all the other ships.

"What is this?" Drake exclaimed, when what he took to be a ghost, or an illusion, appeared before his eyes.

"You must trust me, Captain," Francis said. "However impossible it seems, I really am Francis Bacon, operating with aid from an Ethereal and forces even more powerful. I doubt that you or Dee had time to receive my letters, but I have traveled to the center of the Milky Way and back within the last twenty-four hours, and have been gifted with a means to help us. Tell your own gunner to stand down, I beg you. Tom—bid all the other gunners listen for my voice instead of yours, speaking directly into their heads. Instruct them to relax their limbs, and not to fight me."

Drake, Francis saw, would not have done it. He had insufficient belief in miracles—but Thomas Digges was hesitating in puzzlement. It was Digges' hand that Francis grasped and squeezed. "You see, Tom," he said, in a voice that was not his own. "I promised that we would meet again, and that you would know the truth. I owe you a debt, and am ready to repay it. Go, Francis! You cannot linger here, while the Armada is already dispersing. You must entrust this part, at least, to me!"

It was Francis' turn to hesitate—but not for long. There was no time. "Separate, then!" he said.

Francis' body was, for the time being, a mere simulacrum, but that did not prevent Lumen from emerging from his nostrils like a plume of smoke, which rapidly formed itself into the image of a vaporous moth—and flew, just as rapidly, into Thomas Digges' nostrils.

Drake had seen that before, and had at least some reason to think that he and the other members of John Dee's first crew might not have survived their adventure had the ethereal not chosen to involve itself. In any case, Digges was already giving orders, in a voice other than his own.

"Can you maintain communication with the other gunners without my presence?" Francis asked—aloud, because he was uncertain that Lumen could still hear his silent voice.

"Yes," said Lumen, speaking through Thomas Digges. "Go— and pray to God that you do not need me after all, for you might still have the better part of two hundred vessels to deal with, no matter how effective my aim might be."

Francis took flight again—and saw, once his viewpoint was distributed through the ether again, that he had very little time indeed if he were to catch the Selenite vessels as he intended.

Lumen, fortunately, did seem to be a better aiming-device than the mechanical one his cousin and competitor had provided by way of the black stone. Although Dee's ships continued to sustain losses as the two fleets converged, drawing gradually apart as they did so, while Drake's gunners strove to locate the slowly-dispersing Selenite vessels, the Selenite Armada was now taking much heavier losses. The margin of difference was becoming more conspicuous with every second that passed.

Already, though, a dozen Selenite vessels had passed beyond range of Drake's light-cannon in an Earthward direction. Lumen was correct. Given the difficulty of maneuvering the etherships, somewhere between a hundred and fifty and two hundred were likely to come through that first encounter, and the chances of Drake's ships being able to give chase to them were very slim indeed, even if Drake still had fifty or a hundred ships of his own to make the attempt.

The Selenites had not won yet, though, for they had two barriers yet to overcome: the friction of the atmosphere and the intense affinity drawing them to the Earth's surface. The fleshy crews and cargoes they contained had doubtless been designed with all the alchemical skill at the Selenites' disposal, but the Selenites could not have tested their personnel and products in the field.

Francis knew how foolhardy it would be to hope that the Selenites might simply have made mistakes in designing intelligent insects that could operate successfully in the grip of Earthly affinity; the Arachnids were their superiors in that kind of science, but if the Arachnids could do it, then the Selenites could do it too. Friction was the ally he needed—and, in truth, the only ally he had, for he too could not transport the powers that he now had to the Earth's surface, deep in the punishing well of affinity. When he returned to his native environment, he would have to do so as his ordinary self, with all its limitations.

Until then, however, he was at least half a Shadow, with abilities that exceeded those of an ethereal in the matter of creating storm-winds.

The Selenite vessels were still approaching the Earth on very similar trajectories, but some were slowing down, in order that they could enter the atmosphere at very different points, and fall along a line that would wind twice or three times round the globe, displaced sideways on each circuit. In free fall, they might land anywhere between the tropics, and perhaps some little way outside, on any of the major continents.

Their fall was, however, far from free. Francis could not embrace the globe—or even a tiny fraction of its atmosphere—directly, but he could initiate chain reactions between the molecules of the atmosphere that whipped up winds and whirlpools in the upper strata of the air and the etheric plenum with which it mingled at such heights. He could not act directly upon all the Selenite vessels at once, or even a few at a time, but the time they took to complete their own staggered orbits gave him the time he needed to send deadly ripples after each and every one.

By comparison with the delicacy with which Lumen had plucked attacking insects away from their human victims on the orbital platform, the work that Francis did was very clumsy indeed. Even Lumen could not have played the consummate artist in this enterprise, exercising fine control over every individual action and reaction, but Lumen would not have been a mere child splashing recklessly in the shallows of a placid lake, as Francis regretfully imagined himself to be. Even that clumsy splashing was adequate to its task, however.

One by one, the Selenite vessels descended into the Earth's atmosphere, and were torn apart, one by one by the angry air. Some burned up entire, others fell apart and became showers of smoking debris. Some got much closer to the ground than others—some, perhaps, close enough for their cargoes to stand a chance of reaching the ground without being burned up—but none escaped unscathed. That, Francis was sure, would be enough to ensure that none of them could successfully complete their mission.

There would be no second Armada, he knew; the Fleshcores would see to that, if the rogue machines and the Arachnids could not. The entire galaxy would know before very long what a bone of contention the Earth was, and that it would not lack defenders if it were attacked again. Once the system of hyperetheric links was properly restored, the Selenite blockade would be over, and the Selenites themselves would be dispersed into the vast corpus of the True Civilization.

Francis continued to stir up storms until he was certain that the last of the Selenite vessels had been accounted for; only then did he spare time and attention to rue the residual havoc that might reach the surface, in the form of hurricanes and tornadoes, and the casualties that humankind might suffer as a result—perhaps as many as the casualties suffered by Drake's fleet, whose surviving vessels were now beginning to complete the long loops that would direct them homewards.

Francis waited for the remainder of the fleet, but resisted the temptation to manifest himself in Drake's flagship for a second time. The important task he now had before him was to calm the ether, and then the Earth's atmosphere, in order to smooth the homeward journey of the heroes who had extracted the Armada's sting.

That work was more difficult by far than the work he had already done; destruction, as he was well aware, is invariably easier to sow than harmony, chaos easier to create than order. He was still an infant splashing awkwardly, but he was determined to do what he could. He was no creator, but he knew now what the work of creation entailed, and how valuable intricate chains of cause-and-effect might be. Against the odds, perhaps, he succeeded in calming the ether and the air alike, sufficiently to permit Drake's survivors to descend safely to the surface.

In all, some eighty-seven vessels came safely back to Earth, out of two hundred that had set out. That was a better ratio than Dee and Digges had dared to count on, and a better one than they had promised their crewmen when calling for recruits. More than six hundred men had been lost in the battle—but there was no way to count the number of lives that might have been sacrificed, along with the human species' prerogative of self-development, had the Armada not been thwarted.

All in all, Francis was not dissatisfied.

CHAPTER FORTY-FOUR

Before surrendering his borrowed abilities, as he was bound to do, Francis made one last rendezvous with Lumen, in the placid etheric ocean a few million miles from the gentle turbulence associated with the orbits of the Earth and moon.

"Digges and Drake got safely home with the others," the Ethereal told him. "Poor doubting Thomas did not have time to forgive me, but I think he will look back with gratitude, in time—if you can help him to understand."

"I shall need to understand myself before I can do that," Francis said. "I feel, at present, that the understanding I desire is at the command of my whim, but I doubt that I will feel the same when I am only myself again. All this will seem to have been a dream, no matter how convinced I am of the fact that it was all reality."

"Material memories are so fragile and confused," the ethereal told him, "that I thank God continually for having been born an Ethereal."

"Will Aristocles concede defeat in your game when you confront him?" Francis asked, acidly. "Or will he claim that the intervention of the Shadow rendered the contest null and void?"

"Even if it were still no more than a game," Lumen said, "Aristocles and I would reckon that the matter of who won was far less important than the quality of the contest—and in that respect, neither of us could be disappointed. The intervention of the Shadow was, from that viewpoint, something of a *coup*. The ancients will pretend to be uninterested, and will declare in shocked tones that, had we mastered the Memory, we'd never have been so foolish, but they will not be able to hold that opinion for long. In any case, this is not goodbye. You will doubtless hear from me again—and Kelley will doubtless hear from more than one of us, if he can withstand the pressure of madness."

"Easier said than done, apparently," Francis said. "He has half a dozen apprentice seers in training, but they have all had their difficulties."

"Arachnid alchemy will doubtless help with that," the ethereal relied. "Thomas Muffet is back in England now, and Patience will make a perfect apprentice. You do not need me to warn you, I suppose, to be a little wary of Raleigh—and of Low's golem too, if it chooses to return or is ordered to do so."

"None of these interferers seem to have done us overmuch harm, as yet," Francis said, although he could not yet forgive the Selenite Armada and those who had set in train the chain of causality leading to its launch, "but now we know the extent to which we have been led, I think we will be more determined in future to see to our own guidance."

"And so you should," Lumen said. "The only way, in the final analysis, to avoid being relegated to the status of pieces in other entities' games, is to become players yourselves. You might be able to do that now—provided that the next universal transubstantiation is long enough delayed to grant you the time, or that your species is preserved during the metamorphosis. I shall need to discover the Shadows' purpose, if I can; there may be strange and turbulent times ahead, and not merely for the True Civilization."

"I wish you luck with that," Francis aid. "At least you have had the advantage of meeting one, and sharing in its borrowed powers. Let me know what you discover, if you can."

"It's not impossible," Lumen told him, although Francis knew that it was mere flattery, and probably absurd, "that I shall be the one seeking enlightenment from you."

After that, Francis' return to Earth was swift. Before he went to make his reports to John Dee and Queen Jane, he called in on his brother—who was, remarkably enough, in Stephen Batman's house, completing the task that Francis had begun and then left incomplete.

"I did not know whether I would see you again," Anthony explained. "I thought you might have returned to the heart of the galaxy, or taken up permanent residence on the moon. Now that you can walk through walls and fly through the ether without the need of a ship, London must seem a very narrow arena in which to extend your career as a magician. A task like this is surely far beneath you now."

"I have shrunk to my former three dimensions," Francis assured him. "I have not an atom of magic left in me—less than Ned Kelley, for sure. I am a humble scholar again, and painstaking tasks like sorting Stephen's notes are not beneath me, any more than they are beneath you. You have been outside the Earth as well, and know by sight how tiny it really is."

"But my firebird was only a giant parrot, after all," Anthony replied, "and Low's golem was only some monstrous slug. Even Raleigh is nothing more than a man who has grown an elephant's hide and a little extra hair. Wonders I have certainly seen, but I cannot help feeling that the world seems a little less magical than it did before—all the more so if you are again no more than my little brother, the bane of my existence."

"It was you, was it not," Francis said, "who tried to shield me from the insects when we were taken by surprise, and made sure that I escaped?"

"Mere instinct," Anthony assured him. "The same instinct that guided me in support of de Vere's heroism when we took the platform back. In any case, I could not have saved you the first time without Faust's help, any more than I could have held the platform the second time without de Vere and Marlowe. Faust was the one acting out of duty, and it cost him his life. Kit intends to write a play about him, you know, to celebrate his part in the salvation of the world. Rumor has it, though, that every playwright in London has some similar subject in mind. De Vere says that his will be a comedy, with himself as the hero—although he will have to borrow another man's name for a signature if he does that."

"It *was* a comedy," Francis said. "For which we should all be truly thankful. Had it been a tragedy, as it might so easily have become, it would not be a suitable subject for drama for at least five hundred years. The plays are bound to be dishonest, though—the society to which Marlowe and de Vere belong still exists, even if its figurehead is presently absent; it will be all the more determined to keep its secrets."

"There are no secrets," Anthony told him. "Given the way that the ladies of the court are swarming around Drake, in spite of his antiquity, and Sidney, in spite of his marriage, and even humble Tom Digges, in spite of his being a mathematician, every last moment of what occurred will be common knowledge within a week." He did not mention any attention he might have received himself from the ladies of the court, but he had not been able to make the general point without blushing.

"Oh, there are secrets still," Francis told him. "There will always be secrets—but how insipid would life be, if there were not puzzles to solve, secrets to penetrate and games to play? How could there be change, let alone transubstantiation, without secrets to pursue, and sometimes capture?"

ABOUT THE AUTHOR

BRIAN STABLEFORD was born in Yorkshire in 1948. He taught at the University of Reading for several years, but is now a full-time writer. He has written many science fiction and fantasy novels, including *The Empire of Fear, The Werewolves of London, Year Zero, The Curse of the Coral Bride*, and *The Stones of Camelot*. Collections of his short stories include *Sexual Chemistry: Sardonic Tales of the Genetic Revolution, Designer Genes: Tales of the Biotech Revolution*, and *Sheena and Other Gothic Tales*. He has written numerous nonfiction books, including *Scientific Romance in Britain, 1890-1950, Glorious Perversity: The Decline and Fall of Literary Decadence*, and *Science Fact and Science Fiction: An Encyclopedia*. He has contributed hundreds of biographical and critical entries to reference books, including both editions of *The Encyclopedia of Science Fiction* and several editions of the library guide, *Anatomy of Wonder*. He has also translated numerous novels from the French language, including several by the feuilletonist Paul Féval and various classics of French scientific romance.

www.ingramcontent.com/pod-product-compliance
Lightning Source LLC
Chambersburg PA
CBHW050401260626
47156CB00003B/816